"Just what are your feelings, Claire?"

Philippe murmured, drawing nearer.

Any answer she might have made was lost as he crushed her against his chest and brought his lips down on hers. Instantly, she tried to extricate herself from his embrace, but her efforts served only to tighten the muscular arms around her. Philippe's tongue explored her mouth, ruthlessly at first, then tenderly. When he felt her body responding to his, he lifted his head and regarded her condescendingly.

"You see, *chère,* you're confused. You don't know what to think right now. I'll give you time to consider my proposal."

With an angry shriek, she planted her hands against his chest and shoved. "If you think you can coerce me into marrying you, you—"

"Temper, temper, Claire, or you'll die an old maid. Be reasonable. You *will* marry me. I will not give up without a fight, although why you insist on battles between us, I'll never understand. We have better things to do with our time, you and I."

Dear Reader,

Welcome to Harlequin Historicals, where we hope you'll find a lot to be thankful for this November.

Fans of Bronwyn Williams will be pleased to see that Dixie Browning and her sister, Mary Williams, have written another book in their popular Outer Banks Series. In *The Mariner's Bride,* young seaman Rogan Rawson marries a woman for the sole purpose of keeping an eye on his wayward stepmother, only to discover that nothing is ever that simple.

You will also find *Season of Storms,* from Kate Kingsley (our one hundredth book by the way). It's the tale of a wayward son of the Creole elite and an independent heiress. Readers of contemporary romance will recognize the name Laurie Paige. In the author's first Harlequin Historical, *Wedding Day Vows,* an Englishwoman trades her release from Newgate prison for her hand in marriage.

Last, but not least, I would like to mention Nina Beaumont. This first-time author lives in Austria, and her wealth of knowledge and experience lend a powerful flavor to *Sapphire Magic,* the story of a cynical Austrian count and the woman who melts his heart.

Please keep an eye out for *Historical Christmas Stories 1991.* The collection features Lynda Trent, Caryn Cameron and DeLoras Scott. You won't want to miss it!

Our best to you and yours during the upcoming holiday season.

Sincerely,

Tracy Farrell
Senior Editor

Season of Storms

Kate Kingsley

Harlequin Books

TORONTO • NEW YORK • LONDON
AMSTERDAM • PARIS • SYDNEY • HAMBURG
STOCKHOLM • ATHENS • TOKYO • MILAN

Harlequin Historicals first edition November 1991

ISBN 0-373-28700-3

SEASON OF STORMS

Books by Kate Kingsley

Harlequin Historicals

Ransom of the Heart #72
Season of Storms #100

KATE KINGSLEY

loves to write historical romance. And, having been raised in south Louisiana, she certainly has the background to bring history to life. Kate, who now lives in the San Francisco Bay area, has a strong background in advertising and media; she also does volunteer work at a local hospital, enjoys reading, biking, and especially traveling—whenever she can find some extra time. With her daughter in college, Kate has a bit more time to spend with her husband, an actor and television announcer whose sexy voice can be heard on numerous network and cable programs.

To DD and JD, for keeping the home fires burning

Prologue

New Orleans, 1831

André LeBlanc stood amid barrels and crates and a sea of luggage and wondered what the harbormaster was thinking when he allowed two steamboats to unload simultaneously. The noise was deafening as cargo was heaped onto the dock and passengers from both the *Delphinius* and the *Cher Mignon* were greeted by excited friends and relations.

Street urchins, pickpockets and confidence men worked the crowd that swirled around LeBlanc, buffeting him on all sides. The little horse trader almost wished he had not sent his man-servant ahead with his luggage. Anxiously, he craned his neck, trying to peer through the throng, hoping his client would arrive before he was robbed ... or worse.

At last he spied Philippe Girard, head and shoulders above the crowd, as he strode ahead of a clamoring army of urchins who trailed him, all vying at once for his attention.

"I do not want you to carry my bags, find me a cab or give me a guided tour of New Orleans," the young Creole said, dismissing them impatiently as he drew even with the short, dapper man.

"Go along now, all of you," LeBlanc ordered, wading into the midst of the children, swinging his cane, pleased to stand head and shoulders above a crowd himself. "*Allez.* We have no need of your services."

When the rabble dispersed, the horse trader turned to his young client. "It is a shame. I wager half those children should be in the care of the good sisters at the orphanage."

Philippe was not listening. "I take it they have not un-loaded Cavalier yet?" he asked impatiently.

"*Non*, but it should be soon. Just wait until you see him, Monsieur Girard. He is the finest stallion in five parishes, strong and spirited. I tell you, in all my years as a trader, I have never seen a finer piece of horseflesh."

"I should hope so," the other man responded dryly. "At the price you are charging me, I hope he sires colts of pure gold."

The little horse trader bristled predictably and Philippe grinned down at him impudently. "Do not say it, LeBlanc. You earned your commission. I asked you to get Cavalier for me and you did."

LeBlanc opened his mouth to answer when he was inter-rupted by a terrified cry. From the mouth of the murky hold, one of the *Cher Mignon*'s deckhands was reluctantly emerging with the rebellious palomino known as Cavalier. His voice quaking, the sailor muttered disjointed phrases to calm the high-strung golden stallion, unconsciously gripping the lead rope tighter and tighter as he gingerly led his menacing charge toward the narrow gangway.

After the darkness belowdecks, the sudden burst of sun-light blinded the horse. With each tug on the bridle, the bit in his mouth sawed roughly, infuriating him. Stopping abruptly, Cavalier reared on the precariously rocking gangplank, a mere two feet above the water. The stallion gave a shrill, nervous whinny and pawed the air angrily with his front hooves. Suc-cumbing to panic, the unwilling groom dived for the relative safety of the water.

Ashore all activity ceased as roustabouts and bystanders watched the bucking horse with helpless fascination. Only Philippe moved. Spinning purposefully, he raced down the pier toward Cavalier.

Dodging flailing hooves, he spoke calmly, groping for the lead rope that trailed down the horse's chest. His mouth flecked with foam, the terror-stricken animal snorted and pawed. Fishtailing dangerously on the narrow board, he al-most knocked the man off balance with a toss of his mighty head.

Spreading lithe, sinewy legs to steady himself, Philippe grabbed the lead in a firm hand. He grimaced in pain as the rope slipped with one of Cavalier's bucks, burning his palm, but he held on stubbornly, planting his feet solidly on the rickety gangplank.

Once he captured the rope, the match became a contest of wills between man and beast. The Creole's jaw was set as hard as granite in his determination to win the battle. Although Philippe was tall and slim, he was powerfully built. His shoulders were broad and the muscles of his back were well-defined as they strained under his tailored broadcloth jacket in an effort to control the frightened horse. He had lost his hat in the river, and now a stray lock of black hair brushed his tanned forehead above dark eyes that were focused hypnotically on the skittish horse.

Move for move, he kept up with the stallion, talking quietly and inching toward the solid surface of the dock. Slowly, the tired animal seemed to concede defeat, allowing Philippe to lead him, much pacified, onto the wharf.

"Bring a blanket," the Creole directed a passing deckhand brusquely, oblivious to the cheers of the bystanders. "He has worked up a sweat. I don't want him to catch a cold."

LeBlanc, twirling his waxed mustache importantly, strolled down the pier to join him. "Well done, Monsieur Girard." He nodded approvingly. "I admire your way with horses."

"Merci."

LeBlanc observed as Philippe accepted a soiled blanket from the dripping, apologetic deckhand and threw it over the stallion.

"A magnificent animal, eh, monsieur?" the trader asked.

"He shows a lot of spirit, if nothing else." Philippe patted the animal gently on the flank, watching the skin quiver under his hand.

"If nothing else?" LeBlanc also quivered, drawing himself up in righteous indignation. "Cavalier's bloodlines are incomparable. I assure you, you will never be sorry you bought him."

"I do not suppose I shall," the young man surrendered, laughing. "I need him to add champion blood to my stable. Sound like a good job to you, *mon ami?*" He stroked the horse's velvety nose soothingly, as if looking for a sign of agreement.

"He seems to be calmer now," Philippe said to LeBlanc. "Let us find my groom. He can take Cavalier to my stable while we settle between us. *Oui?*"

"Oui, bien," LeBlanc agreed immediately.

The young Creole led the horse past the passengers disembarking from the steamboat moored at the adjacent pier, toward his groom, who held the sleek, prancing Lagniappe. Philippe had been given the animal, a sickly colt, as lagniappe, something extra, from a breeder. Under his new master's care, the colt had grown to be a powerful black stallion. He nickered happily when he saw his owner.

Philippe's hand tightened on Cavalier's bridle when the palomino sidled nervously, his gait making an uneven rhythm on the wooden dock in counterpoint with the men's smooth strides.

"Just a moment." Philippe halted again, frowning. "I want to make sure he did not injure himself back there."

As he bent to examine the horse's leg, a girl on the deck of the *Delphinius* snatched at her sun hat as a gust of wind lifted it from her dark head.

With a frustrated sigh, she watched the errant hat sail above the wooden planking of the dock before it dropped to cartwheel on its wide stiff brim. Clattering down the gangplank, she nearly caught it before another gust carried it, its yellow ribbons waving giddily, in the direction of the skittish palomino stallion. The frightened horse shied and began to buck and pitch mindlessly.

With a curse, Philippe leapt out of the way of the flashing hooves. While the groom looked on in horror, LeBlanc emitted a strangled yell and scuttled backward. Straining to hold Cavalier's reins, Philippe glared over his shoulder at the girl, who ran toward them, trying to catch the hat before it was trampled.

In a flurry of gingham skirt and childish pigtail, she dived toward the rolling hat as it careened crazily into the path of the rearing horse. Philippe extended one booted foot and neatly tripped her, sending her with a thump and a skid out of danger. Then, stepping astraddle her, he turned his full attention to calming the horse again.

He did not bother to look at her as the girl dragged herself from between his feet and crouched behind him, clutching her battered hat to her bosom. Her eyes, wide with fright, were fixed on the huge stallion.

When Cavalier had settled down, Philippe bent to inspect the horse's leg. Satisfied no great damage was done, he growled over his shoulder at the bedraggled girl, "Are you all right?"

"*Oui, merci.* Are you?"

"*Oui* . . . no thanks to you," he grated, his back still to her. "Damn it, girl, you nearly got us both killed and almost ruined a fine piece of horseflesh in the bargain."

"I didn't mean to. My hat blew away."

"Devil take your hat!" Philippe scowled down at her.

"I said I was sorry." She glared back defiantly.

"What does it take to keep your kind off the docks?"

"What kind is that?" she asked icily.

"Street urchins who have no business on the wharf. If you have a home, I suggest you go to it before I call a constable." He turned to croon gently to the nervous horse.

Silently she rose and dusted herself off. Her temper still narrowly in check, she looked speculatively at the man's muscular back. He had every right to be angry. She knew how close she had come to disaster due to her thoughtlessness.

"Monsieur . . ." she ventured, hoping to apologize.

"Go away before you start more trouble," he snapped.

"*Oui,* go away," LeBlanc interjected arrogantly, discovering his voice had returned.

The girl's eyes flickered over the horse trader, obviously dismissing his threat, but before she could speak again, Philippe snapped, "Begone, or must I call a policeman?"

Glancing over his shoulder, he met her furious, fathomless eyes. Without another word, the girl tossed her plait over her shoulder with a disdainful gesture and marched away.

Philippe handed Cavalier over to his groom and watched the girl disappear into the crowd. Though she was rigid with anger, her skirt swayed provocatively and her long black braid bounced against her back just above nicely rounded hips.

"Nervy as a gnat." LeBlanc sniffed indignantly. "That child should be in a convent until she is old enough to wreak her havoc on a husband."

"*Non,*" the young Creole disagreed softly, "I do not think the convent is the place for that one. And I do not think she is such a child after all."

Chapter One

Standing beside the *Delphinius*'s creaking hoist, Captain John Reed shook his head when he saw Claire Fortier's ominous expression. Every drop of the girl's Indian blood was evident as she stalked up the gangplank. Her head held high on her slender neck, she looked neither right nor left, pride and spirit showing in her very bearing.

The captain went to meet her, wiping his hands on a greasy rag. He had seen the look on her face often enough to know it meant trouble.

"Claire! What's wrong?"

The face she turned to him was golden and touched by the sun. Though her brow was knit in an angry scowl, her natural beauty was apparent. High cheekbones and a delicately chiseled nose gave her face an aristocratic fineness that contrasted with the exotic cast of her dark eyes, which slanted slightly downward.

"What is wrong?" he repeated. "What were you doing off the boat?"

"I was being insulted by a rude man," she gritted. "My hat blew off and frightened his horse. He thought I was a street urchin and threatened to call a constable."

Captain Reed fought a smile as he took in Claire's altered, ill-fitting dress and her begrimed countenance. "He surely did not realize you are related to Monsieur Fortier."

"That makes no difference. There is no excuse for rudeness," she objected stiffly.

"No," he agreed, thinking how much she sounded like his gentle Iris. Had Claire been with them only three weeks? The captain and his wife had become fond of the girl since Father

DuBois brought her aboard at Chouteau Landing, south of Memphis.

Her hair in braids, and clad in a trail-stained buckskin dress, the Indian girl had followed the gaunt priest as he hailed the captain. Stopping a short distance from the men, she waited, trying to ignore the curious stares of the passengers.

"Capitaine Reed, I have come to ask you to undertake a Christian duty," Father DuBois began officiously.

"What Christian duty is that, Father?" John Reed had scowled, disliking the priest's approach at once.

"To see this girl, an orphan, to her uncle in New Orleans."

"She has an uncle in New Orleans?" The captain looked her over skeptically.

"*Oui.* His name is Etienne Fortier."

"Are you sure? He's one of the richest men in Louisiana." Captain Reed looked her over again with heightened interest.

"I am sure," the priest assured him solemnly. "I knew this girl's father, Jules, very well. He was Etienne's younger brother. Though he was a Creole gentleman, he preferred the wilderness to the salons of New Orleans. He became a trapper and married White Sky, a Cherokee woman. They sometimes visited my mission. I baptized Claire when she was born." He nodded toward the girl.

"Jules died some years ago," he continued, "and White Sky, two months ago. Claire has never been accepted by her mother's people. She has nowhere to go now, but to her uncle. I cannot allow her to travel alone. So I beseech you, *Capitaine,* in the name of charity, to take her with you."

"I do not want charity," the girl cut in unexpectedly. "I have some money to pay for my passage. If it is not enough, I will work. I will make my own way."

A soft female voice spoke up suddenly. "I do need someone to assist me, you know, John."

Captain Reed turned to face his wife. He did not know when she had emerged from the cabin behind him, but she had obviously heard the priest's story. Iris Reed was sweet-tempered and gentle, but she had a will of iron once her mind was made up. And he knew she had decided they would take the girl to New Orleans.

Though surrounded by passengers, Iris was often lonely. She and Claire quickly became friends. She was pleased to take the orphan under her wing, altering some of her own clothes for her.

The captain's wife tried to prepare Claire for her new life, and her task did not prove to be difficult. She was delighted to discover the girl had been educated by her father. Claire knew how to read and to write. Her manners were courtly if somewhat dated. Though sometimes stiff-necked and proud, she was an apt student. Even John had been drawn into some of their lessons.

Iris was going to miss Claire, the captain mused. And truth be told, he would miss her himself.

"Did you say goodbye to Iris?" he asked.

"In the cabin." Claire nodded. "She said she would cry if she went with us. Are we going now?" she asked eagerly.

"Yes. Sorry to keep you waiting, but the cargo had to be unloaded." As he retrieved his jacket from the railing nearby, the man was about to suggest that he change clothes, but he saw the look in Claire's eyes. Chuckling, he rolled down his shirtsleeves and drew on his jacket.

They found a run-down carriage whose owner dozed on the driver's seat while flies buzzed around a pair of sad-looking horses that sagged in their harness, lethargic in the heat.

Captain Reed hailed him. "Is your rig for hire?"

"Ah, Monsieur." The man sat up and scratched under his hat sleepily. "I did not hear you coming. I was lost in meditation."

"You must have been deep in 'meditation' to miss all the excitement on the pier," the captain said, grinning.

"I did not miss it. I just paid it no mind," the man retorted with a sniff, climbing down from the seat.

"Can you take us to Fortier House?"

"*Oui.*" The driver placed Claire's meager baggage in the carriage and assisted his passengers into the wobbly rig. Closing the door, he bowed and said grandly, "*Mademoiselle et monsieur,* welcome to New Orleans. Louis Baptiste Renault, at your service."

Back in his seat, he gathered the reins and clucked to the horses. The bony nags stirred reluctantly and trotted toward the broad avenue visible at the end of the wharf.

From the high open vehicle, the waterfront streets appeared a moving river of humanity. Those fortunate enough to ride on horseback picked their way through the hordes of pedestrians who spilled off banquettes, the wooden sidewalks of New Orleans. Louis talked incessantly to the horses when he was not shouting at the throng in a patois that was difficult for Claire to follow.

"Do you understand what he is saying?" the captain asked her.

"It sounds like French, yet it doesn't," she replied, shaking her head.

"It's Gumbo Ya-ya. That means everyone talks at once," Reed explained, "a little French, a little West Indian, a little Spanish, maybe even some Indian. Judging from the reactions Louis is getting, perhaps it is just as well you do not understand."

Gesturing toward the grassy common that ran down the middle of the smooth hard-packed boulevard, Captain Reed said, "This is Canal Street. At one time, it was going to be a canal. Now it's just the dividing line between the old and new sections of the city. The old section, the Vieux Carré, is inhabited by Creoles. The Creoles still call their American neighbors Kaintocks. Makes no difference whether they came from Kentucky or not, or that the frontiersmen were their salvation during the War of 1812. After nearly twenty years, Creoles still see them as outlanders . . . and rough around the edges. Even though many of the Kaintocks are well-to-do now, the Creoles still seem to think they have more money than sense . . . and more sense than manners."

As the carriage clattered onto a cobblestone street, Louis interjected politely, "*Mademoiselle et monsieur,* we are now entering the Vieux Carré. This is Levee Street and you can see, a few squares farther, the French Market."

Her attention caught by cries of the street vendors, Claire gazed curiously toward where people swarmed in front of market stalls. Her head reeled at the sights and the sounds and the scents of the city.

Here a wizened black woman, her gaunt face framed by a yellow *tignon,* sold sugary confections called pralines. There a swarthy sailor threaded his way, his unkempt head crowned by a molting parrot that squawked in vulgar Spanish. On a street corner, four Negro boys played raucous, rhythmic music on makeshift instruments as a tiny girl danced for the coins tossed their way.

"May I offer a short tour?" Louis suggested politely. "You must see St. Louis Cathedral, of course." He pointed with his whip across a lush green park to the magnificent church. "A lovely old building, yes? A bit run-down, but someday it will be restored to its former glory.

"This square is Place d'Armes," he announced as they turned away from the Mississippi, "as it has been known since the days of the Spanish. The buildings on either side of the cathedral are government buildings, the Cabildo and the Presbytère."

Shading her eyes against the glaring sun, Claire examined her surroundings. Its riotous blooms of red, pink and yellow spread before her, Place d'Armes was a place of luxuriant beauty. She breathed in deeply, savoring the heady fragrance. Magnolia trees bloomed above the walkways that cut through the manicured lawn, their huge white blooms emitting a sweet perfume that mixed with the aroma of the muddy river.

"Through the alley by the cathedral, you can see a bit of St. Anthony's Garden," Louis continued, warming to his role as tour guide. The quiet gardens lay behind the stately church, shielded from the outside world by an iron fence and shaded by immense gnarled trees draped with silvery moss. "Many an *affaire d'honneur* has been settled here," he added in reverent tones.

It was hard to imagine death in such a serene setting, but Claire did not ponder the unpleasant thought for long. She spoke little—there was too much to see—but she was glad the captain was with her. New Orleans was a bustling city and rather frightening to a girl brought up in the wilderness.

"The finest stores in New Orleans are along Chartres Street," Louis droned as they crossed a neat street of shops. "Ladies of quality shop there."

Claire's rapt gaze took in every detail. She leaned forward in her seat to peep through tall wrought-iron gates at the cool fountains and luxuriant greenery of narrow courtyards. Her eyes flitted from balcony to balcony, each more elaborate than the last, embellished at each end with *gardes de frise,* curli-cued metal monograms of its owner. The cluttered street with its cramped houses made her feel almost claustrophobic, but she was filled with wonder as the carriage passed through a canyon of cobblestone and masonry. She craned her neck to look toward the sky. Watching her, the captain grinned.

They rode along a street lined with small row houses until they reached Esplanade. On the other side of the boulevard lay the huge town houses of the Creole aristocracy. There, the street names changed, as did the atmosphere. The air seemed cleaner, fresher. The hubbub of the city fell behind and the songs of the birds could be heard. Lines of river oaks stood as ancient sentries, guarding wide streets that meandered among grand estates and small plantations.

Captain Reed watched Claire covertly and wondered what their reception at Fortier House would be. Etienne Fortier had a reputation for being a hard but fair man, he thought. Would he acknowledge the girl as his niece? Would he recognize his blood in her and accept the proof of her identity she brought?

Unaware of the captain's scrutiny, Claire relaxed, at ease in the now rustic setting. But she was instantly on guard when the carriage slowed and passed through a pair of massive iron gates that stood ajar, leading invitingly to the bowered *allée*. The girl shifted to the edge of her seat, her eyes straining for the first glimpse of Fortier House. Her eager face was flushed and her breath caught in her throat when she saw her uncle's home; it was everything her father had told her it would be.

So grand and so big, the girl thought as she stared at the mansion looming at the end of the drive. She took in every detail as a thousand thoughts paraded through her mind.

Her journey's end was in sight. Once she had made the decision to come to New Orleans, Claire had traveled toward her goal, never allowing herself to think of the consequences. But soon she would meet her uncle. Soon she would know whether this immense house was to be her home, whether Etienne Fortier would accept her.

The sturdy, elegant structure sat well back from the road, screened from curious eyes by a wall covered with sweet-scented honeysuckle. Beyond the iron gates, which were adorned with a curlicued *F*, a shell-covered drive circled in front of the house, widening enough at the top of the curve for several carriages to unload their passengers at one time. Tall oaks, their trunks whitewashed, edged both sides of the *allée*, their limbs intertwining overhead. Beyond the trees on either side of the house, plush green lawn spread in an inviting carpet. More shade trees dotted the yard, with vibrant flowers planted around their bases. In the branches of a giant cypress perched a dainty white tree house, a fanciful gingerbread creation.

Like most houses in New Orleans, Fortier House was built along West Indian lines, but on a much grander scale. The main wing was constructed of wood and white plaster with a pitched roof to allow the runoff of heavy seasonal rains. Hurricane shutters framed every window and door, their once-bright colors now muted by time and weather. Boxes abloom with flowers gave the place a giddy dash of brilliance. Above the spacious veranda that shaded the entire front of the house and curved around both sides, lace curtains waved gaily in the breeze wafting through open windows. On the veranda, comfortable-looking rattan chairs were drawn up by French doors that opened to the cool interior.

From the drive, the only sign of the squat brick kitchen was a slender column of smoke that rose behind the main house. The unused *garçonnière,* or boys' quarters, whitewashed slave cabins and storage sheds were all nearly invisible, hidden by a thicket of banana trees. Palmettos lined the path that disappeared toward the stables.

As he handed Claire down from the carriage in front of the stately home, the captain was acutely conscious of the oil that stained his hands and he wished he had taken time to change into more elegant clothing. He took a deep breath, asked Louis to wait for him and escorted the girl up the broad steps to a large oak door guarded by a lion's head door knocker.

"Are you sure this is the right house?" Claire whispered nervously.

"Of course it is." Captain Reed studied her pale face and chided, "You've been so determined, I cannot believe you're having second thoughts now."

"It's just that I've never met my uncle and he doesn't know I'm coming. What if..."

"What if he doesn't want you here?" Gently he pronounced her unspoken fear. Claire glared at him in response.

"Don't be silly," he growled affectionately. "You're his own flesh and blood. He'll want you here."

He dropped the knocker decisively against the big door. The pair stood silently on the veranda, listening almost breathlessly for sounds on the other side.

They heard heavy steps and the door swung open to reveal the biggest, most forbidding man either had ever seen.

"Yes?" The giant's voice rumbled from his expansive chest. Then, scowling at the disheveled pair, he said, "Service and deliveries to the back door."

With a thud, the door closed in their faces.

"Back door!" John Reed yelped in aggravated surprise.

"Yet another person in New Orleans who thinks that I am a street urchin," Claire announced bitterly.

"As you said yourself, there is no excuse for rudeness," the captain told her emphatically as he lifted the heavy door knocker and dropped it again.

The footsteps returned and the door opened a crack. The butler glared at them through the narrow opening. "I told you—"

"I know what you told me," the captain cut in hotly, "but we're not here to make a delivery. We are here to see Mr. Fortier."

The huge doorman looked pained. "He is not receiving visitors this afternoon. Come back another day."

The door was closing when Captain Reed resourcefully inserted his foot into the crack. "I won't be here another day. This young lady needs to see Mr. Fortier today...now."

The servant spared the disheveled girl a glance and repeated stubbornly, "Mr. Fortier is not receiving. He said he was not home—to anyone."

"I believe he will see me," Claire said suddenly, causing both men to look at her with surprise. "I am the daughter of his brother, Jules," she continued imperiously, "and I have come a long way to see him. Please tell him at once that I am here."

The butler opened the door wider to inspect the bedraggled girl skeptically. Looking like nothing so much as a pauper, she carried herself like a princess.

He wavered indecisively, pondering the dilemma. "How do I know you're telling the truth?" he asked at last.

Captain Reed sighed in exasperation. "Do people show up on Etienne Fortier's doorstep every day, claiming to be long-lost relatives?"

"No, but..." The butler groped for a suitable argument.

"*S'il vous plaît,*" Claire demanded impatiently, "tell my uncle I am here."

"But Mr. Etienne said he's not at home. That's what he told me to say," the faithful servant insisted unhappily.

"Then we will wait on his doorstep until he says he is at home," Claire's companion countered.

Suddenly the butler relented. With a shrug of his mighty shoulders, he stepped back and gestured the pair into the cool, spacious foyer. "You may wait in the library," he said gloomily, summoning a pudgy Negro maid. "Beady will take you while I fetch Mr. Fortier."

"You jest missed M'sieur Etienne," the maid said, laughing as she led them into a cypress-paneled room. "Greer gotta go see if he's at th' stables, jest when he got hisself believin' he's not home a'tall."

Clutching a letter from Jules tightly in her hand, Claire explored the pleasant, masculine den. It was filled with books and overstuffed furniture, and a thick Oriental carpet was spread before the fireplace. On it, two well-worn leather wing chairs flanked a low table laden with crystal decanters. On one side of the room, beveled glass doors opened onto the veranda. A massive wooden desk dominated the other side, seemingly anchored by a gigantic globe. Throughout the cluttered room, exotic bric-a-brac—swords, tapestries, ivory carvings—served as reminders of Etienne's role as merchant and importer.

Captain Reed sank into one of the chairs, complaining, "I can't remember a hotter day in all the years I've been visiting New Orleans."

Prowling restlessly, Claire did not answer. Her eyes roamed over leather volumes without really seeing them, her mind was in such turmoil.

The door opened and she turned to see an elegant man, dressed for riding, enter the room. He strode toward the captain without even a glance in her direction. The girl smarted at his slight until she realized he did not see her in the dark corner. She stood there silently, listening to the conversation between the men, feeling almost as if she were eavesdropping. Fascinated, she studied her uncle for the first time.

Etienne Fortier was a handsome, robust man with serious gray eyes that looked at the world with imperturbable skepticism. Thick silvery hair swept back smoothly from a distinguished brow. A hint of jowls, camouflaged by a carefully manicured beard, was the only evidence of age on his curiously unlined face. His dress was immaculate from his polished boots to his crisp stock. Even in the heat of the day, he looked cool and unruffled. His bearing was powerful, his stride vigorous and confident. His entire manner bespoke wealth and influence.

This was Etienne, the older brother Claire's father had respected. Gazing at him, she drew a quick breath at the close family resemblance, which was not entirely physical. Like Jules, Etienne was obviously a man accustomed to living life on his own terms.

"What is this all about, sir?" Etienne inquired brusquely as he joined his guest in the dusky library. "Greer tells me you were most insistent to see me, Monsieur..."

"Reed. Captain John Reed of the *Delphinius,*" the other man supplied pleasantly, rising to shake his host's hand.

"Please sit down, Captain Reed," Etienne invited. His brow knit in perplexity, he asked, "The *Delphinius* ... a steamboat, I believe? Have we done business together before?"

"No, sir."

Before the captain could say more, Etienne sat down across from him and said eagerly, "Greer also mentioned something about Jules. Have you seen him? I haven't heard from him for ten years."

"No, sir, I never met the gentleman, but...er..." Captain Reed's voice trailed off awkwardly, as he nodded toward the girl in the shadows.

"What?" Etienne turned in his seat, his eyes following the direction of the captain's gaze.

Claire stepped into the light hesitantly. Etienne's eyes widened disbelievingly when he saw her and his ruddy complexion turned ashen; shock was apparent in his frozen expression. He swayed in his seat, his breath coming in short gasps, the muscles of his jaw working for control. Suddenly he no longer looked young and vigorous. He was an old man...and ill.

The Creole waved away his guests' offers of assistance and gasped, "I am all right. However, I should be grateful, *Capitaine,* if you would pour me a brandy."

While the man hastened to do Etienne's bidding, Claire bent over the sick man. He leaned against the back of the chair, his eyes closed. His breathing was easier now and the color began to return to his face.

"Are you really all right?" she asked anxiously.

Etienne opened his eyes and looked searchingly into the girl's face. When he seemed to have found the answer to his unspoken question, he sighed deeply and closed his eyes again. Lines of pain were visible, etched around his mouth.

"*Oui,*" he muttered. "You just gave me a bit of a shock."

"I did not mean to upset you."

"Of course not," he answered gruffly. "It is only that you are not who I thought you were."

"Who did you think I was?" she could not resist asking.

Unexpectedly, Etienne sat up and frowned at her. "You are an impertinent girl to ask such personal questions of someone you do not know."

Claire's eyes narrowed. She shot rigidly upright and snapped, "You are right. I do not know you. Perhaps you are my father's brother, but you are a stranger to me." She swept haughtily toward the door. "Come, Captain Reed, I have no place here."

Snifter in hand, the captain watched the scene unfolding before him with interest, noting the older man's bemused expression.

Abruptly Etienne burst into delighted laughter. "*Mon Dieu,* you are a Fortier!"

Claire turned to regard him incredulously. "Of course, I am. I have proof." She thrust her father's letter toward him.

"Later, perhaps." The Creole dismissed the letter with a wave of his elegant hand. "I know you are Jules's daughter, *chère.* I had only to look at you to know, but somehow I thought you would be . . . younger. How the years slip by. You were little more than a baby when last I heard from my brother.

"Come back." He beckoned, then he turned to Claire's companion. "Capitaine Reed, since you are responsible for this . . . er . . . reunion, will you introduce me to my niece?"

Placing a hand against the girl's stiff back, the captain pushed her forward gently. Still apprehensive, she found herself before her newfound uncle.

"Monsieur Fortier," John Reed said grandly, "permit me to introduce Claire Fortier. Mademoiselle, your uncle."

"How do you do?" Claire greeted him, suddenly shy.

"How do you do?" Etienne echoed gravely. "I am delighted to meet you—Claire. Jules gave you a good name. It was your *grand-mère*'s. Did you know that?"

"He told me."

"Did he? And how did you leave your papa?"

"He—he died five years ago."

Pain clouded Etienne's eyes and he asked in a voice rough with grief, "Why did no one notify me?"

"I think my mother always intended to."

"Of course." He did not speak for a moment. At last he sighed regretfully. "Gallant, carefree Jules. How did he die?"

"Of a fever," Claire told him softly. "It came on very suddenly. Mother and I nursed him, but he never regained consciousness. He never even knew we were with him."

"A dramatic end to a dramatic life," Etienne concluded bitterly.

"You have no right to say that," she bristled.

"I have every right. Do not misunderstand. Jules was my brother and I loved him, but we almost never agreed."

Etienne pinched the bridge of his nose, obscuring his eyes, and asked in a tight voice, "And your mother, White Sky?"

"She died two months ago," Claire whispered sadly.

"I see." The man's voice was muffled. Removing his hand from watery eyes, he sat erect in his chair, seemingly marshaling his faculties.

Claire glanced at the captain and wondered if he had seen the pain in her uncle's eyes. Had she caused it by reminding Etienne of the past?

A moment later, she realized the conversation had taken a turn and the men were now discussing her.

"Certainly she will stay here," her uncle declared. "There is plenty of room. Of course, I have never been a family man, but after all, Claire is my brother's daughter. She belongs here. Fortier House was Jules's home. Now it will be hers.

"That is, if such an arrangement is agreeable to you, my dear." He looked questioningly at his niece.

Claire nodded. Why did she feel numb when she had found what she sought . . . a new home, a new life? She felt suddenly tired and too weary for elation.

"How can I repay you, *Capitaine,* for bringing my niece safely home?" the Creole asked.

"Just allow us to call on her sometimes when the *Delphinius* is in New Orleans. My wife and I are certainly going to miss her."

"Will you and Madame Reed join us for dinner this evening?" Etienne invited politely.

"No, thank you, sir, not this time."

"Perhaps on your next visit," his host suggested, pulling a velvet bell rope beside the fireplace.

"We would like that," the captain agreed as the door to the hall slid open and the huge butler thrust his head into the room.

"Greer will show you out, Capitaine Reed. And thank you again."

The servant stepped back to allow the man to pass, but he made no move to escort him to the front door. Instead he looked into the library, pointedly staring at Claire.

"Just show the captain out, Greer," Etienne spoke patiently. "Mademoiselle Claire will be staying."

"For dinner?" The big man looked confused.

"For dinner and for some time to come. This is my niece. Have Beady prepare a room for her. Then take her bag up after you have shown the captain out."

"This way, sir." The butler frowned and guided Captain Reed toward the front door.

Claire watched, feeling strangely abandoned, as John Reed disappeared down the hall. Slowly she turned to face her uncle and they regarded each other warily; family, yet strangers.

As he waited nervously for his niece to come down to dinner, Etienne poured himself another glass of sherry. He had taken the events of the afternoon in stride, he mused, but what was to come? After a lifetime of bachelorhood, he had taken a waif, a stranger, into his household. For years he had been a kind of adopted bachelor uncle to the children of friends, but now he was a real uncle—or worse, a parent!

He had done the right thing, he knew it. Let no one say Etienne Fortier was not honorable and loyal to his family. But damn it, he was too old to become a family man so precipitately.

Mentally, he rehearsed how he would greet the girl when she came downstairs—kindly and cordial, but detached. The man found himself lifting a disapproving eyebrow when she appeared at last. Her face was freshly scrubbed and her hair was combed, but she still wore the wrinkled gingham gown of the afternoon.

"Haven't you another frock to wear besides your... er...travel dress?" Etienne asked critically.

She smoothed her skirt and met his scrutiny with an up-lifted chin. "This is the only one Iris could find to fit me," she replied defiantly, "though I do have a buckskin dress."

Etienne winced slightly at the thought, but quickly recovered. "*Non, non, chère,* you cannot go about New Orleans dressed like a savage. We shall go to the Red Stores tomorrow and outfit you as befits a young lady of quality."

"I have no money for clothes, so if you do not wish me to look like a 'savage,'" she said, her voice dripping with venom, "this dress will have to do." Her knuckles whitened as she gripped the back of her chair.

"Do not be so quick to take offense, Claire, when none was intended," Etienne advised mildly, pulling out her chair. "I shall take care of the bill. I have accounts at all the best stores."

"The ones on Chartres Street where ladies shop?"

"*Oui.*" His gray eyes were round with surprise.

Claire settled herself in her seat and considered the problem. "*Très bien,* I must have clothes if I am to stay here. You may pay for them," she conceded logically, "but I shall repay you as soon as I can."

The man frowned, but if more was to be said about the proposed shopping trip, it was forgotten when Greer brought in a steaming tureen of savory gumbo.

Throughout dinner, Etienne was a charming host. He was polite and discreet, but skillfully he steered the conversation to learn more of his niece's life.

Claire gave him a complete report on Jules's death and answered his questions about her mother, but she volunteered little information about herself.

What could she tell him? she wondered bleakly. That because she was a half-breed, she had not been accepted by her mother's people? That she had grown to be self-sufficient, spending her time rereading the precious books her father had given her? That she had built a wall around herself?

When Claire had revealed as much as she intended, she fell silent. Considerately Etienne took his cue from her and they completed their meal in relative silence.

At the end of the evening, he rang for Greer and excused himself apologetically. "I believe I'll go to bed now. It's been a rather eventful day and I am tired.

"*Bonne nuit,* Claire," he bade her awkwardly when the hulking butler appeared to take her to her room.

"Bonne nuit," she answered briskly and, without a backward look, trotted out of the room behind Greer.

Etienne snuffed the candles and lingered a moment in the deserted dining room. "Sleep well, *ma petite,*" he murmured sadly. Then he trudged upstairs to his own room.

Greer led the girl to her quarters, maintaining a hostile silence. Halting suddenly in front of a door in the long hallway of doors, he rumbled, "Here we are, miss."

Claire extended her hand hesitantly toward the doorknob, then withdrew it. Was this the room she had occupied earlier? The dark corridor had looked different this afternoon.

"Will there be anything else?" the butler asked testily.

"Non, merci." Uncertain what she should do, Claire looked to the big man for direction.

With a perplexed frown he opened the door for her, but he made no move to enter the room. "Beady will be here presently to help you prepare for bed."

"I do not need help." Claire balked in the doorway.

"She'll be here all the same," he said condescendingly, gesturing toward the bedchamber. "Now, if you please..."

The room was indeed the same one in which Claire had freshened up after her journey. But now the enameled bathtub she had enjoyed was gone, and a small fire crackled in the fireplace, chasing away the chill of evening. The *baire*, the mosquito netting, tied back earlier, hung down beside the tester bed. The rose satin bedspread was turned back to reveal clean white sheets and fluffy pillows.

When the butler had withdrawn, Claire slipped off her moccasins and went to draw back the velvet draperies over the French doors that opened onto a small balcony. Stepping out, she looked over the shadowy lawn where wisps of night fog played. After the heat of the day, the evening had grown cool. A golden sliver of moon overhead illuminated silvery Spanish moss, which draped over the limbs of massive river oaks and swayed slightly in the breeze.

"What you doin' out there in your bare feets, mam'selle?" Beady demanded shrilly from behind her.

The girl whirled guiltily. She had not heard her approach. "Just looking," she answered defensively.

Beady dragged her inside and closed the door. "You kin look without ketchin' your death. Ain't no need to be paddin' around 'thout shoes. Step over by th' fire and I'll help you git ready for bed.''

The plump maid herded Claire to the hearth and, despite her protests, helped her out of her clothing and into her nightgown. After a spirited exchange about whose duty it was to brush Claire's hair, the girl grudgingly submitted to Beady's ministrations. At last, she shooed the servant out of the room and nestled comfortably in a big chintz-covered chair to think.

Claire stared into the fire, her feet tucked beneath her. Her chin rested on her doubled knees, which protruded under her made-over nightgown like tent poles too long for the tent they supported. The girl's thick dark hair was straight and loose. A glossy curtain shielding most of her face, it guarded her privacy from prying eyes.

And prying eyes there were, as Beady stealthily opened the door to peep at her new mistress. She started fearfully when Greer lumbered down the hall, making his final inspection of the night.

"Go to bed, Beady," he instructed, seeing her outside Claire's door.

"Mam'selle Claire might need somethin'," she objected, "so I wanna wait here till she goes to bed."

"As you wish," he acquiesced. "But be prepared to do your chores tomorrow. It is wash day, you know."

"But I'm a lady's maid now. Shouldn't hafta do no washin'," Beady sputtered as the big butler disappeared down the murky hallway.

"Beady, is that you?" Claire called from within the room.

"Yes, mam'selle." Beady peered into the room.

"Why don't you go to bed? I can take care of myself."

"Reckon you kin, but you're th' lady of Fortier House," the maid argued stubbornly, her lower lip curling in an injured pout, "and takin' keer of you is my job. M'sieur Etienne say so."

Claire stared wordlessly at her until the little servant fidgeted.

"At least lemme see you all settled in bed, then I'll go," Beady pleaded.

Sighing in resignation, Claire climbed into the feather bed and allowed the maid to pull the light blanket over her.

Drawing the net curtains closed around the bed, Beady whispered, "If you need somethin', ring that bell on th' table and I'll come runnin'." Tiptoeing exaggeratedly, she departed.

Claire tossed, too tired to sleep. In a single afternoon, her life had changed completely. Her old life was over and her new life begun. She had been foolish to think her arrival in New Orleans would solve all her problems, she reflected ruefully. It had simply presented new ones.

Looking for a comfortable position, she stretched out and thought of tomorrow. Tomorrow when she would show her uncle that she expected no charity. She would cook for him; she would clean. She would be a valuable addition to his household. But most of all she would learn to be a lady. She would make him proud.

So much to learn, so much to prove, she thought as she fell asleep, tomorrow.

Chapter Two

The afternoon shadows were long when Philippe Girard urged Lagniappe, his powerful stallion, to a gallop up the *allée* to Bonté, his family home. In a split second, he was forced to rein in tightly as a bright, beribboned form flitted in front of him. Controlling his horse with difficulty, the young man scowled down at his eleven-year-old sister.

"Odette, you little she-devil, I ought to skin you alive. You nearly scared Lagniappe out of his wits," he shouted as he swung down from his mount and tossed the reins to a groom.

Panting from her run, Odette clung to her brother's arm. "I am sorry, Philippe, but I had to see you before you went to the house." She darted nervous glances toward the house and dragged him out of sight into the shrubbery that fringed the drive.

"What is this all about, *chère?* What's so important it cannot wait?" He laughed, dodging limbs as he tried to loosen her grasp.

"I had to warn you. Papa is waiting for you in the study."

"What is it this time?" the young man groaned.

"He shouted at the man, Philippe," Odette babbled. "It was dreadful. I listened at the door. I know it was wrong, but I did, anyway."

"Slow down. What are you talking about?"

Wide-eyed, the girl took a deep breath and began to talk more calmly. "This afternoon a Kaintock came looking for you. Nero told him you weren't in, but the man stomped right into the house, shouting for you. He marched into Papa's office and told him you owed him money and he meant to have it now!"

"I told Johnson I would pay him," Philippe grated. "He did not have to come here."

"Oh, Philippe—" Odette gazed up at her brother through tear-glazed eyes "—how could you borrow money from that awful man? I would have given you the money Tante gave me for a first communion gift—at least, what is left of it." She swallowed bravely.

"I don't need your money, Odette. And I did not borrow from that man. I lost it to him."

"Gambling?" she cried in horror. "After what Papa said!"

"I know, I know. I also remember what he said about eavesdropping on other people's conversations."

Odette hung her head and said nothing in her own defense.

"Just do not make a habit of it," Philippe chided, giving her a brotherly squeeze. "Since you listened to this one, how did it end?" he asked conspiratorially.

"That is what I came to tell you." She sniffled. "Papa flew into one of his rages. He said he would pay for your trans...transgressions this time, but no more. Then he told the man never to show his face here again."

"Is that all?"

"No-o-o," she replied reluctantly. "The man came out of the study, counting his money, but he was still angry. He scowled so fiercely, I was afraid, Philippe. He shouted that the next time he would take your debt from your hide, and Papa shouted back that if there was a next time, he could do just that."

"Where was Maman during all of this?" Philippe asked wearily.

"In her room."

"Saying rosaries for me, no doubt."

"Perhaps you should miss dinner tonight," his sister suggested hopelessly. "Perhaps by tomorrow Papa will forget to be upset."

"*Non.* The longer he has to think, the more he will seethe. I've had enough experience with his temper to know. Better to get it over now. Thanks, though, for the warning."

"Philippe." Odette stopped him as he headed toward the house, and asked in a wavering voice, "You won't tell Papa I told you, will you? Because then he will be angry with me."

"He never stays angry with you, *ma petite.*"

"I know, but . . ." She looked stricken.

"I won't tell." Philippe smiled, throwing a comforting arm around her shoulders. "Now, come on, dinner will be ready soon."

Companionably, brother and sister ambled across the lawn as if they had not a worry in the world.

They were met at the door by Nero, a slave who had belonged to the Girard family for as long as he could remember. Through the years, he had come to know intimately the black rages the master fell into and had often witnessed Pierre Girard's autocratic control over his family, his absolute say over his elder son, René.

Then there was Philippe. Pierre barely tolerated his younger son. Since early childhood, the boy had not bowed to authority, not even his father's. Nero had watched the rebellious lad grow to manhood and observed the unflagging tension between father and son. But never in all his years, the dignified old servant thought grimly, had he seen such a tempest brewing as the one that brewed at Bonté tonight.

"M'sieur Pierre wishes to see you in the study at once," he told the young man politely as he took his hat.

"*Merci.*" Tensely Philippe smoothed his hair, squared his shoulders and strolled toward his father's study.

"There you are, you scoundrel." Pierre sat ramrod straight behind a massive oak desk and scowled at his son through the open doorway. "I have been waiting for you. Come in and close the door. I want to talk to you."

"Now?" Shoving his hands into his pockets, Philippe sauntered insolently into the room.

"Yes, now!" Pierre roared.

"*Très bien.*" The young man shrugged indifferently and closed the door. Lounging against a mahogany table, he braced himself with his palms against its smooth top and stretched out his long legs before him, crossing them at the ankles. He regarded his father with bored expectation.

"Today," Pierre began with scant restraint, "I paid nearly a thousand dollars to settle your gambling debts."

"I heard. I am sorry Johnson made a scene here."

"You are sorry!" the older man exploded. "Sorry you lost, not that you gambled. I have told you again and again, you are irresponsible and immature, but you do not listen. Money slips through your fingers like water. You are twenty-eight years old and you have nothing to show for your life."

"Like René?" Philippe asked, his lip curling contemptuously.

"Like René," his father echoed harshly.

"He works for you. He has the firstborn's claim to Bonté. All I have is Girard Stables and I worked very hard for that. I built it from one colt."

"A colt that was given to you—by your aunt."

"Yes, it was given to me, but I parlayed it into a lot more."

"Keep your gambling language out of this house! I will not have it!" his father commanded. He continued sarcastically, "So you built this empire of horseflesh, yet you can't pay your debts."

"A temporary shortage of funds," Philippe grated defensively.

"You managed to buy a new horse for your precious stables."

"I needed a stud. Cavalier was a bit more expensive than I anticipated. That was unfortunate, but necessary. I put almost everything I make back into the stables."

"And it is necessary that you gamble away the rest?" Pierre asked hotly.

"I was trying to recoup some of my losses," the young man muttered more to himself than to his father. "I could not believe Johnson's horse could be faster than Hyacinth. I still say he would not have beaten her if she hadn't thrown a shoe."

"I do not give a hang about your mare's shoe or your financial reverses," his father snapped. "I just want you to know this is the last time I shall come to your rescue."

"I did not ask you to come to my rescue this time. I would have paid the man."

"And what would you have used for money? Mark my words, boy, the next time this happens I will sell some of your precious ponies to cover my losses."

"They are not yours to sell," Philippe stated flatly.

"Do not tell me what I can and cannot do, you wastrel!" Pierre shouted. Jumping to his feet, he lurched around the desk, his fist clenched and lifted to strike.

Philippe watched his father's violent display with weary indifference, motionless until Pierre swung his fist. Then he easily captured his father's arm and held it in midair.

"I would not do that, Père," he said with a mirthless smile. "We are both men now and the outcome would be disastrous for all concerned."

White-faced and shaken, Pierre glared at his son, then, rage catching in his throat, he wrenched his arm free and turned his back to him. After a long moment, he spoke hoarsely, "I do not know why I even allow you to live here."

"To meet the conventions of polite society, I suppose." Philippe shrugged. "And for Maman's sake, because she wants her unmarried sons nearby, living in the *garçonnière*. God knows you do not keep me here because you love me, and I do not stay because I need a place to sleep."

"What do you mean by that?" His father whirled indignantly.

"What I said—nothing more."

"I know what you meant. Do you think I do not know where you spend your nights? With that whore," the older man spluttered.

"Lila Broussard is not a whore," Philippe protested mockingly. "She is a respectable businesswoman, or hadn't you heard?"

"A respectable businesswoman, my eye," Pierre snorted. "Only because she is kept—and kept well—by Etienne Fortier. Do you know what that means, Philippe? She is another man's property. You steal from Fortier every time you visit his mistress."

"I steal nothing. What Lila offers is freely given, and there is plenty to go around."

"Enough," Pierre bellowed. "Get out of here! Go to your room until dinner."

"Go to my room?" Philippe roared with laughter. "I shall not be home for dinner, *mon père*—tonight or anytime soon." He strode from the room, his cockiness concealing the agitation he felt at another hopeless confrontation with his father.

Slamming the door of the study, he paused in the hall to collect his thoughts. He half expected to find Odette loitering innocently outside the door, but when he glanced around, no one was to be seen.

A muffled sob from the stairs drew his attention and he found himself staring up into his mother's tear-washed face. A pale picture of grief, she swayed on the landing and fingered the beads of her rosary, her sorrowful eyes on her wayward son. Faintly accusing, she bowed her head and turned to trudge up the stairs without a word.

Sadly Philippe watched her go, wondering how much she had heard through the closed door.

"Best you go now, M'sieur Philippe," the butler said quietly from behind him, "before the master remembers something he forgot to say. Your horse has been watered and fed and he's ready to go."

"*Merci,* Nero." Philippe accepted his hat from the old man. "Give my regrets to *ma mère,* will you? Tell her I had important business in town this evening."

"I will, sir."

Jamming his hat on his head, Philippe marched out of the house without a backward look. Evening found him with friends in a café where he drank heavily, but did not eat. Later he played Buck the Tiger at the Palace of Chance, but did not win. As he staggered through the dark streets with his companions, he thought for a moment he glimpsed the girl from the dock, but he was wrong. The night was filled with too much absinthe, too much music and laughter, and too many blurred faces ranged around the gaming tables. At dawn, he stumbled to a bed in a small hotel.

In the distance, a cock crowed and Claire awoke, not knowing for a moment where she was. Then she remembered. Today she was to begin her life at Fortier House.

After dressing quickly, she stepped out onto the balcony to admire the rosy sunrise. The morning was cool and fresh, and birdsong came from high in a chinaberry tree. She inhaled deeply, savoring the aromas wafting from the kitchen.

Downstairs the rooms were still dusky and silent. The girl had not expected that Etienne would be up and about yet, but she was surprised to find no one stirring. Hearing a noise from the backyard, she went to a window and peeped out at the brick kitchen. A wispy column of smoke rose from its chimney. Through the doorway, she could see a teenage slave girl tending the fire, using her skirt to fan the flame one moment and the next to wipe her brow.

In an open shed beside the kitchen, laundry day had begun. Steam rose from the kettles and merged with the last remnants of morning fog. The day promised to be hot as the sun fought to break through the clouds. Many of the women servants were already at work, their sleeves rolled past their elbows, their heads wrapped neatly in colorful *tignons*. Several bent energetically over washtubs, scrubbing, while others wrung the sodden sheets and hung them on lines to dry. The sound of their soft voices floated to the girl on the breeze.

For an instant, she considered joining them, but her step faltered. The distance was too great and she was swept with a familiar feeling, the knowledge of an invisible barrier. This time the line was clearly drawn between mistress and servant. Beady had explained last night that Claire was expected to be the mistress of Fortier House.

Restlessly Claire roamed the main floor of the great house, exploring, reveling in newfound luxury. She peered into the mahogany hutch in the dining room, admiring the china and crystal there. Wandering through the library, she tried the leather chairs. She pulled back the draperies in the formal first parlor, then the lace curtains in the homey second parlor, flooding both rooms with light. She discovered the sliding partition between the rooms that allowed them to become one formal salon. She inspected the marble fireplaces and the gold-framed mirrors suspended above them by silken ropes. In the hall, she ran her fingers appreciatively over the carved newel post at the foot of the stairs.

"'Scuse me, Mam'selle Claire," a pretty Negro maid interrupted, her voice lilting. "I gots to git past you . . . to upstairs. Greer say these towels gots to be put away before M'sieur 'Tienne's bath."

Claire did not recognize her. "How do you know my name?"

The maid dimpled becomingly, her smile barely visible over the stack of linens she carried. "Greer say you are Mam'selle Claire, M'sieur 'Tienne's kin. We mus' take good care of you. If you need anythin' and you cain't find Beady, call for me . . . Lucene."

Curious, Claire followed her upstairs and into a spacious linen closet. The maid answered her questions breezily while performing her duties, and Claire knew she had found a willing subject for her interrogation.

"Have you worked for my uncle long, Lucene?"

"He buy me 'bout five years ago—straight off th' boat from Haiti. He been very good to me," the servant answered judiciously, stacking the towels neatly and arranging plantain leaves between them to keep insects away. "M'sieur 'Tienne is better than most masters, I think."

"Has he always lived here alone with no one to look after him?"

Lucene's pretty face clouded. "Mam'selle, we all take good care of him. He don't want for nothin'."

"No, no," Claire soothed her, "I mean, has he never taken a wife?"

"Don't think so." The maid shook her head. "But he never needed one. He got Greer . . . and Toolah, the cook . . . and me to care for him here. And he keep a *placée* over on th' Ramparts."

"A *placée?*" Claire looked mystified.

"You don't know what that is?" Lucene giggled incredulously. "Why, a *placée*—"

"There you are." Greer's deep voice caught the girls by surprise. They whirled to face the butler, who loomed sternly in the doorway. "What is keeping you, Lucene?"

"I was p-puttin' away th' towels like you said," she stammered.

"I did not tell you to waste your time gossiping, especially when you are needed in the laundry."

"I'm goin' now." Her eyes riveted to the floor, Lucene sidled from the linen closet.

"It was not her fault that she took so long," Claire told Greer heatedly when the maid was gone. "I was to blame for asking her so many questions."

"That is your privilege, miss," he responded stiffly. "But I must warn you, the servants know little, if anything, of your uncle's private life."

She blushed at the well-aimed barb. "I did not ask her anything I would not ask my uncle myself."

"Then perhaps you *should* ask him, miss, and not rely on the gossip of slaves." The butler seized a towel and left Claire's icy stare for the steamy confines of Etienne's bath.

"Just a minute—" Wrathfully, she followed him into the hall, sputtering when he disappeared into a room and closed the door with a decisive click. Her face flushed with anger, she stormed down the back stairs, muttering dire threats in Cherokee, and burst out into the kitchen yard. The sweating servants paused in their labors to whisper among themselves, speculating about the new mistress's abrupt exit from the servants' entrance.

Composing herself, the girl strolled toward the muffled clatter of pots and pans that came from the kitchen. Within moments, Toolah, the rotund black cook, was protesting Claire's insistence that she cook her uncle's breakfast.

"No, ma'am, that wouldn't be fittin'." Toolah pursed her lips and shook her head firmly. "It's my job to fix M'sieur 'Tienne's breakfus' and yours, too.

"Beady," she shouted irritably toward the laundry yard. "Come take your mistress to th' dining room so's she kin eat like a lady." Toolah picked up a tray and backed her ample derriere out of the narrow doorway.

After breakfast, Claire was banished to the garden. Disgusted by her exile, she hardly noticed the brilliant pink of the azaleas or the blue of the Louisiana sky. She wandered through the carefully pruned garden to the lawn beyond. As she paused under a huge cypress tree, a bird fluttered in the branches above, shaking dewdrops onto her head. Gazing upward, she saw that the mighty limbs supported the fanciful white tree house she had noticed yesterday.

Claire mounted the narrow stairs that wound around the massive tree trunk, her fingers trailing against the bark as she climbed. At the head of the steps she found a small octagonal-shaped room—cool, open and airy. Alternate walls were built of lacy white trellis; the other four were uncovered, revealing an unimpaired view of the river in the distance. The sun, now high in the sky, filtered through the foliage, casting dappled shadows on the wooden floor. Several small tables and footstools were set conveniently in front of low benches that ringed the room, their cushions covered with a cheerful cotton print.

Pleased by her discovery, the girl sank onto a bench to enjoy the view. On one side was the glistening river; on the other, stately Fortier House. She felt momentary panic as she considered the enormity of her new responsibilities as the mistress of that great house. Her uncle's expectations of her were greater than cooking, cleaning or washing.

Before yesterday she had never even been inside such a huge home with its army of servants. How was she to run it? How was she even to learn?

She bit her lip in frustration, but forced herself to think calmly. She would learn what she must know in time; until then, the servants would do what they had always done.

Slowly the sun's gentle warmth began to work on Claire. She listened to the soft rustling of the leaves and felt herself relaxing. But her serenity was soon interrupted by a shrill voice.

"Mam'selle Claire! You up there? I been lookin' all over for you," Beady announced when her mistress appeared at the window. Hands on her hips, the maid stared up at her accusingly. "I was 'bout ready to git me some help. I looked in th' garden. I looked in th' yard. I even went back to th' kitchen. I thought sure you wandered off—"

"Why were you looking for me?" Claire asked.

"Your uncle is waitin' to take you to buy some new clothes."

"Has he been waiting long?" Claire cried, jumping to her feet and starting down the stairs.

"Jest whilst I was lookin' for you. I looked ever'-where...." the maid muttered as Claire raced past her toward the house.

"There you are, Claire," Etienne greeted his niece pleasantly. "Did you like the garden?"

"*Oui,* especially the tree house."

"Ah, yes. I haven't used it for a long time, but it's an enjoyable place, as I recall. We must spend an evening there soon, away from the heat and the mosquitoes. But for now, I propose a trip into town for some new frocks and feminine trappings."

Etienne felt unexpected anticipation as their coach rolled through the Vieux Carré. Sitting back, he pulled his Panama hat down over his eyes and studied Claire from under its broad brim. She was an interesting combination, he mused, unusual and exciting, his diamond in the rough.

Much of his mother, the first Claire, could be seen in her— the ivory skin, the aristocratic features. From White Sky, she had inherited dark, slanting eyes and glossy black hair. Although the girl's coltish limbs seemed always to be at angles, she had her mother's natural grace, as well. She was as bright and intelligent as Jules had been—and nearly as tall, he thought ruefully. She might not be beautiful, but she had great potential. Etienne just hoped they would meet no one he knew until she had a decent wardrobe and had had time to adjust to city life.

When the carriage stopped in front of a row of dress and millinery shops, the man opened the door, alighting at once. As he helped Claire to the banquette, he threw covert glances up and down the street. Satisfied that none of his cronies lurked nearby, he steered her hurriedly toward Madame Benoit's Dress Shop.

"Etienne! Etienne Fortier!" A contralto voice rang out down the street, echoing in the doorways of the surrounding shops.

The man cringed but did not stop. Questioningly Claire faltered, but he dragged her toward the shop.

"Come along," he instructed under his breath.

"Isn't it someone you know?"

"It *is* you, you old devil!" The strident voice bore down on them. "Didn't you hear me calling?"

Etienne grimaced and released the girl's arm. Slowly he faced the old woman who strode vigorously in their direction. Tall, erect and portly, she wore a tailored riding habit of very expensive and very wrinkled linen. Apparently unconcerned whether people thought she had a touch of the café au lait to her blood, she wore no hat against the sun. Wisps of iron-gray hair escaped an untidy bun and floated on the breeze around her weathered face.

"*Bonjour,* Madeleine." Etienne tipped his hat and greeted her as if surprised. "What an unexpected pleasure."

"Unexpected perhaps," she rejoined dryly, "but I doubt it is a pleasure."

Etienne brushed her comment aside smoothly. "I had no idea you were in town. Your brother told me you were staying at your plantation out on Bayou Teche."

"That is where he would like me to stay, but I come and go as I please. Always have, much to Pierre's dismay," she added crisply. "You are among the first to know of my return, Etienne. I have not even gone out to see the family yet. I'll wager some of them will be as glad to see me as you were. I thought for a moment you were trying to ignore me."

"I could never do that, Madeleine," he protested lamely.

Standing in the background, Claire stiffened when she felt the old woman's penetrating gaze on her. Deliberately, she lifted her chin and met the piercing eyes proudly.

Etienne missed the silent exchange as he glanced despairingly at the curious faces of passersby, reading disapproval in the expression of every one. He bowed to the old woman and said politely, "It has been good to see you again, Madeleine, but we really must go. We have much shopping to do."

"What?" Madeleine snapped. "You would take your leave before you have introduced your charming companion?" Her liver-spotted hand gripped his arm with surprising strength.

"Ah, yes, my companion." Etienne sighed, drawing Claire forward with reluctance. "Madame Madeleine Delaney, may I present my niece, Claire Fortier. Claire, Madame Delaney of River Oaks."

"Your niece?" Madeleine exclaimed. "Jules's daughter?" She squinted nearsightedly at Claire and crowed, "Yes, by damn, there is a family resemblance. It is a pleasure, *chère,* to welcome you to New Orleans."

"*Merci,* Madame Delaney," Claire stammered, ill at ease at the sudden display of friendliness.

"Call me Tante Delaney, please. Most of the young people do."

"All right . . . Tante Delaney," the girl agreed with a shy smile, "if you will call me Claire."

"I could think of calling you nothing else. 'Tienne," she went on, frowning forbiddingly at the man, "how is it you never mentioned Claire to me?"

"I didn't know her," he explained defensively. "I knew Jules had a child, but I had received no word from him for ten years. Claire arrived yesterday with the news that both her father and mother are dead."

"I am sorry, my dear." Tante Delaney patted the girl's hand comfortingly. "I was very fond of your father in his younger days. He was quite a fellow. Tell me—" she leaned toward her to whisper conspiratorially "—are you the hellion Jules was?"

"Madeleine!" Claire's uncle was shocked.

"Pish-posh, Etienne. You know he was one of my favorites. So handsome and gallant, always at the heart of any scandal or adventure," the old woman reminisced fondly. "He would like to be remembered as a hellion, I think."

"Where have you been living?" she asked Claire.

"Just inside the Indian Territories," the girl answered honestly, hoping Tante Delaney would not ask too many questions.

"How exciting! So your mother was Indian, eh? I should have known, with your dark eyes and marvelous cheekbones." The woman chuckled throatily.

"Madeleine, please," Etienne interjected. "Claire has only just arrived. We have not even had time to purchase proper attire for her. She is not ready for society yet."

"Society, is it? How ready do you suppose she needs to be to sip tea with a bunch of old marsh hens and their stuffed-shirt husbands?" Tante Delaney retorted tartly. "Claire is a natural-born lady. Takes after your mother, I'd say. Except for some window dressing, she looks ready enough for society to me."

Etienne blinked in consternation, but he spoke firmly. "She will have no window dressing if you do not excuse us, Madeleine. Madame Benoit is waiting to fit Claire, and I have an important appointment this afternoon."

"Then run along." Tante Delaney dismissed the distinguished gray-haired man as if he were a schoolboy. "I shall help Claire shop for her new wardrobe."

"That is not necessary, Madeleine," Etienne argued weakly.

"Of course it isn't, but I want to. Besides, I know how men despise shopping. I shall see that she has appropriate attire for every occasion."

"But...but it could take all day," Etienne floundered, out of his element with this strong-willed female. "She must have clothes and shoes and hats and—"

She bristled. "I know what she needs, 'Tienne. I know, too, that many people consider me rather unconventional, but I promise every article of clothing we buy will be quite proper, if that is why you are worried."

"Not at all," he said, surrendering. "If you wish to accompany her, we would both be delighted. Wouldn't we, Claire?" He looked to the girl, who nodded enthusiastically.

"Then it is settled," Tante Delaney exclaimed. "I shall deliver Claire home this afternoon."

"I will leave my carriage, eh, Madeleine?"

"You are just afraid I'll trot your niece home on my mare. But do not worry, I will rent a carriage. Now go about your business while we become acquainted.

"Come along, my dear." Without a backward glance, Tante Delaney swept into the shop, leaving the girl to trail behind.

Etienne patted Claire's hand and admonished, "Charge everything to my accounts and buy whatever Madeleine thinks you need. Do not scrimp or you will have to answer to me."

"Merci." Claire smiled and withdrew her hand gingerly.

"Tell Madeleine I shall send my carriage back for your use. I do not want her to have to hire one."

"Très bien." The girl nodded, turning to go.

"Claire . . ." Etienne stopped her impulsively. "Buy a gown of sky blue. I think it will become you. It looked lovely on your mother. . . ." His voice trailed off. His face red with embarrassment, Etienne refused to meet the girl's curious gaze.

"I have wasted enough time," he concluded curtly, clamping his hat on his head. Striding to his carriage, he got in and barked an abrupt order to the driver.

Claire lingered on the banquette as Etienne was driven away. Why was he suddenly troubled? She had done nothing to bring the sharp tone to his voice, yet suddenly he seemed angry at her.

Perhaps, she thought painfully, he is only kind because I am family. Perhaps he doesn't like me. Perhaps I shall never fit in here, either. No, she told herself fiercely, I will become a lady. I will make Uncle Etienne proud.

As Claire walked slowly into the dress shop, she was unaware of the slitted eyes watching her from behind a window sign, painted black and red:

BROUSSARD'S
Fine Millinery for Ladies

Who was this gawky child Etienne fawned over on the street? Lila brooded, pacing in the empty shop. Surely not a rival. She would tolerate no competition. As arrogant as she was petite and beautiful, the fair-skinned octoroon cursed the unknown girl, halting before a small mirror as if to reassure herself.

She was pleased with the haughty picture reflected. Anger heightened her color and her tawny eyes snapped. She drew herself up, standing proudly erect, chin lifted challengingly. A spot at the base of her throat pulsed and her voluptuous breasts quivered in indignation. Of course she was beautiful, she told herself. Not a woman in New Orleans, black or white, could match her beauty.

Etienne was her protector. He had been since they first met at the Quadroon Ballroom. He had been smitten at once by the dark-haired beauty with golden eyes. The polished, debonair man had become as tongue-tied as a schoolboy when the octoroon, clad in a gown of satin that matched her eyes, flirted boldly from behind her fan. In the glow of a hundred candles, he had swept her onto the dance floor and into his life.

She would never give him up, Lila vowed. Never.

Chapter Three

Impressed by her success, the tiny dressmaker stepped back to admire her handiwork. She, Elise Benoit, had performed a miracle. It had taken hours of fitting and alteration and had kept all her seamstresses busy for the entire afternoon, but the effort had been worth it. She had turned Monsieur Fortier's niece into... well, almost into a beauty. The girl was too tall, too slender, *too different* to be a true belle, but she was at least presentable now.

These basic items were only the beginning, the modiste thought with a thrill. An entire wardrobe was needed, and Monsieur Fortier would expect only the finest.

The birdlike woman twittered and fussed, proudly unfurling rich bolts of velvet and silk for inspection, pulling out rolls of bright ribbon and exquisite lace. Surrounded by extravagant finery, she beamed at her customers, joyfully tallying in her head the cost of the materials alone.

"Deep green for the riding habit," Tante Delaney instructed, "black velvet for a cape, another ball gown of this rose silk. Haven't you something lighter for a morning dress?"

Madame Benoit called at once for muslin in every color of the rainbow.

"What do you think, *chère?*" Madeleine asked Claire as she frowned critically at the offerings. "Do you see anything you like?"

"My uncle wants me to buy a blue dress," Claire mentioned shyly.

"Very good, mademoiselle," Madame Benoit chirped, noting the girl's choice on a growing list.

"You did remember to include a nightgown and a robe in today's order?" Tante Delaney interrupted her pondering.

"*Oui,* madame, and a pair of slippers for lagniappe."

"*Merci,*" Claire said.

"It is nothing," the little shopkeeper responded graciously.

"You must wear that frock home," Tante Delaney suggested, smiling at the girl. "It looks so cool in this heat and that pink is perfect for you. And look, here's a parasol exactly the same color.

"As for this," the old woman snorted, handing the girl's made-over dress to Madame Benoit, "it may be disposed of."

The dressmaker accepted the bundle of worn gingham and disdainfully passed it to one of her assistants. "See this gets to the Convent of the Ursulines' poor box."

"I think that will do for now," Tante Delaney said, gazing at the day's purchases with satisfaction. "An accounting, if you please, Madame Benoit."

"May I wait for you on the banquette, Tante Delaney?" Claire asked, eager to try her new parasol.

"*Oui,*" the woman answered absentmindedly as she inspected the figures the dressmaker presented, "but don't stray."

Elise Benoit's eyebrows lifted. A young lady from a good family out even for a few moments alone? It simply was not done. She started to speak, but thought better of it. Madeleine Delaney was a most unconventional person and she did the most unconventional things, no matter that she was the richest woman in three parishes. What harm in allowing the girl to wait outside? What would happen on Rue Chartres in broad daylight?

Claire stepped out onto the sunny banquette and opened her parasol carefully, positioning it so it blocked the sun's glare. The sunshade felt awkward in her hand, as if she were carrying a torch at midday. Remembering the women she had seen promenading aboard the *Delphinius,* she rested the long handle on her shoulder. Now it felt more natural. She ambled back and forth in front of the shop, twirling the parasol experimentally.

Her movements, mirrored in the shop window, caught her eye. She looked nice, she thought, not beautiful, but nice. Approvingly, she nodded at her reflection, watching the image quaver, distorted by the rippled surface of the window.

Claire's eyes widened when another image appeared beside hers. Tall and lean and dark, the man carried himself with confidence. Thick raven hair was swept back from his sun-browned face, its aristocratic delicacy belied by a powerfully chiseled jaw. A small scar cut a diagonal through one of his eyebrows, giving his handsome face a compelling, cynical look.

"You!" She whirled to face the man from the dock.

"Well, well, the waterfront waif!" Philippe Girard exclaimed softly.

She blushed suddenly, an unbidden picture of muscled thighs, rippling under formfitting breeches coming into her mind.

"I almost didn't know you without dirt on your face," he said, smiling crookedly down at her. "And what do you know? I was right, you're not such a little girl after all."

"I am not," she responded stiffly, "but you are still insufferably rude."

"My apologies, mam'selle." He offered a mocking bow. "I had no idea yesterday I was speaking to a lady."

"And you didn't bother to find out," Claire answered waspishly, turning to go back into the shop. "Good day, m'sieur."

"Don't go away angry, little chameleon," he teased, catching her arm gently. "An urchin one day, a lovely lady the next. I would like to get to know you. Our acquaintance did not start well yesterday, but if you'll give me a chance today, I'll prove what a charming companion I can be."

Claire stared down at the hand encircling her wrist, then she lifted her dark eyes to meet his coldly. "Not today or any day. What kind of gentleman confronts a lady on the street?"

"What kind of lady goes out without a chaperon?" he retorted, meeting her challenge.

Glaring at him in mute fury, she wrenched her arm from his grasp. Then she turned on her heel and marched into the shop.

Surprise was rapidly replaced by aggravation on Philippe's handsome face as the door slammed closed, setting the bell jingling inside. This girl had to be the most exasperating female it had ever been his misfortune to meet, he thought irritably, and still he did not know who she was. He ought to follow her right into that citadel of femininity, Madame Benoit's, and demand to know her name. But he discarded that idea and, with a dark expression, crossed the street to the alleyway beside the millinery shop.

"What's wrong?" Tante Delaney asked when Claire returned so abruptly.

"Nothing. It's hot out there." She did not want to mention her confrontation. That kind of thing did not happen to ladies, she decided.

As Tante Delaney checked Madame Benoit's figures on the bill, the dressmaker watched the parade of boxes being taken out to the carriage, occasionally glancing despairingly at her newest customer. She still had not managed to learn much about Claire Fortier.

How she longed to know about the girl's background, about her sudden appearance at Fortier House. But Madeleine Delaney would not allow even one question.

"You understand the remainder of the order will be delivered by Wednesday of next week, *oui?*" Madame Benoit asked, dogging her customers' steps as they prepared to depart.

"Oui." Tante Delaney did not pause as she herded her charge toward the door.

The dressmaker could not curb her curiosity no longer. "For shoes, I suppose you will go to Greaux, and for hats to Lila Broussard?" she asked slyly. "She will do well for you, I know. She's a great friend of Monsieur Fortier, after all," she added, her explanation directed at Claire.

"Have no fear, Elise, we will find a milliner," Tante Delaney said disapprovingly, her lips tightening. "Come, my child," she commanded, leading Claire onto the banquette.

"Is that where we're going next? To Madame Broussard's?" the girl asked innocently.

"Mademoiselle Broussard . . ."

"Is she my uncle's *placée?*"

"What do you know of *plaçage?*" The old woman peered at her shrewdly. "Very little, eh? Well, never mind. The friendship between that woman and your uncle is no one's business but their own. Such things happen in New Orleans all the time.

"In answer to your earlier question, however, next we'll go to the cobbler, then to *my* milliner, then we must get you home. Come, shake a leg, as the Kaintocks say."

Just down the street, a covey of planters' wives, daughters
and servants approached from the opposite direction. Two
older women led the group, conversing sedately as they
walked. A somber pair, dressed in dark broadcloth dresses and
unadorned bonnets, they were trailed by three young ladies,
the youngest still in braids. The two older girls wore fashionable flower-hued frocks, twirled frilly parasols and smiled
coyly over their shoulders to be sure their admirers were still
attentive, even if at a distance. Two slave women, wearing
snowy *tignons,* brought up the rear, finding a seat on the curb
in the shade when the Creoles entered a banquette café.

"Come, Claire," Tante Delaney said, leading the girl toward the awning-covered café, "I've just changed our plans.
I must have something to drink before I expire from thirst."

As Tante Delaney led Claire toward a seat, she stopped
suddenly at the table where the Creole women sipped lemon-
ade from crystal cups and lethargically wielded fans.

"Emmaline, how are you?" she greeted one of the women
with every appearance of surprise. "How nice to see you."

Madame Hébert smiled graciously. "Bonjour, Madeleine.
It's good to see you, too. When did you return from River
Oaks?"

"This very afternoon. You know, this is a coincidence. I was
just telling Claire—" the old woman nodded toward her companion "—about you and your charming family.

"This is Madame Hébert, Claire, the lady I mentioned earlier," Tante Delaney fibbed, the picture of innocence. "She is
mistress of Belle Grâce, one of the most beautiful—and hospitable—plantations on Bayou St. John. And she throws the
best parties in New Orleans."

Claire curtsied politely, mentally cursing her new friend for
her audacity. She was not sure she was ready to meet anyone
yet.

"Madame Hébert," Tante Delaney continued formally,
oblivious to Claire's annoyance, "may I present Mademoiselle Claire Fortier."

Madame Hébert nodded cordially and introduced the other
members of her party. "This is my sister-in-law, Madame
Yvonne Ledet," she said, gesturing toward the other woman.
"These are her daughters, Isabelle and Marguerite. And this
is my daughter, Anne."

Madame Ledet nodded stiffly, her face unfriendly. The three girls bowed prettily, and Anne motioned to the chair next to her. "Won't you join us?" she invited.

Claire's eyes sought Tante Delaney's, imploring her to refuse, but the old woman dropped into a chair and began to fan herself extravagantly. "We would be delighted, wouldn't we, *chère?*" she rattled. "My, isn't the heat terrible this summer?"

Ill at ease, Claire sat beside Anne Hébert. Next to the diminutive brunette, she felt large and clumsy.

"Mademoiselle Fortier... that is correct, is it not? Fortier? You are not related by chance to Etienne Fortier?" Madame Ledet phrased her opening gambit so it was less a question than the hoped-for-answer.

"He is my uncle," Claire answered quietly, watching the woman blink with surprise.

"Your uncle?" Madame Ledet repeated sharply, frowning at her. "I don't remember that Monsieur Fortier had any brothers or sisters."

"He had one brother, Jules—my father."

"Oh, yes, Jules. Let me see if I can recall. Did he not leave New Orleans in disgrace and become—what? A trapper?"

"A remarkable memory," Tante Delaney commented dryly, "for one who didn't recall at first that Etienne had a brother at all."

Madame Ledet flashed her a look of dislike. "I remember something else, too. Jules married an Indian woman. Was that your mother?" she asked Claire disdainfully.

Then the woman sat back and smiled arrogantly. "No matter. I suppose every family has its black sheep."

"And everyone knows what boils in his own pot, Yvonne," Madame Hébert muttered, arching a disapproving eyebrow at her sister-in-law. Turning to Claire, she said politely, "I am sure, mademoiselle, that your uncle is pleased to have you visiting him. Will you be staying long?"

"Both my parents are dead. I'm living at Fortier House," Claire answered hesitantly.

"I am sorry, *chère,*" Madame Hébert said quietly.

"*Oui,* our condolences," Madame Ledet echoed insincerely. "It is odd, though, that Etienne never mentioned you. He is, after all, a friend of my husband, Charles Ledet."

"Until yesterday, my uncle didn't know about me."

"How exciting," Anne exclaimed, clapping her hands delightedly before anyone else could say another word. "You came all the way to New Orleans to live with your uncle, and you had never even met him! I vow, it is like a French novel, even if he is your uncle. Isn't it, Isabelle?" She looked to her cousin for agreement, which did not come. Isabelle's pretty face mirrored her mother's expression of distaste.

Anne leaned conspiratorially toward Claire. "I've seen your uncle sometimes at balls and I think he is very handsome—for an older man, I mean..." Her voice trailed off and she blushed, as her younger cousin, Marguerite, dissolved into a gale of girlish giggles.

"Anne! French novels, indeed," her mother reproved sternly. "What will Mademoiselle Fortier think of us?"

"She will think you all charming and that it has been a great pleasure to meet you," Tante Delaney interjected smoothly. "But we must go now. I promised to have Claire home before supper and we still have shopping to do."

"How could Madeleine do that to us?" Yvonne Ledet asked dramatically when the pair had left the table. "The girl is half-Indian. She cannot expect to be welcomed by decent folks."

"What's wrong with being half-Indian, *Maman?*" asked Marguerite. "I think it's thrilling."

"Do not be so common, *ma petite.* She's a savage. Do you think that thrilling?"

"*Oui,*" the girl answered breathlessly. "And besides, she didn't look like a savage."

"Marguerite Marie-Thérèse Ledet!" her mother exploded.

"That is enough, please," Madame Hébert said sternly, quelling any further discussion. "A lady is always gracious and hospitable. This Claire may be half-savage, as you say, but she has better manners than some full Creoles I know."

Halting just down the street, Tante Delaney congratulated her young charge. "You did very well, my dear."

"What?" Claire stared at the old woman in disbelief.

"Listen to me," her companion insisted good-naturedly. "You may be Etienne Fortier's niece, but you are an outsider. Creole society is very closed. I know—I married an outsider and it took them years to forget it. They still have not forgiven me.

"The treatment Yvonne Ledet gave you is only a taste of what you have to look forward to among the good women of the Vieux Carré. But you made a good impression on Emma-line Hébert, and she's far more important among *les bonnes familles* than her sister-in-law. Yvonne and her stuck-up daughter—who cares? A shock now and then will do them good.''

Claire drew herself up and looked Tante Delaney squarely in the eye. "I did not come all this way to shock people," she informed her evenly. "I am not a fool to be laughed at nor a child to be ignored. They will like me for what I am. And if they do not..."

"If they do not, they're in for the fight of their life," Madeleine crowed delightedly. "The more I know you, the better I like you, Claire Fortier."

Late in the afternoon, Etienne's carriage, its roof stacked with boxes, lumbered up the drive to Fortier House. A groom appeared immediately to assist Claire from the rig and bear her packages into the house.

"I cannot come in today," Tante Delaney responded to the girl's invitation. "It's late and I must put in an appearance at my brother's home, but I will call on you soon. Tell your uncle his carriage will be returned later."

That evening, Claire stood before the mirror and caught her breath in wonder. Clad in a white silk gown trimmed with blue ribbons, she did indeed look like a lady.

"Perfec'," Beady pronounced with satisfaction.

"It is beautiful," the girl admitted in an awed whisper. "I've never owned a dress like this in all my life."

"One moment," the maid requested, disappearing through the French doors onto the balcony. She returned with a small, newly plucked gardenia. Its delicate fragrance filled the room as she tied a blue ribbon around the stem and painstakingly nestled it in Claire's hair. "More perfec' than before," she breathed admiringly. "Now you better go. M'sieur Etienne is waitin'."

"*Merci*, Beady, *merci beaucoup*." Claire paused for one more quick glance in the mirror, her hand moving in an unconscious gesture toward her hair.

"Don't be touchin' it," the little slave scolded. "Th' petals'll git all brown an' ugly. Go on now, and mind you be keerful with that flower." Following the girl into the hall, Beady watched proudly, new feelings of loyalty welling up inside as her mistress descended the wide staircase.

Carefully Claire glided toward her uncle, who waited at the bottom of the stairs, approval shining in his gray eyes.

"Chère," he said, his voice husky with unexpected emotion, "you are enchanting." Taking her hand, he drew her into the center of the parquet floor and ordered kindly, "Turn around. Let me see you in your finery."

The girl obeyed self-consciously. "Do I look all right... Uncle Etienne?"

"You do indeed," he said with a smile. Although he tried not to show it, the man was shaken. When she arrived on his doorstep, wearing a sack of a dress, she had seemed little more than a child. But in clothes that were properly fitted, she had a figure made for the embrace of a young gallant, he thought a trifle jealously.

She was striking, perhaps not beautiful in the traditional sense, but definitely an arresting presence. Her beauty seemed to rise from within and was mirrored in dark, unfathomable eyes. She had style and grace that had nothing to do with fashion. Despite her innocence, her appearance was disturbingly sensuous.

At dinner, over bowls of crayfish bisque, Etienne asked, "Did you have a good time this afternoon?"

"Oui, merci."

"Madeleine is a difficult woman at times, but she's a good person," he allowed generously. "I knew she would take good care of you. Did you get everything you needed?"

"Yes, thank you very much. I'll repay you as soon as I am able to find employment."

"Claire, I told you before, it isn't necessary for you to repay me," Etienne said firmly, "and it is unheard of for a girl of a good family to take a position in business."

"But I don't want to be idle. I must have something to do."

"Learn to run the house, to be a hostess."

"I will, but I must make my own way."

"I could give you an allowance," he suggested, hoping to put an end to the discussion.

"That's hardly what I had in mind," she contended dryly.

"You're damnably stubborn," Etienne snapped, his voice beginning to rise.

"So are you." Claire glared at him across the table.

"A family trait." The man laughed unexpectedly, easing the tension. "Since you are adamant, I do have a suggestion. I wasn't going to mention it, but as you insist—"

"Are you going to let me help you at your Mercantile?" the girl asked eagerly.

"Whatever gave you that idea?" he asked, the frown returning to his face. "I spend very little time there. And the waterfront is hardly the place for a young lady. However, I may have the solution to our problem," he continued, his expression softening. "Tell me, are you good with numbers?"

"Oh, yes, I helped my father to keep the tally of the pelts he took. And I studied mathematics from the books he left me. I learn quickly."

Etienne smiled indulgently. "I'm sure you do. Well, just today a friend who owns a small business—a Mademoiselle Broussard—told me she needs a responsible person to keep her accounts. If you were to go on Friday evenings to do the books for the week . . .

"Hmm . . . it could work," he mused. "You could earn money as you wish, yet you wouldn't have to deal with the public. People would not even have to know you had taken a job. Ezra could drive you back and forth to Mademoiselle Broussard's home. All perfectly discreet. What do you think?" He turned to Claire for an answer.

A hundred questions were on the tip of her tongue, but recalling Tante Delaney's reluctance earlier to discuss Lila Broussard, she refrained from asking them. Etienne seemed to think it would be a good arrangement—and she did need the money.

"It sounds . . . fine," she replied haltingly.

He did not seem to notice her hesitation. "I'll speak to Mademoiselle Broussard then. She will surely want to meet you."

"You gots ever'thin' you need, Mam'selle?" Beady asked, bustling downstairs with Claire's hooded cape. The little slave clucked like a mother hen when Greer appeared to escort the girl to the waiting carriage.

"She's not going on a world tour, Beady," he said sourly.

"I know, but it's my job to take keer of her," she insisted, following the pair out onto the veranda.

"And it's my job to see her safely there and back. *I* will take care of her." The butler regarded the maid coldly.

"Mind you do," Beady sassed, scampering for the safety of the front door.

So dark was his mood that Greer did not bother to rise to her baiting. He was reduced to playing chaperon, he thought dismally. The master had charged him to watch over the girl and watch over her he would, but he did not have to like it.

As he handed Claire into the coach, he ordered brusquely, "Take us to Miss Broussard's house, Ezra—on Rampart Street."

"*Oui,* M'sieur Greer, I know th' way." The driver chuckled good-naturedly.

The crack of a whip sounded in the evening air and the coach rolled down the drive and through the great iron gates. For a while Claire was silent, listening to the rumble of the wheels on the cobblestone street. But as they approached their destination, her thoughts turned to unanswered questions. Longing to ask Greer about the woman they were riding to visit, she threw frequent covert glances toward him, her lashes veiling the query in her eyes. Finally curiosity proved too much for her.

"Do you know Mademoiselle Broussard, Greer?" she ventured.

The man was quiet for so long that she thought he was not going to answer. At last, he replied tersely, "We've met."

"I understand she and my uncle have been friends for years," Claire persisted, receiving only a noncommittal grunt in response.

She considered giving up, but continued doggedly, "Have you also known her a long time?"

"Long enough," Greer answered, his expression unreadable.

The treble note of the coachman's whistle drifted back to them, and the carriage began to slow.

"Good, we're here," the big butler announced, throwing the door open before they had even stopped.

As she alit from the carriage, Claire brushed futilely at a swarm of mosquitoes that threatened to engulf her. Stepping away from the light that drew the insects, she looked around. They had stopped on a dark street lined on either side by dingy, narrow row houses, and now stood directly in front of an immaculate little cottage, set back from the dusty, shell-covered street. Newly whitewashed, it stood apart from the others in the neighborhood with a kind of bravado, a solitary candle-lit window its only sentinel against the encroaching night.

As the girl waited for Greer to give Ezra his instructions, faint wisps of clouds that obscured the moon cleared away and the cottage was washed in an unearthly light. Claire shivered in the muggy night air, powdery white shells crackling underfoot as she shifted apprehensively. Then the clouds covered the face of the moon again, dimming the ghostly illumination.

She shrugged her shoulders as if to shake off her uneasiness and started along the crude wooden banquette toward the gate. At closer range, the cottage with its white picket fence did not seem such a forbidding apparition. Hanging baskets of pink flowers framed the dark doorway pleasantly, and from where she stood, a minuscule kitchen garden could be seen along one side of the house, its tiny shoots of pale green growth ethereal in the glow from a neighbor's window.

"I'll walk you to the door." Politely Greer guided Claire toward the house.

A stooped, wrinkled Negro woman, wearing a shapeless calico dress and a faded red *tignon,* answered his insistent rap on the door. "Kin I help y'all?" she rasped from the gloom of the murky hallway.

"Concepción, this is Miss Fortier. Miss Lila is expecting her," Greer told her perfunctorily.

"Come in." Concepción opened the door a bit wider. Gripping Claire's arm with a wizened hand, she pulled her inside. Before Greer could follow, the ancient crone blocked his way, saying, "You ain't needed no more tonight, M'sieur Greer. Mam'selle Lila say to tell you she'll make sure M'sieur Fortier's niece gits home jest fine. You go 'long now," she dismissed the butler, shutting the door firmly against his protests.

"Follow, please, mam'selle," Concepción bade in a sing-song voice. "Mam'selle Lila's waitin' in th' drawin' room."

The old woman shuffled painfully down the long shadowy hall, its walls decorated with the massive ornately carved crucifix favored by voodoo worshipers in New Orleans. Claire gazed up at the garishly adorned icon with its ribbons of crimson paint trailing down the suffering face. Shivering, she looked away and followed Concepción to a closed door, where the slave scratched lightly.

"*Oui,*" Lila Broussard's melodious voice answered.

Concepción opened the door and wheezed, "Mam'selle Fortier, Mam'selle Lila."

Nervous at meeting her potential employer, Claire stepped into the room. After the darkness of the hall, she was overwhelmed by light. She faltered in the doorway, momentarily blinded. Then she saw Lila Broussard, clad in a bronze-colored satin robe, lounging gracefully on a fainting couch.

Illuminated by scores of blue candles of all sizes, the small parlor was hot. The candles stood on tables, lined the mantel and filled sconces on all four walls. In their glow, the petite octoroon resembled a pampered golden cat. Toying with a glossy tendril of raven hair that cascaded over her shoulders, Lila looked soft and vulnerable. Only her tawny, unblinking eyes belied that impression, focusing shrewdly on the girl as she entered.

"Come in. You must be Claire. You don't mind if I call you Claire, do you?" the woman purred.

"*Non.*" Claire extended her hand and greeted the reclining woman. "I am happy to meet you, Mademoiselle Broussard."

Although unwilling to shake hands, Lila was charming nonetheless. "Please sit down." She gestured to a low chair nearby.

"So you are Etienne's niece." She chuckled throatily. "I hardly knew what to expect when he told me you had arrived so...suddenly."

Claire tried to make herself comfortable in her rigid seat, sweltering in her cloak, which Concepción had not offered to take. She felt shy and tongue-tied, embarrassed by Lila's scrutiny. In a matter of moments, she had gone from feeling pretty and elegant in her new clothes to feeling like an ox next to this small, graceful woman.

The octoroon ignored Claire's discomfiture and breezily continued, "I swear Etienne was at wit's end about how to entertain you. He told me you were hardly more than a child." She laughed. "But you know how unobservant men are. How old are you? Seventeen? Eighteen? Hardly a child."

"Hardly," Claire replied stiffly. "I'll soon be nineteen."

"Ah, yes," Lila said, laughing again, "*almost* a lady. Tell me, Claire, why do you seek employment?"

"I wish to earn money of my own," the girl answered simply.

"I see..." Lila drawled haughtily. "So you do not feel so much like a poor relation, *oui?*" Casting a sidelong glance, she licked her lips at the perplexity on the girl's face, resembling again a sleek cat. "And you think you could keep my accounts?"

"Yes," Claire responded confidently. Putting aside the doubts the woman had raised, she assured her, "What I do not know I shall learn quickly, I promise you. Already I can—"

Her train of thought was interrupted by a muffled baritone voice lifted in ribald song. It seemed to come from nearby. She started as a heavy, uneven tread reached their ears, followed by a loud crash.

Lila paid no heed to the disturbance, acknowledging the distant ruckus with no more than a slight frown. "I'm sure you're an apt pupil," she resumed. "If you can do the work, I'll pay you a fair price. Your uncle will tell me what that should be. I do not concern myself with money matters. You must, of course, close my books at the end of each week. Are you willing to give up your Friday evenings?"

"*Oui.*"

"Then if you have nothing better to do, the job is yours." Lila shrugged her delicate shoulders disinterestedly. "Today is Thursday, *oui?* Come tomorrow night at seven and you may begin."

The interview concluded, the octoroon rose gracefully and crossed to an embroidered bell rope in the corner of the room. Her diaphanous robe clung to her body, showing its supple curves to their full advantage.

"Wait here and the maid will see you out," she instructed.

A welcome breeze stirred in the room as Concepción opened the door and peered at them. "*Oui, mam'selle?*"

"Show our guest to the carriage, 'Cepción. Tati will drive her home."

"He don't hafta, mam'selle. Greer still waitin'."

"I thought I told you to dismiss him." Lila's cat eyes narrowed at the old woman.

"So I did, mam'selle, but he would not go."

"Très bien." Indifferently she dismissed her new employee. *"Bonne nuit,* Claire."

As Claire followed the stooped servant to the front door, she sorted out her thoughts. This cottage was filled with bad spirits, she decided uneasily. She knew she was being superstitious, but how else could she describe the feeling this place gave her? She glanced up nervously at the crucifix as she passed, almost expecting to see the eyes move. She did feel as if someone were watching her. Drawing on her hood, she quickened her pace, narrowing the gap between herself and her tottering guide.

She did not know that a pair of dark, besotted eyes were indeed watching her exit with keen interest.

His usually sleek black hair mussed and his eyelids drooping lazily, Philippe Girard resembled more a tired little boy than one of the city's most renowned rakes. A silly smile on his handsome face, he lurched drunkenly against the banister at the top of the stairs and gazed down into the foyer with bleary-eyed interest.

Who was that? He tried unsuccessfully to focus. What he could see of the girl as she passed below in a flash of warm velvet was engaging enough. There was something familiar about her, Philippe mused, but it could not be anyone he knew. No Creole family would allow their daughter in the cottage of a *placée.* Perhaps she was a friend of Lila's, a quadroon in search of a protector. He needed a closer look. And he could get it if he were downstairs.

Tentatively, the Creole tested his legs. Still too uncertain to attempt a descent. Just a few moments ago, standing at the bottom of the servants' staircase, he had thought the steps insurmountable. Only with extreme difficulty and some bumbling help from Concepción had he ascended them at all. For now, he reasoned sagely, he would stay where he was. Bracing himself with one hand, he leaned far over the banister to watch the statuesque young woman leave.

"Philippe, get back! What do you think you're doing?" Lila grated from the shadows.

He groaned peevishly. Now he would never get a good look at the mysterious girl. Unsteadily, he straightened and stepped out of the light, looking around through bleary eyes, trying to locate the source of the rebuke. In his rapt observation of

Claire's departure, he had not noticed when the octoroon crept up the back stairs behind him.

Lila had seen how Philippe looked at the girl. Now her chest heaved in anger and she glared at him, her yellow eyes narrowed. But she said nothing until she had heard the front door close.

Deliberately, she walked toward the inebriated young Creole. "Are you mad, coming here like this?" she asked contemptuously. "What are you trying to do? Ruin everything? Do not tell me you didn't see Etienne's carriage in front of the house."

"No one saw me," he answered cockily.

"Concepción saw you."

"'Cepción doesn't count. She knows when to keep her mouth shut," he replied, reaching out to toy with the buttons of the woman's robe.

"How can you be so certain that no one saw you?" She slapped his hand away petulantly.

"Trust me." Undeterred, he playfully resumed his game.

But the octoroon was not to be diverted. "If that ogre of a butler had seen you, Philippe, I hate to think of what tomorrow would hold—for me and for you."

"Don't worry so much."

"The girl may not have seen you, but I know she heard you—all the way in the parlor," she berated him.

"But she didn't see me, did she? What's the difference? She's not Fortier's spy, is she?" he teased.

"Worse, she is his niece," Lila snapped, pulling away.

"His niece?" Philippe echoed incredulously, suddenly sober. "I didn't think the old man had any relatives."

"He does now."

"His niece...well, I'll be damned," he mused wonderingly. "Come to think of it, she did look familiar. It could be a family resemblance, except..."

"Except what?"

"Except she's prettier than her uncle."

"You think she's pretty?" the octoroon pouted.

"Perhaps pleasing would be a better word."

"Do you find her as pleasing as me, Philippe?"

The young man arched a cynical brow. "Jealousy does not become you, Lila."

"I'm not jealous," she said petulantly. "Keep away from her, *cher*, I warn you. Etienne is already protective of her. He won't allow you to dally with her."

"Who said I was going to dally with her, as you so quaintly put it?" the young man snapped.

Her manner suddenly changing, Lila encircled Philippe's waist with her arms and rubbed her face against his starched white shirtfront. "*Non, mon amour,* you do not want anything to do with her," she whispered invitingly, tracing his lips with her finger. "She is just a skinny girl. You need a woman."

"Ah, yes." The Creole smiled arrogantly. "You remind me why I came—I need a woman."

Without another word, he swept the willing octoroon into his arms and lurched toward the bedchamber at the end of the hall.

Chapter Four

Philippe stood beside the bed and gazed at Lila through the *baire*. Even in slumber she frowned prettily, stirring restlessly under the rumpled bedclothes. One tawny arm was thrown across the pillow above her tousled head, and her hair, a mass of black ringlets, partially obscured her face.

Trying in vain to ignore the throb in his head, the young Creole gathered his belongings quietly. He must get away before Lila awoke. He had things to do today.

Downstairs he paused before a mirror in the foyer to tie his limp cravat, grimacing at a reflection that showed the effects of too many long nights. His face was puffy and his eyes were bloodshot. And he felt worse than he looked, he thought ruefully.

Out of the corner of his eye, Philippe saw Concepción shuffling toward him with a cup of coffee.

"Heerd you movin' 'round. So I brung some *café* while your horse is bein' saddled," she rasped, setting the cup in front of him. The aroma of bitter chicory rose in a cloud of steam around his face, nauseating him.

"Merci," he mumbled, still fussing with his tie.

"Make you some breakfust before you go, sir?"

"I don't think so. What time is it, anyway?"

"'Bout half past ten."

"Damn," Philippe swore softly, "I was to meet Henri and Gaspar half an hour ago. I am already late.

"Before you go, 'Cepción," he said hurriedly. "The girl who was here last night—Fortier's niece. What is her name?"

"You mean Mam'selle Claire?"

"That's right, Claire Fortier. She looks familiar."

"Don't think so." Concepción's brow knitted in a frown. "She jest come to town last week."

"Last week, eh? From upriver?"

"*Oui*. You have met her?"

"I think perhaps . . . at the dock," Philippe replied slowly. He had been too drunk to realize it last night, but this girl, Fortier's niece, was the ever-changing young woman who had piqued his interest. "This Mam'selle Claire," he asked after a moment, "is she a friend of Lila's?"

"She is Mam'selle Lila's bookkeeper."

"Bookkeeper? Etienne Fortier's niece?"

"*Oui*. She want a job, but M'sieur 'Tienne, he don't want her workin' so folks knows it. So Mam'selle Lila hired her as a favor. That gal gonna come here ever' Friday and keep track of accounts."

"I see." Philippe sipped his coffee thoughtfully, making a face when the bitter liquid scalded his tongue. Suddenly mindful of the time, he set down the cup with a clatter and strode to the door, calling over his shoulder, "Tell Lila I will see her later."

"I kin tell you now, don't bother comin' tonight, m'sieur. Mam'selle will be gone," Concepción shouted over the slamming of the door.

A popular restaurant, Maspero's Exchange also served as an unofficial post office and clearinghouse of New Orleans. This morning the main room was packed with the usual mob awaiting the mail. They sat at small tables, drinking *café*: businessmen waiting for reports on operations up and down the Mississippi, homesick university boys hoping for letters from their plantation homes, reporters expecting dispatches from distant cities. While they waited, they talked; a hundred conversations producing one muffled buzz.

Philippe poised in the door, searching the smoky interior for his friends, Henri D'Estaigne and Gaspar Boudreaux. The noise and the smoke invaded his head, and his knees were in danger of buckling when he located the men at the crowded bar.

Henri, tall and slender with a copper cast to his unruly hair, posed elegantly, his green eyes scanning the room with lively interest. Clever and droll, the handsome young Creole was as popular with men as with the ladies.

He towered over the dark-haired Gaspar, who was hunched on a tall stool, engrossed in his newspaper. Gaspar was short, plump and always a trifle rumpled. A serious young man with little sense of humor, he was kind and generous to a fault.

The three Creoles had lived on neighboring plantations all their lives and had muddled through their schooling together under the rigid Père Marcus. A year or two younger than Philippe, the other boys had looked to him naturally as their leader. Just as naturally, he had accepted the role, initiating them into all manner of mischief. Their youthful adoration had grown into respect as Philippe taught them, however indirectly, about honor. Time after time, their pranks were thwarted by the wily priest, and Philippe bore the brunt of the punishments without implicating the others. Theirs was a friendship that had lasted a lifetime.

"There he is!" Henri crowed with laughter when he spied Philippe entering the crowded room. He nudged Gaspar, nearly knocking him off his perch. "Just look at him!"

Gaspar glanced instead at the clock behind the bar. "Late as usual," he commented without malice, folding his paper with a snap.

"Over there, Philippe!" Henri indicated a newly vacated table by an open window.

Maneuvering with outrageous agility for one in his debilitated condition, Philippe raced to reach the sunny table ahead of a pair of Americans who had the same idea.

"Sorry, messieurs," he drawled impudently up at them as he sprawled into a chair, "this table is taken." The men paused and looked at each other uncertainly. Muttering, they retreated to the bar when Henri and Gaspar sat down on either side of their friend.

"What kept you, Philippe? It is past eleven," Gaspar chided.

"Yes," Henri teased knowingly, "what kept you this morning?"

Philippe did not answer. Intent on the pain raging in his head, he slumped in his chair and looked around balefully for a waiter.

Instantly, one appeared at his elbow. "Help you, M'sieur Girard?"

"A bourbon, please. Quickly."

"Oui, m'sieur." The waiter disappeared at once.

"Hair of the dog, Philippe?" Henri chortled delightedly.

"They say strong drink the night before calls for stronger measures the next morning," Gaspar counseled, chuckling.

"They say that, do they?" Philippe growled.

"How is the mademoiselle?" Henri pressed blithely.

The waiter reappeared. *"Votre coquetier,* m'sieur," he said. Philippe took the egg cup from the tray and downed the drink in one gulp.

"Another, m'sieur?" the waiter asked solicitously.

"Non, merci, café—noir," Philippe instructed, returning the empty glass to the tray. Revived, he sat back and regarded his companions with an expansive smile. "Well, *mes amis,* it has been a while since we were together here."

"Actually, I don't think I've seen you at all since the ball three weeks ago when you almost called out Neville Johnson to duel," Henri ruminated.

Philippe grinned even wider at the memory. "Too bad Madame Tournay felt compelled to intervene. Still, a gentleman must respect his hostess's wishes, even at a Quadroon Ball."

"That was a close one, if you ask me," Gaspar interjected.

"I've had closer," Philippe retorted.

"If matters had been allowed to run their course, New Orleans would have one less Kaintock to endure," Henri added scornfully.

"That's true, perhaps," Gaspar replied judiciously. "Why, I was reading right here in the *Louisiana Gazette....*" Avidly, he began to unfold the sheet.

"You and your *Gazette!*" Henri cried in good-natured exasperation, snatching the newspaper and tossing it over his shoulder. "You're always reading, Gaspar. Let's not waste time on useless discussions of politics or business."

"What would you rather talk about?" the owlish young man asked peevishly. He retrieved his disarranged paper and folded it neatly.

"Horses," shouted Philippe and Henri in unison.

"Or horses and women," Philippe amended merrily. "What does Henri ever want to talk about?"

The dapper young Creole sniffed disdainfully, turned up his aristocratic nose and looked away, feigning injured feelings.

His friends laughed unconcernedly, accustomed to his pretenses.

With an easy smile, the dandy gave up his act and asked earnestly, "Philippe, how do your horses look for the big race?"

"Never better, *mon ami*," the stable owner replied smugly. "You know I bought a stud from a stable on Grand Teche?"

"I heard."

"He is superb. And last week Hyacinth broke her own record."

"I'd like to have just one runner as good as your Hyacinth," Gaspar remarked wistfully.

"You just want to impress pretty little Anne Hébert," Henri baited his chubby friend.

Gaspar flushed in embarrassment and anger, looking around the room worriedly to see if anyone had overheard. "Don't even speak her name in so common a place," he commanded fiercely. "She is truly a Creole lady and worth any ten—no, twenty—of the chits you pursue."

"No doubt," Henri agreed readily. "Someday I'll wed a refined lady of substance, but for now, Gaspar, I am not so ready as you to settle into the heavy yoke of matrimony. Are you, Philippe?"

"If I could be assured that every night would be as good as last night, I'd die a bachelor," he assured them lightly.

"What? You would have no sons, no heirs?" Gaspar was aghast.

"And no obligations, for that is what a wife is."

"Sometimes I don't know when you are joking, Philippe." Gaspar sighed, shaking his head. "And I vow the many women you sweep off their feet do not, either."

Any retort Philippe might have made was lost when Henri exclaimed, "Look at that!" His friends spun in their seats, craning their necks to see what he was staring at with such interest.

Across the street, Claire Fortier strolled along the banquette. Men who loitered there doffed their hats and stared at her in open appreciation.

Dressed in a simple frock of a pink-sprigged dimity that accented her narrow waist and firm breasts, she seemed completely unaware of the stir she created. Her dark hair was pulled away from her face, but lustrous tresses hung loose in the back, visible under the brim of her white straw hat.

"*Mon Dieu,* I am smitten," Henri breathed.

"She is beautiful," Philippe agreed casually, "in an unusual sort of way."

"But entirely too tall," Gaspar objected.

"Who is she? Do you know?" Henri turned entreatingly to his friends.

"Her name is Claire Fortier," Philippe informed him.

"Fortier... any relation to...?"

"The niece of old Etienne himself."

"What else do you know about her?" Henri asked, continuing to watch Claire.

"Nothing," Philippe replied. "I've never even met her. At least, not formally."

"Then how do you know who she is?"

"I saw her at Lila's."

"You saw her at Lila's?" Gaspar echoed incredulously.

"Keep your voice down," Philippe requested impatiently, his eyes sweeping the café. "Do you want all New Orleans to know I visit Etienne Fortier's *placée?*"

"That could make for some difficulty," Henri murmured distractedly. "My last adventure of that sort found me at the Dueling Oaks at dawn."

"With me as a second," Gaspar grimaced. "I'll be quiet. I do not want to relive that adventure."

"No," Philippe teased amiably, "you'd have to get up early again."

Gaspar returned to his original topic. "Seriously, Philippe, whatever was this girl doing there? Even if she's too innocent to know anything of men's ways, how could Fortier condone it?"

"She probably doesn't know of her uncle's attachment to the inimitable Mademoiselle Broussard," Philippe responded.

"Nor of yours." Henri laughed, turning to his friends when Claire disappeared into a shop. "How did you explain your presence there, Philippe?"

"She didn't see me."

"I don't wonder that you didn't make her acquaintance," the copper-haired Creole said with a smirk. "Lila would scratch your eyes out if you even looked at another woman.

What a shame you will not get to meet the lovely Mademoiselle Fortier, *mon ami.*"

"I *intend* to meet her," Philippe stated confidently.

"Not if Lila has anything to say about it," his friend jeered.

Challengingly Philippe leaned across the table. "Henri, I wager you that I meet Claire Fortier before you do. Perhaps before today is out."

"You can't just accost a lady on the street," his friend objected.

"*Non,* I shall be introduced to her," he insisted, "or I'll meet her in the home of friends. Agreed?"

"For how much?"

"A twenty-dollar gold piece."

"Agreed, although it seems a crime to take advantage of you so." Henri sighed dramatically. "You face a battle not only with Lila, you know, but with the girl's uncle, who knows, no doubt, that you are a ne'er-do-well."

"It is a bet then?" Disregarding his comment, Philippe extended his hand.

Henri shook his hand to seal the wager and nodded at their mutual friend. "You're my witness, Gaspar. Philippe has taken leave of his senses."

"And now I must take leave of you," Philippe announced, rising. "I must get some rest if I'm to make a good impression on the mademoiselle."

Resolutely, Claire forced her attention to the stubborn column of numbers that danced on the page in front of her. Her eyes ached from poring over Lila's books, but she decided not to call Concepción to bring a lamp. There was only a little more to do.

She bent single-mindedly over the figures, so engrossed that she did not hear when the door from the hall opened softly. Some time passed before she sensed the presence of someone else in the cramped, stuffy dining room.

"*Oui?*" she mumbled, glancing up absently. Her breath caught in her throat when she caught sight of the man in the doorway.

With the light from the hall behind him, his features were indistinguishable. He lounged insolently, one broad shoulder leaned against the doorjamb, his face in the shadows. After a moment, he straightened and stepped into the dining room, bringing with him the masculine scents of rum, horseflesh and fine tobacco.

The Creole from the docks, the man who had insulted her on a public street. What was he doing here? Uncomfortably aware of his masculinity, she wondered how long he had been watching her. Seeing his gaze flicker over her appraisingly, she stared at him with open hostility.

"If you're looking for Mademoiselle Broussard," she informed him in a tight voice, "she is not here right now."

"I wasn't looking for Lila." The arrogance in his tone matched his manner. He strolled across the room and perched on the edge of the table, swinging one booted foot casually as he scrutinized her.

"What do you need then?" Claire countered bluntly, rising.

"Please, sit down." He put his hand on her shoulder and gently pushed her back into her chair. "Actually, I do not need anything in particular, except to meet you at last. Allow me to introduce myself," he continued smoothly before she could respond. "Philippe Girard, at your service, mademoiselle." He took her hand in his and kissed it. "And you, I believe, are Claire Fortier."

"How did you know that?" she asked, drawing back her hand quickly.

"Why, you are the talk of the Vieux Carré, *chère*. Everyone seems to find you a subject of great interest. I do myself. In fact, I find you intriguing. Each time I see you, you're different. I take it today you are a bookkeeper?"

"*Oui,*" she replied woodenly.

Philippe seemed amused. "And how long have you been a bookkeeper, Mademoiselle Fortier?"

"I was hired . . . recently." She would not add to his obvious amusement by telling him she was new to the job.

"I see," he said with mock gravity. "And you have always been one?"

"No," she responded curtly.

"I thought not. What then—besides urchin and lady?" he prodded. "A doctor? A lawyer? An Indian chief?"

Claire's temper flared. "I have work to do. I would thank you to go away and leave me alone. And don't make fun of me."

Unfazed, Philippe went on conversationally, "I am also confused on the question of age, mademoiselle. You are not the child I originally thought, but I think you too young to be a bookkeeper. Your eyes are much too clear and your brow unfurrowed."

"I'm nearly nineteen," she retorted heatedly.

"So old!" Philippe feigned horror. "Almost an old maid."

Claire closed the ledger on the table with a bang, causing him to leap from his seat in mock alarm.

"Come now," he said, laughing, "don't be angry. My family and yours are old friends. How is Monsieur Fortier?"

Relaxing somewhat, she answered warily, "He is well."

"And probably quite happy to have such a lovely niece," Philippe said flirtatiously. When the girl did not respond to his compliment, he tried another approach. "Since you're newly arrived in town, perhaps I can be your guide one day soon. I can show you a side of New Orleans you have not seen before," he offered slyly. "Perhaps I could pick you up at your lodgings?"

"I live with my uncle."

"I heard rumors to that effect. But I thought surely an independent woman of the world—a bookkeeper, after all—would have a place of her own," he teased.

Unwilling to spend another moment with the insinuating young Creole, Claire stood and gathered her belongings, plucking her wrap from the back of the chair.

"Don't run away, Claire," Philippe crooned teasingly, capturing the edge of her cape and pulling her playfully toward him. "We have time to get to know each other before Lila comes home and sends you back to your drudgery."

"Monsieur Girard," she snapped, ripping the cape from his grip, "as I told you once before, I have no desire to get to know you tonight or any other time. You are arrogant and rude."

"So you did tell me." He smiled mockingly. "And I told you I could be a charming companion."

"You must be mad or drunk—or both."

"Not at all," he disagreed pleasantly. "I simply wanted to make your acquaintance."

Claire glared at him in amazed anger.

"Very well, Mademoiselle Fortier," he said, sighing and giving up his sport when he heard a carriage stop in front of the house. "We won't get to know each other tonight. But

there *will* be other nights and we *will* get to know each other."
Bowing, Philippe recaptured her unwilling hand and pulled it
unerringly toward his mouth.

Claire yanked it away the instant his lips brushed it, and fled
in consternation. As Ezra helped her into the waiting carriage, she did not look back to see if the sardonic young man
followed. She threw herself against the deep cushions, relieved when the coach door closed.

How dared Philippe Girard humiliate her every time they
met? Philippe with his superior attitude and his irrefutable
good looks. Unshed tears burned her eyes. Three times they
had met; three times he had insulted her; and three times she
had fled.

He was despicable, Claire told herself, willing herself to hate
him. But her cheeks burned with two bright spots of color and
she rubbed the back of her hand absently where his lips had
touched. How could just being in the same room with him
make her heart race?

If she ever met him again, the girl vowed it would be different. She would be unaffected by his presence. She would insult him, mock him as he did her. She would look through him
as if he weren't there. And she would not run away.

"Remember," Etienne instructed his niece when they arrived at the Théâtre D'Orléans, "when you are greeted, just
smile, curtsy and say 'How do you do.' And offer your hand
so gentlemen may kiss it."

"I'll remember," Claire assured him quietly.

"I know you will. Come along now and don't be frightened."

"I am not ... well, perhaps I am a little nervous," she admitted. "There are so many people.

"I'll be fine," she soothed when her uncle stopped short on
the banquette and frowned at her worriedly. "It's just that I
have never been to a theater before."

"All the more reason to enjoy it, *chère*." Taking Claire's
arm encouragingly, Etienne escorted her up the broad steps,
past posters advertising the night's presentation, yet another
revival of Moliere's *Tartuffe,* and into the theater.

From the section of the theater reserved for *gens de couleur,* free people of color, Lila observed when Etienne and

Claire entered their box. She watched her protector seat his niece, resplendent in a rose-colored satin gown. Settling into his own chair, he gazed around the theater, proudly noting each admiring look thrown toward the girl.

Look at him! Lila thought contemptuously. For years she had not shared her protector with anyone. Now suddenly he was a doting uncle. She turned her narrowed eyes on Claire. The girl was tall and plain, naive and unpolished. Yet Lila had learned from Concepción that the first time her back was turned, Philippe had come to the house on Rampart Street especially to meet Claire.

Lila's temper, already high, did not subside when the lights dimmed and the curtain rose. Her eyes, angry glittering topazes, were fixed on the stage, but she did not follow the actors' movements or dialogue. Fury required all her concentration.

In a box above her, Claire was enraptured with the sights, the sounds, the plot. Transfixed, she did not move until the end of the first act.

"It's not over, is it?" she whispered urgently when the curtain fell.

"No," her uncle said, chuckling. "Patience, Claire. As in anything, you will find out the ending eventually."

The curtain rose again and the girl gave herself over to the action onstage. When the lights came up at last for intermission, Etienne stood and suggested, "Let's step out for a breath of fresh air and some champagne to cool us."

Installing Claire next to a potted palm in a corner of the courtyard, he went in search of refreshments. Through the greenery, she stared with unabashed interest as the crowd swirled around her. How often her father had told her about the *Théâtre D'Orléans*. And how exciting it was to be here. Handsome men escorted ladies in dazzling gowns. Gems glittered at the women's throats as they flirted, flashing bright smiles and wielding languid fans.

"Claire!" A voice trilled across the lobby. "Claire Fortier, is that you?"

The startled girl looked around, then smiled as Anne Hébert, clothed in rich ivory lace, glided toward her. Marguerite Ledet dogged her cousin's steps, her braids bobbing behind her.

"You see," the younger girl was chattering, "I was right. Mademoiselle Fortier did come to the theater with her uncle. And is not she beautiful?"

"Indeed," Anne agreed. Grasping Claire's hand, she squeezed it and smiled warmly. "You look lovely, Claire."

"*Merci.*"

"We saw you when you first sat down in your box," Marguerite said excitedly. "Anne waved, but you were talking to your uncle. He is handsome, isn't he? And mature and elegant."

Anne wheeled on the adolescent girl exasperatedly. "Honestly, *cousine,* must you babble so?"

As she turned to face Claire again, the Creole girl's eyes were drawn to the other side of the room. Hurriedly unfurling her fan, she whispered from behind it, "Do not look now, but Gaspar Boudreaux and his friends are coming to speak to us.

"Gaspar is such a kind, sensitive man," she explained, blushing. "I know you'll like him. He has the soul of a poet."

"That's not all he has tonight," Marguerite cried delightedly. "He has that handsome Philippe Girard with him. Isabelle thinks he wants to seduce her. I am not sure what that means, but I cannot see why he would want to do it to Isabelle, can you?"

"Marguerite!" Shock was apparent in Anne's face and voice.

"I don't care. I think he's wonderful, but *mon père* says he's the worst kind of roué. What is a roué, Anne?"

"Not now," Anne warned irritably through a bright smile. "Run along and I'll explain later."

"I would rather stay," the young girl demurred. "How else will I learn about worldliness? The sisters don't teach us anything at the convent." Stubbornly she planted herself beside the palm tree, ignoring the nettled glances her cousin threw her.

While covertly watching the young gallants' approach, the other girls did not notice Claire's chagrin. At the mention of Philippe's name, she had stiffened. She had known this meeting was inevitable. She wanted to remain cool, to ignore him. Turning reluctantly, she found herself staring into his roguish brown eyes.

"*Bonsoir,* Mademoiselle Hébert," Gaspar nervously greeted the object of his devotion. He seemed not to see the other girls. "Are you enjoying the play?"

"I enjoy it more every time I see it, Monsieur Boudreaux." Anne laughed. "And you?"

"Very much. We have excellent seats," the stocky young man explained importantly.

"We know. You're sitting in the dress circle," Marguerite volunteered helpfully. "Anne noticed right away."

Gaspar blinked down at the little girl and choked, "She did?"

Behind her fan, Anne's cheeks colored. "Oh, children," she said quickly, "they say the first thing that pops into their heads, don't they?"

Henri was right, Gaspar thought elatedly. The dress circle was the place to see and to be seen. It was worth ten times the cost of the ticket because Anne had noticed him.

"I am being forgetful," the Creole girl berated herself charmingly, folding her fan with one graceful movement. "My little cousin Marguerite, you all know. But permit me to introduce Mademoiselle Claire Fortier, niece of Monsieur Etienne Fortier. She is new to New Orleans.

"Claire, this is Gaspar Boudreaux of Gran' Pré...." Anne commenced the introductions, gesturing to each man with her fan.

"How do you do, Mademoiselle Fortier." Gaspar kissed Claire's hand, regarding her with mild interest before he returned his attention to the enchanting Anne.

"...Henri D'Estaigne of Cyprès Plantation..."

"I'm delighted to meet you, mademoiselle," the suave Creole exclaimed, bowing and kissing her hand. "I have wanted to make your acquaintance since I first heard of your arrival in our city."

"...and this is Philippe Girard of Bonté," Anne concluded speedily, hoping the rake would behave himself for her new friend.

Philippe also bowed, then, smiling at Claire with an air of assured superiority, he drawled, "We meet again, mademoiselle."

"Again?" Henri echoed, crestfallen.

"Did I not mention it before?" the dark-haired Creole asked coolly. "Mademoiselle Fortier and I met last week at the home of a mutual friend."

Claire nodded in mute agreement. She was greatly relieved when her uncle returned, bearing two cups of punch.

"Ah, Mademoiselle Hébert and her cousin," Etienne greeted the young ladies cordially. "How beautiful you both look tonight."

Anne and Marguerite curtsied graciously.

"*Bonsoir,* gentlemen," Etienne added gruffly, nodding to Philippe and his friends.

"I'm sorry to have been so long, Claire," he apologized, handing her a cup, "but all I could find was some rather tepid punch.

"Mademoiselle Hébert, may I interest you in a cup?" He offered his to Anne.

"*Non, merci,* Monsieur Fortier," the girl refused with a smile.

"Then Mademoiselle Ledet must have it." Etienne turned courteously to Anne's young cousin. The flustered Marguerite accepted with a girlish giggle.

"Are you enjoying the play, Monsieur Fortier?" Henri asked, eager to make a good impression on Claire's uncle.

Claire's attention wandered while the two men talked. She did not notice that Henri's eyes flitted in her direction every few moments. She watched Anne and Gaspar talking softly, their heads close. Involuntarily, she glanced toward Philippe, who stood to one side, scanning the crowd without much interest. Marguerite positioned herself beside him, occasionally tugging on his sleeve to point out a mutual acquaintance.

Claire regarded Philippe through the veil of her thick dark lashes. Her cheeks burned when she recalled their meeting last week. The touch of his lips on the back of her hand had nearly set her skin afire. Without knowing, without trying, probably without caring, he had awakened in her sensations she had never known existed. How could she be attracted to a man who was so cruel and unfeeling?

Each time they met, Philippe mocked her. At Lila's house, he had arrogantly assured her that they would get to know each other, but tonight he did not even attempt polite conversation. Without saying anything at all to her, he compounded her embarrassment.

What did she care what he did? she asked herself resentfully, lifting her chin proudly.

She was disconcerted to discover he was watching her. His eyes lingered for a moment at the bodice of her low-cut gown, then mockingly rose to her face.

"You constantly amaze me, mademoiselle, for you are never what you seem." Philippe moved nearer to speak in her ear. "Tonight you are an alluring woman, but in a matter of one week, I've seen four different Claire Fortiers. Which one are you really, I wonder?" His face very close to hers, he cocked one eyebrow quizzically.

Claire glared at him, but Philippe was spared a sharp retort when a brilliantly liveried page appeared. He called to signal the beginning of the final acts.

"Oh, dear, come along, Marguerite!" Anne exclaimed, herding her cousin toward the door. Over her shoulder, she called, "Please excuse us. We must return to Maman and Papa. We told them we would only be gone for a moment."

"And Isabelle would love to tattle on me," Marguerite mumbled darkly, tugging on Anne's hand.

"I'll call on you soon," Anne promised Claire as the younger girl dragged her away.

"I, too, would like to call on you, Mademoiselle Fortier," Henri asserted hastily. "That is, if it is all right with your uncle." He glanced deferentially at Etienne.

Etienne regarded his niece questioningly. She did not encourage the young man, but she did not appear to object.

"Perhaps you could join us for dinner one night next week, D'Estaigne," he suggested, offering Claire his arm. "*Bonsoir*, gentlemen."

Philippe watched his smitten friends with amusement as the trio trooped back to their seats in the dress circle.

"Did you hear that, *mes amis?*" Henri crowed triumphantly. "Her uncle will allow me to call on *la belle* Claire. I'll bet I shall be her first gentleman caller in New Orleans."

"The bet," Philippe reminded him, "was not who would be first to call, but first to meet her. Pay up." He extended an open palm.

Scowling, the other man dug into his pocket and produced a twenty-dollar gold piece. "You may have met her, my friend," he commented acidly, "but she didn't seem to warm toward you tonight. In fact, she doesn't even seem to like you.

I noticed that she said nothing at all to you the entire intermission, not even when you spoke to her.''

"Who can account for taste?'' Philippe sighed dramatically. "But I wagered I would meet her, Henri, not woo her.
Besides, what chance would I have?'' he taunted. "You made
such a good impression—on her uncle, at least.''

"Yes, I think so,'' the other man agreed happily, missing the
sarcasm in Philippe's tone. He slapped his old friend amiably
on the back as they seated themselves in the dress circle.

Chapter Five

The next day, Friday, dawned clear and warm with a welcome breeze from the river. Knowing she would spend the evening laboring over Lila's books, Claire looked for any excuse to escape the house. When she remembered a pair of Etienne's boots would be ready at the cobbler's in the afternoon, she prevailed upon Greer to let her pick them up.

Claire fled the house, her maid in tow, and headed for the market. Now, as they stood on the corner of Levee Street and Rue Ste. Anne, a great hubbub arose from the Place d'Armes across the street.

"Oh, Mam'selle Claire," Beady breathed in anticipation, "today is Hangin' Day. They gonna hang some of them outlaws from th' Natchez Trace here at th' square. Kin we go watch?"

Claire frowned in distaste. *"Non, merci."*

"But, lissen to th' drum, mam'selle. They mus' be bringin' them out now. Cain't we go?" the little maid wheedled, almost dancing with excitement, "jest for one?"

"You go. I'll get my uncle's boots."

"But you might need me," Beady protested weakly.

"I can find the shop myself. I will meet you here in fifteen minutes, then we can stroll around the market."

"Ain't really proper for you to go walkin' 'round 'thout me," the maid countered dubiously.

"I went walking around without you for nearly nineteen years. I think I can walk to the cobbler's and back," Claire retorted.

The pudgy servant wavered irresolutely for a moment between duty and desire.

"Fifteen minutes," she called over her shoulder as she hurried toward the square, drawn by the hush that fell over the crowd while the charges against the condemned men were read aloud.

Claire ambled slowly to the cobbler's shop, stopping here and there to peer into a store window. At first she did not notice the sharp glances as she neared a group of Creole women. But when she drew even with them and nodded politely, her greeting was rebuffed. As she passed, Claire heard one of the women laugh and say, "That's the one... Etienne Fortier's Indian relation. Do you know what the wags in town are calling her? *Mademoiselle Sauvage.*"

Her head held high, Claire walked into the cobbler's shop, her eyes burning with unshed tears, blind to the admiring glances of the young men who loitered nearby.

A few minutes later, she reappeared on the sunny sidewalk, juggling an unwieldy box. Adjusting her bonnet against the glare, she stepped off the banquette, scarcely noticing when the cannon was discharged at Place d'Armes to emphasize the solemnity of the execution.

Not more than ten yards away, a skittish team of horses hitched to a loaded fruit wagon whinnied shrilly and bolted, dragging the heavy cart behind them. Their driver, no more than a boy, fought for control, sawing frantically on the reins as the vehicle picked up speed. Panic-stricken, he shouted a warning as the huge cart, melons rolling off its back, careened down the narrow street toward Claire.

As the girl lunged desperately toward the gutter, the heel of her shoe caught in the hem of her dress and tripped her. With a cry, she pitched forward, flinching in anticipation of crushing hooves.

Suddenly a sinewy arm wrapped around her waist, arresting her fall, yanking her from the path of the runaway team. She found herself cradled safely against a broad, muscular chest. In the dust, she drew back and looked up breathlessly at her rescuer—Philippe Girard. She blinked at him, openmouthed with amazement.

"Claire Fortier!" He seemed equally surprised. His protective embrace tightened. "I seem to have a talent for saving you from runaway horses.

"Don't be in such a hurry," he advised when she tried to escape his grip. Ignoring curious looks from bystanders, he did not release her. "You should wait until you catch your breath."

"I am fine, thank you," Claire insisted shakily. Her bonnet, hanging loosely by its ribbons, bobbed gently against her back.

Philippe lifted her chin and inspected her face solemnly. "You look faint. Allow me to take you to the infirmary." Hushing her protests with a gesture, he guided her toward his rig, one arm wrapped solicitously around her waist.

Seated across from Philippe in the carriage, Claire set her bonnet firmly atop her tumbled locks and eyed him suspiciously. Glancing nervously out the window as his coach made its way laboriously along the congested route to Hospital Street, she said formally, "I appreciate your assistance, Monsieur Girard, but you can let me out here."

"I wouldn't think of it." He smiled beneficently. "We are some distance from the market, the heat is unbearable for walking, and I am responsible for getting you to a doctor."

"I don't need a doctor."

"You do seem somewhat recovered, but I'd like to keep an eye on you a bit longer."

"Take me back to the market immediately," the girl insisted. "You cannot just . . . just abduct me from a city street in broad daylight."

"Abduct you?" Philippe hooted incredulously. "Mademoiselle Fortier, you never fail to astonish me."

As the carriage slowed to turn onto Hospital Street, he thrust his head out the window and shouted to the driver, "Take us to the lake, François. We need fresh air."

With a smug smile, the Creole settled back in the seat and regarded the sputtering girl humorously. "I've always believed that if I am accused of something, I may as well be guilty."

"Monsieur Girard—"

Philippe cut off her angry objection. "Don't worry, we are only going for a drive to give you time to collect yourself. You should see your face. You have a smudge on your cheek just as you did the first time I saw you.

"Wrong side," he added, chuckling when she swiped at her cheek self-consciously. "Here, use this."

Claire accepted a snowy white handkerchief from him and scrubbed energetically at the offending spot.

"Try not to remove too much skin with the dirt," he joshed gently. "Why are you so nervous?"

"I'm not nervous," she snapped. Suddenly self-conscious, she attempted to stuff her disarranged tresses under her hat.

"Then why are you worried about your hair?" he asked with an intimate smile. Reaching over, he removed her bonnet, causing her hair to cascade over her shoulders. "There, I think it looks lovely like that."

Oddly pleased, Claire clasped her hands in her lap and was silent. At last she asked curiously, "Where are we going?"

"To Lake Pontchartrain, where it is cool," he replied lazily, his dark eyes on her. "Have you been there?"

"No," she whispered, feeling shy under his direct gaze.

"Good, then I shall be the first to show it to you. Maybe I'll even take you to my favorite place. Settle back. I promise the ride will be worth it."

Wordlessly they rode along Esplanade, away from the city, past townhouses and fenced estates. After a while the carriage turned onto the Bayou Road, which ran parallel to Bayou St. John. Staring out the window at the pirogues skimming across the water, Philippe seemed content to think his own thoughts while Claire agonized about what to say to break the silence.

As they traveled, the road grew rougher and the countryside less populated. Glimpses of a cypress swamp were visible through the trees as the carriage rolled past the luxurious fishing cabins of the wealthy, and farther, past the tumbledown shanties of fishermen and trappers. At last they saw no more houses, and the rutted road seemed to be carved through the bayou-laced woods.

"Here," Philippe shouted to the driver. Gingerly, the slave pulled the rig off the road, stopping next to a thicket of rangy pine trees.

"What—what are we doing here? I think we should go back to town," Claire protested as Philippe alit from the carriage and turned to offer his hand.

"You've come this far. Don't tell me you want to miss the main reason I brought you here."

Stepping from the carriage, Claire surveyed the remote landscape tensely. Her anxiety slipped away, however, when she found herself in a world of dappled sunlight and cool breezes, where water lapped quietly against an unseen shore.

It was good to be outside, away from the bustle of the city. She was glad Philippe had removed her hat, she realized, for she liked the feel of the sun on her face and the wind in her hair.

Contentedly, she allowed him to take her hand and guide her across a sandy clearing toward the cool dimness of the woods and the water's edge.

In a dense glade where birds fluttered in the trees above their heads, he halted, placed his hands on her shoulders and judiciously positioned her in the center of the thicket.

"Stand right there," he ordered, tugging at branches, kicking at the undergrowth. "It has grown up a bit since I was here last," he apologized, "but this is what I wanted you to see."

He drew back a pinecone-laden bough, removing the final hindrance to the view, and Claire saw a vast expanse of blue water. Disbelievingly, she squinted toward the horizon, where a steamboat chugged along, a distant speck against the sky. The opposite shore was nowhere in sight.

"This is a lake?" she gasped in amazement.

"*Oui*, Lake Pontchartrain. It covers about six hundred square miles."

"This is how an ocean must look."

"But it is a lake." The young man chuckled. "It opens into Lake Borgne which opens into the Gulf of Mexico, so it's almost an ocean."

"It looks so clear and cool. Are we going swimming?" she asked ingenuously.

Philippe's eyebrows rose and he answered with amusement, "We could, if you wish. Do you like to swim?"

"Oh, yes," Claire murmured, staring wistfully at the blue water. Then, regretfully, she shook her head. "No, I don't think a lady would go swimming."

"I suspect you're right," he said with a grin. "Come sit down." He led the girl to a shady spot, where he spread his jacket on the ground. She sat with her back against a knobby tree trunk while he stretched out on his side beside her. "What do you think of my secret place?"

"It's wonderful," she responded sincerely. Turning her face to the breeze, she enjoyed its caress as it stirred her long dark hair, carrying its sweet fresh scent to the man.

"I don't know why, but I thought you would like it," he declared with a boyish grin. Lazily, he rolled onto his back and cushioned his head with clasped hands. "I knew you would enjoy it without worrying about sand in your shoes, or about mosquitoes or chiggers or snakes."

"You sound as if you have had experience with all those things," she teased.

"Those and worse." He laughed again, rolling to prop himself on one elbow. Suddenly he regarded her seriously. "You know, I have never brought a girl here. Actually, I've never brought anyone here."

The couple fell into an awkward silence until Claire could bear it no longer. "My uncle tells me you own a stable," she blurted.

"That's right. I keep racehorses."

"How did you come to be in the racehorse business?"

"I don't know." Philippe sat up, his brow knit reflectively. "I've always had horses, always loved them. My aunt gave me a Thoroughbred when I was eighteen and I built the stable from that. Or at least, I am trying to. It's been a long hard road."

"But you enjoy it?"

"*Oui,* I spend most of my time at it. It's funny that sometimes what begins as a passing interest can become the passion of your life."

Without knowing why, Claire found her heart was racing. She stared intently at a dragonfly that skimmed across the water. From down the shoreline, the voices of youthful fishermen could faintly be heard.

Philippe picked up a pinecone and tossed it carelessly into the air, catching it as it descended. "Did your uncle also tell you that Girard Stables is the best in South Louisiana—maybe even in the country?"

"You seem awfully sure of yourself," she chided playfully.

"I'm sure of my horses," he countered. "Hyacinth is the fastest filly I've ever seen. She has the makings of a champion. She won the big race last Fourth of July, and that was only the beginning. She'll win next year, too."

"What about the big palomino?" Claire's eyes followed the rise and descent of the pinecone.

The man shook his head. "Cavalier is too old for running, but he was a champion in his day. That's why I bought him for stud."

"He certainly shows spirit." She laughed ruefully, remembering the mishap at the dock.

"Sometimes I wonder whether it is spirit or cantankerousness," he answered with an easy smile, his eyes holding hers for a long moment.

The spell between them was broken by the sound of a splash as a large fish leapt from the lake, catching the sunlight on its scales. Then it sliced through the surface, disappearing to leave only a ring of ripples on the water as evidence of its presence.

Intent on avoiding Philippe's unnerving gaze, Claire stared at the lake's smooth surface, waiting for another fish to appear. She was acutely aware of each movement the man made, shifting his weight so he sat closer to her.

"Claire," he whispered, his warm breath touching her hair.

She was afraid to respond, afraid to move, afraid to meet his smoldering eyes. Closing her own eyes, she still felt his gaze on her as he captured her hand in his. She tried to pull away, but he held her firmly. Her breath came in short gasps, as strange, but not unpleasant feelings flooded through her.

Gently he released her hand and gripped her shoulders to turn her so she faced him. As he leaned slowly toward her, his dark eyes roved over her face for a moment before he kissed her, tentatively at first, then with increasing ardor.

In the heat of his insistent kisses, Claire's senses were aflame. Mesmerized by new sensations, she floated on an unfamiliar tide of passion. Sweet, aching desire took possession of her, engaging every sense, dissolving her will.

He buried his face against the soft, warm flesh of her neck, marveling at the unexpected pliancy of the proud, stubborn girl. Trailing kisses across her jaw to her ear, he murmured her name and eased her to the ground so she lay beside him. Her innocent, unguarded face turned toward his, her lips seeking his. Urgently, his skillful hands began to unfasten the buttons of her dress.

Abruptly Claire's eyes flew open and her body stiffened. "What are you doing?" she gasped accusingly, pushing his hands away.

"Nothing yet." Philippe kissed her and slipped his hand deftly into her open bodice to untie the ribbon of her chemise.

Dismayed, Claire scrambled to her knees and fumbled frantically to refasten the buttons where her dress gaped open.

"Nothing is going to happen," she panted. "I should never have let you kiss me."

Rising to his knees, the man glowered at her. He gripped her arms and pulled her roughly up to meet his body.

"I wasn't the only one doing the kissing," he accused. "You kissed me in return and did a quite tolerable job of it."

"*Non.*" Claire cast about as desperately for escape as she had in the narrow street of the Vieux Carré that morning.

"Damn it, Claire," Philippe growled, "you are not a child. You are a woman—a hot-blooded woman. You try to hide it under that cool exterior, but we both know what you want. Don't deny it."

White-faced, she struggled to her feet. "You have no right—"

"Why?" the man asked scoffingly. "Because you are a lady?"

She nodded her head rigidly.

"Do not be naive," he sneered. "You cannot simply decide to be a lady. You must behave like one, and no lady would have come alone into the forest with a man."

"But you brought me here."

"Your reputation is your responsibility, mademoiselle. I am not to blame if you are careless with it," he concluded grimly.

"Nothing happened," Claire protested hoarsely.

"So you say, but who would know that?" The young Creole shrugged. "And rumor has a way of getting around."

"You—you traitor!" With a choked cry, Claire doubled her fists and launched herself at his chest, pounding impotently before her fury subsided into deep, strangled sobs.

Confounded, Philippe stared down at the angry girl. Then, against his better judgment, he put his arms around her to comfort her, ruefully wondering at his mixed feelings. "Please, don't cry," he murmured soothingly.

Suddenly, Claire broke away and glared at him through redrimmed eyes. "I won't cry," she gritted, "and certainly not because of you." With that, she broke loose and ducked through the bushes toward the waiting carriage.

The ride back to town was long and silent. Claire sat in one corner of the coach, seething. Her pride stung at Philippe's words and she was certain he would betray her. She would never let her guard down again, she resolved, staring balefully at him. The man pointedly ignored her, turning his attention out the window.

When the carriage slowed near the market, Claire scooted to the edge of her seat, prepared to disembark instantly. Before the coach had stopped rolling, she opened the door.

"Wait." He grasped her arm. "I want to talk to you."

"Let me go or I shall scream," she ordered scornfully. "That is what a lady would do, isn't it?"

Before he could answer, she wrenched her arm free and stormed away. As she marched down the banquette, Claire silently cursed the sand in her shoes, the grass on her dress and the hair tumbling around her shoulders. But most of all, she cursed her own bruised and swollen lips that traitorously reminded her she had been kissed by Philippe Girard.

"Mam'selle Claire, I bin lookin' ever'where for you," Beady shrilled as she hurried to catch her mistress. "And jest look at what a mess you are." Bobbing around the girl, she attempted to brush the grass and pine needles off her skirt. She retreated when Claire halted and turned narrowed eyes on her.

"I bin worried sick, is all." The distraught maid's scolding trailed off lamely. "First we heerd you was run over. Then Ezra found your uncle's shoes in th' street. Bootblack on th' corner say you took off with M'sieur Girard after he saved your life."

"I do not want to talk about Monsieur Girard," Claire snapped irritably. "And I expect you to say nothing about this incident to my uncle."

Beady was unlikely to argue, since she felt guilty at having left her mistress alone, but her mind was made up when she caught sight of Philippe over Claire's shoulder. He leaned against a nearby lamppost and, with an impudent smile, placed a finger against his lips.

"No, ma'am," she said, dimpling. "I won't say nothin' to M'sieur Etienne 'bout what happened today."

All the Girards save one had coffee in the parlor after dinner. The silence was oppressive in the big room, relieved only by the ticking of the mantel clock, and the mood was subdued, for Pierre had been in one of his dark moods all day.

His wife summoned a hovering servant nervously. "Naomi, please warm Monsieur Pierre's *café*."

"I do not want more *café*, Clothilde. I shall tell you if I do." Pierre frowned at her. His thin lips tightened disapprovingly when the sound of a jaunty whistle reached his ears from the foyer.

Philippe appeared in the doorway. *"Bonsoir, ma famille."*

"Where have you been?" his father growled in greeting.

"Here and there," the young man answered coolly, sauntering into the room. He bent to peck his mother's colorless cheek before sitting down beside her.

"Papa," Odette blurted, eager to break the tension already evident in the room, "I talked to Marguerite Ledet today and do you know what she said?"

"What did she say?" Pierre smiled indulgently.

"That she saw Philippe at the theater the other night—and he was the handsomest man there." She addressed her brother ingenuously. "Is that true, Philippe?"

"I believe I *was* the handsomest man there," he said with a grin. "I'd never argue with a lady, even when she is my little sister's best friend."

"You know what I mean, Philippe," Odette scolded laughingly. "I mean, is it true Marguerite got to go to the theater?"
"Oui—"

"Handsome, is it, you conceited young rascal?" Pierre snorted, unwilling to let Philippe's joking comment pass. "That's one of the problems with you—too much vanity, too much concern about useless finery." He looked to his pale, black-clad wife for agreement. Unwillingly, almost imperceptibly, she nodded.

"In fact," Pierre continued, his narrowed eyes inspecting his son's apparel closely, "is that a new waistcoat you have on?"

"Oui." Philippe adjusted his elaborate brocade vest studiedly. "Do you like it?"

"I think it's very becoming, don't you, Maman?" René interjected hastily in a futile attempt to avert his father's rage. René received another reluctant nod from Clothilde.

"Whether I like it is not the question." Pierre would not be deterred. "The question is, where did you get it?"

"I bought it." Philippe's voice was soft, but his temper was beginning to rise.

"Bought it with what? I thought all your money went back into the precious stables."

Deliberately, the young man set his coffee cup down and stared at his father. "Not the money I win," he countered evenly.

"A wager! I knew it," Pierre bellowed. "How many times have I warned you against betting on horses?"

"This time, *mon père,* I bet on a woman," his son replied calmly.

Philippe regarded his speechless family with a cocky smile until the shocked, frozen silence was broken by Clothilde.

"Philippe," she moaned softly. "How can you say things like that in your home—in front of Odette?"

"Sorry, Maman...Odette." The reckless smile disappeared.

"This womanizing must stop, *M'sieur Roué,*" Pierre choked angrily. "I will not be humiliated by the gossip on the lips of half of New Orleans. Haven't you had enough brushes with simpering females and their irate fathers?"

Her eyes wide, Philippe's younger sister was a rapt witness, while Clothilde wept silently.

"Pardon, Maman." Grimly, the young man rose and walked to the door through which he had entered only minutes before. "I just remembered some business in town."

Without another word or even a look back over his shoulder, he mounted Lagniappe and galloped away from Bonté.

Chapter Six

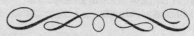

Robert McConnell, manager of Fortier's Mercantile Company, sat on his high stool and stole furtive glances at Claire as she worked. Was it only a month ago that his employer had insisted his niece come to work for him? The middle-aged man's lips twisted in a rueful smile when he remembered how he had objected that the waterfront was no place for a genteel young lady. But Mr. Fortier had been adamant and now McConnell was glad.

Seeing her carriage in front of the office that first morning, the brusque Scotsman had marched across the yard and onto the porch of the office, looking neither right nor left. As he fumbled with the lock, he had heard her soft voice behind him. When he turned, he had looked into Claire Fortier's fathomless black eyes and was lost.

Now he hurriedly turned his attention to his work when Claire looked up and smiled at him.

"I am finished," she said with an air of finality. "You're sure you don't mind if I take the afternoon off? I could come in tomorrow, if you'd like."

"I would nae like," he said curtly. Though it pained him to remember, he recalled her uncle's wishes. The sooner Claire tired of working in the office, the happier Etienne Fortier would be.

"Go on," McConnell said, sighing, "and hae a good time this afternoon. 'Tis what I want for ye."

"I am so glad your uncle allowed you to come with us, Claire. It's not every day you get to see a steamboat race.

Though I vow I'll be glad when it is over. For three weeks, it has been the only topic of conversation," Anne Hébert chattered.

"It was kind of your mother to invite me." Claire smiled at her petite friend. "Your entire family has been so good to me."

"We've enjoyed having you out to Belle Grâce, even *mon père*. I suppose I should be jealous. He says you are the only one of my friends who is the least bit serious, not foolish or flighty. I told him girls have a lifetime to be serious when they are wives and do you know what he did? He laughed and said I am not as flighty as I would have my suitors believe. What do you think of that?

"Oh, look," she cried before Claire could answer, "here come Isabelle and Denise Malveaux. Doesn't *ma cousine* look pretty? I do hope she is not in one of her moods."

Claire turned to watch Isabelle Ledet and her companion picking their way daintily across the open field. Claire and Anne stood with the crowd gathered on the levee to await the arrival of the *Terpsichore* and the *Memphis Lady*, two of the fastest steamboats on the Mississippi.

The air was festive despite overcast skies and the raw chill on the November wind. Carriages and buggies were parked randomly in a grassy meadow. Emmaline Hébert and Yvonne Ledet watched the girls from one of them.

Isabelle and Denise carefully guarded their full skirts from the crowd as they walked, frowning up at a George Walker who strode past them, swaying on his stilts. Dogs barked at him and boys chased him, but their din was nearly obscured by the cries of vendors, who displayed their goods on wagon beds at the edge of the field.

"You look tired, Claire," Anne said, looking at her friend with concern while they waited for the other girls to join them. "Are you getting enough rest?"

Because her uncle had asked her to tell no one about her job at the Mercantile, Claire replied simply, "I didn't sleep well last night."

It was true enough. The evening had been very long. Henri had come to dinner, lingering before the fire in the library for a private talk with Claire. He had demanded at once to know what other callers she had received and what their intentions were. His interrogation and his visit had ended when she tired of his jealousy and her temper flared. The wronged lover had departed then, wrapped in an almost tangible mantle of wounded pride.

"Look over there! Gaspar and Henri!" Anne breathed excitedly. "I think they're going to join us, too."

Down in the open field, the two young Creoles hurried from the carriages where they had stopped to speak to Mesdames Hébert and Ledet. Catching up with Isabelle and Denise, both gentlemen bowed, then escorted them toward the other girls. Isabelle preened, flirting, as they walked, while her mother looked on proudly from the carriage.

Claire steeled herself as they approached. She had met Denise only once, but she did not like her. The short, round Creole girl was charming to everyone she met, but as soon as she left their company, she had a dozen unkind remarks to make.

Isabelle, at least, was not duplicitous, Claire thought wryly. The petite blond girl did not bother to hide her dislike of Anne's new friend. But what Claire especially dreaded, as the small group scaled the levee toward her, was a resumption of last night's scene with Henri.

The handsome young Creole must have seen the apprehension in her eyes for he approached with a repentant smile.

"Bonjour, mesdemoiselles," he and Gaspar called in unison.

"Oui, bonjour, mesdemoiselles." Their greeting was echoed by two more voices. The young people turned to discover the Vidrine twins strolling toward them. Stocky and muscular, André and Antoine were both considered good matches, and both were smitten with Isabelle. Fully aware of her effect on the brothers, she turned to them with a dazzling smile.

The young Creoles halted just before reaching the group and gazed entreatingly toward Isabelle's mother across the field. Their unspoken request for permission to join her daughter was granted with a nod of Madame Ledet's head. Seated comfortably in the carriage, the chaperons watched the young people closely for any sign of misconduct.

Claire was relieved when there was little conversation beyond pleasantries. Gaspar eagerly offered his arm to Anne and they set off on a leisurely walk along the levee. Antoine immediately followed his suit, claiming Isabelle for himself, leaving his slower brother to follow unhappily with Denise.

As Henri and Claire brought up the rear, he asked quietly, "Do you forgive me for last night, *chère?* I had no right to behave as I did. It's just that...well, you know how I feel about you, don't you?"

"I forgive you, Henri." Claire answered only one of his questions. "And I think it would be best if we forgot last night."

He looked at her searchingly for a long moment, then he smiled in acquiescence. "*Très bien.* We will forget it."

For a time the couple walked in companionable silence, savoring the cool November afternoon.

Farther down the curving levee, Lila asked her companion, "Is that not your friend Henri?"

Philippe glanced disinterestedly at the couple who strolled some distance away. "*Oui,* with Claire Fortier."

"Why is he wasting time on that ugly, skinny girl?"

"Lila, you are uncharitable," Philippe answered mockingly as he watched Claire. "Mademoiselle Fortier is far from ugly, and she is an heiress, after all."

"I could understand if he needed the money," Lila said petulantly, "but Henri D'Estaigne is the heir to one of the largest plantations on the river."

Just then the faint sound of a bell claimed her attention. She turned and strained to spot the boats, still far upriver. Unseen by Henri and Claire, Philippe continued to watch them. What was it about the girl that made her stand out in a crowd? he wondered idly. What drew men to her? Henri had confided glumly that he was facing stiff competition in his suit.

Claire became aware someone was watching her. Casually she let her gaze roam, searching for the source of her discomfort. When her eyes met Philippe's challenging stare, she stiffened. She had not seen the Creole since their trip to the lake, several months ago, but she remembered his kiss as if it had been only yesterday. The mere thought of it brought back a surge of unwanted emotion.

Although only a moment elapsed, it seemed to Claire an eternity before she was able to pull her gaze away from his. Philippe's lips twisted into a wry smile at the mixture of emotions apparent upon her face.

Sensing Claire's uneasiness, Henri bent to ask solicitously, "Is anything wrong?"

"I—I'd like to go back to the carriage," she improvised, desperate to escape Philippe's scrutiny.

"But you cannot see the boats nearly so well there," Henri protested in dismay.

To his relief, before they could leave the levee, a cheer rose around them. The couple turned to see the two paddle wheelers, abreast in the wide river as they steamed toward New Orleans. Stripped for racing, the boats moved swiftly on the current, their torch baskets glowing red against the murky sky, spewing cinders into the air. The noise of their machinery as they approached was deafening.

"Oh, they look as if they will explode," Anne cried in alarm, clutching Gaspar's arm.

"There's little danger of that." He tried to comfort her, but he had to shout to be heard. "The captains and crews are even more mindful of safety when racing than when carrying passengers."

The boats passed the crowd, blowing long blasts on their whistles. The sooty-faced crews shouted and waved at the spectators. The paddle wheels churned the water, slapping the surface so hard that Claire was certain she felt the ground shake beneath her feet with their impact. All too soon, the excitement was over. The behemoths disappeared around a bend in the river, leaving only a wake of turbulent water and a plume of black smoke hanging on the wind to show they had been there at all.

As the crowd dispersed, René Girard found his brother on the levee. "*Bonjour,* Philippe. What did you think of the race?"

"It's not over until they reach the Canal Street Wharf."

"True, but surely the *Terpsichore* will take the horns."

"Surely," Philippe agreed easily. "That boat is certainly well named. She seems to dance across the water."

"You had a bet?" René asked unnecessarily.

"Of course."

The brothers stood side by side for a moment, staring at the muddy river without speaking. Suddenly René ventured awkwardly, "You really should come home, you know, Philippe."

"Why? To fight with Père again?"

"Maman wants you to come home. She worries for you. I think she knows—somehow—about Lila Broussard."

With a sardonic smile, Philippe cautioned, "Have a care of what you say, *mon frère.*" He nodded meaningfully toward a lingering figure René had not noticed before.

Excluded from the men's conversation, Lila lolled against a tree a short distance away, twirling her parasol in exaggerated boredom as she stared vacantly at the shadows of the Spanish moss that played on the water.

"How could you bring her here?" René muttered under his breath.

"I didn't bring her. We met. A happy accident."

"It won't be so happy if Fortier finds out."

"Finds out what?" the young Creole scoffed. "That Lila and I happened to be at a steamboat race with two hundred other people? That will certainly make him jealous."

"He is not a fool, Philippe."

"I wouldn't say so," the young Creole agreed mildly.

"I can see it will do no good to argue with you." René drew himself up, stiff with disapproval.

"No good at all," his brother confirmed.

"Then I bid you *bonjour* and ask you to think about what I've said. Maman would like to see you." With that, he turned and marched away.

Philippe watched his elder brother disappear into the crowd and, through the wall of people, he caught sight of Claire again. Pulling a cheroot from his pocket, he lit it and studied her appraisingly.

She was such a contradiction—beautiful in a wild, disturbing way, but naive with seemingly little experience with men. Despite his better judgment, he was attracted to her, the Creole admitted grudgingly to himself.

Suddenly, as he watched her with Henri, he wished she would smile. She did not smile enough, but when she did... Philippe's thoughts strayed to their trip to the lake, recalling Claire's delight in his secret place. When she relaxed, she had been good company. Her face had lost its guarded expression and her dark eyes had been warm and caressing. Her voice was low and pleasant, her laugh clear and infectious. And the kiss they had shared for a moment before she broke away...

Behind him, Lila shivered from the cold and fidgeted impatiently. She had arranged this meeting, had come all the way out here to see Philippe, and he wasn't even paying attention.

"Cher," she summoned teasingly without looking around to see what she interrupted, "I'm getting tired of waiting for you."

When she received no answer, she pouted. Then, trying another tack, she peeped coyly at the man from behind the parasol. What she saw transformed her playful expression into cold fury. Lila flung herself away from the tree and stood with fists clenched, watching Philippe stare openly at Claire Fortier.

The octoroon controlled herself with effort and moved to his side. "I am going to my carriage," she said coldly.

"Good day then." His handsome face was expressionless.

Lila stared up at him in disbelief. Philippe had turned the tables on her. He was not going to protest her leaving. He was not even going to walk her to her carriage. Well, she would not let him see her consternation. Drawing herself up proudly, she said in a tight voice, *"Bonjour,* M'sieur Girard." Then she walked purposefully.

Philippe watched her departure, his face tight with vexation. Lila was becoming more of a bother than she was worth to him, he thought grimly. These "chance" meetings she engineered were dangerous and lost their excitement in the face of her demands. She was beautiful and desirable and they had had some good times together, but she wanted more. Always more. She had to learn—no woman owned Philippe Girard.

Tossing his cigar into the river, he strode toward the carriages where the Hébert and Ledet parties had assembled.

"Philippe," Henri and Gaspar hailed their friend gladly.

"Bonjour, mes amis, André, Antoine. *Bonjour,* ladies." Philippe bowed, his greeting encompassing all the females, young and old. His eyes flickered over Claire, who nodded to him stiffly.

"Were you here for the race, Monsieur Girard?" Isabelle asked at once, offering her most radiant smile. "I didn't see you."

"Not because she didn't look," Denise muttered under her breath. Only Claire heard and shot a curious glance at the Creole girl. But Denise had already turned to chat pleasantly with André Vidrine.

"I wouldn't have missed it, mam'selle," Philippe responded lazily to her flirtatious smile.

"Monsieur Girard—" Anne began.

"*Monsieur* Girard? Aren't we formal, *ma petite?*" The man grinned down at her roguishly. "One would think I was a new acquaintance, rather than the boy upon whom you bestowed your first kiss."

"Philippe!" the blushing Anne and her mother gasped in unison.

"That's better." Turning a remorseless smile on Madame Hébert, who still sat in her carriage, he explained, "Anne was only three years old at the time and, on my honor, she hasn't kissed me since."

"You have always had the most disconcerting habit of saying whatever you please, Philippe." The woman shook her head in exasperation.

"And you have always had the most disconcerting habit of scolding me when I did."

"Someone had to." Madame Hébert laughed unexpectedly. The young people stared at her in surprise as she bantered with the roué she had known all his life.

"You always ruined your sternness by doing something to take the sting away," Philippe reminded her softly.

"*Oui.*" She smiled at the memory. "And to make up for the scolding today, why don't you join us at the town house for an early supper?"

"Oh, yes, Philippe," Anne seconded enthusiastically. "We are having a soiree and it will be such fun if you come."

"Say you will, *mon ami,*" Henri urged. "You've been so busy with your horses and stable that none of us has seen you for weeks now."

"I should be delighted."

The words were hardly out of Philippe's mouth before Madame Ledet rose and descended from the carriage. "We shall follow you, Emmaline," she said, taking the assisting hand André offered. Knowing it was important to please the mother if he was to court the daughter, André escorted the woman to her carriage, leaving Antoine to escort Isabelle and Denise. Isabelle cast quick, inviting glances over her shoulder at Philippe, but he did not seem to be watching. Her pretty face clouded when she realized his dark eyes rested on Claire Fortier.

"Maman has said Gaspar and Henri may ride in our carriage and there is room for you, too, Philippe," Anne suggested, glancing toward her mother for her approval.

"*Merci,* but I have Lagniappe," he answered politely.

"Gaspar and I are going to tie our horses to the back of the rig," Henri said. "If you'll tell me where you left Lagniappe, I'll bring him when I fetch our horses."

"*Merci,* Henri," Philippe surrendered with an easy smile. "You'll find him beside the bakery wagon."

"*Pardon,* Claire. I'll be right back." The copper-haired young Creole set out on his errand.

Philippe was left standing beside the silent Claire. She refused to meet his gaze, her dark eyes following the flight of a graceful egret over the broad river. Seeing that Gaspar and Anne were engrossed in conversation with Madame Hébert, he said quietly, "Here we are, alone again, Claire."

The girl's cheeks reddened at the memory his words brought and she glanced around to see if anyone else had heard.

"Aren't you the least bit happy to see me, *chère?*" he goaded softly. "After all, it's been so long since our tender moment at the lake."

"I do not consider that a tender moment," Claire gritted.

"What do you consider it then?" he asked dangerously.

"A mistake."

"Believe me, it was no mistake when I kissed you. And I can scarcely believe it was one when you returned my kiss."

"If anyone hears you—" she whispered hotly.

"I will swear to them on my honor, just as I did with Anne a moment ago, that you've never kissed me since." He smirked smugly.

"You are without a doubt—"

"Calm down," he advised pleasantly. "Henri is coming and he's sure to ask why you are giving me such a tongue-lashing."

Claire bit her lip to keep from retorting.

If Henri felt the strain between the couple, he did not show it when he joined them. "All set?" he asked, taking Claire's arm possessively and leading her to the spacious brougham where Anne and Gaspar waited, already seated beside Madame Hébert on the bench seat facing forward.

Claire sat between Henri and Philippe as the small parade of carriages returned to the Vieux Carré. Almost knee to knee with Madame Hébert, Philippe engaged the woman in lively conversation, virtually ignoring the girl who sat beside him. Claire answered Henri distractedly when he spoke to her, but her attention was taken up by the feel of Philippe's broad shoulders and his long, lean leg pressing against hers through her skirt with every jostling bump of the carriage.

She breathed a sigh of heartfelt relief when they reached the Hébert town house. The procession of carriages ranged along the banquette and discharged their merry passengers. Madame Hébert led her guests through the passageway from the street to the spacious courtyard where her husband waited.

"*Bonjour* . . . or should I say *bonsoir?*" Monsieur Hébert greeted them. "How was the race?"

It seemed to Claire that everyone tried to answer at once, all but Madame Hébert, who hurried toward the kitchen at the back of the compound to check on dinner's progress.

The girl looked around her admiringly. She loved the openness and grace of the Hébert's magnificent town house, a design common to houses in the Vieux Carré. The parlors, dining room and library formed an ell on the lower floor, their French doors opening onto the private courtyard. A staircase led to a long gallery along which the sleeping quarters for the family were located.

The women of the party followed Anne up that staircase to the guest rooms so they could freshen up after their long ride. The genial host, Monsieur Hébert ushered the men toward the parlor and a brandy.

After making sure her guests had all they needed, Anne called to Claire over the babble of feminine voices, "Shall we go downstairs?"

The tall girl nodded gratefully and headed for the door. The women of the Héberts' party all seemed either to know one another or to be related. They had not been rude, but they had not been particularly friendly. They responded politely to Claire when Anne introduced them, but then they returned to their earlier conversations.

As Claire followed Anne out onto the gallery, she heard Denise Malveaux's stage whisper, "And they call her Mademoiselle Sauvage!"

Claire closed the door and glanced at her hostess, relieved that she had not heard. Though she longed to confront the venomous Denise, Claire did not want to ruin Anne's party. Cautioning her friend to keep quiet, the vivacious Creole girl leaned over the railing to see who was in the courtyard below.

"No one," she reported, straightening disappointedly. She had hoped to sweep majestically down the stairs and take Gaspar's waiting arm.

The babble inside the guest room reached the girls clearly for an instant as the door opened and Isabelle and Denise emerged.

"*Pardon,*" the blonde said haughtily, brushing past them. Making the sweeping descent Anne had wanted, she disappeared into the parlor in a swirl of pastel-blue skirt.

"Isabelle is never happy unless she can make an entrance," Anne said, envious of her cousin's confidence.

"And she is not likely to be happy unless she can make Philippe Girard notice her," Denise remarked cattily behind them.

For an instant, a flash of dislike flickered in Anne's eyes. Then she turned to Denise and smiled sweetly. "But *chère,* if Isabelle concentrates on Philippe, that leaves both the Vidrines susceptible to your many charms."

Completely missing the uncharacteristic sarcasm in Anne's voice, the plump, plain girl brightened. "*Mais oui. Pardon,*" she said hastily. Squeezing past Anne and Claire with difficulty on the narrow gallery, she, too, hurried downstairs.

From the moment she entered the parlor, Claire could feel Philippe's eyes on her, but it was Henri who hurried to meet her. He stayed by her side through the buffet dinner and during coffee, his constant presence and attentiveness discouraging other admirers.

At last, as the couple sat in matching chairs near the door, Gaspar called jovially to his friend from across the room, "Henri, come and tell Monsieur Hébert about our adventure when we went boar hunting near Pearl River."

"Do you mind?" Henri asked Claire softly.

"Not at all," she replied, pleased for a moment to herself.

"You are sweet," her suitor murmured as he stood. "I won't be long."

While Henri launched into a lengthy, merry description of the guide he and Gaspar had used on their ill-fated trip, Claire rose silently and crept out to the dark courtyard.

The night was chilly, but the fresh air felt good after hours in a stuffy room overheated by the presence of too many people and a score of candles. Pleased by her solitude, the girl inhaled deeply and gazed up at the night sky appreciatively. The clouds of the day had cleared and now hundreds of stars shone overhead.

From inside the house, she could faintly hear piano music and muffled laughter as Henri embellished his tale, but she did not feel a part of the festivities. Alone in the courtyard, Claire realized how much she relished her moment of freedom from manners and customs and proprieties. Though she was cold, she could not face going back inside.

Wrapping her arms around herself to keep warm, she wandered farther from the noise and the light, strolling toward the fountain in the shadowy center of the courtyard. As she approached the huge magnolia tree that overhung the fountain, a figure materialized from the darkness at her side.

"Claire, what are you doing out here?" a familiar voice asked.

"Philippe," she gasped, startled. She did not want to see him now, she thought, panic-stricken. She did not want to be alone with him, not after what had happened the last time. His very presence in the dark garden brought a storm of turmoil to her.

She sought to cover her agitation with truculence. "I was trying to get away from the noise and the heat . . . and the people," she said emphatically.

"I thought for a moment I unnerved you, but I see I did not." In the faint light from the house, Claire saw the flash of white teeth as he smiled. "I take it I am one of the people that rather pointed barb is directed against?"

"Take it however you wish," she said tersely, about to return to the house.

"Don't go." The man stepped quickly in front of her to block her way.

"Let me pass, monsieur," she demanded unsteadily. She had to get away from him, for when he was near she never knew what was going to happen.

"Stay, Claire," he urged quietly. "It seems you are always running away from me. Do I frighten you so much?"

Claire strained to see Philippe's face clearly. His voice was serious, but with his back to the light, she could not see if he mocked her.

"I—I'm not frightened of you," she said after a moment. It was only half a lie. She feared her reaction to him as much as she feared him.

"Then why are you shivering?" he asked, strangely gentle.

"Because it is cold out here, you idiot," she answered through chattering teeth.

"That's a fine way to talk to the gentleman who is about to give you his jacket," Philippe railed playfully as he stripped to his shirtsleeves. Over Claire's protests, he stepped close and draped the heavy jacket over her shoulders.

The garment still held the warmth of his body, and it smelled pleasantly of tobacco and the bay rum he wore.

"Merci." She smiled up at him, glad he had moved so she could see his face as he gazed down at her. But at the look in his eyes, she felt that her knees would give way and she would be drawn against him as if he were a magnet. She fought the urge to sway toward him, to close the distance between them. Instead she summoned the strength to step back.

"Are you running away again?" he asked chidingly as he advanced another step.

"N-non." She forced herself to stand her ground, but would not look at him. "I really should go inside," she said desperately.

Placing his hands on her shoulders, he said lightly, "I suppose I could promise not to kiss you."

"Would you?" she asked, lifting her face to look at him hopefully.

"No," he whispered. His hands slid over her shoulders to the slim column of her neck, feeling the pulse race there as his mouth dipped to claim hers. Claire was not as unaffected as she pretended to be, he realized with a thrill.

But sensation replaced thought for Philippe when Claire began to respond to his caresses. Her lips parted under his tender pressure, inviting him within. His tongue tasted the sweetness of her mouth and it seemed to the man as though he would never be sated.

Lacing his fingers through her hair, he cradled her head in one big hand as he kissed her closed eyes, the sensitive spot below her ear, then returned to her mouth.

She stiffened in his arms when the sound of Henri's voice reached them. The young Creole stood in the parlor door, silhouetted by the light from within, and peered out into the dark courtyard. "Claire, are you out there?" he called.

Clasping Claire tightly in a one-armed embrace, Philippe put his hand over her mouth and commanded in a whisper, "If you do not want to be the subject of malicious gossip tomorrow, don't answer. It would never do for you to be found kissing a man in a dark courtyard."

When Henri had gone back inside, Philippe loosened his grip. Claire broke free at once and glared up at him, confusion and reproach in her dark eyes.

"You promised not to kiss me," she accused in a strangled voice.

The man did not appear to be listening. "Go around the long way and go into the parlor as if you are coming from upstairs," he ordered, "so no one will know you've been out here with me."

Claire's anger turned to surprise. Philippe was worried about her reputation? Was it possible he could be a gentleman after all? She didn't take time to ponder the questions.

"*Merci,*" she said simply, returning his jacket.

"And remember, Claire," Philippe called softly before she was out of earshot, "I didn't promise not to kiss you."

If she answered, he did not hear her. Philippe's set face did not relax until the girl had stolen through the shadows and entered the house unnoticed. Drawing on his jacket, which now smelled faintly of Claire's scent, he repeated to himself grimly, "I didn't promise. And, damn it, I don't think I could have if I wanted to."

At the edge of town, Lila made her way through the night to knock on the door of a shabby cottage.

"*Entrez,*" a quavery voice responded.

Stepping inside, Lila found Sanité Dédé, queen of voodoo in New Orleans, wrapped in a quilt, sitting beside the fireplace.

"Mama Dédé," she greeted the old woman respectfully. "I need some advice."

"Knew you'd come tonight," Mama Dédé croaked. "You gots man troubles, hein?"

"How did you know?"

"Killt a chicken and read what the obeah say."

"What did it say?" the octoroon coaxed.

"That you mus' take keer, chile," the old woman answered gravely, "for they's one who will steal 'way what's precious to you."

"Is that all?" Lila breathed anxiously.

"One thing more. This gal—you think she cannot ketch a man's eye. I warn you, she may ketch a heart. And not even voodoo knows what a heart will do."

Chapter Seven

It was time to put his foot down, Etienne thought, stabbing his grapefruit with a spoon. He had allowed Claire to spend too much time away from the house. Now, on this beautiful Saturday morning, she was still abed, exhausted from her week at the Mercantile and the Friday evening accounting job. Lately he didn't even have a bourrée partner for these long winter evenings.

Although the man's face was stern, he dreaded the speech he would deliver and the explosion that would follow. Every time he thought his niece was becoming biddable, her damnable temper destroyed the illusion.

"May I take it in to him, Greer?" Claire's voice rang from the hallway.

"Bonjour, Oncle." She swept into the dining room and dropped an envelope on the table in front of him. "A boy just delivered this for you."

"So glad you could join me," Etienne said curtly, looking down his aristocratic nose at her. "I thought you were going to spend the day in bed."

"And miss my favorite meal of the day with you?" She smiled brightly at him. Washed by November sun, she looked feminine and graceful in her purple velvet dressing gown, her dark hair cascading over her shoulders. Alone with her uncle, she showed none of her earlier uncertainty. Only with strangers did any awkwardness return, but she had learned to disguise it by moving slowly, bringing to her motions a regal quality.

Etienne shook his head in exasperation. Then he returned the smile in spite of himself, allowing his pique to slip away. In a more congenial mood, he picked up the envelope and opened it.

"Another blasted invitation to another blasted ball," he grumbled after a moment, pitching the note onto the table. "The ladies of the Vieux Carré seem to believe I've nothing else to do."

"Someday they will realize you do not attend balls and they'll stop sending you invitations. Then you won't have any mail at all to open in the mornings. What will you do?" his niece teased.

"What will I do, indeed?" he responded absently, retrieving the discarded envelope.

Despite his apparent distraction, Etienne's mind was working calculatingly. He had yet to introduce Claire to society. What better way to overcome her insistence that she have a job than to introduce her to a score of marriageable bachelors? Young D'Estaigne seemed to be getting nowhere with her. Perhaps she would meet someone at the ball or perhaps a bit of serious competition would hasten Henri's pursuit. Claire's nineteenth birthday had come and gone last week, and she seemed completely unconcerned that she was headed for spinsterhood. Something had to be done.

"The prospect of no mail at all is grim," he jested, suddenly jocular. "I must take precautions. We shall attend this ball."

"You are going to a ball?" Claire asked incredulously.

"*We* are going to a ball—'a masked ball,'" Etienne read from the invitation, "'to raise funds for the proposed medical school.' It takes place in a fortnight, so you must order an appropriate dress right away. This will probably be the event of the season. Every ball seems to be," he added drolly.

"Surely there is something in my wardrobe that will do," the girl floundered.

"You amaze me." He stared at her wonderingly. "I have a position to maintain in this city. You must have a new outfit—gown, shoes, half mask."

"But, Uncle Etienne, you have already given me so much."

"Obey me in this, Claire. I wish to go the ball. I wish you to go with me. Go this week and buy a gown."

"I can't take time from work," she muttered obstinately.

Her uncle arched a cynical brow. "Shall I take it up with McConnell?"

"Non," she mumbled. "I will go."

"Très bien." Etienne regarded her speculatively. Strengthened by one victory, he decided to try for another. "Claire, would you consider giving up your position at Mademoiselle Broussard's?"

"Oui." When the man's gray eyes widened in surprise, she explained, "Once they were organized, Lila's books are almost always correct to the picayune. I don't believe she needs a bookkeeper now, and I'd rather spend my evenings at home with you. Do you think she will mind?"

"Not at all," Etienne assured her, glowing with pleasure. He sat back to finish his breakfast, a happy man.

"Bonjour, Mademoiselle Fortier," Madame Benoit greeted Claire pleasantly. "How may I help you today?"

"Bonjour, Madame Benoit. I need a gown for the charity ball."

"Oh, mademoiselle, surely you cannot expect me to make a new gown for you by next Sunday." The dressmaker gasped dramatically.

"But you made my entire wardrobe in little more than a week," Claire protested in dismay.

"Oui, but then I did not have so many other orders. *Everyone* wants a new gown for this ball."

"Then I suppose I'll wear an old gown after all," the girl murmured, glumly imagining what Etienne's reaction would be when he learned that she had procrastinated a full week before going to buy a new dress.

"I am sorry, Mademoiselle Fortier, I—" the seamstress was apologizing when a voice called from the back of the shop.

"As much as I like it, Madame Elise, it's simply too big." Anne Hébert sighed, peeping out from behind the curtains of the dressing room. Her pretty face brightened when she saw Claire.

"Claire, what are you doing here?" As usual, Anne did not give her friend a chance to answer. "Come and see the most beautiful petticoat in the world that simply will *not* fit me," she urged, opening the curtain a bit.

Claire stepped into the cramped dressing room and was engulfed by petticoats of every color and description, hanging from pegs on the walls: dainty pink ones, embroidered yellow ones, even one that looked as if it were spun from silver spider webs.

Swallowed by an elaborate golden petticoat, the petite Anne stood amid the disorder, regarding herself sadly in the huge mirror. The strapless bodice, much too large for her, drooped lopsidedly to reveal her chemise underneath. Gingerly, she tugged at the fragile fabric of the bodice, only to have it sag again. Sighing wistfully, she ran her fingers over the gilded lace that ran in vertical rows down the front from the narrow waist, curving to form a border along the bottom.

"It's hopeless," she moaned.

"Couldn't you cut it down to fit?" Claire ventured.

"*Mais non,* what a waste that would be!" the Creole girl exclaimed, shocked by the idea. "My dear Claire, this is the finest Brussels lace and it is gilded, at that. No, there is nothing I can do," she conceded practically, squirming to allow the heavy petticoat to slide over her hips to the floor.

Madame Benoit, entering with fresh samples for Anne, narrowly missed stepping on the discarded garment. Claire stooped to pick it up while Anne resumed her position before the mirror, a petticoat in either hand. She held each one in front of her critically before turning to her friend.

Her eyes wide, she nodded at the golden bundle Claire held and said excitedly, "That petticoat would look lovely on you. Gold would be just the right foil for your dark hair. Hold it up and let me see."

Shaking the wrinkles from the crumpled garment, Claire did as she was asked. As she gazed in the mirror, she was stunned by the effect. Months in New Orleans had softened her dusky coloring to a creamy ivory, making her dark hair and eyes seem even darker. Above the golden petticoat, her face seemed to shine with an inner light, her cheeks and lips glowing a healthy pink.

"*Oui, oui!*" Anne clapped her hands gleefully. "It is perfect for you. Madame Elise," she sang out gaily, "come and see how pretty Claire is."

The dressmaker bustled into the dressing room. "Oh, mam'selle, she is right. You are exquisite in that color," she gasped, clasping her hands, elated at the prospect of selling one of the most expensive items in the shop. "Now that you've selected the petticoat, surely I have something we can alter for you."

"I know just the dress," Anne suggested, "the one that is the color of fine wine."

"The red one?" The woman recoiled in genteel shock. "Oh, *non, chère,* that is the latest style from Paris—hardly suitable for girls your age."

"But it would look wonderful on Claire," Anne insisted.

"Mam'selle Anne, you know unmarried girls wear pale, delicate colors to the ball, so they look like beautiful, feminine flowers."

"Claire would look like a flower—a lovely red rose. Just wait and see," Anne maintained.

Madame Benoit searched the Fortier girl's face for a sign of disagreement, but she saw none. Instead, she saw how Claire fingered the delicate lace admiringly. Greed overcame sensibility and the shopkeeper hurried to fetch the dress.

"Put the petticoat on," Anne instructed Claire. "You can't tell how they will look together unless you try the dress over it." She cleared the only chair in the cramped dressing room and plopped down to await the outcome.

Claire obeyed her friend and discovered the petticoat fit as if it had been made for her. Madame Benoit returned with the opulent wine-colored dress and helped her put it on. After arranging the skirt in becoming swags that revealed the spun gold of the petticoat, the woman stepped back to admire the effect.

The fitted bodice of the gown seemed to be cut just to show off Claire's slender white shoulders against the voluptuous red fabric. The low décolletage draped softly, exposing a daring expanse of soft bosom. Speechlessly, the girl stared at her reflection. She knew from her short experience that she had never looked lovelier and she was dazed by the knowledge.

"*Très jolie,*" the others exclaimed softly.

Suddenly Madame Benoit became very businesslike, summoning one of her employees to measure Claire for alterations. "I can have the gown ready for a final fitting on Thursday," she announced briskly, "if that's all right with you. And I have a gold lace fan which matches the petticoat... for lagniappe, of course."

"*Oui, merci.*" Claire sighed gratefully.

As Claire changed into her street clothes, Anne perched on the chair and chattered, "You're going to be the belle of the ball, Claire. I imagine even Philippe Girard will be smitten. I'll have to spend all evening trying to get the boys even to look at me," she lamented teasingly. "I swear I shall be jealous."

"You have no reason to be jealous, Anne, when Gaspar Boudreaux cannot keep this eyes from you."

The Creole girl colored prettily. "I do not know what you mean," she fluttered coyly. Then suddenly dropping all pretense, she looked up at Claire and giggled. "Do you really think so?"

"*Oui*. I think he will try to keep you all to himself."

"I hope so." Anne sighed. "Then you must dance with all the other gentlemen."

"That will be a problem," Claire responded tensely.

"Why? Don't you like to dance?"

"I never learned."

Anne was aghast. "Never learned? Well, don't worry." She patted Claire's hand comfortingly. "There is still a week before the ball."

"A whole week." Claire laughed in spite of herself. "I must go now, Anne. I have many things to do today."

"Is it true," the other girl asked, "that you work all week in your uncle's office and have only Saturday and Sunday for pleasure?"

"It's true," Claire admitted, unwilling to lie to her friend.

"I heard rumors that you worked just like a man." Anne bounced excitedly in her seat.

When Claire remained uncomfortably silent, the Creole girl blurted, "Oh, you mustn't think I disapprove. I think it is thrilling—at least, until you find a husband," she concluded innocently.

Claire was spared from replying when Madame Benoit bore in another armload of petticoats for Anne. The petite girl bade her friend farewell and doggedly returned to the tiresome business of trying them on.

Rain pelted on the veranda when Claire returned to Fortier House. The candles were lit against the gloom, and the girl had just settled in front of the fireplace to read when she heard a commotion from the hall.

"Where's the fire? I am nearly frozen!" Tante Delaney trumpeted over the roll of thunder. The rawboned old woman swept into the room with Greer on her heels as he tried in vain to take her sodden cloak.

"Tante, what are you doing out today?" Claire rushed to lead her friend to the warmth of the hearth.

"Seeking sanctuary from the storm. Like a fool, I rode into town this morning. I should have known it would rain."

"Mrs. Delaney to see you, Miss Claire," Greer muttered despairingly, hoping the mistress understood it was not his fault the lady had arrived unannounced and now stood in the middle of the parlor, the drips from her cloak soaking into the carpet.

Removing the soggy garment, Tante Delaney thrust it at him and requested, "Close the door when you go, please, Greer." When he had withdrawn, she turned to Claire. "Now, what is this I hear about you not knowing how to dance?"

"News certainly travels fast in the Vieux Carré," Claire said ruefully.

"Always. I received this information in strictest confidence, however, because Anne thought I might help with a lesson or two.

"So don't be shy. We'll try a waltz first. It's the latest rage." Gravely the old woman molded Claire's stiff arms into the right positions. "Now follow me. One-two-three, one-two-three..."

They circled the room inexpertly, dodging pieces of furniture in their path. Concentrating so intently she hardly dared to breathe, Claire watched her feet, noting the motion and pattern. "One-two-three, one-two-three..." she whispered.

"What we need is music." Tante Delaney halted midstep.

"Greer!" she shouted, bringing the butler at once. "Come and make yourself useful. Push the furniture against the wall and pull out the piano where I can get to it."

When Greer had meekly complied, the old woman seated herself and began to play a simple tune in slow, measured three-quarter time. "Now," she said, smiling, "try again."

"One-two-three, one-two-three..." Claire bobbed around the room. Gradually the music seemed to transmit itself to her feet and she seemed to float on air. She beamed in triumph.

"Wonderful," Tante Delaney called from the piano. "Now—a good, old-fashioned reel." Wasting no time, she plunged into the raucous opening chords of a song usually heard only in taverns near the waterfront. "My nephew, the rascal, taught me this tune. It has a good rhythm for dancing, don't you think?''

Later, when Greer opened the door for his master, Etienne seemed to be blown into the house by a gust of rain-soaked wind. As he divested himself of his sodden cloak, a burst of loud music, drowning out even the thunder, drew his attention to the parlor.

"What is that unholy din?" Etienne asked, frowning.

"Mrs. Delaney is visiting Miss Claire, sir."

"Madeleine, eh?" The man looked toward the closed doors with interest.

"Yes, sir. I believe Miss Claire is having a dance lesson."

"A what?" At first Etienne was startled, then a look of understanding slowly crept over his face. He should have known Claire did not know how to dance. That explained her reluctance to attend the ball.

With unnecessary stealth, he crept to the parlor and slid back the wooden door. What a scene met his eyes! In the corner, Madeleine Delaney pounded mercilessly on the piano, her face flushed from the exertion. Her head bobbed wildly, causing her gray bun to teeter even more precariously than usual on top of her head. In the center of the makeshift ballroom, Claire gamely gathered her skirts in one hand and sallied forth to meet an imaginary partner.

"Etienne, you old devil," Tante Delaney crowed, catching sight of the man beaming with paternal pride in the doorway. "Come dance with Claire."

"But—but I haven't danced in years," he sputtered.

"Then it's high time you did," the old woman retorted. "If you're going to the ball, you probably need the practice."

"Uncle Etienne," Claire greeted him gaily as he joined her on the dance floor. "You're dancing!"

"So are you," he said, chuckling, "and quite well, I might add."

They danced buoyantly, stepping forward and back, bobbing, whirling and spinning in time to the music, until they collapsed, laughing, into armchairs at the end of the song.

"I swear, Claire, I haven't felt so young in ages."

"You certainly moved sprightly enough, 'Tienne," Tante Delaney puffed from the piano bench. "Claire must be a good influence on you."

In the hallway, Greer nodded in mute agreement. He had watched the merriment with wonder. The master had not looked so happy in all the years he had served him.

The butler experienced a twinge of conscience when he remembered he had not been kind to the young mistress when she first arrived. But he had been watching over Mr. Etienne, trying to protect him. Now Mr. Etienne loved Miss Claire, and life was good at Fortier House. Greer decided with a satisfied nod of his head that he would watch over both of them—always.

Trying not to show her nervousness, Claire accompanied her uncle into the Orleans Ballroom. In the deserted, candle-lit reception hall, the latecomers were greeted by a black butler, who gestured imperiously for maids to take their cloaks. Her eyes fixed on the huge double doors at the end of the hall, Claire did not see Philippe as he emerged from the men's cloakroom nearby.

Hastily, the young Creole stepped back into the shadows and watched as the Fortiers waited to be announced. Etienne beamed down at his niece with pride, oblivious to the disapproval of the butler, who belonged to one of the organizers of the ball.

Philippe's eyes drifted over Claire appreciatively. Her velvet gown, the color of rich red wine, bared shapely shoulders. Gilded lace spilled over her low décolletage and from under the skirt of her dress. Her black hair was simply arranged and tied back with a golden ribbon. Around her neck she wore a shimmering choker of faceted garnets. Tiny cascades of garnets and diamonds sparkled at her ears.

She looked lovely, Philippe thought. But he was determined to stay away from her tonight, for she seemed to bring out the worst in him. When he was with her, he either insulted her or kissed her—though he didn't set out to do either one. He still thought her too tall, too dark and too direct, but Claire was always...interesting.

And in that dress, she should set plenty of tongues to wagging tonight. He chuckled in anticipation.

When the music ended inside the ballroom, the butler motioned politely for Claire and her uncle to take their positions in the doorway.

"Monsieur Etienne Fortier et Mademoiselle Claire Fortier," he announced grandly, drawing every eye as the pair entered the ballroom.

"Do you see..."

"...simply not done."

A tide of whispers washed over the packed room, only to be drowned out when the band began to play for the next dance.

"I do not see one single person I know," Claire said, looking around apprehensively as her uncle took her in his arms.

"I do not know all the people I see here," he replied comfortingly as he guided her skillfully around the dance floor, "but you may be sure you'll see your friends. We just have to find them in such a large room."

While Claire and Etienne danced, she unconsciously looked for Philippe's tall, erect figure, feeling almost disappointed when she did not see him. She did see Tante Delaney smiling encouragingly, nodding in time to the music. Nearby Anne danced with a young man Claire did not recognize.

With another swirling turn, Claire caught a glimpse of the disconsolate Gaspar at one side of the room with Henri by his side. When her most determined suitor caught her eye, he smiled broadly and bowed in her direction.

As the dance drew to a close, Claire spied Philippe near the entrance to the ballroom and her breath caught in her throat. Like Henri, he smiled at her, but his smile was aloof. His manner when last they met could hardly have been described as cool, she thought. Why was he so unpredictable? It seemed as if he delighted in keeping her off balance.

But she did not have time to dwell on thoughts of Philippe. Henri was at her side the moment the music stopped.

"Bonsoir, monsieur et mademoiselle." Kissing the girl's hand, he complimented, "You look lovelier than I thought possible, Claire. Will you honor me with the next dance?"

Etienne watched approvingly while the two danced. "They make a handsome couple, eh, Madeleine?" he asked as the old woman joined him.

"Handsome, yes, but I don't think Henri is man enough for Claire," Tante Delaney responded bluntly. Clad in a deep green gown that was already rumpled, she looked, despite her best efforts, as if she had just come in from a day's hunt.

"Ah, I see the gossips are already at it," she snorted, her eyes flicking over a knot of Creole women, who stared at

Claire with incensed expressions on their patrician faces. "This is partly your fault, you know, 'Tienne."

"My fault?" the man sputtered, taken by surprise.

"You should not have allowed Claire to wear that dress."

"Why not? She looks lovely."

"*Oui,* but red is not the color for maidens, nor is velvet the fabric."

Etienne looked around at the other girls in their pastel gowns, as if seeing them for the first time. "I—I didn't realize...."

"Of course not. Men do not notice such things. And Claire did not know. I shall have a word with Elise Benoit for selling that creation to her. And to think you were worried when *I* took her shopping. But never mind. What we must do now is be sure Claire is introduced to some of *les bonnes familles* before those old cats ruin her chances."

When the music ended, Henri lingered on the dance floor, his hand still at Claire's waist. "*Merci* for the dance, *chère,*" he whispered.

"My pleasure." The girl smiled at him. Then, seeing the amorous gleam in his green eyes, she stepped back. "Should we not return to my uncle now?"

"*Non,*" the handsome Creole demurred, scowling toward a group of young men gathered around Etienne, obviously waiting for an introduction to his niece. "Let's dance again and again and again," he invited Claire softly, capturing the dance card that dangled from a ribbon around her wrist.

"I do not think—" Edging away slightly, she threw a nervous glance toward her uncle and was relieved to see him beckon. "I'm sorry. Uncle Etienne wants me. And there is Tante Delaney. I really must go."

"Oh, very well." Henri sighed with ill-disguised impatience. He walked Claire to where their elders waited, careful to place himself between the girl and the cluster of would-be admirers.

"*Pardon,* D'Estaigne," Etienne told him politely, "but I must reclaim my niece. There are some people she must meet."

"May I sign your card before you go, Mademoiselle Fortier?" one eager young man interjected from nearby.

"And I," said another.

"And I," Henri added hastily. With a frown, he watched as several young men surrounded Claire, petitioning to sign her dance card. Elbowed to the back of the crowd, he managed to claim one of the last dances of the evening. Finally Tante Delaney shooed them all away and led Claire and Etienne to Emmaline Hébert.

"Emmaline, you know Monsieur Fortier's niece, Claire, of course." The old woman spoke loudly, aware that everyone in the ballroom observed.

"Of course. In fact, Claire has been our guest several times since her arrival in New Orleans. How are you tonight, *chère?*" Madame Hébert greeted the girl graciously, determined to make the best of the situation despite the scandalously improper gown.

"Very well, thank you." Claire dipped in a polite curtsy. "And I'm glad to see you again, Madame Hébert."

Emmaline turned to Etienne. "Monsieur Fortier, *bonsoir.* I am glad you could finally attend one of our balls."

"My pleasure, madame." Bowing respectfully, Etienne kissed her hand.

"Doesn't Claire look beautiful, *Maman?*" Anne's voice rang out gaily, cutting through the murmured conversations around them. They turned to see the girl approaching, curls bobbing on either side of her head as she walked, mindful of her white gown with its yellow bows. "You look just as beautiful as I said you would," she told her friend, missing the shocked expression on her mother's face.

"*Merci.*"

"Isn't this just the perfect dress for Claire, Gaspar?" Anne demanded of the moonstruck young man who dogged her steps.

"Perfect," he agreed, never taking his eyes off Anne.

"Monsieur Boudreaux was just telling me he wants at least one dance with you—weren't you, Gaspar?" she entreated prettily.

The young man's expression was pained. He had hoped to monopolize the petite, pretty Anne for the entire evening, and he would look ridiculous on the dance floor with Claire, he thought miserably. But catching the appeal in Anne's eyes, he gallantly resigned himself to his fate.

"The next dance would be nice, Mademoiselle Claire," he suggested politely as the band struck up a lively reel. At least, he would not have to embrace her and be dwarfed by her.

To Gaspar's surprise, his dance with Claire proved to be pleasant, but he did not have the opportunity to tell her so. Before the music had died, he was tapped on the shoulder by her next partner. The girl's evening passed in a blur of changing partners, tall and short, young and old.

The hour was late when Philippe lounged near the door, considering whether to call it a night. His dark eyes followed as Claire whirled past in the arms of an admirer. Engrossed in conversation, she and her attentive partner circled the dance floor, swirling past Henri without realizing he was there. The copper-haired Creole swayed on his feet at the far side of the ballroom, his green eyes never leaving her.

Usually a ladies' man, the handsome young Creole did not seem interested in anyone tonight but the tall girl in red. He brooded in a corner, ignoring the curious glances thrown his way by several disappointed young ladies and their mothers.

Philippe eyed his friend with interest, noting his downcast expression and unsteady stance. Best not to leave Henri in his current condition, he decided, strolling casually across the floor to join him.

"'*Soir, mon ami*,'' Henri greeted him with an inebriated grin. He pulled a silver flask from his pocket. "Offer you a l'il something for your p-punch?"

"It looks as if you've already had a little something," Philippe commented dryly.

"Jus' killing time till my n-next dance with Claire," Henri mumbled. Half-turning his back to the revelers, he sloshed more rum into his cup.

Cursing under his breath, Philippe quickly moved to block the view from the ballroom. "This is not like you, Henri. Don't you think you should go home?"

"Not till I dance with Claire 'gain," Henri insisted, drinking deeply.

"You won't be able to dance, if you don't lay off the rum," Philippe cautioned. "Let's go up to the gaming room to wait."

"'M not drunk, if tha's wha' you think."

"You're not?" his friend asked incredulously.

"'M sober 'nough. I haven't challenged ev'ry man who dances with her...th-though I wanted to," Henri hiccuped.

"A duel might be more interesting than this soiree," Philippe said grimly, "but you're in no condition for swordplay."

"P'raps," the intoxicated man conceded. "Tell the truth now, Ph'lippe. Isn't she *magnifique?*" he asked, nodding toward Claire.

"I suppose the mademoiselle has a certain appeal."

"She's beautiful." Henri turned a belligerent, unfocused gaze on the other man.

"Whatever you say." Philippe shrugged indifferently.

"I say Claire Fortier's the mos' beautiful woman here!" the copper-haired young man insisted loudly, drawing the attention of several bystanders.

"Keep your voice down, if you do not wish to make a scene," Philippe commanded under his breath.

"M-make a scene if I wish. Call you out, if I wish." Assuming an arrogant posture, Henri rested his hand on the hilt of his *colchemarde* for effect.

"Think twice what you wish, *mon ami,*" Philippe warned softly. "Do you truly want to meet me in St. Anthony's Garden?"

"Non," Henri muttered. Fumbling in his pocket, he withdrew his flask again. "We've been f-friends for too many years."

"That's precisely why I'm going to relieve you of this," Philippe growled, plucking the flask from his hand.

Henri stared down at his empty hand stupidly. "Wha'—wha' are you doing, Ph'lippe?"

"You have had too much to drink already, Henri. Since I don't wish to duel with you nor to serve as your second, I'm taking you upstairs."

"Très bien—but only 'cause you're *mon ami.*" Henri hiccuped again and allowed himself to be led toward the gaming room.

As the young men ascended the stairs, the copper-haired Creole halted suddenly on the landing and peered down at the ballroom, his bleary eyes locating Claire in a swirl of red and gold. Shaking his head as if to clear it, he mumbled, "I've never known a girl like Claire before."

"I daresay that's true." Philippe snorted unsympathetically. "She is certainly one of a kind." A forbidding frown knit his brow as he stared down at her. "Come on now."

Unaware of Henri's shaky departure, Claire continued to enjoy the attentions being paid her for the first time in her life. At last she found herself dancing with Tee-Jean, Anne's young cousin. After a clumsy attempt, the lad suggested they sit out the dance. Winded and weary, she accepted. They ducked off the dance floor and Tee-Jean deposited Claire in the first seat they came to while he went to fetch the obligatory cup of punch.

Hearing loud voices from nearby, Claire glanced over her shoulder at a small cluster of Americans, who had been invited to the ball because it was a fund-raiser for charity. They seemed ill at ease. They were not accepted by New Orleans society and they knew it.

So these were *Kaintocks,* Claire mused. Having never ventured far from the Vieux Carré, she had never really seen them. Covertly, she inspected them as they sat apart in a tight knot; all attention was being given to a burly, red-faced man who swayed drunkenly in their midst and held forth on the natural superiority of the North over the South. Although none of his audience seemed to notice her presence, Claire realized with a start that the speaker was gaping at her through red-rimmed, unfocused eyes.

She shifted apprehensively when, without changing his belligerent tone, the drunkard announced his intention to dance. Immediately all eyes were on the girl, as she looked around in alarm for Tee-Jean.

Hitching up his pants importantly, the man started to swagger toward her, but he tripped over his own feet.

"Hell, Neville, you can't hardly walk. How you gonna dance?" one of the men guffawed as the females of the group shrieked with shrill laughter.

"Shut up," the man called Neville snarled, struggling to gain his balance.

Claire craned her neck, trying to catch sight of her uncle, but he was nowhere to be seen. Desperately, she glanced at a group of Creole men standing nearby, willing them to look her direction, but they stood with their immaculately tailored backs carefully turned toward the outsiders. Chatting among themselves, they seemed unaware of what was taking place behind them.

Neville staggered to stand before her. "Let's dance," he commanded.

"No, thank you, monsieur," she refused politely.

The big man's face darkened and he grasped her wrist roughly to pull her from her chair. "I said let's dance."

"And I said no, thank you." She wrenched her arm from his grasp.

"Who do you think you are?" he bellowed. "Just because your last name is Fortier. Or is it? For all anybody knows, you could jest be the old man's Injun chippie."

The girl erupted from her seat, her narrowed eyes fixed unflinchingly on his bloodshot ones. Neither of them was aware when one of the Creoles nonchalantly detached himself from his company and ambled toward them.

"Ah, Johnson, as charming with the ladies as ever, I see." His manner casual, Philippe thrust himself between them. "I could not help but overhear, and I believe you owe Mademoiselle Fortier an apology."

"For sayin' what everybody thinks?"

"Not everybody," Philippe contradicted coldly.

"Keep out of this, Girard, unless you're lookin' for a fight."

"I'm not looking for a fight—tonight," the Creole drawled, his dark eyes glinting dangerously. "I am looking for my dance partner. And here she is." He nodded coolly toward the girl.

"She's goin' to dance with me," Neville Johnson blustered.

"*Non,* m'sieur, she is not." With that assurance, Philippe offered his arm to Claire and started to lead her away.

"Stay here and fight, you bastard!" Johnson's enraged roar was warning enough that he was about to charge. Philippe whirled in time to see the other man lurch toward him, hamlike fists clenched and swinging. He waited until his opponent was nearly on him, then he sidestepped nimbly and watched the drunken man collapse in a sodden pile on the floor.

"We'll fight another time, M'sieur Johnson—when you are sober," he murmured contemptuously and steered Claire toward the dance floor.

Behind them, they could hear Neville Johnson thrashing against the restraint of his friends, shouting, "When I'm sober, Girard, I'll fight you. When I'm sober, I'll kill you."

"Kaintocks." Philippe grimaced in disgust as he swept the girl into a waltz. Deliberately, they ignored the consternation of the Creoles who had witnessed the confrontation. And neither of them noticed Tee-Jean, standing forlornly at the edge of the crowd, balancing two cups of punch.

Claire's mind was awhirl. Philippe had rescued her—again. It seemed at times that he barely tolerated her, yet he always seemed close at hand when she needed him. It must be coincidence, she told herself realistically. The attraction between them was undeniable, she admitted unwillingly to herself, but she would not let him know she felt it. Had he felt her tremble when he whisked her into his arms tonight?

He had sworn to himself he was going to leave Claire alone, Philippe was reminding himself as they danced. Now here she was in his arms and she fit as if she were made for them.

Disgusted by his thoughts, the Creole asked curtly, "Are you quite recovered, mademoiselle?"

"Oui, merci," she murmured, wondering whether he was angry with her or with Neville Johnson. She knew she should thank him. Steeling herself for his ridicule, she looked up at his unsmiling face. His eyes were fixed on some point in the distance over her shoulder. His jaw was set as if it were carved from granite, making him look remote and forbidding. If he felt her scrutiny, he did not show it.

Claire allowed her eyes to roam over his face, to follow the minute smile lines around his mouth. She blushed slightly, disconcerted by the memory of those lips on hers. The same lips sneered at her as often as they kissed her, she told herself. Her eyes drifted upward, noting that one eyebrow was higher than the other, its line interrupted by the tiny scar running through it. At close range, she could even see the white line on his tanned neck that gave evidence of a recent haircut.

Philippe's muscled back felt warm and solid under the dovegray brocade of his jacket. Reflexively, her finger traced the line of his velvet collar against the nape of his neck. His arms tightened around her in an almost involuntary reaction.

Another involuntary reaction followed when Claire lifted her gaze to meet his bemused stare. Confronted by a rush of feeling, she quickly averted her eyes, nearly missing a step.

Judging they were far enough from the Kaintocks, Philippe quickly released the girl and said sarcastically, "Here you are, safe and sound—again."

Uncertain what to say, Claire smiled and offered her hand. "Thank you very much for what you did, Monsieur Girard."

"No thanks are necessary, mademoiselle. I didn't do it for you," he responded, ignoring her friendly gesture.

Her smile faded as the familiar surge of anger toward him washed over her. "I see," she gritted, glaring at him, "you had to protect your honor and do your duty as a gentleman."

"Honor had little to do with it—yours or mine," Philippe disagreed indifferently. "I have a long-standing difference with M'sieur Johnson that will resolve itself eventually at the Dueling Oaks, I'm sure. Tonight I only evened the score a bit. Perhaps I should thank you for the opportunity to see him fall on his face."

"No thanks are necessary," she parroted icily. "*Bonne nuit*, Monsieur Girard."

The girl wheeled, her head held high, and walked to a nearby row of chairs. Angry red splotches burned on her cheeks and unshed tears blinded her. Biting her lip, she attempted to collect herself. She had told Philippe at the lake that he would never make her cry. And he wouldn't, she thought fiercely.

Claire started when a hoarse voice sounded at her elbow. "I vow I haven't danced so much in ages."

Absorbed in her anger, she had not noticed anyone else was near. Now she discovered Tante Delaney beside her, fanning wildly, her gray bun wobbling precariously with each movement.

"What's wrong, *ma petite?*" The woman's wrinkled face creased in a concerned frown and she ceased her fanning. "You are on the brink of tears."

"I think Philippe Girard is the most insulting person I have ever met," Claire blurted, as surprised by her intensity as by the admission she made.

"Philippe, rude? Well, I'll have something to say about that." The old woman rose purposefully, scanning the room for him.

"Oh, no, Tante Delaney!" Claire cried in horror. "Please don't say anything to him."

"It's all right, *chère.*" She patted her young friend's arm. "But I will not tolerate rudeness from a nephew of mine."

"Philippe is your nephew?" the girl choked as Tante Delaney summoned him from his flirting with dainty, blond Isabelle Ledet.

"Philippe, a word with you, *s'il vous plaît*," the old woman said peremptorily.

Hiding his annoyance, the young Creole excused himself to the prettily pouting girl and sauntered toward his aunt.

"*Tante?*" He bowed and, towering over her, awaited her pleasure.

"Philippe, did you insult Claire Fortier?" She frowned up at him.

"Why do you ask?" he said innocently, despite the truth of his aunt's claim.

"Because she is obviously upset."

"I see." Philippe glanced toward the girl, who stared woodenly at the revelers on the dance floor. "And what am I supposed to have done?"

"She didn't say. She said only that you are a rude fellow."

"And you believe her."

"I know you too well, Philippe. You are unpredictable. You are a roué and—" his aunt's manner softened "—you are my favorite. Because you're my favorite, I'm asking you to apologize to her."

"*Très bien,*" Philippe sighed in defeat, "but only because I know you well. If I don't apologize, I shall never hear the end of it."

"Never," Tante Delaney agreed affably. "Now, go and be charming. You're good at that."

Philippe approached Claire with a mocking smile. "I understand that I owe you an apology, mademoiselle."

"Not at all," she replied, refusing to look up at him.

Zut, she was not going to make it easy. Concealing his ire, Philippe edged to stand in front of her. Her view of the dance floor obscured, the girl was forced to look up at him.

"Imagine my embarrassment," he went on caustically, "when my aunt told me I had offended you in some way."

"There's no need for embarrassment, monsieur. You spoke your true feelings. There can be no harm in that."

"Ah, if there's no harm in honesty, why not tell me what you feel right now?" he challenged her, cursing himself as he did so. He had intended this to be a simple, if insincere, apology.

Claire glared up at him for a long moment before she took his dare. "I think..."

"Go on," Philippe goaded her, "you think..."

"I think that none of this would have happened if you had minded your own business," she snapped.

"And left you to fend for yourself? That's gratitude."

"Henri would have claimed me for the next dance."

"Henri is upstairs, passed out on a chair—and all for jealousy of you. In fact, I danced his last dance with you. Didn't

you even notice your faithful admirer's absence? For shame."
A scornful smile curled his lips.

"I could have taken care of myself," Claire countered hotly.

"*Au contraire*, mademoiselle, since I met you, *I* seem to be
the one who takes care of you. I stepped in this time because I
saw the situation was about to deteriorate into a common
brawl. Besides, I couldn't stand by and watch a fair flower of
Creole womanhood be mauled by a drunken Kaintock, could
I?"

"You've made your apologies, Monsieur Girard. Please
leave me alone now," Claire dismissed him coldly.

"With pleasure." His voice was steely. Glancing pointedly
toward his aunt, who was watching, he bent to kiss Claire's
hand. "Be assured," he murmured darkly, "the next time I
shall mind my own business."

The girl yanked her hand from his. "*Bonne nuit*, monsieur."

"Mademoiselle." He bowed and left her alone with her anger.

Swallowing a lump in her throat, Claire rubbed the hand he
had kissed and desperately looked around for her uncle. It was
time to go home.

Chapter Eight

Etienne rode past the warehouses that lined the levee on his way to the Mercantile, trying to ignore a dull pain in his chest. Perhaps he should have paid more attention to Dr. Perez's warnings, he thought, but he was hardly ready to be an invalid now that his life had become interesting—and yes—happy. These past months, Claire had changed his habits, his attitude, his very existence.

That was not to say his niece was perfect, he admitted to himself. But she was a model student, quick and eager to learn. She looked lovely and behaved well—at least when her temper wasn't flaring or she wasn't being contrary and proud. It was true she refused to consider marriage, but that would pass. If only he could convince her she did not need to work...

Etienne's frown lessened when he remembered that his niece had gone out with Madeleine Delaney today. Perhaps her absence from the Mercantile for even one day was a good omen.

Under gathering clouds, the man rode slowly into Mercantile yard, ashen-faced and shaky. Reining his horse to a halt, he made no attempt to dismount, but sat for a moment in the saddle, glad no one was around to see him while he collected himself. As he swung to the ground, he heard McConnell's shout from the warehouse behind him. "Mr. Fortier, good afternoon to ye."

"*Bonjour*, McConnell."

"I'm just checkin' a cargo that's aboot to go oot, sir," the manager called. "I'll be but a moment. There's fresh coffee in the office, if ye'd like."

The wind that swept in from the river carried on it a thick mist. Suddenly chilled, Etienne welcomed the idea of a cup of hot coffee. He went inside and helped himself, sniffing the thick black liquid approvingly as he fumbled in his pocket for a cigar. McConnell must be taking lessons, he mused, for the Scotsman had never been much of a coffee drinker and even less of a coffee maker.

Picking up a long sliver of kindling from the bin beside the potbellied stove, Etienne opened the grate and held it over the fire until the end flared. Rapidly he withdrew it and used it to light his cigar. As he bent to close the stove's door, the man's eyes lit on a tiny, singed scrap of paper lying on the floor.

When he glanced down at it, Etienne's face froze disbelievingly. He picked up the paper and slowly walked to the window where he held it up to the light. There was no doubt—it was McConnell's handwriting. Claire's name decorated the entire surface, entwined with hearts and bits of moonstruck doggerel.

Etienne wadded the paper in one hand and flung it into the stove. Who would have thought McConnell would become smitten with Claire? he brooded. But from the looks of this doodling, love had indeed come to the confirmed old bachelor.

A scowl on his face, the Creole drew deeply on his cigar. McConnell was a good man, but he was no prospect for Claire. As her uncle, Etienne could do no less than remove the girl from the office and, at the same time, remove temptation from an old fool.

His mind in turmoil, Etienne went out into the drizzle and mounted his horse. As he turned his steed homeward, he did not see his Mercantile manager emerge from the warehouse to stare after him with a perplexed frown.

Etienne had other things on his mind. He had to speak to Henri D'Estaigne. A match between him and Claire would be a good one. The D'Estaignes' holdings were nearly as extensive as his own. Furthermore, Henri could give Claire respectability and quite a comfortable life. The time had come for the young Creole to declare his intentions.

Long lines of ebony men and women snaked in and out, intertwining in the waning sunlight. Their feet shuffled over footworn ruts in the ground as they surged back and forth with primitive grace, drawing near one another, yet never touching.

Clad in bright calico with feathers in their hair and bells on their ankles, the slaves had come to dance in Congo Square. They writhed and swayed, their minds, their very souls given over to the all-consuming rhythm of the music.

Heedless of the cold or the curious white faces surrounding them, the slaves gyrated, moving to the hypnotic beat of homemade drums. Sweat poured down their faces as the pulsing music built toward a climax. As their shadows grew long in the dust, they danced, thinking of nothing else. Today was Sunday, their day, and for a while they were free again—free to dance the Bamboula.

When the dance reached its frenzied zenith, the women's monotonous chant built to a keening wail that hung in the frosty air until the dancers came to a slow reluctant halt.

The throb of the drums continued in the ache of Claire's head. Looking around dully, she noted that the sun was losing its feeble battle to break through the overcast. The intensity of the dance had dissipated and the girl was suddenly cold. She shivered in her fur-lined cloak and shoved her hands deeper into her nutria muff.

There was concern in Henri's green eyes as he peered at her over the soft folds of a huge gray muffler. He led Claire toward an open area at the back of the throng, explaining, "It will be a while before they start another dance. Come, I'll buy you something hot to drink."

Due to the chill of the afternoon, the stalls that sold coffee, hot cider and chocolate were thriving. Groups of people in beaver coats, heavy woolens and knit scarves huddled around braziers of live red coals. Vendors elbowed aggressively through the crowd, hawking their wares. Stridently, they offered feathers, potions and powders for all manner of voodoo rites.

"I gots th' blue candle for th' good lovemakin'," a fat black woman shouted lustily. Her voice dropping to a sepulchral whisper, she intoned, "I gots black for bringin' death to your enemy."

As the couple made their way toward a coffee stall, Henri caught sight of Philippe through the crowd and hailed him.

A puzzled expression on his face, the dark-haired Creole scanned the throng for a familiar face. When he spotted Henri over the heads of the crowd, he waved a leather-gloved hand and edged toward him. His step faltered when he saw Claire, but he rapidly collected himself and strode confidently to where they waited.

"Mon ami." Henri extended his hand in a hearty greeting. "I didn't expect to see you here today."

"Nor did I expect to be here," Philippe responded dryly. Solemnly, he bowed to Claire. *"Bonjour,* Mademoiselle Fortier."

"Bonjour," she answered with unmistakable coolness.

"What are you doing here today, Philippe?" Henri questioned congenially as his friend fell into step with them.

"I promised Odette long ago I would bring her to the Congo dances and she never let me forget it."

"Ah, the lovely Odette. Where is she?" Henri made a show of looking around in vain.

"I left her with Gaspar and Anne." Philippe nodded toward where the music had started again and dancers undulated in the center of the circle. "Ever her faithful and obedient servant, I was dispatched to fetch her a cup of hot chocolate."

"She has always had you wrapped around her little finger." Henri chuckled. While the two friends talked familiarly, Claire absently perused the shifting crowd and wondered who Odette was. One of Philippe's passing flirtations? One of his seemingly countless feminine admirers? Or a childhood sweetheart? He seemed to know her well—very well.

She frowned, suddenly annoyed at herself. Why should she care if someone named Odette had Philippe wrapped around her finger? She was more than welcome to him. He was arrogant and rude, and Claire could not summon adequate words to describe her loathing for him.

"Take care of Mademoiselle Claire for me while I get her some *café,* will you, Philippe?" Henri was saying when the conversation reclaimed her attention. "It's not a good idea to leave a lady alone here even for a moment, you know."

Desperately, Claire shook her head in silent dissent, but she was unable to catch Henri's attention.

"Of course," Philippe agreed accommodatingly. When they were alone, he smiled at the girl. "I seem to find myself responsible for you again."

"I'm perfectly capable of taking care of myself, *merci,"* Claire responded tartly.

"So you've told me, but I've yet to see proof of it," the Creole countered. He watched the weaving columns of dancers through the crowd, missing the murderous glint in Claire's eyes.

"When you have not come here for a long time, you forget what a spectacle the Congo dances are," he remarked conversationally. "The drums—the bamboulas—evoke a certain primitive stirring in almost everyone. I'm sure you must enjoy it." His voice was heavy with irony.

"Why? Because some people call me Mademoiselle Sauvage behind my back? I know and I don't care." She lifted her chin challengingly.

"A name is not everything. I would never mistake you for a savage, *chère*, but you do have a wild streak in you, I think."

"What do you mean by that?" Claire reacted hotly.

"That you attract danger wherever you go—rearing stallions, runaway wagons—" he paused for effect "—dire threats to your reputation."

"My reputation is my business, and I thought you agreed the last time we met to mind yours."

"Touché." Philippe laughed unexpectedly. "And truce, if you do not want Henri to think that anything is amiss between us. He would probably insist that he and I settle it under the Oaks. Then one of us would be dead, and what a waste that would be for womankind." He heaved a tragic sigh and smiled insincerely at her.

"There you are, *mon ami*," Philippe greeted his friend, as if the conversation of the past few minutes had not taken place. "I hate to rush off, but I must. Au revoir." He bowed and departed before the incensed girl could say a word.

After they had sipped steaming coffee and eaten the savory little fried pies Henri had bought, the copper-haired Creole escorted Claire back toward the dancing.

Stopping impulsively, she suggested, "Let's find Anne and Gaspar, Henri, just to say hello."

"If we see them, we shall certainly stop and chat," he granted indulgently, "but I don't want to go in search of them. I'd rather have you all to myself."

"Are you ashamed of what this—Odette might think of me?" Despite her efforts, she could not keep the accusation from her voice.

Henri looked mystified. "Why should I care what Philippe's little sister thinks? She is only a child. Besides, I would never be ashamed of you, Claire," he added gently. "You know how I feel about you. I'm just selfish and don't want to share you with anyone."

"I'm sorry, Henri," she apologized, blushing.

"Never mind, *chère*. Come along, we're missing the dance," he insisted, leading her to the front of the crowd of spectators.

After a while, Henri laughed and pointed to a group of spectators clustered on the opposite side of the square. "Look, there's Anne."

The petite brunette stood with Gaspar at the front of the crowd. Beside them was an exquisite child, who regarded Claire through interested gray eyes. Not much larger than the young girl herself, Anne bounced on her tiptoes and waved her handkerchief. With more reserve, Gaspar tipped his hat and nodded at the pair across the square.

Flanked by Isabelle and Marguerite Ledet, Philippe stood at the back of the group, his hand placed lightly on his sister's shoulder. His attention seemingly fixed on the dancers, he appeared to take no more notice of Claire than he did of Isabelle's frequent flirtatious glances. He reacted only to Odette, his lean brown face transformed by a smile each time he looked down at her. When she spoke, he bent forward obligingly, chuckling at her comments.

But when he straightened, Philippe watched Claire, his eyes hidden beneath the broad brim of his hat. Unaware of his scrutiny, she waved at Anne and talked animatedly with her companion. Henri's head was close to hers as his ardent green eyes caressed her.

How blatant Henri's devotion was even to a casual onlooker, Philippe thought scornfully. What was wrong with him? To flirt was one thing. All red-blooded Creole males enjoyed the chase; they were as bred to flirtation as the females of their culture. Henri was a ladies' man, better at the game than most. But he had done the unthinkable, he had fallen in love with a woman who did not know the rules.

It was not enough Henri's heart was there for the taking, Cyprès went with it. Could Claire be unaware of it? Philippe had to admit he could see no coquetry, no ulterior motive in her manner. There was nothing in her eyes when she looked at his friend beyond amiable affection. How could poor Henri have chosen so poorly? Why did he care for this one?

Narrowing his eyes, Philippe fixed the girl with a critical stare. Despite what he had told Henri at the ball, he did find her disquietingly beautiful. Though he wished it otherwise, the image of her face stayed with him, sometimes even haunting his dreams.

Enough of that, Girard! The Creole grimaced impatiently. Dreams would not solve Henri's problem. Problems. Mentally, Philippe ticked off her faults. Claire was too tall, too intelligent, too serious. She was proud and unyielding, quick to anger. And the steel just below her surface would be most disconcerting to a man like Henri, accustomed to pliant women.

What was a friend to do? He could not save Henri from himself and he had already rescued Claire at every opportunity, Philippe chided himself wryly. She did not want to be rescued again.

But the fleeting memories of the few times he had held her in his arms, of the kisses he had stolen, returned to him unbidden. He knew now that beneath her rigid exterior was a warm, yielding body. He knew her lips were sweet and soft and inviting.

Unconsciously, Philippe's hand tightened on Odette's shoulder, causing her to turn to him questioningly, but he did not notice. His mind was on Claire and her animosity toward him. She hated him and showed it in every word, every move she made toward him.

His brow knit in a dark frown, Philippe concentrated on the dancers and tried not to think of the girl. His attention was soon demanded by a clamorous request from his sister. When his gaze returned to the spot where Henri and Claire had stood, they were gone. Over the tops of heads, he saw the couple beyond the crowd as Henri led the girl toward his carriage.

"The dances will be breaking up soon. The slaves must be home by sundown," Henri was explaining as they walked. "I wanted to leave early because I wish to talk to you."

He assisted Claire into his phaeton, then sat next to her on the narrow seat. He arranged lap robes around them, and when they were settled in the open carriage, he instructed the driver to take them along the River Road.

The wind from the river was cold and penetrating as they turned onto the deserted thoroughfare, driving through sparse patches of fog that swirled near the ground. Huge barren limbs partially shaded the road, blocking the sun's feeble warmth as they drove under them.

Huddled under the blankets, Claire glanced at Henri, wondering whether she should ask where they were going. She refrained when she saw his preoccupation. Shivering, she thrust her chin deep into her fur collar and was silent.

"Stop here," Henri called suddenly. The phaeton lurched off the road and halted by the earthen levee that curved in a huge crescent with the meandering of the river. Stepping to the ground, the young man held out his hand in invitation. "Come with me. There is something I want to show you."

He lifted the girl and set her on the ground, his hands lingering on her trim waist. Then, taking her gloved hand in his, he led her up onto the grass-covered levee.

At the top, they paused next to a graceful willow tree and Claire took in the peaceful vista. Where they stood, the Mississippi took a sudden bend westward before continuing south. Within the curve the muddy river made, huge gnarled cypress knees bleached white from the sun jutted through the rippling surface of the water. Through the dusk, Claire saw a house just upriver, a stately, imposing structure with massive whitewashed columns.

"That is what I wanted to show you," Henri murmured reverently. "Cyprès, my home."

"It's beautiful," the girl breathed in admiration.

"Oui," the heir to Cyprès agreed without conceit. "One day it will be mine. It could be yours, too—if you wanted."

When she looked at him uncomprehendingly, he said hoarsely, "I love you, Claire. I want you to marry me." He gazed at her expectantly for a moment, then he leaned toward her, his lips brushing hers tenderly.

"Oh, Henri." Claire sighed, looking out at the river. "I don't know what to say."

"Say you will," he suggested promptly.

"I cannot," she answered reluctantly.

"Why not? Because you don't love me?" With a gentle hand, he tilted her face toward his. "You could learn. And I would be a good husband to you."

"I know you would," she answered with a sad smile, "but I'm not sure either of us would be happy."

"I would. We'd be a good match," Henri maintained. Suddenly the entreaty etched on his face dissolved, and he withdrew stiffly. "I want to marry you, Claire, but I will not beg. Just tell me—is there hope?"

"Of course, there is always hope." The girl ached at the pain she had caused him.

"And there is no one else?" he demanded, his green eyes an intense reflection of his jealousy.

"No one." Determinedly she pushed away the troublesome, unwanted memory of Philippe.

"Then I will make you love me," Henri muttered and led Claire back to the phaeton.

He handed her into the carriage just as lovingly as before and arranged the robes. But on the long ride to Fortier House, he did not say a word.

Peering at his aristocratic profile from the corner of her eye, Claire wished she could say something to comfort him, but she could not find the appropriate words. Instead she left him to his thoughts, watching quietly as the sun set behind the clouds, illuminating them with a fiery red glow. The distant peal of the curfew bell sounded as they passed slaves who trudged, tired but happy, toward the homes of their masters.

"Did you and Henri have a good time at the Congo dances?" Etienne inquired pleasantly at dinner.

"*Oui, merci.*"

"You returned rather late," he probed casually.

"*Oui.*" Claire sipped her wine.

Her uncle rolled his eyes heavenward. If he was to find out anything, he must take a direct approach. Deliberately, he placed his fork on his plate and asked, "Did you do anything special?"

"We went for a drive along the River Road."

"Yes?"

"To Cyprès because Henri wanted to show it to me." Before her uncle could comment, she added, "Since you're set on knowing the details of my day, you should know that he proposed."

"Well, well, well..." Etienne leaned back in his chair and tried to look surprised. "What did you say to that?" He beamed with satisfaction.

"I said no."

The man's benevolent expression abruptly faded and his face grew mottled with contained anger. "You said what?" he choked.

"I said I wouldn't marry him," the girl replied calmly.

"And why not, may I ask?" Etienne's face turned a deeper shade of red as he struggled to control his temper.

"Because I don't love him."

"Claire Fortier," he scolded, fixing his niece with a steely gaze, "there are more important things in life than love. What about security—and position?"

"What about them?" She glowered at him.

"Henri can give you a good life. He can make you mistress of Cyprès, one of the finest plantations on the river."

"Those are not reasons enough that I should marry him. I don't want his plantation or his money," Claire retorted stubbornly.

"That takes care of security," her uncle snapped. "What of position? Don't you understand how important it is in the modern world?" He did not wait for her answer. Instead he pounded the table in frustration. "I vow, you are the most impossible bit of baggage I have ever come across."

A moment of tense silence ensued while Etienne fought to regain control. "You must marry someone, Claire. Why not Henri?" he asked persuasively, rushing to override her protest. "Don't tell me you will bide your time and continue to work at the Mercantile. That cannot be, for you're not employed there anymore."

"Why not?" she flared. "Because I won't marry Henri?"

"No, I was planning your early retirement even if you had agreed to marry him."

"Even if I had agreed?" Claire echoed disbelievingly, accusation in her flashing eyes. "You knew Henri was going to propose today. You probably forced him into it."

"That's not true." Etienne suddenly found himself on the defensive. "Henri wanted to propose. He had already persuaded his family and was waiting for the right moment to ask for your hand. I just sped things up a bit by speaking to him first."

Becoming even more outraged, Claire shouted, "I don't need you to speed things up. When I'm ready to marry, I'll marry. In the meantime, I will live my own life."

"Live your life, if you will," Etienne roared, unleashing a Fortier temper to match Claire's, "but do not plan to spend any part of it at the Mercantile. From this day on, you will stay at home as any proper young lady should. And that is final!"

Drawing herself up, Claire returned her uncle's glare. Then, with dignity, she rose from the table and stalked from the room, leaving the irate man to finish his meal in solitude.

The next morning, she did not go down to breakfast. She kept to her room until she heard Etienne depart for the day. At her window, she watched as he rode out of the front gate.

Hastily, she threw on a riding habit and dragged a brush through her unruly hair. Opening the door a crack, she surveyed the deserted hall, then scurried down the back stairs before Beady could stop her with a lecture about young ladies who go out without chaperons.

At the stable, Claire ordered a dubious groom to bring her the high-spirited filly deceptively known as Violette. There was nothing shy or shrinking about the horse as she pranced skittishly out of the barn.

"Alls I kin find is a reg'lar saddle, mam'selle. If you wait, I'll try to find you a sidesaddle," the groom assured her nervously. "I reckon that's what your uncle would wan'."

"Go and look." Claire took the bridle from him and when he disappeared into the murky barn, she grasped the high-strung filly's mane and nimbly mounted her bare back. Before anyone could interfere, she wheeled Violette wildly out of the paddock gate and galloped her toward the wooded countryside behind the house.

The girl exulted in the rippling power in Violette's muscles, the warmth of the horse's hide through the fabric of her habit, the feel of the cold wind, biting at her face, ripping at her hair. Galloping across the open field, she felt wild and free for the first time in months.

When Claire reached the bayou that served as the boundary line between Etienne and his neighbors, she slowed Violette and allowed her to walk. Reveling in the crisp, sunny morning, she tried to keep from her head all thoughts of last night's confrontation, but it was impossible.

Why couldn't Etienne understand that she did not want to marry the first man who would have her? Now secure in her uncle's love, Claire knew he would not force her to marry and he would not send her away. They needed to talk, but talk

would lead to another shouting match unless she first dealt
with her anger.

Life had certainly been simpler before her arrival in New
Orleans, she mused. In their secluded cabin, her family had
seldom seen anyone. No strangers, no Creoles, no men . . . no
complications.

Turning homeward, Claire reined her filly to a halt at the
edge of the wide, open field.

"All right, Violette," she said, "let us run with the wind."

With an exuberant cry, she urged the filly forward. She
leaned close to her neck and felt her tensions slip away.

At Bonté, Pierre Girard's reign of terror over his family began at the breakfast table. He scanned the faces of his assembled family. His wife sat at the other end of the long table,
René to his right, and the treasure of his life, Odette, sat demurely beside her mother. But Pierre's baleful gaze lingered on
the vacant chair to his left.

His thin lips tightened disapprovingly when the tardy young
man appeared.

"Bonjour," Philippe greeted his family cheerfully.

"You're late," his father pronounced at once.

"Am I?" The young man's expression was bland as he set
about filling his plate.

When the apology Pierre expected did not come, he said
accusingly, "You were out late last night, too, Philippe."

"Oui," he agreed, offering as little explanation as he had
apology. A leaden silence filled the room until Philippe asked
his sister conversationally, "Did you have a good time at the
Congo dances yesterday, 'Dette?"

"Oh, *oui.*" The girl nodded emphatically, her eyes round.
"It was exciting, wasn't it?"

"I thought so, but that was because I was in the company of
the prettiest girl there," he answered playfully.

"Do you know what we did afterward, Papa?"

"What, *ma petite?*" Pierre smiled indulgently.

"We stopped at the racetrack to visit Philippe's horses. One
of his mares is going to have a baby and Philippe says I can
have it if it's a filly."

"Now you're so successful, you can give away horses?"
Pierre charged his younger son sourly.

"Only to Odette." Philippe grinned, refusing to rise to the bait. "I am successful enough, however, *mon père,* that I can repay what you gave Neville Johnson." He laid a bank draft on the table and slid it over to his father.

"Where did you get this money?" Pierre asked. He scowled down at the paper without picking it up.

"I don't know why you would care, as long as I didn't steal it," Philippe said evenly, his temper beginning to rise.

"Gambling—that's where it came from, isn't it?" the older man asked, setting down his coffee cup with a clatter. "You pay back money you foolishly lost with money you won from some other damn fool?"

"That money is the winnings from a good race. And not one damn fool was entered, as far as I know," the young man retorted.

"Pierre, Philippe," Clothilde moaned.

Pierre did not spare his wife even a glance. "I knew it was from a wager," he bellowed. "I have told you repeatedly, young man, I will not support your gambling."

"You don't have to," Philippe said coldly, rising and stalking toward the door. "I don't want you to. I never asked you to. And I just paid you back."

With an enraged bellow, Pierre charged from the dining room, his napkin still wadded into a tight ball in his hand. He followed his son onto the sun-dappled veranda.

"Take my advice, you young rascal, give up horse racing or marry a wealthy wife, for you'll get no more money from me," he yelled as Philippe threw himself on Lagniappe's broad back.

Cursing under his breath, Philippe galloped the huge steed down the lane toward town, ducking off the main road onto a dirt trail that served as a shortcut to the road leading to the racetrack and his stables.

Fleecy clouds, carried by gusts of winter wind, slid across the sky, casting vast shadows across the open fields. Philippe relished the feel of the powerful horse under him. His spirits lifted a bit and he allowed the huge beast to run.

Lagniappe's hooves flung clods of dirt skyward as he hurdled over low fencerows with ease. Still eager to race, the great steed pranced restlessly when Philippe reined him up tightly and guided him to the edge of one of the fields.

There, charging at breakneck speed across the landscape, was Claire, riding bareback on one of Fortier's most spirited fillies. Philippe watched appreciatively as, with dark hair streaming out behind her, she handled her skittish mount skillfully. One with the horse, the girl was a creature of wild beauty.

Suddenly the solution came to Philippe. He would heed his father's advice and marry a rich woman. He would marry Claire Fortier. She would inherit a fortune from old Etienne. And what better revenge on his father than to bring Mademoiselle Sauvage into the genteel Girard family! He laughed softly in anticipation.

Philippe had never seriously considered marriage before, but he felt this one could work. Claire would have to understand theirs would be a marriage of convenience, for he needed her more than wanted her. But she seemed a practical girl, and she needed a husband as much as he needed a wife.

She might resist at first because she had a strong will and an inner fire. Like a spirited horse, she would need to be broken gradually, but he could do it. And what fun would be the taming!

Chapter Nine

"M'sieur Philippe sure gonna like the way you look today." Beady admired her handiwork as she put the finishing touches on her mistress's hair.

"*Merci,*" Claire answered, frowning at her reflection in the mirror, "but I don't care whether Philippe likes it or not."

"How come you wanna be sayin' that 'bout your beau, mam'selle?" Beady asked sensibly. "I never seen a man so taken in my life. If you runs fast 'nough, you might ketch him."

"I don't want to 'ketch' him," her mistress snapped. "I do not even like him. The only reason I'm going riding with him this afternoon is to humor Uncle Etienne. You know how he keeps pushing the roué at me."

"Yes'm," Beady agreed with an insincere grin, and opened the door for her. "But th' master mus' not think M'sieur Philippe's no roué if he's lettin' you go ridin' with him alone."

Occupied with her thoughts, Claire did not seem to hear her maid. "Tante Delaney is as bad as Uncle Etienne," she muttered to herself, "making sure we are seated next to each other at her dinner party. And now it seems that everywhere I go, Philippe is there. I cannot rid myself of him for a moment. It's as if he knows my plans before I do." Jamming her hat on her head, she halted in the doorway and regarded the plump maid speculatively.

"You best go down now," Beady urged hastily. "You don't wanna keep him waitin'."

She followed her mistress into the hall with a dreamy look on her face. No doubt M'sieur Philippe was a rake. He sure had a way with women folks, even ladies' maids. He just better be good to the *maîtresse,* the little slave thought darkly, or he'll get no more information for love, money or bright cotton scarves.

Poised at the top of the stairs, Claire wished she were as sure of her feelings about Philippe as she sounded. An uneasy truce had existed between the couple for the past few weeks, but she remained on her guard.

Claire was finding Philippe a surprisingly patient and persistent suitor. She had finally come to accept his companionship and even at times to enjoy it. Still, she could not trust him, would not marry him, no matter what her uncle urged. But at the same time, she realized uncomfortably she was no longer sure she wished to banish him from her life.

"*Bonjour,* Claire," Etienne greeted her in the foyer. "Ready for your ride, I see, now that the morning rain has passed."

"*Oui,* and I mustn't keep my beau waiting," she answered sarcastically as she opened the door to leave.

"Claire..." Frowning worriedly, he stayed her progress.

"Yes?" she responded without looking back.

"Do you not wish to go riding with Girard?"

Slowly the girl pushed the door to, so it was almost closed, and faced her uncle. "I thought I had made myself clear," she answered evenly. "I do not want Philippe Girard as a suitor."

"Then why did you accept his invitation today?" Etienne glared at her through narrowed eyes.

"To please you, to keep peace," she stormed.

For an instant, the man looked startled at her vehemence. "I didn't realize you disliked him quite so strongly."

"Apparently not. You keep trying to marry me to him."

Etienne's jaw worked with anger as he bit back a retort. "You know I only want what is best for you," he growled at last.

"I know, Uncle Etienne." Claire sighed, the fight suddenly leaving her. "I wish I knew what was best. I think sometimes I don't even know my own mind. Philippe's behavior has changed so much toward me recently.... I could almost believe he likes me."

"Of course, he likes you. Don't think I haven't seen how he looks at you."

Her gaze riveted to the tile floor, Claire did not answer.

"We'll talk later," Etienne said gently. "I must know what you want. I think Philippe may ask for your hand."

"I hope not." She shook her head sadly, dreading the discussion and the decision. Opening the door, the girl stepped outside.

On the damp veranda, the subject of their conversation eavesdropped bleakly. Philippe slapped impatiently at his boot with his riding crop. This was a fine fool's game, he berated himself, setting out to wed a woman who did not want him. Women and their ways were no mystery to him, but how to woo Claire baffled him.

For weeks he had courted her, calling every day, ingratiating himself to her uncle, bribing her maid. But Claire refused to succumb to his charm. *Mon Dieu,* he had never had this problem before and his masculine pride smarted.

It made no difference, he told himself, as long as she agreed to marry him in the end. It was damnable luck that he needed her to complete his plan. And she did not seem to understand she needed him, too, for social position and respectability and to ensure an heir to the Fortier fortune. They each had much to gain.

As a Creole, Philippe knew he was not likely to find love in an arranged marriage, even in one he arranged himself. What did it matter if his bride nurtured any tender feelings toward him? He would do what he must to wed her, not thinking past the wedding, when he would live with her scorn. For now, all that was required was a thick skin and the knowledge that his efforts would soon be worthwhile.

Absorbed in his thoughts, he barely heard Claire's subdued farewell to her uncle. He had scant time to pose indifferently against one of the whitewashed columns that lined the veranda. With a forced smile, he greeted the troubled girl. Involuntarily she glanced back at the door before her guilty eyes met his. It had been open, she realized, and Philippe had heard every word.

Blushing, she looked away, but she greeted him graciously, "*Bonjour,* Monsieur Girard, we have a beautiful afternoon for our ride after all, *oui?*"

"*Oui,*" Philippe said with a nod, leading her to her horse. Violette pranced skittishly as the girl swung into the men's saddle she had insisted upon. Attired in a fawn velvet riding habit, Claire presented a striking picture astride the sleek filly. Head high and slender back erect, she handled the horse expertly.

She watched covertly as Philippe mounted Lagniappe. The hard muscles of his back rippled under his jacket as he controlled the powerful stallion. His strong, brown hands lightly grasped the reins as the horse reared, sending the groom to the safety of the veranda. On the huge beast's back, his master swayed and bobbed easily with the motion as if they were one.

"Shall we go?" Philippe smiled at Claire and turned his spirited steed toward the gates.

She urged Violette down the drive at a brisk canter. Catching up with Philippe at the gates, she slowed her mount to ride at his side along the tree-lined road. They began the now familiar, guarded process of warming toward each other. Soon the distance between them lessened and they became simply two young people who enjoyed each other's company. Listening to Philippe's anecdotes, Claire relaxed and savored the warmth of the sun on her shoulders as it peeped through dense, fast-moving clouds, reflecting in puddles and creating dappled patterns on the road.

Spying a break in the shrubbery, Philippe suddenly ducked off the road with a high-spirited shout, "Follow me!"

Violette charged through the undergrowth on Lagniappe's heels and Claire found herself in the open field where she had ridden bareback a few weeks before. Her eyes lit mischievously.

"I'll race you to the big oak," she challenged gaily and pointed to the tree half a mile away. Her words were lost on the wind as she flew past Philippe.

"You think because you have a head start you can win?" he called good-naturedly. Kicking his horse to a gallop, he raced across the muddy turf after her.

Hooves pounding in the quiet field, the pair hurtled toward the goal at breakneck speed, laughing and shouting taunts at each other as they hunched over their saddles. Claire's cloak billowed behind her and the breeze tore her hat from her head so it dangled by its cord down her back. Philippe thundered behind her, his stallion gaining ground with every stride.

"Come on, Violette," she urged the little filly as Lagniappe passed them with a smooth, effortless stride and what seemed to be a disdainful snort.

Philippe reached the tree first. With an exultant whoop, he spun his horse and watched Claire. The race lost, the disheveled girl slowed her filly to a trot. Strands of dark, tangled hair twined through the golden hoops she wore in her ears. Transformed by a broad grin, her face was flecked with mud thrown up by Lagniappe's hooves as he had passed her. Her cheeks were pink, whether from excitement or the brisk air, Philippe did not know. Windblown and carefree, she was a sight to take a man's breath away, he thought admiringly. The prospect of marriage was suddenly not altogether unpleasant.

"You win this time," she conceded. "I should've known better than to race the owner of racehorses."

"You gave me a good run." Laughing, he offered a snowy handkerchief. "Now, wipe the racecourse off your face."

"My face is dirty again?" Mildly chagrined, she accepted the handkerchief.

"Your filly is fast and you handle her well," Philippe complimented her as she scrubbed at her face. "We must have a rematch one day."

"Très bien," she agreed easily, patting the horse's shoulder. "Violette and I accept."

"Let's walk the horses and I'll show you something." Philippe led the way along the bayou and through a sparse stand of trees.

Ahead of her, Claire saw a white jewel of a manor house, set on lush green lawn. The riders approached it from the side. Halting silently in the thicket, they surveyed the home. Faint afternoon sunlight filtered through the clouds, giving the scene an ethereal glow.

In front of the main house, a long drive wound between massive shade trees to the broad veranda. Dotting the lawn were flower beds, ablaze with color. Behind the house, female slaves, dressed in calico, bent over vines in the kitchen garden. Beyond the bean pickers, a spry old Negress brandished a huge ladle, the mark of her station, and supervised from the doorway of the squat, brick kitchen.

"This is beautiful," Claire murmured, "almost as beautiful as Fortier House."

"I take that as rare praise, indeed," the Creole thanked her wryly.

"Is this . . . ?"

"Bonté," he finished for her, "my home."

"It is lovely, Philippe," Claire assured him sincerely, unaware of the ease with which his name slipped from her lips.

Philippe noticed and was encouraged by it. Perhaps he could win the elusive Mademoiselle Claire, after all. With only a glance toward the darkening sky, he asked, "Would you like to see more?"

"Very much."

The couple skirted the big house and followed the drive past the garçonnière, spring house and carriage house.

"Is this where you keep your horses?" the girl asked with interest as they approached the stables.

A shadow crossed Philippe's face. "*Non.* Some are at the track, the others on a farm nearby. These are not my stables. My brother René will inherit Bonté."

Beyond long rows of slave cabins, the couple rode along a dirt road that was hardly more than a rutted wagon track. "*Mon père* has great plans for this land. This will be another field soon," Philippe said as they paused to watch a small army of slaves labor beside mules to pull stumps from the rich brown soil. The overseer astride a bay horse nodded a pleasant acknowledgment of the master's younger son.

At last, they came to another bayou, where Philippe dismounted and helped Claire from her horse. "Come, I want to show you my favorite fishing spot as a boy." He tethered the horses to a frail-looking scrub pine and took the girl's hand, maneuvering her over a plank footbridge that seemed on the brink of collapse. From the bridge, an almost invisible footpath led into the murky forest.

Claire balked. "I don't think we should."

"Don't worry," he said, deliberately misunderstanding her. "I know these woods like the back of my hand."

"I mean I do not think we should go alone."

"It's all right—this time." He grinned roguishly. "Your uncle knows you are safe with me."

The girl forgot her uncertainty, watching Philippe shed years and troubles before her very eyes as he rediscovered the haunts of his boyhood. Hand in hand, they hiked, inattentive to time or weather. Finally they rested on a fallen log where Philippe's recounting of long-forgotten childhood escapades was interrupted by an ominous roll of thunder.

"I haven't been watching the sky," he confessed, peering through the ceiling of tree branches, "and it looks as if I should have. It is about to pour."

As they prepared to run for their horses, a gust of wind swept the storm in their direction. They heard the onslaught of the downpour as huge raindrops hit the roof of leaves over their heads. Big cold drops spattered on them slowly at first, then in sheets of water seemingly shaken from the trees by deafening claps of thunder.

Beaten by the wind, they fought their way through the woods to the edge of the bayou, which was already swollen and menacing. Claire could not locate the narrows where they had crossed. No sign of the rickety bridge showed the roaring water had ever been spanned.

Straining to see through blinding rain, the pair watched helplessly as their horses on the opposite bank pitched and reared at each brilliant slash of lightning across the dark sky. Jerking free of the tiny pine, the animals bolted madly up the dirt track whence they had come.

"There's no way across!" Philippe shouted to make himself heard above the wind. He grasped Claire's hand and dragged her back toward the forest. "Come, I know where there is shelter."

Her sodden garments lashed against her by the storm, Claire stumbled behind him. Through the downpour, she barely discerned a tiny cabin set among a grove of orange trees in a clearing ahead of them. Sliding in the mire and holding on to each other, they staggered across the muddy yard to a rough wooden door.

They were propelled into the cabin by a savage gust of wind. Bracing himself, Philippe fought to close the leather-hinged door against the raging weather as Claire surveyed the abandoned cabin, her dripping clothes flooding the hard-packed dirt floor. The young man went immediately to the crude wooden bunk and retrieved two blankets spread upon it.

"Here." He tossed the blankets on the dusty table. "Get out of those wet clothes." Without waiting for a response, he turned his attention to building a fire.

Resolutely disregarding all good sense, Claire decided not to undress. Lectures on ladies and propriety... from her father, from Iris, from Etienne—from Philippe himself—rang in her ears.

Regretfully, she smoothed her drenched skirt with cold hands and wrung water from its sodden tail, succeeding in leaving a larger puddle on the floor. With a sigh, she perched on a rough-hewn log chair and hugged herself to conserve her body's warmth.

His back to her, Philippe concentrated on his task and instructed distractedly, "Make yourself comfortable."

"I don't plan to be here that long," Claire objected. "We can go as soon as the rain stops."

"It won't stop soon," he muttered, his eyes on a tiny wisp of smoke that rose from the kindling. "It may not even slacken for a while—maybe not until morning."

"Morning! I cannot stay here all night with you."

"Why this sudden streak of prudery?" he snorted derisively. "Since the storm shows no sign of letting up, there's not much choice. You saw yourself, the bridge is gone. Perhaps you'd enjoy a swim in an icy bayou, but I would not. We'll wait until morning."

Rising from his task, he glanced at the shivering girl and scowled. "I thought I told you to take off those wet things."

She returned his frown and did not obey.

"As you please—" the man shrugged "—but I don't intend to catch *my* death of cold." Removing his jacket, he hung it on the back of one of the chairs. Then, pulling the chair in front of the fireplace, he sat down and tugged on his soggy boots.

Claire watched him indignantly, making no move to follow his more sensible suit. He placed his limp boots fastidiously to one side of the hearth where their damp leather began immediately to steam from the heat of the fire. Lackadaisically, he unbuttoned his shirt. As he peeled off the clinging garment, he cocked his head and observed the girl.

Her fascinated stare skipped hesitantly across his smooth, broad shoulders, burnished gold by the firelight. The muscles underneath rippled with every move. With effort, she lifted her eyes from his furred chest and diffidently met his amused gaze.

"At least come closer to the fire," he suggested with a lazy grin, "until your clothes dry out."

She shook her head and edged away, putting the table between herself and the half-naked man.

"Oh, all right," he said, sighing in exasperation and draping one of the blankets over his shoulders like an oversize shawl. "I recommend, however, that you follow my lead. I'll turn my back while I see if I can find some *café*, or something to warm us."

"Très bien," Claire surrendered, her teeth chattering. Her eyes riveted to Philippe's blanketed back, she began to undress while he rummaged through the shelves. First her boots went, then her jacket. Soon layer after layer of clothing was spread across the crude trestle table to dry. By the time she reached her damp chemise, the girl felt considerably warmer. Enveloping herself in a blanket, she sidled to stand before the crackling fire.

"Ready?" He was careful not to look until she gave the word.

"Ready," came the affirming echo.

Philippe turned and inspected her approvingly. "Much better. Now, look what I found for you." He held out a wooden comb, then presented a grimy bottle with a flourish. "And some brandy, well aged, I'd say, and a cup."

"You seem to know this cabin well," Claire ventured, wincing as she dragged the comb through her wet, tangled hair.

"I've spent a lot of time here. It was the home of a fisherman—a Yugoslavian named Povich. My brother and I called him Thor when we were boys. He was huge, with big mustaches, and we were frightened of him for years." Philippe chuckled. "But it was Povish who taught us these woods and bayous. He taught us how to hunt, how to set a crab pot and, one disastrous night, how to drink rum. Oh, I was sick the next morning." He rolled his eyes expressively, causing the girl to laugh.

"When it froze in the winter, René and I helped him set out smudge pots to save his precious oranges. We had some good times here," he reminisced, looking around nostalgically.

"What happened to him?" Claire asked hesitantly.

"He died two years ago. His fishing boat was caught out on the Gulf during a hurricane. He didn't even have time to make port. He left this cabin to me. I call it Bons Temps."

"Good Times, that is a good name." She smiled up at him.

"Yes." Philippe's expression was unreadable for an instant as he watched her by the flickering firelight. She accepted the brandy he poured into a battered tin cup and sipped it, knowing it would warm her.

"Here, sit down." Suddenly remembering he was her host, he pulled a braid rug from its place in front of the bed and positioned it so she could bask on the warm hearth.

"Speaking of names, I'm curious," he said, lowering himself to the floor beside her. "I know Indian names mean something. What is yours?"

For a long moment she was silent, then she answered reluctantly, "Night Storm."

"Night Storm—a wonderful name," the man murmured, taking her hand in his. "It fits you. There is something as wild and exciting as a storm about you."

Self-consciously, Claire withdrew her hand and passed the cup to him. Swathed in the homespun blanket, her feet tucked under her, she looked young and vulnerable. The powerful, protective feeling that was becoming too familiar and quite inconvenient surged up in Philippe, conflicting with his ambitious goal.

He nearly groaned aloud at the realization. He was in the perfect position to seduce the girl, bed her and simplify his entire plan. But here she sat, gazing trustingly into his eyes, and he found to his dismay he could not. He drained the cup with a bitter scowl, furious with her, with the situation, with himself.

"Are you going to marry Henri?" he demanded suddenly, surprising even himself with the question.

"*Non,*" Claire said with a sigh. "I know Henri is your friend, but you must understand I don't love him."

"You don't know what love is," Philippe scoffed, seeking an escape from his own mixed emotions.

She stiffened predictably and snapped, "I suppose you do?"

"You forget my reputation and the name of my cabin. I have had more than a few tender moments with the ladies," he drawled arrogantly, hating himself as he did so.

"I suppose you drag them here," she accused, staring knives at the young man beside her.

"They come willingly enough. Some even stay the night," he teased cruelly.

As soon as he had spoken, Philippe knew it was a mistake. The girl jumped to her feet, struggling to hold the blanket closed over her short chemise. Frantically she began to gather her clothing. For an instant, he felt a grim satisfaction. He had gotten a response from the aloof Claire.

Then the unwelcome protective instinct surged through him again. She was just a frightened girl, ready to run, dressed in damp garments if she must. He longed to hold her in his arms, to reassure her. *Zut,* what had she done to him?

"It's still pouring rain," he protested, rising to take the bundle of damp clothes she held. "Be sensible, *chère.*"

Poised for flight, the girl watched warily as he laid her things on the table.

"Claire, Claire." Philippe's dark eyes caressed her as his fingers gently outlined her full lips. "Why do we always fight? Do you not want me as much as I want you?"

The anger in her rigid body melted to a warm, rapturous wonder as he wrapped her in his arms and kissed her hungrily. Emotion and sensation blotted out all thought. She wanted only to feel, and she had never felt anything to compare to Philippe's touch. The tentative tenderness in his kiss was soon swept aside by an urgent wave of molten fluid passion.

She moaned in wordless pleasure as his fingers twined in her hair, drawing her head back to expose her arching neck. She whispered his name huskily as his kisses traced a burning path up her throat, lingering where her pulse fluttered under ivory skin. Her lips sought his insistent mouth as a flower seeks the sun. Warmer and more yielding than the man thought possible, she clung to him, molding her body naturally to his. Her smooth arms slid sensuously under the blanket to encircle his waist; her fingers playing lightly over his spine created spasms of delight and longing. Staggered at the intensity of her ardor, Philippe drew a ragged breath and gazed down at her in awe.

With a low, questioning whimper, the girl moved closer to him and nuzzled his neck where it joined his muscular shoulder. The blanket slid to the floor and lay in a rumpled pile at her feet, leaving her satiny shoulders and legs bare to gleam in the firelight. Unthinking, she turned her face to him, inviting his lips again. Her eyes were closed and a half smile was on her lips. Dark-fringed lashes shadowed her cheeks, making him think for an instant of a peacefully sleeping child.

And though she was a woman, he realized with a jolt, she was still as innocent as a child.

With a choked curse, he broke from her embrace. "Go to bed," he commanded hoarsely, his face contorted as a battle raged within him. "You take the bed. I'll sleep on the floor."

Tenderness changed to alarm and alarm to rage in Claire's eyes as she watched the young man stalk to the fireplace. Picking up a poker, he stabbed the logs viciously and tried to sort out a maelstrom of emotion he did not care to feel.

Standing amid the crumpled blankets, she fought tears, her chest heaving. Anger and unfulfilled desire caused her breasts to strain against the flimsy material of her chemise. Philippe muttered over the fire, refusing to look at her.

After a long, silent moment, Claire retrieved her cover and wrapped it tightly about herself, then sank miserably into the feather ticking of the bunk.

She lay rigidly on the narrow bunk, her emotions in turmoil. She would never understand Philippe, she thought bitterly. First he was kind, then he was cruel. First he wanted her, then he did not. But even harder for her to fathom were her own feelings. How could she expect to understand him when she no longer knew herself? Her hatred was close to the surface now, but moments before she would have given herself to him.

Her face grew warm at the memory of his kisses, burning with shame when she remembered how he had thrust her away from him. Turning to the wall, she feigned sleep, but she was still awake when he opened the door and stepped out onto the porch.

Now that the worst of the gale had passed, he did not even want to be in the same room with her, she brooded. He would not have to tolerate her presence much longer. She would leave as soon as the storm subsided. She listened drowsily until the steady rain lulled her into a troubled sleep. Wistfully she dreamed that Philippe returned and tenderly tucked the blankets around her.

Claire awakened at dawn to a bird's song. Sitting bolt upright in the unfamiliar bed, she gazed around in confusion. Then her eyes fell upon Philippe's lean figure wrapped in a cocoon of blankets before the dying fire. The storm, the trapper's cabin . . . she remembered.

Rising, the girl dressed quietly to the muted accompaniment of water dripping from the trees. Holding her breath when Philippe stirred in his sleep, she stole from the cold cabin and set out across the clearing, picking her way between vast mud puddles. As she walked through the forest toward the bayou, she sniffed the wind appreciatively. Conflict and confusion had clouded her mind last night. Now it was cleansing and comforting to smell the air after the rain.

She stopped at the edge of the swollen bayou. In a field on the opposite bank, she saw the muddy, bedraggled Violette, grazing safely in a patch of sunshine, her reins dragging in the muck under her hooves. But how to reach her?

Claire searched for stepping stones or a narrow place she could wade. Her gaze roamed upstream, suddenly freezing disbelievingly on one spot. There, undamaged, stood the bridge that Philippe had assured her was washed away. Looking as rickety and unreliable as it had the previous afternoon, it still appeared passable.

Wrathfully, she stalked toward it, turning a deaf ear to Philippe's calls as he plunged through the forest after her. The rushing water inches below her feet, she marched across the span.

"Wait, Claire, I must talk to you!" he shouted, bursting from the brush a little downstream. "Don't go."

She halted midspan and turned a stony face toward him. "Don't go?" she spit. "I stayed with you last night because you told me the bridge had washed out. You knew it had not."

"How could I know in such blinding rain?" he contended as he sauntered toward her. "Did you see it last night?"

"No, but I don't 'know these woods like the back of my hand,'" she countered crossly.

"Touché!" The man laughed. He did not bother to deny her accusations. His hand extended in entreaty, he stepped on the first plank of the bridge.

"Don't come near me. Just tell me why you tricked me," Claire requested sorrowfully.

"Listen to me, *chère*." Philippe covered the distance between them in three long paces, stopping so near that Claire could feel his warmth.

"I will not listen." She backed away, glaring balefully at him. "I can't trust you. Everything you say is a lie."

Philippe lunged forward and caught her arm, pulling her toward him. "You will listen," he insisted quietly, "and you will trust me—because my kisses didn't lie, did they?"

Before she could answer, he brought his lips down on hers. She responded for a moment, then all the anger and frustration Claire felt toward this arrogant, confident man overpowered the pleasurable sensations his kiss gave her.

With a strangled cry, she shoved him away, wrenching from his grip. As Philippe teetered on the edge of the narrow bridge, she pivoted and ran toward the bank. She did not slow her pace even when he uttered a colorful curse and plunged with a splash into the icy water.

Capturing Violette's trailing reins, Claire was relieved the horse had not had the sense to run home the night before. She mounted and, without a backward glance, galloped down the narrow trail toward home.

Philippe slogged through the cold muddy water and hauled himself up on the soggy bank. He damned Claire, damned her stubbornness and damned himself for the fool that he was.

With a black scowl, he trudged along the rutted track to Bonté.

Chapter Ten

The rain started again before Claire was halfway home. Her teeth chattering from cold, she was glad to see, through the light, wind-driven shower, Fortier House's iron gates. Turning up the *allée,* she guided Violette around fallen limbs and debris of the night's storm and galloped to the house, where horses and men were gathered.

When Etienne spied his niece, wet and bedraggled, he felt nearly limp with relief. He rushed to greet her as she dismounted. The cares of the night etched on his haggard face, he enfolded her gratefully in his arms.

"Claire, my child, where have you been?" His voice shook with emotion. "I've been so worried. I ordered Greer to organize a search party while I rode to Bonté to see if you were there. Are you all right?"

"I'm fine," she answered, her voice muffled against his shoulder. Then she drew away gently. "But I would like some breakfast and a hot bath."

"Where is Philippe?" Etienne asked, walking her solicitously to the veranda.

"I don't know and I don't care," she grated tensely, striding toward the house.

For a second, Etienne looked puzzled, then the puzzlement turned to fury and he followed his niece inside. "Just a moment, young lady," he roared, catching her in the foyer. "What has that young blackguard done? I'll kill him with my bare hands—"

"He didn't do anything, with the possible exception of ruining my reputation," Claire snapped. "We got stranded by the storm and spent the night in a cabin. Nothing happened," she added hastily, seeing her uncle's murderous expression. "But surely you understand, I do not want to see Philippe Girard again."

"Look at me, Claire," Etienne commanded gently. His gray eyes searched her weary face. "He didn't . . . harm you?"

"Non."

"Très bien." He accepted her answer. "You are wet and cold and tired, *chère*. We'll talk about this later."

With a troubled expression, he watched his niece go up to her room. Greer hovered behind him, looking as grim as his employer.

Before Etienne had another chance to speak to Claire, Philippe arrived at Fortier House, riding just ahead of roiling black thunderheads. Alerted by the butler, Etienne met him on the rain-washed veranda.

"I trusted you, Girard. You had better have a good explanation for what happened last night, or I'll see you under the Oaks," he greeted the young Creole over the howling of the wind. "I should dislike having to kill you, my boy. I was just beginning to like you."

"I'd dislike it as much as you, sir. I can explain."

"Then come in." Etienne stood aside and allowed the dripping man to enter the house. "There's a fire in the library and we can speak privately there. You look even worse for wear than Claire."

"She was not dunked in the bayou," Philippe growled, missing a flicker of surprised amusement in the older man's eyes.

In the study, the young Creole paced before the fire, telling his story of the night before while Etienne listened judiciously.

"So you see, monsieur," he concluded, "it was my fault we were caught by the storm, but it wasn't intentional. I assure you nothing happened. Claire slept on the bunk, I slept on the floor. You know your niece and you must believe this."

"I believe you," the older man replied quietly, "but . . ."

"But what will other people believe?" Philippe finished the thought for him. "That's why I've come today, sir. I want to marry Claire."

"I see. Very honorable." Etienne's tone showed he was unimpressed.

"It's not just because of honor that I ask for her hand. There are other reasons. I think Claire and I are well suited to each other. I'm fond of her. And though I don't believe she loves me now, perhaps love will grow in time. I think we could be happy together." He stopped in front of the fireplace and regarded her uncle hopefully.

"Sit down, Girard," Etienne instructed brusquely. "Your proposition warrants some thought." Preoccupied, he stared into the fire, scarcely noticing that the young man obeyed, sipping his brandy, watching him guardedly.

Etienne wanted nothing more than Claire's happiness, he told himself. He also wanted her to marry. Examining the problem, he believed that Philippe could make her happy—if they could work out their differences—for they certainly seemed to be attracted to each other. Etienne even believed that Philippe loved Claire, though he had not said so when he asked for her hand.

These young people, Etienne thought, and sighed gustily. Philippe was as blind to his feelings as Claire was to hers. But did it matter? Love had been known to grow between a couple after marriage.

Another consideration, Etienne mused, feeling almost guilty at the thought, was that if word of last night got out, Philippe's proposal might be Claire's last offer of marriage.

"Though I'm not opposed to it, arranging a marriage between the two of you may prove difficult," he spoke dryly at last, "since Claire told me this morning she never wanted to see you again."

The young Creole stirred in his chair and grimaced ruefully. "I imagined as much. But I'd like to try to change her mind."

While Etienne went up to talk to his niece, Philippe congratulated himself. Even without seduction, his scheme was falling into place. He had been so persuasive in his talk with Claire's uncle, he had almost convinced himself that the marriage was his heart's desire. Now to convince his bride-to-be.

But his smug expression faded when the indistinct sound of voices reached him, rising to an angry crescendo, then dropping. In the library, the young man strained to hear over the gale. After a few moments, it became quiet again upstairs.

A few minutes later, Claire entered the library warily, closing the sliding doors behind her. Though she was clad in dry clothes, her hair was still heavy and wet from her bath. Philippe watched her appreciatively with his back to the fireplace as he warmed himself.

"Good morning again, Claire," he greeted her, bowing elegantly. "Thank you for coming down to see me."

"My uncle was unusually insistent." Her lips formed a scornful downward curve. She was disgusted with herself when she noticed how handsome he looked, even in damp clothing and muddy boots.

"Aren't you going to come in and sit down?" he asked, virtually daring her.

"I shall stand, *merci*." She refused his challenge, but she stepped nearer, glaring up at him.

"Did your uncle tell you what I want to talk to you about?"

"He told me that you had some idiotic idea about marriage," she snapped.

"Well?" One eyebrow lifted, he met her gaze uncompromisingly.

"Absolutely not. I will not salve your sense of honor or whatever it is that prompts your proposal," she declared positively.

"Once again, honor has little to do with it." The man shrugged carelessly.

"*Non*—or last night would never have happened."

Philippe's jaw worked with restrained fury. How did she always manage to get under his skin so quickly? "You think I took you riding with the plan to be stranded at the cabin?" he grated.

"I think you had no scruples whatsoever at putting me in such a position," she accused coldly.

"What position?" Philippe countered. "You were hardly seduced and abandoned last night. You know I could have made asking for your hand an unnecessary formality. It would have been easy, Claire. You were certainly willing enough."

Stung, the girl opened her mouth to protest, but he silenced her with a gesture.

"I didn't make love to you," he concluded magnanimously, "because I had already decided to marry you."

"You wanted a virgin bride, so you didn't take advantage of me. How nice," she commented acidly. "But who will believe it?"

"All the more reason for us to wed," he replied in clipped tones. "I'm asking you to marry me. Will you give me an answer now, or do you need time to think about it?"

"I don't need time. The answer is no. Now, if that is all..." She turned on her heel and prepared to leave the room.

"That is not all," Philippe growled, capturing her arm.

"Stay away from me," she ordered, struggling against his hold.

He would not be deterred. "Not until we talk about this. Why do you refuse my offer of marriage? Because you don't love me? Love is not everything, *ma petite,*" he taunted. "Many marriages are loveless. Besides, if you received me as warmly today as you did last night, we wouldn't need love."

"Put last night out of your mind, Philippe," she spat. "It should have never happened. I thought I made my feelings clear this morning at the bridge."

"And just what are your feelings, Claire?" he murmured dangerously, drawing even nearer.

Any answer she might have made was lost as Philippe crushed her against his chest and brought his mouth down on hers. Instantly, her body stiffened and she tried to extricate herself from his embrace, but her efforts served only to tighten the muscular arms around her. Philippe's tongue explored her mouth, ruthlessly at first, then tenderly as he sensed her resistance wane. When he felt her body responding to his, he lifted his head and regarded her condescendingly.

"You see, *chère,* you're confused. You don't know what to think right now. I'll give you time to consider my proposal."

With an angry shriek, the girl planted her hands against his chest and shoved. Obligingly, Philippe released her, laughing harshly when she put a chair between them.

"I would not marry you, Philippe Girard," she pronounced furiously, "if you were the only man to ask for my hand—ever!"

"After last night, that's entirely possible."

"If you think you can coerce me into marrying you, you—"

"Temper, temper, Claire, or you'll die an old maid. Be reasonable now and consider this. You need a husband, I need a wife. Your uncle is determined to see you married, and I'm equally determined to see you married—to me."

"Why are you doing this?" she whispered disbelievingly. "For my uncle's money?"

"It's not his money I want."

"What then?"

"You. Our marriage will give me independence to build my stable, and security that I do not have as a second son. It might even lend a touch of respectability to both of us. And I won't mind having my name removed from the list of eligible bachelors kept by the mothers of the Vieux Carré. But most important—" he grinned charmingly "—I think you and I could have a good time together."

"But not much of a marriage," Claire maintained coldly.

"As much as we need." He shrugged nonchalantly.

"What you are proposing is a marriage of convenience."

"Call it what you like."

"I call it an impossibility. For the last time, I will not marry you." Without understanding why, Claire felt compelled to explain. "I want a husband who will want me because—"

"I *do* want you. I thought you knew that," he interrupted.

"I understand you want a lot of things, Philippe, but I don't believe you want me because you love me."

"Will it satisfy some desire of your maiden heart to hear me babble some pretty words? If I went to the trouble to compose sonnets about your eyes or lips or—" his mouth twisted in a cynical grin "—your gentle manner, would you believe them? I choose to speak frankly with you, Claire." Philippe's dark eyes held hers. "You will marry me. I will not give up without a fight, although why you insist on battles between us I'll never understand. We have better things to do with our time, you and I."

The girl's mouth worked for a moment as if she would speak, then mute with fury, she whirled and fled the room, leaving her suitor smiling cockily.

In the days that followed, Claire's uncle intervened, trying to reason with her. Finally, in the face of her obstinacy, Etienne's pleas for rationality turned to blustering anger. His ire ignited her own hot temper and she stormed away, refusing to speak of Philippe's proposal anymore.

She took to locking herself in her room, listening each night as her uncle welcomed Philippe to Fortier House. Every time he came, the young Creole brought gifts; every time, she refused to see him. The men were spending a great deal of time together. If nothing else, they were becoming fast friends, she thought bitterly.

Claire bolted from her seat to pace irritably in front of the French doors. A jingling sound cut through the steady patter of rain, drawing her attention. Surely even Philippe was not foolish enough to be out on a day like this.

The girl stepped to the window and peered down at the drive below, feeling vaguely disappointed when she saw it was Etienne. He was returning from Maspero's, where he went each day, as if grateful for a refuge from the tempest that raged at home.

Cautiously, she pulled back the curtain enough to watch him. Wearing a sodden cloak, its collar turned up against the cold rain, Etienne trudged toward the house, leading his horse around the shallow puddles that had collected along the shell-covered *allée*.

Claire felt an unexpected pang of guilt. She was responsible for the weariness and discouragement visible in his sagging shoulders. She suddenly missed her uncle acutely; they had grown accustomed to each other's company and were so happy together—when they were not at odds. Though her self-imposed isolation wore on her, she was afraid to resume her daily routine. Etienne would undoubtedly take it as a sign of surrender and resume his pressure for her to marry Philippe. She ducked from view when Etienne raised his gray eyes toward her window.

Late in the afternoon, a rap sounded at her door. "Open up, mam'selle. It's me, Beady. I mus' tell you somethin'."

Claire opened the door a crack and peered out suspiciously.

"It's jest me," the maid said defensively. "Your uncle say—"

Her mistress frowned at her. "If my uncle wishes to speak to me, let him do it. It's not your job to deliver his ultimatums."

"Don't know nothin' 'bout no ol' tomatoes," Beady responded dubiously, "but M'sieur Etienne say you kin have supper downstairs tonight if you want. He won't be here."

Claire opened the door and gaped at her with surprise. "He won't be here?" she repeated, concern apparent in her voice. "Where is he going in this weather?"

"'Out' was all he say," the pudgy maid answered. "Reckon you'll be safe, 'cause M'sieur Philippe ain't comin' neither. Want me to tell Toolah you gonna eat in th' dinin' room?"

"Oui, s'il vous plaît," Claire replied distractedly, crossing to the window, where she watched torrents of rain spill from the pitched roof to the empty *allée* below.

Beady lingered a moment outside the door, pleased when Claire did not close it. This was a good sign, she decided gleefully, because once the mistress came out of her room, maybe peace would return to Fortier House.

After dinner, Etienne lounged in a chair before the fire, pleasantly lulled by the sounds of Lila's cluttered sitting room. Although the rain had stopped, the monotonous drip from fresh-washed trees outside provided a fitting counterpoint to the crackle of the fire and the quiet ticking of the mantel clock.

The man rested his eyes on his mistress, contemplating her proprietorially. She sat demurely, as if unaware of his inspection, bent over the needlework hoop resting in her lap. With a sigh of contentment, he reached toward the small table at his side upon which were placed a snifter of brandy and a fine cigar.

"You think of everything, Lila," he complimented the octoroon.

She met his gaze with a sad smile. "I must take care of you when I have you to myself, Etienne. Did you like your meal?"

"It was a fine dinner, *chère.*"

"I'm glad you enjoyed it. You've appreciated the pleasures of this house little enough of late."

He shot her a pained look and applied himself to the task of lighting his cigar. "I explained to you, Lila," he said patiently between puffs, "it has taken a while to get my niece settled. Until recently, I spent a good deal of time trying to find a suitable husband for her."

"You have found one, then?" the woman asked casually, counting her stitches diligently in an attempt to disguise her interest.

"I haven't found one that Claire deems suitable," Etienne answered dryly. "Last week, young Girard asked for her hand, but she would have none of him."

"Philippe Girard?" Lila gasped as she jabbed her finger savagely with her needle. She glanced up to find the man eyeing her shrewdly.

"*Oui.* Do you know him?"

"How would I know him?" she countered the question with a brittle laugh. "I know of him, of course."

"Of course."

Lila laid aside her needlepoint and folded her shaking hands in her lap. Worriedly, she scanned her protector's face and tried to read his expression as he leaned back in the chair and blew smoke rings toward the ceiling.

Did Etienne know about Philippe's visits here, she wondered apprehensively, or about their clandestine trysts? Perhaps she had been too reckless. Her heart pounded with the fear of discovery. Surely he did not know, she decided, or he would not sit so contentedly in front of the fire.

Returning to her sewing, the octoroon gave Etienne a sidelong glance. When she discovered he was dozing, she cradled the hoop in loose, idle hands and allowed her thoughts to range freely. Her glowing yellow eyes narrowed and her generous lips grew tight as her mind settled on Philippe. He could not intend to wed Claire.

Still, she had seen how he looked at her. Tears burned her eyelids, and she gripped the hoop tightly.

"What are you thinking, *mon amour?*" Etienne broke the silence, causing her to jump guiltily and drop her work.

"I—I thought you were asleep, 'Tienne."

"Just napping." He straightened in his seat and stretched. "What unhappy thought furrows your brow, Lila?"

His placée hesitated a moment, then with a deep breath, she plunged into the topic she knew he had no wish to discuss. "I know you think your niece's marriage is none of my affair, *chère,* but everything is my business when your happiness is concerned."

Etienne regarded her fondly. "Don't worry your pretty head, *ma petite.*"

"But, 'Tienne, I cannot believe you would consider letting your niece marry Philippe Girard."

"Why not? He comes from a fine family."

"But he is the black sheep. And what a reputation he has!"

"Has he?" The man rose, frowning, and flicked the ash from the end of his cigar into the fireplace. He turned to face

Lila. "How did you manage to gain such an uncommonly close knowledge of his reputation?"

"I know only what I hear. The ladies who come to the shop, they talk," the octoroon replied lamely. Recovering herself, she added coolly, "They say he is always in need of money."

He looked at her with a thoughtful expression on his aristocratic face. "I've given it a great deal of thought, and I don't believe Girard is a fortune hunter. He has built up a substantial business for himself. But I don't care if he's a pauper. I plan to take care of Claire as long as I live and to leave her well provided for at my death.

"No, what the girl needs now is marriage, and some children to keep her busy." Etienne seemed to be talking more to himself than to Lila.

"But you say you seek respectability for your niece. Surely someone else would be a better match for her," Lila argued. "Why not the elder son? Wouldn't the heir be a better match?"

"René is not the Girard who wants Claire for a wife."

"What of Henri D'Estaigne then? Is he not a regular caller at Fortier House? I hear he's willing even to defy his father to marry for love."

"You hear a lot in that hat shop of yours," Etienne grunted, inspecting the end of his dwindling cigar. "Claire says she does not love young D'Estaigne."

"She loves Philippe?" Lila whispered hoarsely.

"I think so, though I find it most vexing that she won't admit it, not even to herself."

"Oh, Etienne, you mustn't let her marry him," the woman blurted, unmindful of the desperation in her voice.

He stared at her in astonishment. "I thought it was your fervent wish that Claire marry anyone who would have her. Have you not professed concern many times that she would become a spinster?

"Now," he continued exasperatedly, pacing before the fire, "you tell me I shouldn't allow her to marry well when opportunity—a good opportunity—presents itself.

"Women! You never fail to amaze me. I am sick unto death of ceaseless nagging and fits of pique. I sought to escape such behavior when I came to visit you." He fixed his *placée* with an accusing stare.

"You take no note of what I say, anyway," she said, pouting. "I think since that girl came to New Orleans, your Lila is no longer important to you."

"That's not true, *mon amour.*" Etienne visibly softened. Taking the octoroon's dainty hand in his, he drew her out of her chair and held her in his arms tenderly.

"It is true," she insisted, shrugging from his grasp. "I don't believe you love me anymore, Etienne."

Petulantly, she flounced from the room. With a violent movement, the man pitched the remainder of his cigar into the fire.

He knew this game well, he thought wearily. He knew all the rules. Now he was supposed to go upstairs, where Lila waited for him with tearstained face. He was supposed to apologize, to give her some money for a trinket. Finally, she would relent and melt into his arms, whispering endearments. She would lead him to the tall tester bed, turn down the lamps and the game would be over—until next time.

The only problem was that he was too tired to play. Trudging into the hall, Etienne bade Concepción to bring his hat and cloak.

Up in her room, his exquisite mistress sat before the mirror, brushing her hair. Vainly, she practiced the appropriate pout for the situation. But her expression changed to one of cold fury when she heard the sound of the front door closing and the man's tread on the porch.

Rushing to the window, the octoroon watched with tiny fists clenched as he stepped into his carriage without even a backward look. The carriage door swung closed behind him, and Ezra, giving a loud whistle, urged the team down the street and out of sight.

"Concepción," Lila shrieked. "Concepción, come here!"

"Mam'selle?" The old slave materialized in the doorway.

"Bring that bundle I brought from Mama Dédé's this afternoon."

Concepción made no move to leave. "Mam'selle Lila, you cannot put no gris-gris on M'sieur 'Tienne," she argued quietly.

Lila wheeled on her servant, her face contorted with rage. "Who says I cannot?" she screeched.

"Jest me," the old woman said placatingly, "but he been good to you. You don't wanna use no voodoo. Would be a sin to hurt him, *oui?*"

"I'm not going to hurt him, 'Cepción," Lila crooned, ambling toward her. "I'm just going to make him do my bidding."

She stopped in front of the slave. Suddenly her hand lashed out, catching the old woman full force across the mouth. "Go and get that bundle now, or do I have to put the gris-gris on you?"

"No, mam'selle." Blood dribbling down her chin, Concepción swayed in the doorway and made the sign of the cross on her bony chest. "I'll git it for you."

"Wake up, miss!"

Claire was jolted from sleep by the urgency in Greer's voice. He leaned over her, his face grave and worried.

"What is it?"

"It's your uncle. He's ill and wishes to see you."

"What is wrong?" she asked, rising immediately.

"I don't know, miss. After he returned this evening, he was reading in his room when he clutched at his chest and began to breathe hard."

"Have you sent for the doctor?" Claire padded barefoot behind the butler, drawing on a robe as she went.

"No, ma'am, Mr. Etienne won't allow it. He says he's had these pains before and they pass."

The anger of the past week forgotten, the girl rushed to her uncle's room, where the only sound was Etienne's labored breathing. He lay on his back, his face ashen against the white bed linens.

Kneeling beside the bed, she whispered, "I'm here, Uncle Etienne. Are you all right?"

With a mighty effort, he opened glassy eyes and focused them on her. His lips curved into a pained smile.

"I knew you'd come, even if you are angry at your old uncle," he joked feebly.

"I'm not angry," she whispered soothingly, taking his hand in hers. "You're the one who should be angry. I'm so stubborn sometimes. I'm sorry." She bowed her head, fighting tears.

"Now, now, *chère.*" Etienne stroked her head with a shaky hand. "Forget our little differences and tell me that you love me."

"I do love you. You know that."

"*Oui.*" He smiled weakly. "But I've been thinking, I've never told you how much I care for you or how glad I am that you came to live with me. You're the daughter I never had. You might have been mine, you know, if I had spoken my love one time." A shadow crossed his haggard face.

"You look so much like her," he whispered painfully, "like White Sky. Before I started the Mercantile, Jules and I tried our hand at trapping. We met your mother. I loved her, but I didn't tell her. Jules told her of his love and he won her. I never told her..." His breath came in short gasps. "And now I have no one."

"You have me, Uncle Etienne," the girl soothed him.

"Ah, yes, thank *le bon Dieu*, I have you." The sick man returned to the present. "You taught me how to love again, Claire. Let me teach you the most important lesson I know." Turning his head toward her, he rasped, "Follow your heart, *ma petite*. Follow when and where it tells you. Do not hesitate or you will lose. Philippe won't wait forever."

Claire drew back involuntarily, as if burned, her mind reeling. How little Etienne understood of Philippe's motives. She gazed down at her uncle, pale and wan against the pillows, and could not tell him. She nodded and squeezed his hand lightly.

"He truly wants to marry you, you know," Etienne whispered.

"I know." Her throat burned with unshed tears, but she did not argue.

"Then you'll marry him?"

"I'll consider it."

"That's all I ask for now." He settled back on the pillows and closed his eyes before concluding wearily, "I don't want you to marry Philippe because I wish it, Claire. If you love someone else, marry him instead."

"There is no one else."

"I didn't think so," he said with certain satisfaction. "Philippe is the man for you." His voice trailed off as he listened to the clock downstairs striking the hour.

"Three o'clock? I've kept you awake half the night. Run along to bed now, *chère*." Releasing her hand, he patted it fondly.

"I'd rather stay with you."

"Then neither of us would get any rest. Greer will stay with me tonight, and I'll see you in the morning." Etienne dismissed his niece with unexpected firmness.

When she had gone, Greer stood by his master's bedside, his broad face openly displaying his concern. "Won't you let me send for Dr. Perez now, sir?"

"No," Etienne snapped. "I have a pain in my chest. I have had many pains in my chest and they always go away. Besides, Perez would tell me to quit smoking, quit drinking, quit eating. He is well-intentioned, but he might as well tell me to quit living."

The big butler did not argue. Silently he turned down the lamp and sat beside the bed to keep his vigil through the night.

"Greer," Etienne spoke suddenly in the darkness, "if anything happens to me . . ."

"Nothing is going to happen to you, Mr. Etienne," the other man assured him gently. "I will tend you."

"Of that I am sure. Nevertheless, if something should happen to me, I want you to be sure Claire is cared for. Will you do that?" he asked patiently.

"Yes, sir. Now rest," Greer insisted.

"You're right," Etienne admitted grudgingly. "I'm more fatigued than I thought."

The loyal servant sat for a long time before he surrendered to a restless sleep. It seemed to him that only a few moments had passed when Lucene bustled in with the master's breakfast tray. His body stiff from a night in the chair, Greer stretched and blinked groggily at the maid.

"*Bonjour,*" she whispered loudly. "How th' patient this mornin'?" She indicated Etienne's still form with a nod of her head. The man lay on his side, quiet and motionless, his back to the pair.

Lucene set the tray on a table and swept back the heavy draperies. Outside the sky was leaden and overcast. The feeble sunlight did little to alleviate the gloom of the cold bedchamber.

"I'll rekindle the fire whilst you see if M'sieur Etienne will eat a bite," she announced.

"Mr. Etienne, Lucene has brought your breakfast." Greer leaned over the sleeping man and touched him on the shoulder. When Etienne did not respond, the butler shook him gently. When he did not move, he shook him with more energy. Slowly, the expectant light in Greer's eyes dimmed to dull comprehension. He stood erect and gazed down at his master, tears glazing his eyes.

"Lucene," he bade quietly, "go and fetch Miss Claire."

"What's wrong?" Wide-eyed, she came to stand next to the butler. Her brown eyes became even wider as she looked down at the inert figure on the bed with growing horror. "He ain't dead, is he, Greer?"

"Yes. Now go get Miss Claire."

"Oh, no!" Wailing, the maid ran in search of the mistress of Fortier House.

Chapter Eleven

In the miniature city of gleaming white tombs that was the St. Louis Cemetery, a score of mourners clustered around an elaborate casket. Most were men, friends and business associates of Etienne Fortier's. But one figure stood out from the rest—slender, black-clad and female. Although women in New Orleans did not attend funerals, Claire, the dead man's niece, had insisted on being present.

Flanked by Philippe and Henri, she stared unseeingly at the flower sprays covering the coffin. Their colors melted into one another in her fixed gaze, and their sickeningly sweet scent carried on the brisk March wind. She scarcely heard the droning voice of the priest. Claire's mind was empty but for one aching thought. Her uncle was dead.

Behind the Creoles, another woman stood alone, separate. Red-eyed under her heavy veil, Lila had come to see for herself that her protector was really dead. It could not be her fault, she reassured herself. She had not known Etienne had a weak heart, and the spell she left on his doorstep by the light of the moon had not been a strong one. She was not to blame.

Lila's yellow eyes rested resentfully on the polished mahogany coffin. It was true that Etienne had left her well-fixed; the house and the shop were hers. But he had left her alone and a woman needed a man.

She had thought Philippe would become her protector, but perhaps it was too soon for him to approach her. He did not, however, seem to think it too soon to carry through his plan to marry Claire, she thought bitterly, watching the grief-stricken girl beside the tomb.

Swaying slightly on her feet, Claire asked herself the same question she had asked over the long days while she observed the stilted customs of white society. She had longed to pull her hair and howl her sorrow aloud as her mother would have, but in her new life she could not. Instead she had sat in the parlor beside her uncle's casket, greeting callers and agonizing. Had she hastened Etienne's death by her stubbornness?

The priest paused to allow the mourners to pay their last respects. Her back stiffly erect, Claire stepped forward and laid a white rose among the other vivid flowers atop the casket. Then she stood unmoving, staring down at the blossoms through tear-blurred eyes.

Philippe took her elbow solicitously and led her back to stand beside the glowering Henri. Unwilling even to think of the young Creole's jealousy, she refused to meet his green eyes, oddly grateful for Philippe's comforting presence beside her.

On the other side of the grave, Greer lingered sadly. No one had ever been as kind to him as Mr. Etienne and now he would reciprocate with loyalty that went beyond the grave. It was up to him to care for Miss Claire as the master had asked.

The big butler studied the girl apprehensively over the blanket of flowers, feeling a protective surge when he noted the dark circles beneath her eyes, visible even behind the black veil. She must rest when they returned home, he resolved. But his thoughts were interrupted by the harsh, final noise of the coffin being slid into place inside the open tomb.

Philippe escorted Claire toward the gate of the cemetery, past mourners who waited, respectful of her loss. Greer fell into step behind the pair as they led the way toward a black-draped carriage.

Numb with grief, Claire did not recognize Lila's black-clad figure, stark against a background of whitewashed tombs, but Philippe nodded almost imperceptibly in her direction. With a sudden intake of breath and a jerk of her head as if she had been slapped, the octoroon pivoted on her heel and strode away.

Behind Philippe and Claire, the butler quickened his step to close the gap between his mistress and himself. He had no idea why the exchange unsettled him, but no one must cause Miss Claire any more grief.

* * *

Claire waited silently on the steps while Greer locked the door to the Mercantile and retrieved a small lantern that hung on a post nearby. "I don't think you should work such long hours, Miss Claire," he muttered disapprovingly as he lit the way to the waiting coach.

"Now you sound like Robert." The girl smiled wearily at the big servant through the twilight.

"Mr. McConnell is worried about you, too."

"I know, *mon ami,*" she said softly as she climbed into the coach. "Tell Ezra to take the River Road home, will you?"

"It's late and that's the long way," he protested.

"Tell him to drive slowly."

"Don't you think we should go on home so you can rest?"

"I don't need to rest, Greer. I need to think."

When he had given the order and handed over his lantern, the big man joined Claire in the carriage. As Ezra urged the horses through darkening streets, Greer sat in the murky dimness on the other side of the carriage and frowned worriedly at his mistress. Her pale face, so thin since her uncle's death, was illuminated in the glow of a street lamp.

"Miss Claire—" he rumbled tentatively.

"Try not to worry so much, Greer." Her voice floating to him in the darkness cut off his lecture.

He grunted in response. Then, crossing his brawny arms over his chest, he settled back, so that the seat creaked under his bulk. He was silent for a few minutes, then a soft snore came to Claire over the quiet croaking of the tree frogs, which was carried on the June breeze.

Thank God for Greer, Claire thought as she stared out at the dark tangled woods along the River Road, where fireflies flitted among the trees. She had been surprised and touched by his steadfast loyalty since her uncle's death.

During those past three months, Claire's life had been turned upside down—from the moment Prosper LaBiche, Etienne's unctuous attorney, had read the will. Except for bequests to servants and employees and a generous settlement for his *placée*, Claire inherited her uncle's considerable estate—or would inherit it when she married.

In verbose legal terms, the document echoed her uncle's dying wish that she follow her heart in choosing a suitable mate—soon. At least, she reflected ruefully, she did not inherit Philippe as a husband, although undoubtedly Etienne would have liked that.

As if the burden of grief had not been enough to cope with, suddenly Claire was an heiress. LaBiche, the squatty lawyer with greedy eyes and an insincere smile, took an interest in her and her inheritance, calling almost every day. He had counseled her to leave the operation of the businesses to him. She remembered the remainder of his advice with a shudder: concentrate on seeking a husband and on presenting only the most decorous face to society. New Orleans was ever ripe for scandal. After all, she had come from nowhere to live with Etienne and now he was dead. She should not worry because there was talk, he concluded, she should just take care not to fuel a scandal.

As much as she hated to admit it, the lawyer had been right. Gossip had spread like wildfire through the Vieux Carré and had to be extinguished by the dead man's physician. In an interview in the *New Orleans Gazette,* Dr. Perez had flatly stated that Etienne Fortier died of heart failure and there was no reason to subject his niece to an inquest.

Even so, tongues still wagged when Claire walked down the street. But after a while, they stopped, thanks largely to her friends. Tante Delaney and Anne were kind, loyal companions, spending time with her whenever possible, for they knew how she missed Etienne. That Fortier House now belonged to her was little solace. Without the warmth of her uncle's presence, the big house was stark and silent.

Henri had begun to call again last month. A proper Creole gentleman, he had waited to allow Claire privacy to grieve. Now he came to Fortier House almost every day in fervent hopes of persuading its mistress to marry him. Petulantly, he accused her of fickleness and demanded she no longer see Philippe. Although Henri obviously adored her, Claire came to dread his visits, for his spiteful, childish behavior wore on her more each time. She was glad when he was called to Baton Rouge for a few weeks on business.

Unfortunately, he was not the only sullen person in her life. Day after day, she faced Robert McConnell's dour frown. The Mercantile office had become her refuge, but the gruff Scotsman still believed business was not the fitting place for a young lady.

Though she did not have full control of her fortune, Claire insisted on making as many of her own decisions as possible. There were so many things to manage and so many people who wanted to manage them for her. The lawyer, McConnell, Henri...

How strange she would have thought it three months ago, Claire realized, if she had known Philippe would become an ally. He offered no judgment, no recriminations. Surprisingly, the Creole ladies' man seemed content to sit on the veranda or in the tree house after dinner, engaging Claire in conversation when she wished it and lapsing into comfortable silence when she did not.

The only strain between them was his continued determination to marry her. Because he did not press, however, she gratefully accepted his company, appreciative that he made no demands on her. But she was careful to make it clear that she did not plan to marry him, or anyone else at the moment.

She knew she must marry eventually, but whom? She must keep her promise to Etienne. If only she knew what to do, Claire brooded, as the carriage bounced along the dark, rutted road toward Fortier House.

Reviewing the field of potential husbands, she immediately ruled out the host of Creole gallants who hoped to win an heiress. And she omitted Philippe. Even after all this time, her pride stung at the memory of his proposal.

Henri was in love with her, but she did not love him. Nor did she think she could live with his petulant demands, intimations, and pouting. Besides, she suspected he was not strong enough to handle the Fortier businesses—or the Fortier woman.

She would not marry Monsieur LaBiche, who fancied himself a contender for her hand. McConnell was also rejected. Though he was a good man who had her best interests at heart, he was a confirmed bachelor and old enough to be her father.

Claire's stomach gave a sudden turn when she realized Philippe was the only logical candidate. He wanted the same thing she wanted—independence. He did not seek to control her. Theirs would be a business arrangement...a marriage of convenience.

But it was hard to surrender the idea that a marriage should begin with love and be built on trust, as her parents' had been.

Those qualities certainly had no place in a marriage with Philippe.

Stubbornly Claire envisioned his mocking eyes and the superior expression he wore when insulting her. But those memories were crowded out by remembrances of gentle caresses and kisses.

With effort, the girl wrenched her mind from its foolish reverie. The attraction between them was not reason enough for marriage. She was mad even to consider marrying him.

With a sigh, she reviewed her catalog of potential suitors again. At the end of her evaluation, the outcome was the same: Philippe was the only reasonable choice—even though he loved her no more than she loved him.

As the horses turned onto the *allée* to Fortier House, Claire considered the advantages of a match with the young Creole. Philippe came from a good family. He was intelligent and strong—strong enough to be her partner and to manage the bulk of the Fortier interests, but with his own stables to look after, he would not be constantly in her way.

Also he had been her uncle's choice for her. He paid little attention to gossip, which surely there would be. He was handsome, charming when he wished to be, and a good companion. But most important, he wanted to marry her.

She would do it, she decided sensibly; she would marry Philippe. Besides being an ideal partnership, it would allow her to keep her vow to her uncle that she would marry. Claire was troubled by Etienne's wish that she follow her heart. She did not know what her heart urged, but logic told her this marriage was the solution to her problems.

People would undoubtedly say she was rushing through her period of mourning, but her uncle had wanted her to marry, she thought with resignation, and that was what she would do. There was no need for coyness, no reason to delay. She and Philippe were both adults; they would enter the arrangement with their eyes open.

Feeling as if a burden had been lifted from her shoulders, Claire decided she would tell him of her decision tomorrow when he was to take her out for the first time since Etienne's death.

* * *

"*Bonsoir*, Philippe," Claire greeted the man in the parlor formally. "I'm sorry to have kept you waiting."

"*Bonsoir.*" He bowed and kissed her hand. "It was well worth the wait. You look lovely."

"Do you think my gown is proper?" Ingenuously, she spun for his inspection, her heavy burgundy moiré dress belling gently as she turned. "It's not too bright, is it? I couldn't bear to wear another stiff black dress tonight."

"I can't see how you could have chosen better." He looked her over approvingly. "I've always liked you in that color, even when I haven't liked *you*."

Her narrowed eyes met his amused gaze as both he and she remembered another, more dazzling dress she had worn at the charity ball.

"If looks could kill, I should be dead," Philippe teased. "But look, *Mademoiselle Sauvage*, I brought you a peace offering." He drew a minuscule black box from his pocket. Casually flipping it open, he handed it to her.

Claire forgot her annoyance as she admired the perfectly matched pair of creamy-white pearl earrings. "They're beautiful, but I cannot take these, Philippe," she demurred.

"Of course you can," he assured her, closing her hand around the box. "Pearls were made for a dark beauty like you."

"But I can't," she protested adamantly.

"Why not?" He scowled, certain Claire was impossible to please. "Are they not to your liking?"

"I—I told you, they're beautiful," she stammered, "but I can't accept such a magnificent gift."

Philippe positioned the girl in front of the mirror over the fireplace. "At least try them on," he insisted, standing casually with one arm propped against the mantel. "If you like them, we'll call it a trade."

"A trade?" Claire frowned up at him uncomprehendingly.

"*Oui*, I'll give you the pearls in exchange for these dreary things." His hand brushed her cheek lightly as he touched the black jet earrings dangling from her earlobes.

Claire drew back as if burned and snapped, "I am in mourning."

"I know, but tonight we're going out," Philippe argued, unfazed by her vehemence. "Life is too short to be spent lamenting the dead. Your uncle wouldn't want you to waste your life grieving. It's time to get on with life, Claire. Why not try on the earrings?''

"If you insist," she acquiesced grimly.

"Oh, I insist," he drawled. "It would be a shame to waste these magnificent pearls on a bit of blond fluff who wouldn't do them justice."

Her face stony, Claire removed her earrings with fingers made clumsy by anger and tossed them onto the mantel. Leave it to Philippe, she fumed. She tried to look her best for him, but her best was not good enough. Then he had the nerve to throw blond, petite Isabelle Ledet in her face. Her task completed, she turned rigidly so he could admire his gift.

"*Magnifique.* You will recall, however," he reminded her, extending one palm, "that it was a trade."

Resentfully, she seized the jet earrings and slapped them into his hand, hoping the wires would jab him.

If her petty act caused him any pain, Philippe did not show it. Instead he pocketed them with one hand, offering his other arm. "Shall we? My carriage is waiting."

His injured hand jammed in his pocket, the man was glad Claire could not know the discomfort she caused him. His thumb gingerly massaged his palm, as inwardly he cursed her stiff-necked pride. Settling the girl in his carriage, he steeled himself for the evening to come.

Seated in the elaborate dining room of the popular restaurant, Claire watched Philippe peruse the leather-bound wine list. A slight frown on his handsome face, he summoned a nearby waiter. Her attention strayed as he questioned the man about a particular vintage.

Now that her ire had cooled, Claire considered the fineness of Philippe's gift and the thoughtfulness that had inspired it. Absorbed in watching a crowd of new arrivals, her hand strayed to one of the smooth gems at her ears and absently stroked it.

"You do like them, don't you?" Philippe asked confidently.

Claire shifted her eyes to his knowing grin and fought the impulse to respond contrarily. Summoning a smile, she conceded, "They're lovely, Philippe. *Merci.*"

"You're most welcome, *chère.* And what I said before is true," he continued in a bemused voice, "pearls are perfect for you. Next I believe I'll give you a strand of pearls to wear around your neck.

"No," he amended huskily, "two strands—with a magnificent ruby clasp to nestle in the hollow of your throat. That would be pretty, indeed."

A shiver ran up Claire's spine as his dark eyes held hers. Tearing her gaze away, she protested feebly, "You really shouldn't buy another expensive gift."

"Whether I should or not, it's what I want to do. And what would be better than pure white pearls to convince you of the sincerity of my suit?"

The girl bit her lip to keep from sighing with relief. He had brought up the subject of marriage for her, making it easier than she had anticipated to reach an agreement.

"As a matter of fact, Philippe, that's why I wanted to talk to you tonight," she began carefully, avoiding his quizzical gaze.

"Claire! Philippe!" A squeal of delight sliced through their conversation.

The man rolled his eyes impatiently before composing his face in a welcoming smile. Anne swept toward them in a flurry of ruffles, dragging Gaspar in her wake.

"*Bonsoir!* How good to see you," the vivacious brunette called excitedly.

"The pleasure is ours, Anne." Philippe rose politely. "*Bonsoir,* Gaspar."

"Good evening, Philippe, mademoiselle," the flustered young Creole responded.

"I am so glad you're here tonight, Claire," Anne bubbled. "Gaspar and I want you and Philippe to help us celebrate."

"Anne, we really must find our table," Gaspar objected. "We can't interrupt their dinner."

"But, Gaspar, we've already interrupted it," Anne countered merrily.

"Please join us, if only for an aperitif," Philippe invited with a gracious smile. Looking around, he beckoned and instantly two waiters appeared with chairs for the newcomers.

Smiling at her elated friend, Claire forgot her frustration at the interruption and asked, "What are we to celebrate?"

"Why, our engagement," the Hébert girl said with a giggle, gesturing between her companion and herself. "Gaspar and I have been secretly betrothed for nearly a year, but now we have the blessings of both our families. Is it not wonderful?"

A moment of silence followed, then everyone at the tiny table began to talk at once.

"That is wonderful, Anne! I am so happy for you."

"Congratulations," Philippe cried, pumping Gaspar's hand. "This does call for a celebration. Sit down, sit down."

"*Merci*, but we cannot stay," the other man responded politely, perching on the edge of his seat. "We are to meet our parents for dinner."

"But we could have some champagne," Anne suggested with innocent candor.

"Of course." Philippe laughed and nodded to the waiter. "Champagne it shall be."

"Anne!" Her fiancé's shocked, owlish expression conveyed his disapproval, but it had no effect on the unrepentant girl.

"Oh come, *chère*," Anne railed gently, "Philippe and Claire are our friends. Besides, it'll be such a solemn meeting as our parents determine our futures. All the talk of dowries and inheritances. Let's have just one glass of champagne," she cajoled prettily, "to celebrate."

"All right, one glass." Gaspar's resistance melted into an indulgent smile.

Anne's exhilaration touched them all, and a number of toasts were drunk and good wishes fondly conveyed before the couple rose to leave.

"You didn't tell us," Philippe reminded them, "when the happy day will be."

"Not until December." Anne pretended to pout, but she could not hide the sparkle in her eyes. "I always wanted a June wedding, but I think I'll be the happiest Christmas bride you've ever seen."

Philippe watched the couple depart, then he turned to Claire as if their earlier discussion had never been interrupted. "You were saying?"

She drew a deep breath, wishing the champagne had made her braver. "You've said that you wish to marry me...." she ventured.

"*Oui*." He nodded, saying nothing further to assist her.

"The first time you mentioned marriage—" she paused, blushing at the memory "—you offered an arrangement... for convenience. Do you remember?"

"I remember, but—"

"Please, let me say what I must say," Claire implored. "Since that time, I've given it a great deal of thought and I realize that although you do not care for me, nor I for you..."

In her haste to finish her speech, she did not notice how Philippe's face darkened at her words.

"...what you offered could indeed benefit both of us," she continued in a rush. "Therefore, if you will consent to take me on my own terms, I accept your proposal of marriage."

"And just what are your terms?" the man grated.

Claire faltered, taken aback by the cold anger in his stare, but she had to finish what she had started.

Steeling herself, she stated simply, "I know that under Louisiana law whatever I own becomes the property of my husband to control and dispose of as he sees fit. But my uncle left the house and the businesses to me. I want everything to be held jointly. And I would like to live in my own home."

"And where am I supposed to live?"

"I suppose you could live at Fortier House. Or you could take an apartment in the Vieux Carré. I understand that's often done."

"Fortier House should do nicely." Philippe's fury was close to the surface, but his voice was mild. "Go on," he prompted.

"You can manage most of the businesses if you wish, but I want to manage the Mercantile. Also, if you decide to sell any of the businesses at any time, I should have a word in it."

"You *have* thought a great deal about this."

"I—I wanted everything to be clear from the start."

"I see. Is there anything else?"

"*Oui.*" She paused nervously before plunging ahead. "I want to continue to be my own woman. My life—my body— are my own."

"And what do I receive in return?"

"Other than half my possessions?" Claire's temper flared, even as she struggled to control it.

"Besides a partner in business," Philippe corrected, his voice cold and flat.

"I thought a partner was what you wanted." The girl looked confused, but she rapidly collected herself. "All I can promise is that I will be chatelaine and hostess in your household and a good companion to you."

"What more could a man ask?" Philippe said caustically. "I suppose you wish our attorneys to meet to draw up a contract for this 'arrangement'?"

"Perhaps that would be a good idea," she snapped. "At least that way there could be no questions."

"I have no questions, but I have a term or two of my own that do not need the meddling of a lawyer."

"Oui?" Claire nodded warily.

"First—in public our marriage must seem as any other. I'll appear to be a proper bridegroom and you, the demure bride."

"I thought you didn't care what other people think," she challenged.

"People will gossip. As a rule, I don't care, but I don't wish to live with rumor and innuendo for the rest of my life, either," her prospective husband declared definitely.

"Second—we will post our banns tomorrow after I've bought you an alliance ring. Such haste is rather unconventional, but we are rather unconventional people. The wedding should be performed next week. A small, private ceremony would be best," he persisted, quashing her attempted protest.

"And, finally, I'll abide by your wishes. We'll live at Fortier House, but it will be *our* house," he asserted forcefully. "Understand from the beginning, Claire, I will be master of my household. Do you agree?"

She hesitated for a long moment, chewing her lip in indecision. "I agree," she whispered at last.

"Good." Philippe smiled unpleasantly across the table at his new fiancée. "Let's order dinner, then. I find that becoming engaged makes me ravenous."

Smothering a retort, Claire lowered her head and studied the fine weave of the damask tablecloth. Tears blurred her vision. What had she expected? Theirs would be a business arrangement with no room for personal feelings. She herself had prescribed the limits of this ... marriage.

Resolutely, she forced the pain and the urge to lash out at him from her mind. Some things were better left unsaid.

Chapter Twelve

"Mam'selle Claire, want Greer to close them big shutters before this gale turn into a full-growed hurricane?" Beady asked as the wind rattled windowpanes.

From the shadows, Claire glanced over her shoulder at the maid, who was working Anne's shiny hair into a mass of ringlets. Reflected by the mirror, they sat in a circle of light cast by lamps that had been lit against the sullen gray afternoon.

"No, I want to watch the storm," the ivory-clad girl replied over the rumble of thunder. Her marriage approached, she mused fancifully, borne on menacing, rolling thunder-heads—not exactly a fortuitous sign.

Leaning her forehead against the cold windowpane, she surveyed the windswept lawn. Illuminated by a jagged bolt of lightning, the garden was alive with growth. Clusters of daffodils lifted their golden heads stubbornly to buffeting winds. Against dark clouds, the white tree house was visible, seeming to tremble in the gloom as leaves skittered around the base of the tree and down the empty garden path.

"Don't worry if it rains, *chère*," Anne said cheerfully. "Nothing could spoil your wedding day, not even a little shower." Smiling, she caught Claire's eye in the mirror. "You do make a lovely bride. Your uncle would be proud."

"*Merci*," the other girl muttered miserably. She did not feel lovely. She felt ashamed—ashamed that she had been so foolish.

When Philippe came to Fortier House on the first day of their engagement, he had taken her into the formal first parlor and given her, with uncharacteristic shyness, an engagement present, a magnificent ruby ring.

"Perfect," he murmured, slipping it onto her finger. Then he kissed her chastely on the cheek to seal their betrothal.

At first the couple had gone everywhere together—riding, to a soirée, to the theater. Philippe took Claire to his stables to meet his sleek racehorses, Thoroughbred beauties with names like Hyacinth, Magnolia and Wisteria. He even spent an afternoon at Fortier House, getting to know the servants, the mansion and its grounds.

Claire sometimes discovered her future husband watching her with an appreciative gleam in his eye, and for a time she had actually believed he might care for her. She had believed, at least, until Lila came to call.

Claire had been lingering over a cup of coffee at the breakfast table when she heard voices at the front door. Going into the hall, she heard the butler brusquely turn someone away.

"Who is it, Greer?" Clad in a plain housedress, she was not dressed to meet callers, but she hurried toward him, recalling her first experience at Fortier House.

"Someone who should go to the back door if she is to call at all," Greer muttered, never taking his wary eyes from the unseen caller as he started to close the door.

"Let me see." She motioned for him to open it. On the threshold posed Lila Broussard. The octoroon immediately glided into the house, presenting herself haughtily to its mistress.

She nodded in perfunctory greeting. "Claire, I told this great baboon I must talk to you, but he wouldn't let me in."

"It's n-not fitting," the butler sputtered in protest.

Claire glanced over the tiny woman's shoulder at the agitated man. "It's all right, Greer," she said soothingly. "I will speak with Mademoiselle Broussard."

As she led Lila to the parlor, Claire cursed herself for deigning to talk to the woman. The octoroon had an infuriating way of making her feel like a gangly child. That Lila outshone her today, there was no doubt. Her dress was made of vibrant yellow-and-black-striped satin, its bodice so tight it threatened to force her breasts up over her décolletage. Her face was pale under her black-lacquered hat, her delicate jaw set purposefully.

In the parlor, Claire bade her uninvited guest to sit down. She remained standing, waiting for the octoroon to begin.

"I wasn't sure you would see me," Lila said, looking up at Claire coolly. "I thought perhaps you had learned more genteel ways by now. I should have known better."

"I saw no reason to be rude," her hostess replied evenly, "and I see no reason for you to be. I agreed to see you because my uncle cared for you."

"Ah, you've heard the rumors." The woman shrugged negligently. "There's always gossip. People enjoy talking about me, perhaps because I am beautiful."

The tall girl shifted impatiently. "I haven't much time, mam'selle. Why did you wish to see me?"

"For two reasons. First, because I wish to protect myself."

"To protect yourself?"

"*Oui*. You took Etienne away from me. Now you would take Philippe and I won't allow it. You *must* be aware he doesn't love you. He loves me and I want him."

"Let me see if I understand," Claire replied with an innocent calm she did not feel. "Philippe loves you, but he wants to marry me. And you want him to marry you. Is that right?"

The octoroon flushed with anger. "Don't be naive. We both know he can't marry me. But you must realize you'll be his wife in name only. Understand now that Philippe loves me and it will save you much embarrassment later."

"You said you came for two reasons," Claire reminded the other woman in clipped tones.

"*Oui*. I have a wedding gift for you." Lila's delicate face was contorted momentarily by a malicious leer. Then the hateful expression was banished by a victorious smile as she pulled a tiny box from her reticule and handed it to the girl.

Claire took it, dreading what she would find, and opened it. Nestled in white velvet were the jet earrings Philippe had taken in exchange for the pearls she wore this very minute. He had given her earrings to his mistress. Speechless, she met Lila's gloating amber eyes.

"I thought you might like to have them back," the octoroon crooned. "Philippe left them at my house the night you two became so romantically...engaged."

Claire closed the box with a snap. "If there is nothing else," she recommended in a tight voice, "you will leave my home, Mademoiselle Broussard, and never return."

"I've accomplished what I came for," Lila jeered, sweeping toward the door. "Remember what I told you. You will have his name. I will have Philippe."

That evening when her fiancé arrived for dinner, Claire met him at the door, leading him at once into the library.

"We had a visitor today," she announced coldly the moment the door was closed.

"A well-wisher?"

"Hardly."

"Who then?" Philippe asked, his brow lifted in surprise.

"A friend of the groom's—Lila Broussard."

"So Lila came to call," he drawled, leaning casually against the desk. He crossed his arms on his chest and watched the irate girl with guarded amusement. "What did she want?"

"To give me a wedding gift." Yanking the box from her pocket, Claire opened it and tossed it onto the table. "Jet earrings. Do you like them?" she asked sarcastically.

The man glanced at them without apparent interest, then he reached out to lift a glossy lock of her hair from her neck. "I must say, I prefer the pearls, *ma belle.*" He grinned wickedly, tracing circles on her cheek with his thumb.

Recoiling, Claire exploded. "You gave her my earrings! You cannot deny the evidence of your misdeeds."

"What misdeeds are those?" Philippe's dark eyes narrowed dangerously. Trust Lila to stir up trouble, he fumed inwardly, and trust Claire to believe her. It would do no good to explain that he had not given the earrings to the *placée.* She must have taken them from his pocket that night.

His memory was muddled as to the events after he took Claire home from the restaurant. He had drunk, whether in celebration of the success of his plans or in frustration with the impersonal arrangement, he did not know. The acquaintances with whom he drank had merrily deposited him at the octoroon's cottage when he could no longer stagger along with the hardier drinkers.

He had awakened the next morning with a headache, surprised to find himself there. He had managed to escape while the household slept, avoiding a confrontation with Lila. But the witch must have searched him while he slept and now she bedeviled him with what she had taken.

"*What misdeeds?*" Claire hissed, bringing him back to the present. "You gave my earrings to your—your whore. I will not be treated in such a manner. I will not marry you. When I wed, I will be treated as a wife."

"Then perhaps you should practice behaving like one." Gripping her shoulders, Philippe jerked her toward him, almost lifting her from the ground to meet his lips. His rough kiss smothered her protest and stirred her blood as she struggled against his chest.

Then unexpectedly, she yielded. Unable to deny her passion, her body became soft and pliant. Her arms wrapped around Philippe's waist while her fingers traced warm patterns on his spine. She moaned softly, her mouth warm and inviting against his.

The moment Claire yielded, he tore from her embrace, setting her back on her feet so hard she rocked on her heels. Breathing hard and reeling with the suddenness of the release, she drew back her hand and slapped his face.

With a rueful expression, Philippe rubbed at his reddened cheek and bowed, murmuring, "I won't be staying for dinner after all, *chère*. But heed my advice. Practice behaving as a wife—because you *will* soon be mine."

After a long, sleepless night, Claire knew what she must do. Rising just after dawn, she rode to the racetrack to find Philippe.

The June morning was sunny and promised to be hot and humid, but Claire scarcely noticed as she galloped along the narrow dirt road, mentally rehearsing what she would say to the man.

At the track, she paused beside the empty racecourse, its surface dotted with puddles, before riding into the deserted stable yard. Dismounting at Philippe's tiny office, she tried the door, but it was locked and no one answered when she pounded on it.

Violette's reins still held in her hand, she stood for a moment, debating whether to go to Bonté. Philippe had said little about his family, but she knew they were opposed to his impending marriage. Would they be happy to see her if they knew she had come to break the engagement?

Just then she noticed the door to the barn that housed Philippe's Thoroughbreds standing partly open. Tethering Violette nearby, she went to peer into the murky interior. Perhaps one of the grooms would know where to find the young Creole.

Horses nickered softly from nearby stalls when Claire appeared in the doorway. Afraid she would startle the skittish animals, she did not call out, but stepped quietly inside, looking around.

Suddenly she was showered with hay from the loft overhead. With a muffled cry, she looked up just in time to see more hay flung into midair overhead. Sidestepping it, she called out.

Philippe's head became visible at the edge of the loft. Bright sunlight pouring through a window above caused his face to be shadowed as he looked down, but Claire knew he was grinning as he apologized insincerely.

"Sorry, I didn't know anyone was down there, least of all my future wife."

"Philippe, I need to talk to you," she said stiffly, trying to brush the hay from her velvet riding habit.

"Talk."

"Aren't you coming down?" She scowled up at him, craning her neck.

"*Non.*"

"Then I am coming up," she announced determinedly, scaling the ladder to the loft, where she found Philippe, barechested, wielding a pitchfork expertly.

"What's the matter?" he growled when she hesitated at the top of the ladder. "Haven't you ever seen a man work before?"

"Not..."

"Not a Creole gentleman," he curtly supplied the answer for her. "Well, this gentleman owns racehorses, and they must eat whether he can afford to hire another stable boy or not. Pardon me if I do not don my jacket, mademoiselle, or even my shirt. They are down below, where you should be."

"Philippe, please, I must talk to you," Claire insisted, trying not to look at him too closely. She stepped onto the springy wooden platform beside him.

"I'm listening." He halted his work and leaned against his pitchfork, a politely bored expression on his lean face.

"I've been thinking," Claire began tensely, pacing the narrow space as she spoke, "And I want to call off our engagement."

"I see." His voice was devoid of expression.

Halting beside him, she held out a tiny bundle. "I must ask you to take this back."

Philippe did not answer, but took the bundle, carefully untying the knots in one of Claire's fine linen handkerchiefs. Inside he found the ring he had given her.

He cradled it in his cupped palm, admiring the way the magnificent ruby caught the light. "You return my ring and our agreement is canceled, *oui?*" he asked mildly.

"*Oui,*" she agreed, relieved their meeting was going so smoothly.

He laughed harshly. "Do you really think I'll release you from your promise so easily?"

"But—"

"Our engagement stands," he said determinedly.

"Surely after last night you see a marriage between us cannot work," Claire argued hotly.

"After last night I see that I'm going to have a jealous wife," he countered with a lazy grin.

"Don't be ridiculous," she snapped. "I was not jealous."

"*Bon—très bon,*" Philippe murmured, stepping toward her. "Why should there be jealousy in a marriage of convenience?"

"I can think of no reason." She sidled nervously, but she did not retreat.

"Nor I. Ours is a business arrangement, *oui?*" He advanced another step, seemingly enjoying himself.

"Oui." Suddenly Claire's heart was pounding, but she would not let him know. "It's only a business arrangement," she maintained firmly, "and nothing more."

"So we must keep our minds on business." The man now stood very near, but he made no move to touch her.

"Just on business," she affirmed, nearly choking.

"Then we arè agreed? A marriage between us will work."

"I—I suppose."

"Shall I return this ring to your finger where it belongs and we'll start again?"

After a moment, Claire wordlessly offered her left hand. Philippe slid the ring easily into place on her finger. Then, his eyes holding hers, he bent to kiss her cheek, as chastely as he had the first time.

"We're partners, then?" His breath stirred her hair.

"Partners." Ducking her head, she studied the ring on her finger as if it had just appeared there.

"Claire," Philippe said gently, "things will go much better between us if we can manage to get along. Am I forgiven?"

She lifted her gaze to his, her dark eyes searching his face. *"Oui,"* she whispered.

Knowing even as he did it that he should not, Philippe kissed her lingeringly on the lips. A gesture of reconciliation, he thought before the kiss deepened. Then his arms closed around her, the business agreement between them forgotten.

This was mad, rationality told him, but he was driven by a soft moan of desire that came from deep within Claire. Sinking into a pile of hay, he drew her down with him.

Mindless to all but sensation, Claire returned his caresses. She stroked the warm flesh of his muscled back with open palms as they rolled so Philippe lay atop her. She savored his scent, the scent of bay rum, the out-of-doors and sweat. She reveled in his touch when she felt his hands slide inside her open jacket. His skillful fingers had worked the buttons free and now smoothly untied the ribbon of her camisole.

"Claire," he whispered thickly, "sometimes you drive me mad with wanting." Cupping one bare breast, he lowered his lips to it, drawing a ragged breath as her body arched instinctively beneath him.

"Where are you, Philippe?" A masculine voice reached them from downstairs.

"Damn, it's my brother," the man muttered grimly, cautioning the girl in his arms with a glance.

"Are you up in the loft?" René called.

"Oui, I'll be down in a moment, *mon frère!"* Philippe shouted. He gazed down at Claire, uncertain whether he felt relief or regret at the interruption. The girl's heavy, almost drugged expression had fled, replaced by one of confusion and fear of discovery.

"I want you to meet René, Claire," he said softly, "but not today, not like this. Wait here until I can get rid of him." Rolling off her, he stood and ran his hand through his hair with a weary, harassed air.

Her eyes large in her face, she watched as Philippe descended the ladder. Then she sat up, fumbling to pull the front of her jacket together. Gratefully, she listened to the men's voices fade as they left the barn for Philippe's office.

Hurriedly she stood, arranged her clothing and combed the hay from her tumbled hair. Her face aflame at what she had just done, she struggled to regain her composure. It made no difference that Philippe was her intended husband. She had just behaved shamelessly, nearly letting him take her in the hayloft!

Creeping to the edge of the loft, she looked down into the barn, making sure it was safe before she climbed down. On the ground, she peered out at the sunny stable yard. The men were nowhere in sight. With a mighty sigh of relief, Claire raced to where Violette waited patiently. Then she rode as if pursued all the way to Fortier House.

"You can come out now," Philippe called, frowning up toward the loft when Claire did not answer. "It's all right. René is gone."

When there was still no reply, he climbed the ladder swiftly, knowing what he would find when he reached the top. Claire was gone. He should have known she would not wait. She had looked so frightened and ashamed by what had nearly happened. How had she felt? he wondered guiltily. Humiliated? Shaken by the passion she had obviously felt? Or just angry?

Just because they had stolen a kiss in the barn, it did not mean he had ruined the girl, the young Creole told himself impatiently. Besides, he was going to marry her.

But he found he needed to talk to her, to apologize, to explain. From past experience with Claire, he doubted she would even give him the opportunity.

He did not want things to begin this way between them, Philippe realized suddenly, sitting down heavily on a bale of hay. He noticed Claire's handkerchief on the floor beside him and picked it up. It was delicate and light in his large hand and scented with her fragrance. Shoving it into his pocket, he rose decisively and went to saddle Lagniappe.

At Fortier House, Claire had just emerged from her bath when Lucene knocked at her door. "Mam'selle Claire, M'sieur D'Estaigne is downstairs, sayin' he gotta see you."

Wrapped in a towel, Claire perched on the broad lip of the bathtub and deliberated. Henri must have received her note on his return from Baton Rouge and was surely here to protest her marriage. She must talk to him sometime, but why did it have to be today? After the scene this morning with Philippe, she felt ill prepared for one of Henri's emotional outbursts.

"What you want me to do, mam'selle?" the maid nervously called through the door.

"Take him to the library. I'll be down as soon as I'm dressed."

She found the young Creole standing braced against the mantel of the cold fireplace, his back to the door.

"Henri?" she said hesitantly.

"Claire!" He whirled, her note clasped in his hand, and crossed the room toward her in three long steps. "I must talk to you. I didn't believe your note at first, but I hear it is true. Please tell me it's not. Tell me you are not going to marry Philippe."

"I'm afraid it is true," she said softly.

Taking her arm, he guided her to one of the chairs in front of the fireplace. "How can you do this when you know how I feel about you?"

Dropping to his knees beside her, he took her hand in his and pleaded, "Listen to me, my darling. I love you. I always have. I told you that when I proposed nearly six months ago. Only give me the chance and I'll be a better husband to you than Philippe."

"I'm sorry, Henri." Claire could think of nothing more to say.

"You're sorry that you don't love me, aren't you? I told you before I will make you love me." He slid one arm around her waist and looked up at her hopefully.

"You cannot make one person love another," she demurred gently.

"Do you love Philippe?" he demanded, his green eyes searching. Suddenly he shook his head and buried his face in her lap. "Don't answer," he said, his voice muffled against her skirt. "I can't bear it."

Claire sat helplessly for a moment, unsure how to comfort him. Then, hesitantly, she smoothed his crisp copper hair.

"Well, well." Philippe's soft drawl came from the doorway. "This seems to be your day for compromising situations, *mon amour.*"

Loosening his grip on Claire, Henri lifted his stricken face and looked at Philippe. The couple had not even heard him approach.

"Go upstairs, Claire," her fiancé ordered quietly. "I want to talk to Henri."

Her face mutinous, Claire rose. "Philippe, I—"

"He's right, Claire." Henri got to his feet wearily. "I'll explain."

"There is nothing to explain," the girl said hotly.

"Not even why I find my bride-to-be in the arms of another man?" Philippe asked tauntingly.

"Please go." The urgent note in Henri's voice could not be ignored. Furious with both men, Claire whirled and left the room, slamming the door behind her.

Philippe spoke before Henri could. "Please do not do anything foolish such as challenging me to a duel, Henri. I'm in no mood for heroics and might take you up on it. As you said yourself once before, we've been friends too long for that."

"How could you do this, Philippe? You knew that I love her."

"I knew," the other man admitted. "But I also knew she doesn't love you, *mon ami.*"

"And she loves you?" Henri snorted disbelievingly.

"She's marrying me tomorrow." Philippe shrugged casually in response, then he added softly, "I warn you, for the good of all concerned, stay away from Claire."

"I'll stay away from her, Philippe," Henri answered harshly. "I'll stay away until she realizes what a mistake she has made. In her despair, she'll turn to me, for she knows I love her." With that bitter pronouncement, he threw open the French doors and strode across the lawn without a backward glance.

His brow knit with a frown, Philippe fished in his pocket for a cigar. His fingers found Claire's handkerchief instead and he pulled it from his pocket. Suddenly remembering why he had come to Fortier House, he barked with laughter. He had wanted to apologize for kissing her, while she had sought so-lace in another man's arms.

He bounded up the stairs and confronted Beady in the hall. "Where is Claire's room?" he demanded.

Her eyes wide, the maid pointed with a shaking finger.

Philippe knocked on the door. When there was no answer, he bellowed, "Open the door, Claire! I want to talk to you."

"Go away. I'm sure you and Henri did enough talking for all of us."

His jaw working with anger, he tried the knob. The door was locked. "You may lock me out today," he shouted, "but to-morrow you'll be my wife and there will be no locked doors. So heed me well, Claire. I don't ever want to find you alone with Henri D'Estaigne again."

Suddenly the door flew open and his bride-to-be glared up at him, her face pale with rage. "I will see whom I want, when I want, Philippe Girard. I do not take orders from you. You are my partner, nothing more. We made a business agree-ment—remember?"

"I remember," he said hoarsely, "and I'm already begin-ning to regret it."

Claire listened bleakly to the sound of hoofbeats as he thundered away on Lagniappe, and wondered again if she was mad to marry such a man.

And now that man waited downstairs to marry her—a man she hardly knew, did not understand . . . and did not love.

Absorbed in her thoughts, Claire did not hear Tante Dela-ney enter the room. She started when the woman touched her shoulder, and blurted apprehensively, "Is it time already?"

"No, child." Tante smiled. "As Philippe's only relative present today, I come to bring his bridal gift to you." She pre-sented a slender velvet box.

"Bridal gift? But I received his *corbeille de noce.*" She nodded toward the exquisite basket Creole grooms tradition-ally gave their brides. It was filled with flowers, perfume and a coral choker with matching earrings.

"This is something he says he promised you," the older woman told her.

With shaking hands, Claire opened the hinged box. Inside lay a lustrous pearl choker, its double strands held by a fiery ruby clasp.

"It's beautiful," Claire whispered, sadly remembering the night Philippe had given her his last gift of pearls.

"*Oui*, and pearls are perfect for you," Tante Delaney pronounced. Busy fastening the necklace around Claire's high collar, she did not notice her pained expression.

"See how lovely it looks." She drew Claire to the mirror, where the girl gazed at the reflection of a stranger. The lace dress and the fragile veil were unfamiliar, and she hardly recognized her own face. Above pale cheeks, her eyes were haunted. Her lips were bloodless and dark shadows below her eyes evidenced a lack of sleep. She hardly looked the part of joyful bride.

Claire's head felt light and her knees were weak. Gripping the bedpost tightly, she closed her eyes and sat down heavily on the bed.

"Are you all right, *chère?*" Tante Delaney's alarmed voice seemed so distant.

Opening her eyes, Claire met her anxious gaze. "Just nervous," she assured her. "I'll be better as soon as the wedding is over."

"It's not too late to change your mind, you know," the old woman said hesitantly. "Philippe would murder me with his bare hands if he heard what I said, but you don't have to marry if you do not wish to."

"But I . . ."

"You promised." Tante Delaney harrumphed. "Etienne wouldn't hold you to some ridiculous deathbed promise. If you don't love Philippe, don't marry him."

"I wish things were so simple," Claire said, sighing.

"You must make your own decision." The woman shrugged. "But I can do this much for you—I'll go down and seat myself at the organ. If you appear at the head of the stairs within five minutes, I'll play. If not, I'll send everyone home. You don't even have to come downstairs. All right?"

"*Merci,*" Claire agreed with a sigh of relief, "thank you for everything."

"I just want you both to be happy." The old woman smiled warmly. "And I believe you will come downstairs because I believe you love my nephew."

In the library, Philippe sprawled in a chair, downing his third glass of brandy since lunch. Gaspar lit a lamp against the murkiness of the afternoon and hovered worriedly over his friend.

"The wedding will begin any minute now," he reminded Philippe anxiously. "I know you needed it after last night, but don't you think you've had enough to drink now?"

"There's so much to celebrate, *mon ami,* I've hardly even started," the bridegroom said, laughing uproariously and twirling the cravat he held casually around his finger.

"Philippe," Gaspar almost wailed, "why are you doing this?"

"Because, *mon ami,* marrying Claire Fortier is a part of my plan. But then you do not know about my plan. You must take my word for it, everything is working out exactly as I wanted."

Unsteadily, Philippe rose to refill his glass. With the cork in one hand and the decanter in the other, he looked up in surprise when the door flew open. Henri poised on the threshold, his face stark and pale. His hair was mussed and his usually immaculate clothes looked as if he had slept in them.

"I want to talk to you, Philippe," he grated as he marched into the room.

"We talked yesterday, Henri," the other man replied with a reckless grin. "Why don't we toast the happy bridegroom today?"

"I would talk to Philippe alone, if you don't mind, Gaspar," Henri insisted, grasping the smaller man's arm and propelling him toward the door.

"It's all right, Gaspar," Philippe reassured his protesting friend. "This won't take long. Even in my current state, I can see Henri is a man with a mission."

Gaspar departed, casting dubious glances at his two oldest friends as they faced each other across the room. With a sad shake of his head, he closed the door softly behind him.

"Are you sure you wouldn't care for a brandy, Henri?" Philippe offered genially. "It's excellent, Etienne's best."

Grimly, Henri shook his head.

"Well then, sit down." The bridegroom gestured to the chairs in front of the fireplace.

Henri's green eyes were pained as he surveyed the familiar room. "I'd prefer to stand," he replied curtly.

"Suit yourself." His host sighed with resignation. "But you'll excuse me if I sit." Lurching to a chair, he slouched into it. "Now what is so important that you burst in here today? I thought you agreed to stay away from Claire—for the time being," he added sarcastically.

Henri refused to rise to his baiting. "I have stayed away from her. It's you I came to see."

"Why?"

Henri took a deep breath and plunged ahead. "Yesterday we spoke of Claire and whether or not she loves you. But what I must know is whether you love her and will care for her."

"She'll want for nothing," Philippe assured him, drunkenly expansive. "You know well, Henri, we Girards always take care of what is ours."

Henri's jaw worked with suppressed emotion, but he continued doggedly, "I know. But do you love her, Philippe?"

"Why do you insist on knowing this?" the raven-haired man countered arrogantly, struggling awkwardly upright in his seat.

"Because Claire should have been mine." Henri's voice was ragged. "I loved her from the moment I saw her. I wish we had never made that foolish wager that you would meet her first. You took her from me. You forced yourself on her. Don't think I don't know about the night you spent at the cabin."

Philippe's dark eyebrows shot up with surprise, but he did not attempt to stem the other man's tirade.

"I know you seduced her," Henri grated. "And I still offered to marry her."

"But she chose me," Philippe muttered incredulously.

"Yes, she chose you, you bastard. And I demand to know—do you love her?" the rejected suitor roared.

"All right, if it will make you feel any better," Philippe murmured sympathetically, "our marriage is to be nothing more than a business arrangement."

"A business arrangement!" The other man's cry was anguished. His shoulders sagged as his clenched fists lifted and dropped convulsively.

"Damn you, Philippe!" Henri sighed wearily, his voice hoarse. "It would be better if you loved her, if she loved you."

"Undoubtedly," the bridegroom agreed wryly.

"Claire deserves to be loved. I would have loved her," Henri muttered.

"Don't say anything more, Henri," Philippe interrupted. "You may regret it later. We've been friends for a long time."

The proud young Creole drew himself up as some of his old spirit returned. "We are friends no longer, Girard," he spat. "If I ever find that you've hurt Claire in any way, I will kill you."

The jilted lover stormed from the room, nearly colliding with Gaspar, who lingered just outside the door.

Hesitantly, the stocky man peered into the room. "Philippe, the priest asks if you are ready."

Considerably sobered, Philippe stood and drained his glass, setting it on the table with a clatter. "*Oui*, I am ready," he mumbled, pulling on his coat and tying his cravat. "Let us get this wedding behind us."

At the organ, Tante Delaney sighed in relief and began to play when the maid of honor appeared. With a measured tread, Anne walked toward the flower-bedecked bay window, where the groom waited unsteadily, Gaspar by his side. Oblivious to the reproachful glance of the priest, the young Creole stared unseeingly down the aisle past the handful of guests.

He watched as his bride, looking pale and drawn under her veil, paused in the doorway. Her head held high, she did not falter as she walked down the aisle. She approached the altar slowly, looking neither right nor left, her eyes riveted to a spot over the heads of the wedding party where the first drops of rain streaked the leaded-glass windowpanes.

Irrationally, he felt the heat of anger rising. Claire agreed to keep up appearances. She wore his gift, but she would not even look at him. Why did she have to look so beautiful . . . and unattainable? Filled with disgust at the wave of longing that washed over him, he resolved to be as detached through the ceremony as his bride seemed to be.

Claire willed herself to set one foot in front of the other. In only a matter of moments, the wedding would be over and her promises—to Etienne and to Philippe—would be fulfilled.

The priest nodded when she took her place beside Philippe. They were a handsome couple, he thought smugly, from two fine old families. Etienne Fortier should have lived to see this day. But where was the groom's family?

Setting his spectacles perilously close to the end of his nose, the priest began to read the ceremony, enunciating the Latin words grandly. Suddenly, his voice was drowned out by the ominous clatter of hailstones as the storm's fury broke over Fortier House. He stopped abruptly, his pince-nez dropping onto his open Bible as everyone shifted uneasily and peered toward the windows.

Then, as rapidly as it had begun, the storm abated. Adjusting his spectacles, the priest cleared his throat and continued, but his reading was rushed as if he felt unconsciously that the storm had been a sign from God, a portent of a bad marriage. Tension filled the air as his droning voice raced through the rites.

Mechanically, the couple responded, kneeling and rising as necessary. When the time came to hand the ring to Philippe, Gaspar fumbled nervously, nearly dropping it. Calmly, Philippe took the simple gold band and slipped it onto Claire's finger, where it nestled against the fiery ruby. In turn, she repeated her vows without emotion.

The priest hastily concluded the ceremony, lifting his hands in benediction. Then, with false heartiness, he added in French, "You may kiss the bride, my son."

Philippe planted a perfunctory kiss on his wife's cheek and turned to greet the well-wishers who surged around them. Disregarding Claire's strained face, the groom laughed and greeted each guest, congenially accepting their congratulations and slaps on the back.

"Take care to look the radiant bride, *chère,*" he whispered in Claire's ear. "Don't forget we have made a bargain.

"Come, Madame Girard," he spoke jovially so all could hear, "let's lead our guests to dinner." Ignoring the murderous glint in her eye, he offered his arm to his wife.

Chapter Thirteen

Claire entered the bedroom just ahead of Anne, relieved to escape the sumptuous bridal banquet taking place downstairs and the endless rounds of toasts, each more suggestive than the last.

"You must know how honored I am to be your bridesmaid, Claire," Anne was saying, "and to be the one who helps you prepare for your husband."

"I am glad you're with me," the bride answered, going quickly to close a door to another room. Her back against it as if to ward off intruders, she dragged off her rumpled veil with one hand.

"You're so pale. You're not ill, are you, *chère?*" Anne asked anxiously, leading her to a chair.

"I'm fine."

"Those are Philippe's chambers?" She nodded toward the closed door as she loosened the high collar of Claire's bridal gown.

"*Oui,*" her friend sighed.

"Don't be frightened," Anne said soothingly. "I know that a bride should be shy on her wedding night. Perhaps you will think me improper, but I think it will be wonderful."

"How would you know?" Claire was suddenly exasperated by Anne's constant fancies.

"I wouldn't know, exactly." The petite girl pouted for a moment before her face was wreathed with a mischievous smile. "But what I've read in French novels sounds so...romantic. Besides," she added, helping Claire out of her dress, "you're so beautiful—no, no, do not disagree—and

Philippe is handsome. The two of you make such a lovely couple. Think what beautiful children you'll have.''

Claire bit back a reply as the other girl helped draw a flimsy white nightgown over her head. Anne would not understand that she was not frightened. This wedding night presented no threat—or promise.

Through the folds of fabric, she heard Anne's tentative voice. ''Claire...will you tell me if it is really like a French novel? I must know if I'm to marry Gaspar.''

''I've never read a French novel,'' Claire said, laughing in spite of herself. She thrust her head through the neck hole.

''Well, if you had, you might not have nearly swooned tonight,'' the Creole girl pronounced loftily. ''Since you've never read one, I can only tell you not to be frightened. I'm not.''

''You're not the one who wed today.''

''*Non,* but when I do, I know it will be...''

''Wonderful?'' Claire interjected cynically.

''Wonderful,'' Anne echoed, blushing. She bent and kissed her friend on the cheek. ''*Bonne nuit,* Claire.''

''*Merci,* Anne. Thank you for everything,'' the bride murmured, watching her little friend tiptoe from the room.

For a long time, Claire sat before the fire, brushing her hair, the distant rise and fall of voices reaching her from the dining room. Downstairs Philippe was already acting as master of Fortier House, she brooded, displeasure drawing her lips down in a frown. He acted as if he owned the place—and her. How dared he remind her of their business arrangement while they still stood at the altar? Only yesterday, he had said he regretted it.

At least the wedding was over, she thought with a sigh. Now life would settle back into a routine. Everything would be better after a night's sleep. Claire went to lock the door between the rooms, grimacing when she set her bare foot on the cold wooden floor. Outside it had stopped raining, but the night was chilly, and in her room a small fire crackled in the fireplace.

As she stood with her hand on the latch, Claire realized that her bed linens had been turned back with care and her nightgown had been spread atop them in preparation for the wedding night. Had the servants assumed the new master would spend the night in her room?

Opening the door a crack, she peeped into the adjoining bedchamber. By the flickering light from his fireplace, she saw Philippe's bed still neatly made, his dressing gown laid upon it.

The servants had assumed wrong. Stubbornly, Claire went in to turn down his bed. When she had finished, she surveyed Philippe's new domain. He had refused Etienne's suite, choosing instead the empty room next to Claire's. It was a mirror image of hers, but where her room was decorated in the colors of roses and fine red wine, his contained the hues of the out-of-doors. A green velvet spread embroidered with gold and piped with brown satin covered the tester bed. Heavy gold damask draperies hung at the windows. The Turkey carpet in front of the hearth was as lush as the forest floor.

The brick fireplace, its mantel lined with silver loving cups won by Philippe's horses, was faced by a pair of wing chairs and a small table. The table drew Claire's attention, for it held an assortment of his belongings, brought to Fortier House that very afternoon.

A volume on veterinary medicine lay open, its place held by the handkerchief in which she had returned his ring. Was it only yesterday? A leather cigar case lay beside a pair of framed miniatures.

Bending close, Claire inspected the pictures. One was a portrait of Odette; the other must be his mother. A softer version of Philippe's dark eyes stared out at her from a solemn feminine face. Were his eyes ever as gentle as his mother's? she wondered.

The girl started violently when an amused voice cut into her reverie. "Well, wife, I'm gratified to see you are impatient."

She whirled to find Philippe watching her ironically from the doorway to the hall.

"If I had known what a pleasant surprise awaited me," he drawled, "I would've come upstairs earlier."

"What—what are you doing here?" she asked breathlessly.

"The guests are gone and I came up to my room. At least, I think it's my room." He stepped inside and made a show of looking around. "Yes...these are my things. This is my room. What are *you* doing here?"

"I came to turn down your bed," she retorted, glaring at him.

"I'm touched you're already tending my needs." The man's tone was mocking, but the cocky smile had left his face.

"I hope you'll be comfortable." Claire smiled icily and turned to leave.

"Don't go yet," he commanded, stepping toward her.

Unconsciously, she retreated. His face darkened, but he halted, unwilling to chase her away. Did she not know what an alluring picture she presented?

Every curve of Claire's supple body was clearly outlined through her nightgown as she poised before the fire. Her loose gown had slipped, dipping wildly toward one smooth firm breast, leaving her shoulder bare. She had forgotten to remove the pearl choker from around her neck. Its ruby clasp nestled in the hollow of her throat, winking in the firelight at every beat of her pulse. Her long thick hair was loose, hanging in a dark, glossy cascade down her slender back. In her surprise, her black eyes looked even wider in a pale face touched with gold by the fire's glow.

Set on having a closer look at this enticing vision, Philippe walked slowly toward her.

Although her heart pounded, Claire did not retreat. Inwardly, she cursed the turmoil she felt when he was near. Attraction battled the hurts and confusion of the past week. His cavalier acceptance of her business proposition had been only the beginning. Then he had changed the rules of their agreement to suit him. When she resisted, the skirmishes between them had become a game he enjoyed. This man—her husband—cared nothing for her or her feelings. Had he not shown her often enough?

Yet the memories receded as he approached, his desire evident. His intentions were reflected in his eyes, which held hers with a mesmerizing intensity. For the moment, there was only the present. Dully, Claire shook her head as if to break the spell.

She must never give in to him. She clung to the thought. She was a conquest not yet made, nothing more. He might desire her, but he did not love her. And if she ever allowed herself to love him, she was lost. Claire looked away from his riveting stare, willing her legs to carry her from the room before he reached her.

He came to stand so near she felt his brandy-scented breath on her hair. Gently cupping her chin, he turned her face so he could see it. "You were a beautiful bride," he whispered.

"The guests have gone," she protested uneasily. "There's no further need for pretense."

"What I say is not pretense," he assured her. Sliding his fingers gently along her jawline, he twined them in her dark, lustrous tresses. "You were lovely. And you're even lovelier in the firelight."

Realizing suddenly that she wore only a flimsy nightgown, Claire tugged at the shoulder in an attempt to cover herself. "We have an agreement, monsieur," she began doggedly.

"Agreement be damned, madame," he murmured, pulling her close. "You are my wife now." His fingers tightened in her hair, tilting her head, leaving her slender white throat invitingly exposed.

He left a trail of molten kisses upon her neck, lingering for a sweet moment where her pulse fluttered wildly. He ensnared her body against his as his mouth found hers.

The heat of his kiss sparked a hidden fire within the girl. Struggling against his chest, she sought to stay the fluid warmth that flooded her limbs, replacing the will to escape his passionate embrace. As if he sensed imminent surrender, Philippe loosened his grip. Cradling her gently in his arms, he murmured her name. Tenderly he cupped one breast and bent to caress it through the fabric with his lips.

In one last rebellious gesture, Claire broke free and retreated. "How dare you!" she panted. "You have no right—"

"I have every right," he answered, seemingly unperturbed. He made no move to pursue her. "I have the rights of a husband."

"Sharing your bed was not part of our agreement."

"Neither was finding you in my chambers." He grinned wickedly. "I thought you wanted to resume where we left off yesterday—when we were so rudely interrupted."

Claire's face flushed with color. "I told you, I came to turn down your bed. You can find someone else to warm it," she threw spitefully over her shoulder as she stalked toward the door between their chambers.

"I am surprised at you, *chère,*" Philippe chided, a twinkle in his eye, "suggesting that I visit a whore on my wedding night."

"That's not what I said." She stopped short and glared at him indignantly.

"I should hope not, when I find so enchanting a woman in my bedchamber."

"Must I remind you again that you said we were to have a business arrangement?"

"Was that before or after you said you wished to be treated as a wife? I forget," he crooned dangerously. "We've had this conversation so many times before."

"What difference does that make? A wife shouldn't have to worry that she will be accosted every time she ventures from the safety of her own room."

"True—but mark me well, Claire." Philippe's voice was serious and caused the defiant girl to turn, her hand on the doorknob. "When we made our agreement, I said I would be master of my own home. So I tell you now, because I know what you're thinking, we may have separate rooms, but there will be no locked doors between us. You invite trouble if you try that course."

Removing his jacket, he began to unbutton his shirt. "Now, madame," he dismissed his wife patronizingly, "unless you care to watch me undress, you must return to your own chamber, for I wish to retire."

Ignoring Claire's venomous glare, he sat down and tugged at his boots. He did not look up when the door clicked shut behind his furious bride.

Awakening early from a troubled sleep, Philippe lay still for a moment and wondered where he was. Then he heard whispers from the next room that brought him to his feet. His head pounding from the aftereffects of last night's celebration, he dressed quickly and stood poised on his side of the door to listen.

"How 'bout this dress?" Beady was exclaiming. "It'll make you look like th' beautiful new bride you are."

Claire sniffed disdainfully. "That hardly matters at the office."

After an incredulous silence, Beady's dismayed voice shrilled, "You cain't go out today, mam'selle. You jest got married. Didn't Mam'selle Anne 'splain it to you? You ain't even s'posed to stick your nose outta th' house for two weeks. What will people think if you go traipsin' off to th' Mercantile today?"

"They'll think what they want. They usually do," Claire snapped.

"One thing they will not think," her new husband corrected, opening the door, "is that Philippe Girard cannot keep his wife at home. You're not going to the office."

Whirling guiltily, Claire snatched a gown from Beady and clutched it to her chest in a futile attempt to cover herself.

Fully clothed and prepared for the day, Philippe surveyed his wife arrogantly. Despite his dapper appearance, he looked haggard. Beneath furrowed brows, his eyes were bloodshot and darkly circled. No smile relieved the stern expression on his face.

"Why are you whispering in here?" he quizzed, fixing Claire with a suspicious stare. "Were you trying to make an escape already?"

"I was dressing and didn't want to wake you." She glared at him, returning his disapproval in full measure.

"Don't worry about that," the man replied curtly, trying to ignore the fact she wore only lacy undergarments behind the dress she used to shield herself. Glancing toward the hovering maid, he ordered, "Beady, leave us."

"*Non,* stay," her mistress countered. "I need you here."

"As you wish, madame," Philippe said as the slave gingerly retreated behind a door of the wardrobe. "Then hear me well. You are not going to the Mercantile today—or anytime soon. Custom demands that you go nowhere without me, that you have no callers, for the first two weeks of marriage. Do you understand?"

"Is this how you keep your bargain?" his wife raged. "We agreed that the Mercantile is mine to manage, did we not?"

"We did. But you recall, you agreed to keep up appearances. Therefore it's impossible for you to go to the office so soon."

"And when will it be possible?" Her voice was icy.

"In two or three months," he allowed tolerantly.

"Two or three months!" she exploded. "How am I to manage the business if I'm absent that long?"

Philippe looked mildly shocked by her vehemence. "Your manager handled it well enough in the past. He can continue to handle it."

"And what am I supposed to do?"

"Learn to be a wife." His dark eyes, glinting dangerously, caught and held hers.

Claire refused to be intimidated. "I'll learn to be a wife when you learn to be a husband."

"I tried last night, remember?" He paused, grimly enjoying the show of color that crept up her slender neck to her face before he continued, "I'm more liberal than most, Claire. In a week or so, I would have no objection if you began to work at home. Use the library as your office, but don't go to the Mercantile."

"What about the books and correspondence I'll need?"

"Have McConnell bring them to you."

"I can't ask him to drop everything and come all the way out here," Claire argued.

"Why not? He came when your uncle summoned. And he works for you now." Certain he had effectively swept away every obstacle to his plan, Philippe turned his back on the conversation, missing the stubborn set to Claire's jaw.

While his back was turned, the girl slipped into a robe and sat down to brush her hair. "I told Beady to have your breakfast sent to your room, Philippe," she informed him crisply. "Or would you prefer to join me in the dining room?"

"Neither. Beady," he addressed the maid directly, "run and tell the cook I'll stop in the kitchen for *café* and a *beignet* on the way to the stables."

"Where are you going?" Claire's hairbrush halted midstroke and she regarded him accusingly in the mirror.

"To ride the fields," he explained.

Beady rushed from the room as if flying before a storm.

"It's not fair for you to go out while I stay at home." Claire glared at her husband with renewed hostility.

"I could stay, if you'd like. We could become more intimately acquainted," Philippe suggested with a wink and a lecherous leer.

At the look in Claire's eyes, he hurriedly stepped out into the hall and closed the door on a scorching tirade. What was a man to do with such a woman? Scowling, he set out for the kitchen.

A week later, he was still asking himself the same question. It was only midmorning, but the day was hot and humid. Philippe's jacket seemed molded to his broad shoulders, and a drop of sweat trickled from under his Panama hat. Turning Lagniappe toward home, he wondered sourly whether a visit to the Fortier overseer was worth such discomfort. Then he admitted to himself that the time used to go over plans with Monsieur Chauvin had been well spent. The man had welcomed his ideas and offered some of his own.

Almost everything was working smoothly now. At the house, Toolah pampered him outrageously, Greer offered grudging respect, and the young groom, Xavier, was his constant shadow. Why, then, was it so difficult to win over the mistress of the house?

In the past week, nothing had changed between the newlyweds. Their marriage seemed as doomed as it had on their wedding day. He and Claire seemed to do nothing but match wills. And what a will she possessed.

He had hoped things might be different when he discovered her in his room on their wedding night. He should have known it was too good to be true, he told himself bitterly.

She had looked sweet and willing, and her disarray had made her seem all the more inviting. His blood pounded at the memory. But there had been no invitation in her lips when he kissed her. He had met rigid, unyielding resistance beneath that soft exterior.

Philippe cursed under his breath. Which was the real Claire? The cold and unattainable business partner or the passionate woman he glimpsed when she let her guard down?

His first, almost irresistible urge that night had been to take her in spite of her protests. She was his wife, after all. It had taken all his will not to carry her to his bed. He could have taken her, he thought savagely, and no one would have thought less of him for it—except Claire.

No, Philippe admitted reluctantly to himself, he could not live with himself if he had forced her. He had never taken a woman against her wishes and he did not intend to start now—especially with the vexing mixture of innocence and steel he had wed.

One day, he vowed hotly, she would come to him, but he would not bed her until she asked him. That was what he wanted, what he had unconsciously desired since he saw her riding alone across the fields. That was what he would wait for.

Chapter Fourteen

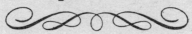

Trying not to think, Claire turned all her attention to polishing a table in the foyer. But her exertions did not keep her mind from Anne's visit that morning.

Claire had welcomed her friend gladly. It was not fair, she thought rebelliously, to be forced into two weeks of isolation without even Philippe for company. He came and went as he pleased, using business as his excuse. He rose early, eating in the kitchen before he rode out to the fields or to his stables, and stayed away all day. She seldom even saw him, and when she did, she discovered the cold, mocking Philippe had returned. She didn't mind that he seemed to go out of his way to avoid her.

But Claire said nothing of this to Anne, listening instead as her guest excitedly described the elaborate preparations for her own wedding. After a time, the conversation trailed off and the Creole girl seemed distracted.

"What's wrong, Anne?" Claire asked gently.

"Nothing, really," the other girl mumbled, staring fixedly out the window.

"You're upset about something."

"Perhaps I am a little."

"What is it, then?" Claire probed gently. "Is it Gaspar?"

"*Non*, it's Philippe," Anne announced in a rush, turning to her friend with concern in her eyes.

The color drained from Claire's face. "Philippe? What has happened?"

"You do love him. I can tell." Anne sighed with relief. "I knew the stories couldn't be true."

"What stories?" Claire asked, careful to mask the turmoil she felt.

"Just rumors. I didn't want to tell you, but I realized, as your best friend, I must. And I must lay them to rest."

"Tell me," the new bride requested quietly.

Under Claire's calm questioning, Anne recounted reports of Philippe's reckless behavior over the past week—drinking at the Absinthe House, unofficial moonlight races around the dark racetrack, grim losses at the Palace of Chance. "You must make Philippe understand there will be gossip, if he behaves as if he were still a bachelor," she concluded imploringly.

"Is that all?" Claire asked, dreading the answer.

"No," the Creole girl whispered sorrowfully, her face turning a deep red shade. "I do not believe it, but there is talk that he visits Lila Broussard, the octoroon."

Claire felt a stab of pain, almost physical. Then to her amazement, she found herself soothing the other girl and, inexplicably, lying for her husband. "Don't worry about rumors, Anne," she reassured her. "I learned when my uncle died that the world will make gossip of anything. And you know Philippe's and my marriage was not well accepted by some."

"That must be it," the Creole girl cried in relief. "The gossip will die when everyone sees how happy you are."

After Anne left, heartened that all was well, Claire sat brooding. Again and again, she told herself that she did not care when—or if—Philippe came home, but he had insisted they keep up appearances. Why was he undermining her efforts? Why was she working harder at this marriage than he? she asked herself resentfully.

Craving activity to take her mind off her problems, Claire summoned Greer. If the big butler had known what awaited him, he might not have responded so quickly. She issued a series of rapid-fire orders, mustering stable boys to wash the windows, dispatching maids for brooms and mops. Once her house was in order, Claire decided, she would worry about her marriage.

Under her direction, the big house was transformed by a flurry of cleaning. Doors were thrown open and the scents of lye soap, beeswax and pine oil filled the air. Kneeling beside Lucene, Claire helped the servants polish every inch of the ornately carved banister. She supervised when the chandelier was taken down so every crystal could be washed and dried.

Trusting no one else to perform that task, Greer mounted a ladder and lowered the huge light himself. He lingered on his perch for a moment, his muddy brown eyes resting on the mistress. Bent to her task, she looked like a kitchen wench as she brushed back a stray lock of hair. Shaking his great head indulgently, he descended to do whatever she bade.

The last rays of daylight glinted on the spotless chandelier and created a glow on the polished parquet floors before Claire was willing to pronounce the house clean. Wearily, she dismissed the laborers and sat down on the bottom step of the staircase.

"Is there anything else, miss?" Greer asked, unaware of a smudge that ran across his nose from one sunken cheek to the other.

"A bath . . . and bed." She tugged her scarf from her head and allowed her hair to tumble free.

"Beady is already preparing the water," the butler informed her. "And Toolah will send a tray as soon as you are finished."

"*Merci,* Greer." The begrimed girl smiled as she rose and went upstairs. Within moments, she was soaking gratefully in a high-backed tub of steaming water.

"Take some time and enjoy your bath, mam'selle," Beady whispered and departed. Claire closed her eyes and felt the weariness seep from her muscles.

Perhaps she dozed, she did not know. But after a time, a muffled sound nearby intruded on her relaxation.

"Are you back already?" she murmured without opening her eyes.

"That's a fine way to greet your husband," a teasing masculine voice complained.

"Philippe!" Claire gasped, sitting abruptly upright in the tub. Ignoring the water that splashed onto the carpet, she shot a panicked look toward the door between the rooms. "What are you doing here?"

"Enjoying the view." He grinned and focused pointedly at her bare breasts bobbing above the soapy waterline.

"Go away," she commanded with as much dignity as she could summon and sank in the water to her chin. "I'll be out in a moment."

"No hurry." Philippe ambled into the room. "I'll just sit here and talk to you." Removing her towel from a nearby chair, he sat down and folded it neatly in his lap.

His wife glared at him inarticulately and slid farther into the tub, irritatedly aware that the water, lapping at the nape of her neck, had begun to cool.

"Just what is it you wish to talk about?" she snapped.

"First the amenities, *chère*," he scolded playfully. "How are you?" Only the mischievous gleam in his eyes told her he was aware of her discomfort.

Under the cover of lush bubbles, Claire's hand groped for, then tightly clenched a bar of soap. She shifted for better aim as she considered throwing it in Philippe's mocking face.

"You know," he went on casually, "it's been too long since we sat and talked. We've both been so busy."

"I've been here. You're the one who has been away on 'business,'" she replied sarcastically.

"You've noticed my absence." His eyebrows lifted in mock surprise. Then he frowned down at her and offered the towel solicitously. "Are you sure you won't get out now?"

When she did not respond, he refolded the towel properly and hunched forward in his chair for a better view. Claire slid farther into the tub, dampening her hair, gritting her teeth to keep them from chattering, though whether from anger or cold, she was not sure.

"It is true I've been away too much," he said with a charming smile, "but that's about to change."

Claire regarded him cautiously from the tepid water, ready to fire the bar of soap at the first provocation.

"Two weeks is long enough to play the parts of newlyweds. Since we can now receive callers, we must have a dinner party.

"We'll begin simply," Philippe continued, blissfully ignorant of the danger that had just passed as she released the soap. "Just my family—and my Tante Madeleine. You seem to enjoy her company. Perhaps you'd like to include Anne and Gaspar?"

"Not this time." Claire sighed, relieved that a dinner party was all her husband sought from her. "I shall take care of it."

"*Très bien.*" Philippe stood and dropped the towel onto the chair. Lingering beside the bathtub, he gazed down at her, an odd expression in his eyes. For a moment it seemed as if he would speak, but he did not.

Claire sat up warily in the cooling water and watched him saunter toward his own room. When he turned abruptly in the doorway, she snatched the towel to her breast.

"It's nice to come home to such a picture, *chère,*" he said huskily. "It would be very nice to stay, but I can't. One of my mares is about to foal and her time is near."

Flooded with unexpected disappointment, she leaned back in the tub, the wet towel plastered to her breast, and glared at him.

"Don't stay too long in that cold water. You might catch a chest cold." Her husband smiled wickedly, indicating the sodden towel with a nod of his head. Then he went into his room and left her to finish her bath.

"Mam'selle, please," Lucene wailed, "I mus' ax you a question."

"*Oui?*" Claire turned to the frazzled servant expectantly.

From the landing above the foyer, Philippe watched his wife surrounded by a bustling army of servants. Her cheeks were pink from heat and exertion, and a thick plait slapped heavily against her damp back as she rushed from one room to another. The sleeves of her cotton dress were rolled to her elbows and her arms were covered with a sheen of perspiration.

The man's eyes lingered on the base of her throat where her open collar plunged in a V, its point disappearing behind the calico apron she wore. The effect was decidedly domestic, he decided, and it invited closer inspection.

"Claire!" he called over the hubbub as he descended. In the midst of the frenzied activity, he dodged and ducked, managing to catch hold of his wife's arm before she could disappear.

The mistress of the house spun and glared at him, but irritation was supplanted by surprise. "Philippe! I didn't realize you were still home."

"You would have, madame, if you paid attention to me, instead of the upstairs maid," he teased.

"I just want everything to be right for our guest tonight," Claire apologized with a weak smile.

"Don't worry so much," Philippe chided gently. "Our guest is just Tante Delaney."

"But—"

"Everything looks wonderful," he assured her. "You've done well."

Scanning the preparations with satisfaction, the man missed the pain that clouded her eyes for a moment. Then, resolutely, she put aside the hurt at receiving the Girards' tersely worded refusal to her invitation. She almost shuddered aloud, remembering the wrath on her husband's face when he crumpled the response in one white-knuckled hand. But his anger seemed to have passed.

She stole a covert look at Philippe from the corner of her eye and was disconcerted to find him watching her.

"I said you've done well," he repeated softly.

"Merci," Claire replied, glowing at the praise. Acutely aware of his nearness, her heart pounded and her knees felt weak, but she would not let him know the effect he had on her. "I promised I would be a good chatelaine," she reminded him.

"So you did," he responded dryly. The brief moment of warmth was past. He never knew what to expect when he looked into those unfathomable eyes.

"I came to tell you that I won't be here this afternoon," he asserted testily. "I must time Hyacinth for next week's race."

"Of course," his wife agreed distractedly. "Tante will be here at eight o'clock and dinner will be served at eight-thirty. You will be back in time, won't you?"

"Mais oui." He bowed mockingly. "I'm the host."

"Yes..." Claire's mind was on other matters. "Please don't be late," she requested, headed for the dining room. Lucene trailed in her wake, bombarding her with questions.

"Non, madame." Philippe's smoldering eyes followed Claire. "I shall not be late. And *merci,"* he added sarcastically under his breath, "for taking the time to talk with me. I am, after all, only your husband." Jamming his hat onto his head, he stamped out to where Xavier waited with the horses.

Throughout the day, the mistress of Fortier House arranged and rearranged until satisfied with her preparations. Finally, late in the afternoon, she yielded to Beady's distressed clucking and went to her room to get ready for dinner.

When she was dressed, Claire stood before the mirror. In the last glow of the evening sun that filtered through the window, her skin resembled warm, polished alabaster against her pale coral gown. Creamy lace adorned its skirt and edged its décolletage and tight-fitting sleeves at the wrists. The coral choker Philippe had given her on their wedding day rode at the base of her throat and the earrings peeped from below wings of sleek dark hair.

Suddenly mindful of the time, she asked anxiously, "Has Monsieur Girard returned, Beady?"

"No, ma'am, but don't worry. He's sure to be here soon."

"Have his clothes been laid out?" Claire fretted.

"No, ma'am. Want me or Greer to do it?"

"I will." Her petticoats rustling, Claire stepped into Philippe's room and went to his ornate, double-doored chiffonier. But she faltered in front of it. She knew nothing of his belongings or where he kept them.

Opening the carved doors, she scanned the neat row of clothing that hung inside and selected a dove-gray jacket, a pair of dark blue breeches and a vest of blue and silver brocade. Searching through the drawers of the chiffonier, she found a crisp white shirt and the ebony box that held his stocks. Opening the box, she chose a pale blue cravat.

Carefully she arranged the clothing on the bed, then she went downstairs for a last-minute check before their guest arrived.

The dining room table was set with the best china, crystal and silver. A fire burned on the grate in the first parlor, and the cherry wood furniture shone warmly with its reflected glow. The room looked elegant, she decided, fluffing the pillows on the stiff horsehair sofa. Elegant and beautiful.

Her smug smile faded when the clock on the mantel caught her eye. Philippe had promised not to be late, yet it was nearly eight o'clock and he was not home.

Hearing sounds from the *allée,* Claire went to the window to discover Tante Delaney was arriving a few minutes early. She welcomed Philippe's aunt in the foyer, studiously ignoring Greer's displeasure at being deprived of the opportunity to announce the guest formally.

"Claire, how good of you to invite me to dinner!" Her face beaming with pleasure, Tante Delaney hugged the girl. Noting her nephew's absence, she peered over Claire's shoulder at Greer, raising her eyebrows in mute question. Silently, the butler shrugged his broad shoulders and shook his head.

"A glass of sherry, Claire, *s'il vous plaît,*" Tante Delaney requested as Greer took her cloak. "I must collect myself for, I vow, the streets of New Orleans become bumpier every day."

Instantly solicitous of her guest's comfort, Claire led her to the parlor. "I don't know what is keeping Philippe," she apologized, handing a delicate crystal glass to Tante Delaney. "He should be here any moment."

"No hurry," the woman assured her kindly. "His tardiness gives us a chance to visit. I've hardly had a chance to chat with you since the wedding."

For nearly an hour, Claire listened distractedly to Tante Delaney. One ear cocked to the window, alert for the sound of Philippe's return, she responded mechanically to the woman's small talk.

"And the only thing Emmaline can talk about these days is Anne's wedding," Tante Delaney was saying with a laugh. "I never thought that woman could turn into as much of a flibbertigibbet as her daughter."

Smiling wanly, Claire rose. "If you'll excuse me, I must check on dinner."

She found Greer in the dining room, stationed at a window overlooking the front of the house. "Is there any word from Philippe?" she asked without preamble.

"No, ma'am."

"How long can Toolah keep the dinner warm?"

"At least until Ezra returns," the butler replied. "I imagine Mister Girard has lost track of time, so I took the liberty of sending Ezra to fetch him. They should arrive shortly."

"Thank you, Greer," the girl murmured gratefully and returned to the parlor, determined to put a good face on Philippe's tardiness. She sat down opposite Tante Delaney and resumed the conversation with much more enthusiasm than she had shown previously.

At last, she heard the sound of hooves on the drive and she visibly relaxed. As soon as Philippe joined them, they would go in to dinner. The evening would not be a disaster after all.

Claire looked up expectantly when Greer appeared at the door. "Excuse me, ma'am, may I see you for a moment?"

In the hall, he turned unhappily to his mistress. "I'm sorry, Miss Claire, but Ezra says the master is not at the stable. No one is. Would—er—would you like me to send him out again to see if he can find him?"

"No," she said, sighing in resignation. "Just serve dinner."

Had she ever truly doubted the gossip? Claire wondered bitterly. Philippe was surely at Lila's cottage. To drag him from his mistress's arms was the last thing she wanted.

"Men!" she exclaimed with a hollow laugh, going in to face her husband's aunt. "I'm sorry, but I just received word that Philippe has been unavoidably detained. There's no reason to wait any longer. Shall we go in to dinner?"

Throughout the meal, Tante Delaney kept up a steady stream of conversation, filling each awkward silence. If the exquisite dishes were dry from lengthy reheating, the old woman gave no hint of it. She ate with great appetite, even helping herself to second servings of turkey and truffle dressing. Painfully aware of the empty chair at the head of the table, Claire scarcely ate at all.

Finally, Tante Delaney murmured, "You mustn't think too much of Philippe's not being here tonight, *chère*. I'm sure he had a good reason."

"I'm sure," her hostess agreed with a stiff smile.

"Besides, a man is entitled to one little lapse, isn't he?" She stabbed energetically at her dessert and gave the nettled girl a sidelong glance. "When you find Philippe perplexing, try to remember his life has been hard."

"Philippe's life hard?" Claire blurted skeptically.

"He's known little of love," his aunt explained gently. "His mother is devoted to her devotions. My brother, Pierre, is a tyrant who tries to run his children's lives. With some success, I daresay, looking at René. That boy wanted to be a doctor, but Pierre insisted his firstborn would inherit and run Bonté. So René is destined never to fulfill his dearest dream. Philippe is a different story. He may never have Bonté, but he does have dreams. And he will do as he pleases—always has." She chuckled.

The reminiscent expression on her angular face was replaced by one of canny understanding. "The poor boy knows what he does *not* want in life, but he is not sure what he *does* want."

"'The poor boy' is no longer under his father's control," Claire argued unsympathetically. "His life is his to live—on his own terms."

"His terms, your terms, it makes no difference," Tante Delaney contended. "Life has not worked out as he planned."

"Our marriage is as we planned."

"Plans change. I hate to say it of my own nephew, but I don't think he meant to care for you."

A long moment of silence ensued as the girl fastidiously measured sugar into her coffee cup. She had no intention of debating Philippe's feelings with his aunt.

"You probably think I am a meddling old woman, and perhaps I am," Tante Delaney acknowledged quietly, "but I want you to think about what I've said."

"I will," the girl responded grudgingly. "And I don't think you meddlesome. But let's talk of something else now," she requested, steering the conversation to less painful subjects.

Later, when she was alone, Claire wandered into the library and settled moodily in a chair to await Philippe's return. Where could he be? she asked herself again, certain she knew the answer.

The mantel clock measured minutes and seconds, its ticks punctuated by the crackle of the dying fire. Curled in the big leather chair, Claire dozed at last.

She did not hear when Philippe rode wearily past the house to the stable yard, trailed by a tearful Xavier. When they dismounted, Philippe patted the exhausted groom's shoulder.

"It's been a hard day, Xavier," he said kindly, "but don't skimp on your attention to Lagniappe. Give him all he needs. Then get some rest yourself. I won't need you in the morning."

"*Oui,* m'sieur," Xavier said, nodding dazedly as the man disappeared in the shadows at the back of the house.

A hard day indeed, Philippe reflected somberly as he walked. He would not have believed how many calamities could occur in so short a time. His pace did not slow when he passed the kitchen. Although he had not eaten since breakfast, he had no thought of food. What he needed was a drink and bed.

The huge house was dark and silent as Philippe tiptoed through the hallway. Passing the servants' quarters, he heard a deep snore from Greer's bedroom where the butler napped in front of the fire, waiting for the master to come home.

Wearily, he groped his way to the library. The faint glow of embers illuminated the area around the hearth and he could see the brandy on a side table. As he passed one of the wing chairs, he nearly tripped over a pair of outstretched legs.

Steadying himself with a hand on the high back of the chair, Philippe smiled incredulously. Claire—he hadn't thought she would wait up for him. Admiringly he gazed down on his wife as she slept, noting with satisfaction she wore the coral jewelry he had given her on their wedding day.

Tenderly, he bent to kiss her forehead, drawing back in shock when her eyes flew open and narrowed with undisguised rage.

"So you decided to come home at last," she greeted him hotly.

A look of consternation flitted across Philippe's tired face only to be replaced by rigid anger. Straightening stiffly, he ordered hoarsely, "Don't start, Claire. It has been a long day."

"And a long night as well." She glanced meaningfully at the clock.

"Yes, and a long night as well." Philippe poured a healthy shot of brandy into a snifter.

"Where have you been?" she asked in spite of herself.

"I've been busy." The man threw back his head and downed nearly half the brandy in one swallow.

"You weren't at the stable," she accused from the shadow of the wing chair.

"You presume to check on me now, madame?" he inquired coldly, pouring another brandy, sloshing the amber fluid on the table in his haste.

"I was not checking on you," Claire retorted. "Greer sent Ezra to the stable to fetch you for dinner. When you weren't there, I could have told him where you were."

"And where would that be?" he gritted.

"We won't go into it tonight. You're drunk."

"*Non*, madame, I am not drunk, but I will be very soon." Scooping up the decanter, he stormed from the room.

White faced and shaking with anger, Claire slumped in the chair and listened to her husband's heavy footfalls on the stairs. She stared bleakly at the dying fire, stirring only when Greer loomed in the darkness at her side, his hair mussed and his jacket hastily donned.

"Monsieur Girard has just retired, Greer." She rose wearily. "Please lock up for the night."

* * *

Sunlight flooded the dining room the next morning when Claire came down to breakfast. Her strained face mirrored the effects of a sleepless night.

Discreetly, Greer shooed the other servants out of the room, then leaned near to pour a cup of coffee. "Mr. Philippe won't be down this morning," he informed his mistress.

"That's hardly surprising," Claire responded tersely. "I'm sure he must feel what he drank last night."

"I don't think he drank so much, Miss Claire," the butler disagreed with quiet obstinacy. "I think he drank enough to sleep and—and to forget what happened yesterday."

"What happened?"

"From what I've learned from Xavier, yesterday was a most unfortunate day. There was an accident at the stables. Billy Barron, Mr. Philippe's jockey, was badly injured and taken by ambulance to the infirmary. The master went with him."

"Will he be all right?" Claire asked with a concerned frown.

"Xavier says he may never walk again. And he says Mr. Philippe took it very hard."

"I'm sure," she said gravely. "Did Xavier say how it happened?"

"It seems to have started with Maeger—"

"The new trainer? But he came to Philippe well recommended."

"Recommended or not, when it came time yesterday to run Hyacinth, Mr. Philippe found him asleep in the tack room, smelling of rum. When he woke him, the man swore that he had spilled rubbing alcohol on himself. Mr. Philippe is a fair man," Greer offered a rare insight, "and since he couldn't prove misconduct, he warned Maeger against drinking on the job. Then he told him to have Hyacinth saddled.

"Apparently Maeger was certain Mr. Barron had reported him. He tried to pick a fight with him in the stable yard. When Mr. Philippe stopped it, the bully went inside and told the groom that no one but the trainer should handle a champion filly. He saddled Hyacinth himself. A cinch was missed." Greer shrugged sadly.

"During the trial, the saddle slid and tangled in the filly's legs. She tripped, throwing Mr. Barron, then fell on top of him. Besides his injuries, both of her front legs were broken."

"Oh, no! Hyacinth was Philippe's favorite," Claire moaned, tears welling up in her eyes.

"I think that's why he put her out of her agony himself. Afterward he went to the infirmary and stayed with Mr. Barron until the sisters made him come home."

"What about Maeger?"

"The master fired him and threatened to beat him within an inch of his life if he shows his face at Girard Stables again."

"Poor Philippe. And I was so..." She faltered, casting about for the right word.

"Unsympathetic?" Greer supplied helpfully.

"*Oui,* unsympathetic," she agreed uncomfortably, wishing the butler were not so exceptionally candid this morning.

She had not shown herself to be much of a wife last night, she mused regretfully. She had done Philippe an injustice. In the space of one afternoon, his favorite jockey was badly injured; his stable was without a trainer; his fleet, beautiful champion was dead. And his wife had harassed him about a dinner party.

He had needed someone to talk to and she had accused him of drunkenness. He had needed understanding and she had shouted at him for being late. If she could, she must make it up to him today, she decided. She must try to make him forget last night's unpleasantness.

Claire was soon forced to put her resolutions into action. She smiled tentatively as her husband's uneven tread in the hallway announced his arrival. The Philippe who appeared was not the immaculately groomed man she knew. Despite Greer's claims to the contrary, the young man's entire being bespoke hangover. Haggard and unshaved, he was clad in a rumpled dressing gown.

"*Bonjour,* Philippe," she greeted him. Summoning Greer, she instructed, "Please tell Toolah to cook breakfast for Monsieur Girard. She knows what he likes."

"*Non,* no food," Philippe objected, raising a shaky hand. "I only came downstairs to get some *café.*"

"You should have stayed in bed. Lucene could have brought it to you."

"And miss the kind attention of my loving wife? I assure you, *mon amour,* your tenderness last night lingers in my memory."

Claire flushed to the roots of her hair. "About last night, Philippe—" She glanced desperately at Greer. Correctly reading her plea for privacy, he set a cup on the table across from her, pulled out the chair and withdrew.

Philippe sank into the chair, shrinking from the aroma of the steaming coffee. He clasped his hands on the table, his arms encircling his cup. Cocking one eyebrow, he regarded his wife balefully through bloodshot eyes and did not utter a single word to ease her discomfiture.

"I—I apologize for my behavior when you came home last night." She paused. When he did not speak, she continued defensively, "I thought you were inebriated."

Philippe stared stonily at her.

"Perhaps if we talked about it. . ." she suggested awkwardly.

"I have nothing to say that was not said last night."

"But, Philippe, I know now what happened yesterday," she went on doggedly, swallowing her pride. "Xavier told us and I was very sorry to hear it. And I know, too, that you weren't drunk."

"I was not," came Philippe's curt affirmation. "Nor was I wherever you seemed to think I was."

"I know," she whispered contritely. "And I'm sorry."

"You should be," he grumbled uncharitably.

Biting her tongue, Claire allowed him his anger. After a time she asked softly, "How is Monsieur Barron?"

"Poor Billy." The man sighed and ran a tense hand through his tangled hair. "I don't know. He's in a great deal of pain. And last night the doctors didn't offer much hope of recovery." His anguished eyes met his wife's concerned gaze.

"Perhaps it was early to tell." She reached across to pat his arm consolingly. "He may be better after a night's rest."

"Perhaps," Philippe replied, as if seeing her for the first time. "I'll find out when I go back to the hospital this morning. But first I believe I'll have some breakfast, after all." Almost casually, he laid his hand across hers and looked around for a servant.

Just then, Greer entered with a tray laden with food. "Thought you might like a little something to eat, anyway, sir," he suggested.

"Greer, you're a mind reader." Philippe shifted in his chair, adjusting slightly to make room on the table for the plate. But he did not release Claire's hand.

The butler set his breakfast in front of the man, then handed him a small white envelope. "This came for you a few minutes ago, Mr. Philippe."

"Merci," the young Creole answered distractedly. Without so much as a glance at it, he tossed the envelope aside and attacked his breakfast with surprising appetite.

When he went upstairs to dress, Claire lingered contentedly over her coffee. Warmed by the sun filtering through the dining room windows, mellowed by her conversation with her husband, she was considering what she would do with her day when her eyes fell on the envelope.

Philippe had forgotten his note. Perhaps she should take it up to him. Smiling indulgently, Claire picked up the envelope, but her smile faded when she recognized the handwriting on its face. Lila—she had seen that elaborate script often enough in the octoroon's ledgers.

Shaken, she struggled for control. She would not allow her imagination to run wild as it had last night. After all, Philippe had hardly incriminated himself when he received it. He had not even looked at it. Was it because he sought to avoid a scene? Or perhaps, she thought hopefully, because he did not care for the petite octoroon anymore and did not care what she wrote?

But perhaps, a nasty little voice whispered in her head, he had not looked because he knew who sent it and what it would say.

Claire had no time to weigh the evidence before she heard Philippe's footfall on the stairs. Leaving the note where she found it, she fled to the garden, determined not to quarrel with him while he had so much on his mind. Deliberately she turned a deaf ear to his call and sequestered herself in the tree house until he gave up the search and left for the day.

Chapter Fifteen

Shoving back her straw hat, Claire peeped up at the sun, already a white-hot orb in the morning sky. Hopelessly, she surveyed her arid garden, its foliage wilting and dusty in the sweltering heat. Summer in New Orleans was always hot, but this year the weather was unusually dry. No rain had fallen for more than a month—since the day she and Philippe had married. Only tempers seemed to flourish in this weather.

It seemed as if the quiet moment Claire had shared with her husband last week over breakfast had never happened. Perhaps she should have confronted Philippe about Lila's letter then, for now she found she could not. Neither could she rid herself of suspicion. Her aloof behavior took its toll on the fragile relationship, and life at Fortier House was as it had been before—or worse.

Turning her attention to a drooping rosebush, Claire poured water on the ailing plant and spaded the dry soil at its base. Then, mud streaking her arms halfway to her elbows, she felt around the root ball, breaking up the dense pockets of dirt with her fingers to allow water to reach roots.

When the ground became soft, she was determined to remove a healthy weed that grew beside the bush. Planting her bare feet solidly, she yanked on the stringy stalk. Suddenly her feet began to slide, making furrows in the slippery mud. She lost her balance and sat down hard on the ground. But in her fist she triumphantly held the weed, its roots showering clods of dirt onto her skirt, which rode up around her thighs.

"A word with you, madame." Philippe appeared at the edge of the rose bed, carefully ignoring his wife's ignominious position.

Claire nodded coolly, her only concession to the absurd situation to pull her skirt down over her knees.

"I thought you should know we'll be attending a ball on
Saturday," he informed her.

"Saturday?" She gazed up at him haughtily, but found
herself squinting against the sun. She rose with as much dignity as possible and brushed herself off. "That's only two days
away," she said testily. "Isn't this rather short notice?"

"Not really. I received the invitation some time ago, but I
just decided we'll go."

"I see." She hid her annoyance. "And whose ball is this?"

"Skylar Prentiss's."

Claire frowned distractedly. "I cannot place him."

"He's a horse breeder from Virginia."

"We're going to a Kaintock ball?" she asked in amazement.

"*Oui.*" Philippe nodded. "Prentiss has a filly I wish to
purchase, but he's asking a great deal. I hope to convince him
to come down in price."

"For a friend?" she baited him.

"For a friend," Philippe growled. "As it happens, I do like
Prentiss. He's fair and I've never known him to be judgmen-
tal. One could do worse for a friend," he concluded accusingly.

"I agree." She sighed. "Of course, we shall go to the ball."

"*Très bien.*" Pivoting sharply, he strode toward the stable.

The next morning Claire and Beady rode to the French
Market to buy ribbon to match the gown Claire would wear to
the ball.

It was good to be out, Claire decided before her carriage had
even reached the end of the *allée* at Fortier House. After weeks
of isolation, she relished the ride into the bustling Vieux Carré.

Alighting on the banquette of Rue Royale, she paused, listening to the faint shouts of the vendors coming from the open
market. She spent a leisurely moment, ambling along the
sunny street, trailed by her maid, before performing the errand for which she had come to town.

When Claire finished her shopping, she summoned Beady.
"Come, I feel a great need for a praline, and I think the

woman who sells them on the steps of the cathedral has the very best, don't you?"

"Best in the Vieux Carré." The maid followed happily as her mistress led the way toward Place d'Armes, the heart of the French Quarter.

As they approached St. Louis Cathedral from Rue Conde, their way was blocked when a carriage pulled from the traffic to stop in front of them.

"Claire!" Henri called.

"Bonjour, Monsieur D'Estaigne," Claire greeted him cautiously. She had not seen the young Creole since the emotional day before the wedding. Though the smile on his face was sad as he looked down at her, Henri was as handsome and elegant as ever.

"Will you join me for a ride around the park?" he invited.

She sidled nervously in the face of his grave eagerness. *"Non, merci."*

"Why not? Because it isn't proper for you to be alone with me? We shall scarcely be alone." With a nod, he indicated the steady flow of traffic, as fashionable Creoles rode in carriages around the square. "Who could object to your riding with me in an open carriage right here in broad daylight? Please," he implored urgently. "I must talk to you."

"Henri, try to understand—"

"I understand that if you do not get into this carriage, I am getting out," he interrupted forcefully. "And I will follow you wherever you go today until you agree to talk to me." Opening the door of the phaeton, he offered his hand, confident of what her answer would be.

Sighing, Claire pressed a coin into her maid's hand. "You go and get a praline. I'll ride around the park once with Monsieur D'Estaigne, then I'll meet you at the carriage."

"But, mam'selle—"

"I'll be fine, Beady," she cut in quietly before the maid could object. "Monsieur D'Estaigne is right. Who could object to my riding with him in a crowd in broad daylight?"

Beady watched Claire step into Henri's rig. Her worried eyes followed the phaeton as it rolled past the cathedral and the government buildings, joining the traffic that looped slowly around the park.

"I'm glad you decided to ride with me, *chère*," Henri murmured, admiring Claire's profile beneath the straw brim of her hat.

"You gave me little choice," she replied stiffly. "I didn't want a scene on a public street."

"Is that the only reason you came?"

"*Oui*," she snapped. Then, because she could not bear his dejected demeanor, she amended, "*Non*, I've been worried about you, Henri. It's good to see you looking so well."

"Is it?" He gazed wistfully into her eyes.

"We've missed you at Fortier House," she explained hastily, looking away.

"Not Philippe," he muttered.

"*Mais oui*, Philippe. You're one of his oldest friends."

"We stopped being friends when he took you from me."

"He did not take me from you," she argued gently. "I couldn't marry you because I didn't love you."

"And you love him?" Henri demanded skeptically.

For a long moment, Claire stared at the pedestrians crisscrossing the square. At last she murmured, "I suppose I must."

"Just because you married him doesn't mean you must love him," he insisted. "I know yours is a marriage of convenience."

"And just how do you know that?" she inquired coldly.

"Philippe told me you had a business agreement. A business agreement," he repeated painfully, "when you could have had love."

"Philippe told you that?" A wave of fury swept over Claire.

Framing his earnest plea, Henri did not notice her heightened color or the tears of anger in her eyes. "Listen to me, *chère*," he begged, "you don't have to accept his shabby treatment. I've heard about his recklessness and how he already neglects you. It's shameful."

"And it's no affair of yours," she responded tersely.

"But I love you. I could take you away...to Paris or—"

"Stop, Henri, please. I am a married woman."

"How good of you to remember," an icy voice cut in, and a shadow fell across Claire.

She looked up to discover her husband, astride Lagniappe, riding alongside the carriage. So engrossed were they in their conversation that neither she nor Henri had seen when Philippe passed them. Already in a bad mood after a trip to Prosper LaBiche's office, he had wheeled his horse with a curse in the middle of the narrow, crowded street and set off after the couple.

Now, rising in his stirrups, he loomed over his wife, scowling furiously. One strong arm snaked around her waist and he scooped her roughly from the carriage seat, holding her so her back was pressed against his saddle and the lower half of her body dangled against his lean flank.

"You'll pardon Claire, *s'il vous plaît,* Henri," Philippe said politely. He nodded in farewell and urged Lagniappe to a trot, causing Claire's teeth to jar with every step.

She shifted in his grip, seeking a more stable position. Philippe's arm tightened around her waist and he put his mouth close to her ear to murmur, "Do not even think of struggling, *ma petite,* or I'll drop you on your fine derriere right in the middle of the street."

"Whether you drop me or I fall," she gritted, "the result will be the same." Her face burning, Claire felt herself being hauled up into the saddle in front of Philippe, the pommel poking her, as bystanders pointed from the banquette.

Claire stiffened in her precarious, uncomfortable seat, sitting erect in order to touch the man as little as possible. She demanded, "How could you humiliate me this way?"

"I might ask you the same question," he snarled.

"I? Humiliate you?" Claire repeated disbelievingly. "How on earth did you reach that conclusion?"

"People talk when a wife carries on with a man other than her husband in public," Philippe answered tersely.

Claire did not bother to point out that riding with a man in his carriage was not quite the same as "carrying on." Instead, she countered coldly, "People also talk when a man hangs his wife from his saddle like a bag of rice."

Philippe did not reply, but now that his fury was past, he saw how passersby gawked at Lagniappe and his double burden with genuine amazement. The people of the Vieux Carré would not soon forget this sight.

"Where are you taking me?" Claire asked icily.

"To your carriage. I saw it as I rode in." He was silent for a moment, then he asked, "What did you and Henri have to discuss that was so important you made a laughingstock of me?"

"I didn't make you a laughingstock," his wife responded. "You did it yourself when you yanked me from the carriage. Perhaps you could tell me why you told Henri of our agreement."

"The one in which you agreed to play the role of proper wife?" he growled.

"I play the part of wife much better than you play husband.... Husband," Claire jeered. "I see my role as spouse, not hypocrite. My visit today with Henri was open for all to see. I do not creep around to *placée* cottages after dark."

"Is that what you think?" the Creole asked incredulously.

"Don't tell me Lila Broussard is not your mistress," she snapped. "I've heard the rumors."

"And you believe them?" he asked flatly.

"Do you deny them?"

"Would it matter?" he grated. "I suspect nothing I say would make a difference to you."

They approached Claire's carriage, where Beady waited. Her mouth stuffed with sticky praline and her eyes bulging nervously, the maid watched as Philippe reined Lagniappe to a halt and deposited Claire on her feet beside the rig none too gently.

"Take Madame Girard home, Ezra," he commanded the coachman curtly. "Straight home."

Then, wheeling his horse, he disappeared down the sun-baked street in a cloud of dust. Cursing Claire's unbending will under his breath, Philippe urged the huge animal around the corner as if pursued by demons. Lagniappe sensed his master's agitation and danced and reared nervously. The man reined him to a halt and, speaking softly, tried to calm him.

While he waited for his mount to quiet, Philippe mopped his brow and looked around. A reckless glint came to his eye. It was fate: he was in front of Lila's shop.

If he was accused, the Creole mused, he might as well be guilty. He had not seen the octoroon for months. And after his latest confrontation with Claire, he could not think of why he had stayed away. Lila was a soft, yielding woman and she had said in her note—was it last week or the week before?—that she wanted to see him. He had neglected her, but he would correct that failure now.

Tying his horse to a hitching post, Philippe strode up the steps to the raised banquette.

Lila was standing near a window when she saw him. Her eyes widened, and without a word she opened the door. The man glanced quickly up and down the deserted street, a practice born of habit, and ducked into the shop. Impatiently, he waited while she pulled the shades and locked the door.

Unable to contain her delight, Lila threw herself against his chest. "Oh, Philippe, you shouldn't have come," she gushed, rubbing her cheek against his crisp white shirt, "but I'm glad you did."

Philippe wrapped his arms around the woman, who molded her body to his. He ran his hands over the familiar contours, feeling her warmth through her silk dress. But to his astonishment, no passion overcame him, no mindless arousal, no feeling at all. He stood very still, his arms wrapped awkwardly around her and a puzzled expression on his face.

The octoroon did not seem to notice his quandary. She gazed up at him adoringly. "I knew you'd come back," she whispered. "I'll be the best *cher amie* a man ever had, I vow to you."

"I'm not here to speak of vows," he muttered.

"Why are you here?" she asked suggestively, her voice husky with desire.

Frowning, he looked down at her. She was the reason he had come—the woman in his arms, ripe and ready for loving. Her seductive amber eyes and full lips held the unspoken promise of pleasure. Why the hell didn't he feel something?

Crushing her to his chest, he kissed her, his demanding lips bruising hers. Brutally, he sought the soaring passion that had marked their lovemaking, but still he felt nothing.

With a frustrated groan, he thrust her from him. Lila's eyes flew open and she regarded him with hurt surprise.

"What's wrong, *cher?*"

"Nothing. Nothing is wrong, but I can't stay here." He made his way hastily to the front of the shop.

"Will you come to my house later?" The petite octoroon rushed after him, trying to match his long strides.

"Soon," he lied.

"Tonight?"

"Not tonight."

"*Très bien, mon amour* . . . soon," she said, sighing dejectedly.

The man planted a cursory kiss on top of her head and left the shop before she could say another word. Lila watched sadly as the door swung closed behind him, the shade fluttering crazily in the breeze.

The next evening at Fortier House, Claire appeared at the top of the stairs, clad in a simple pale blue gown. Diamonds shone at her ears, but no necklace marred the expanse of white skin revealed by her plunging décolletage. Her sleek dark hair was swept back and woven with silvery ribbons. To her waiting husband, she looked like an ice queen as she descended.

She had not spoken to him since the day before and her eyes, as they rested on him, were cold. What would melt her frosty exterior? Philippe wondered. Provoked by his troublesome thoughts, he snapped, "Come, we'll be late if we do not hurry."

The man brooded on the ride to the American section of the city, angry—at whom he was not sure—about the incident with Lila. What was wrong with him? He had always done what he wanted. But now, to his amazement, he no longer wanted Lila. Somehow that lack of desire was connected to Claire. What was she doing to him? He shifted his eyes toward his wife accusingly. She leaned back in the seat with her eyes closed. As if she had not a worry in the world, he thought sourly.

Claire's eyes were indeed closed, but she was painfully aware of the baleful looks her husband directed at her. She was tired—tired of scenes and arguments and recriminations. If only they could forget their differences, even for one night.

She was able to put her problems away for a while when the carriage pulled up in front to the enormous house on St. Charles Avenue.

"Girard, you old horse thief!" Skylar Prentiss boomed, detaching himself from a cluster of people near the door and coming to greet the new arrivals.

"*Bonsoir,* Skylar." Philippe grinned as his hand was swallowed by his host's ham-sized fist.

"Glad y'all could make it tonight, my boy." He slapped his guest on the back and pumped his hand enthusiastically.

The big, middle-aged man was as imposing as his home. His elegantly cut coat did not hide the power of his impressive figure, tall with a girth to match. His handsome face was friendly under a thatch of blond hair and he smiled down at Claire with undisguised admiration.

"So this is your wife. Skylar Prentiss at your service ma'am." He made a courtly bow. "I heard you were lovely, my dear, but the word doesn't do you justice. Come along and meet my own beautiful wife. Nancy," he bellowed, elbowing his way through the crowd to throw an arm around the shoulders of a short, dumpy woman.

To describe their hostess as plain would have been charitable. Plump and florid with dark eyebrows that nearly met over her twinkling blue eyes, it was obvious Nancy Prentiss had never been a beauty. It was just as obvious her husband adored her.

"Who do we have here, Skylar?" She peered at the couple through stubby eyelashes.

"Philippe and Claire Girard, Nan," he announced officiously before dropping his voice to a whisper. "The newlyweds I told you about. Folks, this is my Nancy."

"Welcome!" A warm smile transformed her face, and she motioned to her companions. "Madame and Monsieur Girard," she said, awkward with the French greetings, "may I present Mademoiselle Monique Freneau of the American Theater Company. This is Mr. Chase, our neighbor, and here are Leland and Bettina, our son and daughter-in-law."

"What about us, Aunt Nan?" a male voice asked teasingly.

"Yes," bellowed another, "we thought we were the reason for this jubilee."

Claire and Philippe turned to see two young men strolling toward them. Tall, muscular and blond, the twins were identical right down to the dimples that framed their affable smiles.

"Mr. and Mrs. Girard, these handsome rascals are Skylar's sister's boys, Luke and John Bennett," Nancy said fondly. "They're visiting from Richmond."

From inside the ballroom, a fanfare sounded. "Time for the festivities to start," Skylar announced, peering at his pocket watch. "C'mon, Nan, they're waitin' for us to dance the first dance.

"Hope you'll save the first reel for me, Mrs. Girard," he said as he offered his arm to his wife. "If y'all will excuse us— come, my love."

"But I'm not ready, Sky. I've been greeting guests and haven't even looked at a mirror," the woman fussed, patting at her graying hair. "I probably look a sight."

"Darlin', you're as lovely now as on the night we were wed." The man's serious reply floated back as he escorted her to the dance floor.

Bemused, Claire allowed Philippe to lead her into the ballroom. In its center, Skylar bowed and his Nancy curtsied prettily. When the host and hostess had made a complete round of the floor, other couples joined them, forming an ever-shifting kaleidoscope of silk skirts and sparkling jewels.

"What are you thinking?" Philippe asked, noticing Claire's thoughtful expression as they danced.

"That they really love each other," she blurted, then blushed at revealing her thoughts.

"Do you think marriage is a battle for everyone?" He regarded her wryly.

"No, just for us, I suppose." She sighed.

"Perhaps we should call a truce this evening, madame," her husband suggested softly.

Concealing her surprise with a smile, Claire agreed. "A truce, Philippe."

Smiling himself, the man waltzed his wife through the open doors and out onto the veranda.

"What are you doing?" she questioned.

"Seeking a private place where we may seal our pact." Philippe was no longer dancing, but he continued to hold her in his arms.

Claire's heart raced as she remembered the last time they had sealed a bargain—in the hayloft. Shyly she met his eyes. In them she saw no arrogance, no challenge, as he bent to kiss her, his lips claiming hers tenderly. The kiss they shared was like none before and when they parted, both were shaken.

"Claire, I—" Philippe began huskily.

"Where's my partner?" Skylar's voice carried over the lively tune coming from the ballroom. "Claire Girard promised me the first reel!"

Grimacing good-naturedly, Philippe released his wife and they went inside, hand in hand.

"There you are! What're you two up to?" their host greeted them. "C'mon, gal, time to shake a leg."

While Philippe paired off with Nancy, Skylar led Claire onto the floor for a rollicking Virginia reel. By the end of the dance, the horse breeder was flushed and breathless.

"Stand back, Uncle, and give a younger man a chance," one of Skylar's teenage nephews suggested. "That is, if it's all right with you, ma'am."

"I'd be delighted," Claire agreed graciously.

"Good, good," Skylar boomed. "Hope you don't mind, but I have to discuss some business with that husband of yours. Luke here—"

"John," the lad corrected.

"John'll take good care of you. We won't be too long."

"Merci."

"No, ma'am, thank *you*." John grinned and swung her onto the floor energetically.

The twirling couple did not see Philippe's ominous expression as he watched them, considering whether to reclaim his wife. But before the young Creole could act, Skylar hailed him.

"Philippe, I'd like to talk to you about that filly you seem so interested in. Would you join me for a brandy?"

"My pleasure, sir," he responded cordially.

"Don't worry about Claire," his host reassured him. "I figure the twins'll take good care of her."

"So I see," Philippe muttered, staring at his wife and the young blond giant. Suddenly, he knew the answers to the questions he had asked himself earlier. He had been without a woman for longer than he cared to consider; now he realized the only woman he wanted was Claire. He wanted her to desire him as much as he desired her. He wanted to go to her now. He wanted to tell her, but his pride would not let him. Philippe Girard had never been jealous in his life.

As he and his host made their way to the library, they were stopped several times by Skylar's guests. A hospitable man, the big Virginian had a moment for everyone. Each time they were delayed, he glanced apologetically at Philippe, but the young man did not seem to notice. His eyes were fixed on his wife as she stood, smiling, between the Bennett twins, who vied good-naturedly for her attention.

"You see, ma'am," Luke was saying, "our parents kinda got a New Testament theme goin'. Our older brothers are named Matthew and Mark. Then there was us—Luke and John.''

"So they started worryin'. If we had a younger brother, should they name him Acts of the Apostles?'' John interjected.

"They were so relieved when our sister was born—'' Luke said.

"That they named her Gloria Anne Bennett,'' John picked up the story again. "We call her Glory-B.''

Claire's laughter died when she looked up and saw Philippe glowering at her from across the room. She still tingled at the memory of his recent kiss, but now her heart sank. The look on his face surely signaled another battle to come.

"Don't look now, Girard,'' Skylar whooped, "but I think we've got a clear shot for the library. Run for it, boy!''

Hoping to catch Claire's eye again, Philippe glanced toward where she had stood, but she was no longer there. He did not have to search to know she was dancing with one of the Bennetts. Wrathfully, he stalked behind Prentiss to the study.

When the Creole emerged from the study, Claire was waiting for him. "There you are,'' she greeted him, tucking her arm into his. "It's nearly time for the midnight supper and I was afraid I was going to have to eat alone.''

"I imagine there was little fear of that,'' he answered curtly.

"I thought we had a truce this evening, Philippe,'' she reminded him in a subdued voice.

Swallowing another harsh remark, he answered contritely, "So we do, *chère.* I'm sorry.''

Quietly, the couple joined the other guests at the buffet. With full plates, they joined a small group clustered on chairs and benches in a corner of the ballroom, chatting while they ate.

Seated beside Philippe, Claire could not help but notice Monique Freneau sat very close to him on the other side of the long bench they shared, seizing any opportunity to lay a hand on his arm or to cast an inviting glance toward him. Philippe met the actress's flirtation with a lazy grace, gratified to feel a tinge of annoyance in Claire's manner.

"Oh, a waltz!'' Monique clapped her hands with delight when the musicians began to play again. "Monsieur Girard, I think you are the only man here tonight who has not danced with me.''

"Then let us rectify that mistake, mademoiselle," Philippe answered smoothly. "You will excuse me?" He bowed politely to his wife and led the other woman onto the dance floor, determined to give Claire a taste of her own medicine.

She did indeed feel a flicker of anger as she watched them leave the small party in the corner, but she did not have time to dwell on it. She was soon joined by her host and hostess.

From the dance floor, Philippe watched Claire, chatting with Skylar. Half-listening to the voluble Monique, he suddenly wished the music would end and that he had never set out to make his wife jealous. For all the good it did, he thought bitterly. She did not even seem to notice his absence.

When the waltz was over and one of Monique's admirers had claimed her, Philippe made his way toward Claire, who now sat alone, watching the dancers. Before he could reach her, his view was blocked by two identical muscular backs.

"You have to choose one or the other of us, Miss Claire, or break both our hearts," one of the Bennetts was saying as Philippe approached.

"Gentlemen, how can I make such a difficult decision?" she asked merrily.

At her jesting tone, her husband's eyes narrowed. He tapped one brawny shoulder impatiently. "*Pardon,* monsieur."

The twins turned as one. In the space between them, Claire was revealed, her beaming face upturned. Her smile faded when Philippe announced, "It's time to go home, madame."

"Must you?" Luke cried in disappointment.

"We must," Philippe grated, taking Claire's hand and dragging her from her seat.

"Wish you didn't have to leave. The ball won't be nearly as much fun without the belle," John said gallantly.

"It is not the custom in New Orleans for a married woman to be the belle of the ball," the Creole snapped.

"I reckon me and my brother aren't too up on your customs yet," John replied slowly. "We didn't mean any offense. We just thought Miss Claire was the prettiest gal here tonight."

"In that case, there's another custom of which I should make you aware," Philippe explained arrogantly. "One man does not pay court to another man's wife."

"Well, we've got a custom, too, mister," Luke interjected hotly, towering over Philippe. "If a fellow gets too cantankerous, we invite him out back and beat some manners into him."

"Or to the Dueling Oaks?" the Creole asked dangerously.

"If you want."

"Enough!" Claire exploded. "Luke, John, I believe your aunt is looking for you."

The young men looked around, seemingly relieved by the break in the tension.

"It was a pleasure to meet you both. Please tell Madame Prentiss that we regret we must leave so suddenly," she continued with a glance at Philippe, who was white-faced with fury. "I fear I'm developing a headache and must go home at once." Taking her husband's arm, she regarded him imperiously. "Shall we?"

Not a word was spoken between them until the couple settled into their carriage. At last Claire ventured tentatively, "When I talked to Monsieur Prentiss earlier, he said you and he are to meet on Monday."

"So you also interfered in my business?" Philippe turned a harsh face toward his wife.

"I don't know what you mean."

"You know damned well what I mean. I can tend to my own business and fight my own battles. I do not need my wife to fight them for me."

"I didn't fight your battle. I stopped it." Undaunted, Claire met his narrowed stare.

"It amounts to the same thing." The man stared moodily out at the dark landscape. "I warn you, don't ever interfere again."

"Have no fear, Philippe," she assured him through clenched teeth. "The next time, you and your opponent can cut each other to ribbons for all I care."

With that, Claire settled into the corner for the long ride back to Fortier House.

The sound of hammers rang in the twilight as carpenters hurried to finish the new grandstand in time for the big race. Alone in his cramped office, Philippe did not hear them. He brooded, his feet on his desk, his chair propped back on two legs. No lamps were lit, but the door was open to admit the waning light as the sun dipped behind the buildings of the stable yard. A cooling breeze wafted into the office, mingling with the pungent odors of tobacco and liniment.

Philippe's ancient chair creaked as he opened a drawer in the cluttered rolltop desk. Pulling out a bottle of bourbon and a battered tin cup, he poured himself a healthy drink and settled back to gaze dolefully around the tiny room. Through the tack room door, he could see the narrow cot on which he had slept for the past week, his eyes lingering on it in disgust.

Damn Claire, he thought peevishly, he could not live with her, did not want to live without her. He was miserable here in self-imposed exile among the gnats and mosquitoes. And for what? She was so damned proud and inflexible, she had not even bothered to inquire about his whereabouts.

Perhaps it was partly his fault, he admitted grudgingly to himself. He had been hard on her the last time they met. But she should never have interfered in his business.

Philippe had recognized Claire's meddling that sunny Monday morning after the ball when he inspected the filly in the stable yard behind Skylar's house. When he made an offer, the Virginian did not dicker or balk. He almost gave the horse away.

Philippe needed the filly—badly. Hyacinth's death was a loss that could prove disastrous to the future of his stables. Forced to face facts, he drew himself up, swallowed his pride and nearly choked with the effort.

"You have a deal, Monsieur Prentiss." Philippe offered a reluctant hand to seal the bargain. "If you'll draw up the contract, I'll send a bank draft this afternoon. And my groom will pick her up tomorrow."

"Agreed." Skylar shook hands firmly, his eyebrows raised questioningly at the young Creole's formal manner.

As Philippe galloped away, Nancy appeared in the back door, wiping her hands on her apron. "What on earth?" she asked.

"Philippe Girard." Skylar walked up the steps, shaking his head. "I think he's perturbed that I didn't haggle. Guess I made it too easy.

"I don't know," he sighed. "Creoles are proud and that boy is as Creole as they come. Sometimes I wonder why I do business with those fellers at all."

"Why did you sell that filly? You said she's going to be one of the finest racehorses in Louisiana."

"Part of the reason I sold her," he replied enigmatically.

"Talk sense, Sky." His wife frowned up at him.

"Well, you see, my love," he explained, throwing an arm over her shoulders, "I've got the best with Sweet William. Rose of Sharon is showing lots of promise, too. But I like competition. What fun is racing if you know which horse is gonna win? Besides, I like Girard. A man who names his horses after flowers can't be all bad."

"So you've told me for years," Nancy teased. Companionably, the couple went into the house, forgetting about the young Creole and his injured dignity.

The wounds to Philippe's pride festered through the sultry day. When he returned home that evening, he sought his wife on the veranda where she sat, hoping for a breeze.

Taking the seat beside her, he propped one booted foot on the railing and announced, "I bought that filly from Prentiss today."

"That's wonderful, Philippe." Claire smiled toward where he sat in the darkness.

"You don't seem surprised."

"I knew you'd work it out."

Certain his suspicions were correct, he scowled at her. "You knew?"

"I supposed you would." She frowned perplexedly.

He pounced on her answer. "Which was it? You knew or you supposed?"

Anger flared in her eyes. "Get to the point, Philippe."

"You knew Prentiss would nearly give me the filly—because you asked him to."

"And when am I supposed to have done that?"

Philippe shrugged expressively. "You danced with him. You talked to him. Did you tell him the fate of Girard Stables hangs in the balance? I'm sure a word from the distressed bride, especially one as lovely as you, would make all the difference to a chivalrous Virginian."

Claire got to her feet furiously, but Philippe blocked her way. The frustration he had contained for weeks bubbled to the surface and his temper erupted in a flood of angry words.

"Prentiss is as big a fool as I am, if that's possible," he roared. "He fell victim to your charm, thinking you and I are loving partners in marriage, in business, in everything." He laughed bitterly. "We share a name, madame, and that's all."

Claire winced at his words, glad he could not see her clearly in the darkness, but she said coolly, "Don't say anything else, Philippe. We may both be sorry later."

"I'm already sorry." The man prowled the veranda. "I'm sorry I met you, sorry I married you, and sorrier still that we make each other miserable.

"You avoid me." His argument veered in a new direction and he returned to his wife, his closeness daring her to retreat. "Yet Henri D'Estaigne, one of my oldest friends, threatened to kill me over you. Even those pups, Prentiss's nephews, were smitten. And all because you encourage every man who comes near you. Why do you do it?" He seized her arms and stared furiously into her eyes.

"I do not encourage anyone," she snapped, wresting her arms from his grip. But she did not retreat. Her chest heaved with anger and Philippe was dimly aware of the heady scent of her perfume, but he would not be deterred from his rage.

"*Non,* you do not encourage men, madame, not even me," he snarled. "Mark me well, Claire, I will not be manipulated by any woman, especially by a wife who won't share her bed with me."

"You share your bed with someone else, m'sieur," she hissed. "Surely you remember that, although it is of little import to me."

For an instant, Philippe loomed over his wife, rigid with rage. Then, abruptly, the fight seemed to leave him and he stepped back. "If that's what you choose to believe, I cannot dissuade you." He sighed wearily.

Imperiously, she swept past him toward the door.

"Claire," he called softly, set on firing the parting shot.

A slender silhouette framed by the candle-lit doorway, she looked back at him.

"You know a funny thing, my love?" he drawled quietly. "Prentiss names his horses after flowers, too. This filly's name is one you should appreciate."

"What is it?" she asked dully.

"Touch-me-not." Her husband chuckled mirthlessly. "He named her after a cold Northern flower, Touch-me-not. You're beautiful kindred spirits, *oui?*"

Without a word, Claire went into the house.

The memories of that exchange were bitter and ugly when Philippe awakened the next morning. They stayed with him the entire sweltering day. He returned home from the track, hoping to speak with Claire, but she refused to see him.

He ate alone in the huge dining room, then he rode to the stables to spend a lonely night in his office, vowing not to return to Fortier House until he had made peace with his wife. Tomorrow, he thought, tomorrow they would put an end to the fighting.

Six tomorrows had passed and he was still sleeping at the stable, Philippe thought dismally, pouring another drink. He should have known better.

As the night air cooled the stifling office, it carried with it the sweet scent of pine and unbidden recollections of a trip to the lake. Suddenly the man sat his chair down with a thud. Things could not go on this way. He needed to see Claire. He had to talk to her, to see if her eyes held indifference or anger or the unconscious tenderness of an unguarded moment. It could be worth the chance he took if he could put aside his pride for one hour.

Chapter Sixteen

"Mam'selle, it's near dark. Don't you think you better come on down?" Slapping at mosquitoes, Beady hailed her mistress in the tree house.

"I'll be in later," Claire called down, appearing at the rail.

"Gonna be real dark soon," the maid argued gloomily, "when *loup-garou* prowls. You kin hear him bayin' at th' moon sometimes."

"I don't believe in werewolves."

"Don't say that," Beady begged, looking around uneasily. Then she issued a more practical warning. "If th' *loup-garou* don't get you, the skeeters will."

"Not up here." Claire's answer floated down to her.

"I s'pose," she agreed dubiously, slapping a fat insect that threatened to drain her ankle dry. It was getting darker by the moment. "Well," she said with a sigh at last, "I'll be in th' house."

In her latticework tower, Claire stared moodily at the sunset reflected in watery, open patches of hyacinth-covered marshlands in the distance. Moss-hung trees jutted through the water here and there to break up the flat expanse of horizon. Above them, the fleecy clouds were tinted scarlet and orange, which faded gently to rose and purple, then to the dusky blue of the evening sky.

How could she have done it? she pondered miserably. How could she have fallen in love with Philippe? How could she love an arrogant, unpredictable man who was sorry he had married her? Confronted with the enormity of the lie she had been living for the past few months, she admitted to herself that she had married him because she wanted to, because she loved him, had always loved him—in spite of herself.

But Philippe had left Fortier House in a rage and she had not seen him since. All week, her pride had not allowed her to summon him from the house of his *placée*. Now it was too late.

Claire's thoughts turned suddenly fierce. She would do just fine without him. She should be glad her sham marriage had ended so soon. But the tears she shed alone in her bed at night were first tears of sorrow and loss, only later of anger.

Anger was the reason she had returned to the Mercantile. After several lonely days, she had decided to go on with her life. She would argue it out with Philippe when—or if—he came home.

As if beckoned by her melancholy thoughts, the man rode slowly up the shadowy *allée* toward the lantern-lit veranda. From the tree house, Claire could not see the way Lagniappe's sides heaved or the lather that flecked his hide, evidence he had galloped all the way from the track. It seemed to the girl that the horse and rider ambled leisurely as if they were returning from no more than a pleasant evening's ride instead of a week's absence.

Philippe dismounted in front of the house and handed the reins to a groom, lingering a moment. Then the master of Fortier House strolled across the lawn toward the tree house. Claire saw him clearly in the moonlight, her heart pounding at his presence. She drew deeper into the shadows and watched through the branches beneath her as he paused to light a cigar.

Afraid to breathe for fear of discovery, she willed him to walk on, but he found a location to his liking, facing the house. Loosening his cravat, Philippe leaned one muscular shoulder against the massive tree trunk and smoked.

He was very still so his peace would not be disturbed by the swarms of insects that could be seen against the illumination of the house. Claire could smell the smoke and, if she craned her neck to peer over the half wall, she could see the glow at the end of his cigar brighten, then dim in the darkness.

"Claire," he said in a hushed voice, almost as if he were talking to himself.

"*Oui?*" Disconcerted at being discovered, she struggled to keep her voice as quiet as her husband's.

"We'll be going to the celebration at the track tomorrow."
His voice drifted up to her with the smoke.

"I'm in no mood to celebrate, Philippe."

"Touch-me-not is running, so it's important that I be
there," he explained calmly. "All New Orleans will be there
and my wife must be at my side." His tone made it clear there
was no room for discussion.

"I will not go to that hot, dusty track just to be window
dressing for you," she responded calmly, without malice.

Philippe flexed his shoulders tensely, but he did not look up.
Chewing impatiently on his cigar, he growled, "You have no
choice, madame. You must go."

"I won't be bullied, Philippe."

"Then do as I say."

"Is this why you came home? To quarrel?" she asked sadly.

"I came to tell you we're going to the track tomorrow," he
answered.

"I still say I'm not going."

"And I say you are." With a sudden violent movement, he
tossed his cigar into the darkness, the bright ember descend-
ing end over end until it disappeared from view. Turning, he
glared up at his wife, her face a pale blur in the tree house.

"You'll go tomorrow, Claire, if I have to carry you there,"
he warned dangerously.

"You wouldn't!" Her voice lashed out.

"Wouldn't I?" Deliberately, Philippe mounted the circular
staircase around the tree trunk. His face, white and set under
his hat, became visible through the trapdoor entrance, followed by broad shoulders.

"What are you going to do, Philippe?" She rose defiantly
and looked her husband in the eye, her very bearing a challenge. "Toss me around as if I were a bag of rice again, the way
you did at Place d'Armes?"

"If I must," he said hoarsely, seizing her shoulders. "I
swear, sometimes I just want to shake some sense into you."

In the dimness, he could see her upturned face very close to
his. Lips parted, she waited breathlessly to see what he would
do. With a soft curse, he lowered his mouth to hers. Her lips
met his tentatively, and they shared a kiss that was achingly
sweet and tender. His grip loosened and he slid his hands down
her arms lightly, causing her to shiver at his touch.

In awe of her emotions, she withdrew and rested her head on his shoulder. Cupping her chin, he lifted her face and gazed down at her, his passion unmistakable in his dark eyes.

"I want you, Claire," he whispered. "No other woman will do. No other woman makes me feel as you do."

"No other woman?" Suddenly Claire's enraptured expression disappeared and she jerked away from him. After a week's absence with no word, he expected to come home, kiss his wife and pick up where he had left off. And all the while, he would be comparing her to another woman—to Lila.

"No other woman...." Philippe repeated, baffled by her abrupt change of manner. "What is wrong with you?"

"I'll tell you what's wrong," she spat. "You come to me from the arms of your *placée* and expect me to believe that you love me."

"Perhaps I should set the record straight once and for all," he drawled mildly, fixing his wife with a level gaze. "First, I have no *placée*. And second, I said nothing about love."

"No, you didn't," Claire murmured, mortified. Then she bolted down the stairs, leaving him alone with a longing ache.

Philippe slumped on a cushioned bench and lit another cigar. Why did Claire have this effect on him? No other woman made him so angry. No other woman haunted his thoughts. *No other woman,* he thought savagely.

When the light was extinguished in Claire's room, Philippe left the tree house and trudged to where Lagniappe waited. As he rode into the night, he did not know that his wife stood at her darkened window and sadly watched him go.

It was still early when Claire padded downstairs, barefoot and sleepy and sluggish from the heat. To her amazement, Philippe was waiting at the breakfast table, crisp and cool in his best clothes.

He frowned when she slumped into her chair. "Why haven't you dressed yet? I told you last night, we must leave early."

"And I told you, I'm not going," she answered, sipping her coffee.

One eyebrow arched cynically, her husband set down his cup with a clatter. "Don't oppose me, Claire. Don't you remember what I said last night?"

"I remember," she retorted.

"Well?" He smiled at her in arrogant expectation.

"Well?" She mimicked his expression defiantly.

Without a word, Philippe folded his napkin and laid it beside his plate. Then he rose calmly and walked around the end of the table where he loomed over her. When he spoke, his tone was pleasant. Only the flinty gleam in his eyes revealed his annoyance.

"I told you, my darling wife," he said softly, "that I would carry you to the track if I had to." In one smooth move, he hauled her from her seat and slung her over his shoulder as if she weighed no more than the sack of rice they had discussed the night before.

Claire was motionless for a moment, taken aback, gasping to catch the breath his unexpected maneuver had knocked out of her. The blood rushed to her head, reaching her brain the same instant as the heat of fury, and she began to fight, kicking her feet and pummeling his back with doubled fists.

"Philippe Girard, you put me down!" Planting one hand firmly against his muscled back, she braced herself and arched her body in an attempt to straighten.

"I warned you, but you wouldn't listen." He swatted her squirming derriere vigorously and carried her into the hall.

"Greer," Philippe addressed the astonished butler as if his rebellious burden were not at all out of the ordinary, "please have some *café* sent up to my wife's room. She won't be joining me for breakfast this morning. Because," he proclaimed loudly, setting her on her feet with a thud at the bottom of the stairs, "she'll be upstairs, dressing for the races.

"Now," he told the dumbfounded girl, "go and prepare yourself. The carriage will be ready in twenty minutes. No more, no less. Don't make me come for you," he advised when she opened her mouth to protest, "because I will."

Biting back an angry retort, Claire spun on her heel and ascended the stairs with as much dignity as she could muster. In the hall, away from his view, she rubbed her stinging posterior and marched to her room. Slamming the door as hard as she could, she locked it behind her.

Claire paced in front of the fireplace, muttering. Her husband was a cad; he was abusive; he was— Her bravado evaded her when a knock sounded at the door.

With relief, she recognized Beady's voice. "Mam'selle Claire, lemme in."

"Are you alone?" Claire asked suspiciously.

"*Oui.* I gots you some *café.*"

Claire opened the door as little as possible and yanked the maid into the room. Rapidly she clicked the lock back into place.

"Careful, *mam'selle,*" Beady scolded, her eyes fixed on the cup and saucer in an effort not to spill the hot liquid. Placing it carefully on the table beside the bed, she turned to look at her mistress and her eyes widened in dismay.

"Why ain't you gettin' dressed?" she said with a gasp.

"Because I am not going," Claire explained calmly.

"But you gots to," Beady argued. "And M'sieur Philippe is gonna be real mad if you make him late."

"No, he won't. Because you're going to tell him I have a headache and can't go."

"Oh, no, mam'selle. Please don't make me do that."

"Don't worry." She hauled Beady heartlessly to the door and thrust her into the hall. "If Philippe is angry, he'll be angry at me."

Poised at her locked door, she listened for Beady's reluctant footfall on the stairs. Then she settled in a chair by the window with her coffee.

Claire's tranquillity was soon disturbed by a bellow from downstairs. Almost at once, she heard Philippe's booted feet pounding up the stairs.

"What's this foolishness?" he shouted, beating on the door. The knob jiggled and the infuriated yell came. "Open this door!"

"There's no need, my darling husband," she answered sweetly. "I told you several times, I'm not going to the races. You go ahead."

The silence from the hall was ominous. "Claire, I'm warning you. Open this door," he ordered.

She refused to answer, hoping he would give up and go without her. Suddenly the door gave way in a shower of splintering wood. Claire scrambled to her feet, sending her coffee cup flying, and regarded Philippe with consternation. Framed by the doorway, he stood, one polished boot still raised. The terrified Beady peeped out from behind him for a split second before she bolted for the stairs.

Composing himself, Philippe straightened his vest and stepped over the ruins of the door. "I told you there would be no locked doors between us," he reminded his wife mildly.

She recovered enough to reply, "It seems there no longer are."

"I see you're still not dressed." He looked her over disapprovingly. She glared at him, her mounting anger overcoming the awe she felt at his display of fury.

"Can you not find something to wear? I'm sure you must have something." He flung open her chiffonier, smiling grimly when he saw the array of gowns and petticoats inside. Pulling them out in an untidy, multicolored mass, he held them out questioningly.

"Nothing here pleases you?" He tossed his load carelessly onto the bed and returned to the wardrobe. "Why not one of these?" He grabbed more and threw them on top of the others, then more and more before he began to rummage through the shelves, ignoring Claire's sputtering protest.

"Choose a dress, *chère*." He gestured absently toward the rumpled heap on the bed. "I'll find a hat for you."

Livid with anger, Claire watched as he cleared the shelf of hatboxes with a sweep of his arm. They tumbled to the floor and rolled, spilling a profusion of ribbons and feathers. Treading on her favorite bonnet, he inspected the neat rows of shoes aligned on the closet floor. Seizing handfuls of slippers, without regard to where their partners were, he hurled them on top of the pile of clothes on the bed.

"And let us not forget pantaloons," he said grandly, headed toward the bureau.

Pushed to the limit of her tolerance, Claire pounced at him. "Are you quite finished?"

"Almost." Philippe halted and scooped her into his arms, eliciting a howl of outrage from her as he dumped her onto the bed.

His hands on his hips, he scowled down at his wife as she sprawled atop the colorful heap of garments. "Now, madame," he snarled, "dress yourself, or by God, I will do it for you."

"I will. Just get out." She glared at him and shifted to dislodge the heel of a slipper that prodded her backside.

"You have fifteen minutes," he grated, "before I come back and carry you to the racetrack, dressed or not." With that, he stomped from the room, contemptuously ignoring the shoe that whizzed past his head.

Claire scrambled off the bed and ran to close the shattered door with shaking hands. She wasted no more time attempting to repair it than she spent trying to understand what had just occurred. Her stomach roiled and her head ached in truth now.

Numbly, she sorted through the conglomeration of clothes on the bed until she found a suitable gown for the August heat, a cool muslin dress of pale yellow.

"I found this in th' hall," Beady mumbled as she returned. She would never understand these two, she thought as she offered Claire one white pump. "Guess y'all lost it when you and M'sieur Philippe was . . . er . . . talkin'."

"Come and find the other one," her mistress ordered frantically. "I have to get ready now!"

Obligingly, Beady assisted her, and within fifteen minutes Claire was miraculously dressed and downstairs.

"Where is Monsieur Girard?" she asked Greer.

"He . . . er . . . said he had to be at the track early, so he's already gone," the butler informed her, looking as if he wished he were anyplace else. "Ezra's waiting to take you in the carriage."

After that deplorable scene, Philippe was not even here, Claire fumed. She toyed briefly with the idea of staying at home, but discarded it. If he came back for her, it would be even worse.

Brandishing her furled parasol like a weapon, she charged out to the carriage, leaving Greer on the veranda, looking baffled but relieved.

Claire found herself relaxing as the carriage drove along the Bayou Road to the track. On either side of the road, among massive trees whose limbs were shrouded by Spanish moss, white egrets waded in green, brackish water. The water's surface was barely visible between patches of purple and white water hyacinths, so abundant they looked as if they could be walked upon. Dragonflies, or mosquito hawks, hovered above them, the sun glinting on their iridescent wings.

At last the strange, unearthly beauty of the swamp gave way to a solid, substantial clearing, where carriages were discharging their passengers. Elegant Creoles gathered around a flagpole upon which a pennant drooped dispiritedly in the sweltering heat. The rush was just starting when the Girards' rig pulled into the line of vehicles in front of newly built grandstand, draped with bunting.

Stepping down from the carriage, Claire was met by her husband. *"Bonjour, chère,"* he greeted her pleasantly, his lips brushing her cheek. "I'm so glad you could join me today."

Acutely conscious of the bystanders, Claire returned his salutation with a brittle smile. "I could hardly do otherwise with your new filly running." Turning her attention to the unfurling of her parasol, she managed to hide her ire from the watching eyes.

"Come, I'd like you to meet some people." Unconcernedly, Philippe offered his arm and led her to a congenial mob of Creole cousins and cousins several times removed. After a while, he made their excuses and took his wife with him to the stable yard. Promising to return soon, he showed her to a shady bench and disappeared inside the barn.

Claire surveyed the yard with interest. The sunbaked expanse of dirt between the barns was usually a lazy spot, occupied only when grooms cooled weary horses under the watchful eyes of their trainers, but today it was a hotbed of activity. In various spots, horses were islands in a sea of dust as packs of grooms, trainers, jockeys and owners eddied around them.

Most of the powerful animals seemed indifferent to the shouts and tension that filled the air. They submitted to currycombs and last-minute checks of their hooves, ignoring the bustling humans as much as possible, hardly reacting when saddles were placed on their backs with precision. The horses' harried trainers tripped over touts and enthusiasts who wandered through, contributing to the confusion. Jockeys, nodding at the owners' murmured instructions, tightened cinches, tested them, then tightened them more. Intent on their tasks, the gentlemen of New Orleans prepared for the upcoming races.

Enthralled by the activity around her, Claire did not mind waiting for Philippe. She was surprised and touched when a small man, using crutches, greeted her. "Good day, Mrs. Girard. I'm William Barron."

"Monsieur Barron," Claire said, smiling warmly. "What a pleasure to meet you at last. I was sorry to hear about your accident. It's good to see you out and about."

"Thank you, ma'am. Wild horses couldn't keep me away today, not from Touch-me-not's first race. Wasn't much time for training, but she's a fine filly and Mr. Girard and I spent enough time this past week planning." Propped on his crutches, he grinned shyly. "I want to thank you, ma'am, for being so understanding about all those evenings the boss spent with me after I got out of the infirmary. It was kind, you being newlyweds and all."

"You're w-welcome," she stammered in surprise. Had Philippe been with his jockey every evening and not with Lila?

"It wasn't just his company that meant so much," the little man was saying, "though God knows I needed it. But the most important thing . . ." He paused, his eyes misty. "When the doctors said I'd never walk again, Mr. Girard helped me out of bed and walked me around. He had these crutches made for me. I may never be a jockey again, but he showed me that I'm no cripple."

Engrossed in their discussion, Claire and Billy started almost guiltily when the subject of their conversation hailed them from across the stable yard.

"I'm glad you two have met," Philippe called, striding toward them, "though I probably should worry what kind of mischief you're up to."

"We were scheming about how to lure you out here, but now perhaps our desperate plan won't be necessary," Claire bantered, earning a grateful look from the abashed Billy.

"You wouldn't have time to carry it out." Her husband laughed. "Billy is needed in the barn this very moment."

"Pardon me, ma'am," the man excused himself.

"Not so fast, *mon ami*." Philippe laid a hand on his shoulder. "I think you should know that Touch-me-not is living up to her name today. She wants nothing to do with any of the grooms. Only the trainer for that one or she'll refuse to run, I fear." He smiled and extended his hand in congratulations.

"The trainer? Me?" Billy breathed disbelievingly. His face lit with joy, he braced himself and pumped the Creole's hand. "I'm Touch-me-not's trainer?"

"You're Girard Stables' trainer," Philippe affirmed.

"I—I don't know how to thank you," the other man sputtered.

"Just go take care of my filly." Grinning, he watched as the new trainer navigated the yard with amazing agility, his crutches leaving a track in the dust.

Claire glanced covertly at her husband's handsome profile, noticing the lightly etched lines near his eyes that crinkled appealingly when he smiled. Her eyes lingered on his mouth. The upturned corners transformed his face, giving it a boyish charm.

"Philippe," she ventured, "what you did for Monsieur Barron was kind and generous."

"He deserved it." He quickly changed the subject. "Sorry I took so long. Shall we find our seats?" He held his wife's hand in a loose grasp as they strolled toward the grandstand.

Near the crush of people disembarking from carriages, Philippe halted beside the rail fence surrounding the racecourse. "I hate to leave you again, but I must go to the judges' stand and make sure Touch-me-not's entry papers are in order. I wouldn't want them to award the purse to Skylar by mistake." He squeezed her hand lightly before releasing it. "I'll try not to be too long."

Claire nodded understandingly, content to wait. From beneath her parasol, she surveyed her surroundings and mused over the contrasts in her husband's behavior. She loved Philippe, but had she ever really known him?

Her eyes sweeping the arriving carriages, Claire saw Anne and Gaspar, accompanied by Henri, step from an open phaeton. Anne waved gleefully when she saw her friend. Henri excused himself with a hasty word to his companions and strode toward her. There was nothing Claire could do but steel herself for another scene.

"Claire, are you all right?" the young Creole greeted her anxiously.

"I'm fine," she answered brightly. "How are you?"

"*Non*, I mean, are you all right since that terrible day when Philippe snatched you from my carriage?"

"I'm fine," she repeated. "But, Henri, I don't think it would be a good idea for him to find you here talking to me."

"I must talk to you," he insisted. "I must know if you are happy."

"*Oui*." She said what she knew she must, and was surprised to find she meant it—today.

"You love him, don't you?" Henri asked sadly.

"Yes. I'm sorry if it hurts you."

The aristocratic young Creole stared over her shoulder at a crew of Negro boys who labored to smooth the track before the races. "I couldn't bear it when Philippe told me you weren't marrying for love," he murmured more to himself than to Claire. "It seemed worse than if he had told me you were passionately in love. Does that make sense? Knowing that you do love each other, I suppose I'll forgive Philippe in time. I only wanted what was best for you, you see."

Claire remained silent.

"Do you know when I knew he loved you?" Henri turned sad green eyes on her.

"When?" she asked, unwilling to explain that her love was not returned.

"That day at Place d'Armes. I've never seen him act that way over any woman."

"If bad behavior tells you that a man is in love, Philippe must be mad about me," Claire said dryly. Shifting her parasol, she realized with a start that he stood only a few feet away, an odd expression on his face. Apprehensively she wondered how much he had heard and whether his temper was about to erupt.

But her husband's curious mien was not due to anger or even jealousy. His face reflected the awe he felt at Claire's words. She loved him. She had said it—not to him, but to Henri. Did she mean it? Or did she say it to prevent a scene with her rejected lover?

Composing himself, he strode toward the pair with a confidence he did not feel, trying not to think of his past few meetings with his old friend. "*Bonjour,* Henri."

"*Bonjour,* Philippe," Henri muttered with a feeble smile. "I just came to say hello."

"I'm glad you did," Philippe said pleasantly. "We've missed you at Fortier House. Why don't you visit us some evening?"

"Perhaps, some evening," the other man agreed noncommittally. "It's good to see you . . . both. I must be getting back to Anne and Gaspar now." Kissing Claire's hand in a hurried farewell, he disappeared into the crowd.

As Philippe led his wife toward the box seats, a bundle of petticoats and lace pantalets launched itself at him with a screech of joy. In a flurry of coltish limbs, Odette wrapped her arms tightly around her brother's waist.

"What are you doing here, *ma petite?*" Philippe laughed and returned her hug before disentangling himself enough to look at her.

"Papa brought us. It's my birthday. But of course, you know that." Beaming up at him, Odette bubbled, "Oh, Philippe, the colt is so beautiful. *Merci beaucoup!* I'm naming her Desirée. Don't you think that is a good name—even for a horse?" In her excitement, the girl did not give him time to answer.

"Maman and Papa are over there." She pointed toward the cluster of Creole cousins. "Will you go and talk to Papa? I know he said he'd never forgive you, but I think he might."

Philippe glanced toward the group and discovered his mother's limpid eyes fixed longingly on him. He smiled and tipped his hat respectfully at the dark-clad woman before answering his sister, "I'd like to speak to Maman, Odette, but I don't wish to fight with Père, especially on your birthday. Besides, Claire and I were on our way to our box."

"Ohhh," the lovely child squealed delightedly as she whirled around and took note of Philippe's companion for the first time. "Claire! I am Odette." She bobbed in a proper curtsy.

"How do you do. I'm pleased to meet you." Claire returned the curtsy gracefully.

"It was terribly impolite of me not to greet you earlier," the girl apologized, "but I was so happy to see *mon frère,* I didn't see anyone else. I knew he'd be at the races, you know. That was why I wanted to come. And because it *is* my birthday.

"Oh, you are *très jolie.*" She had changed the subject without even a pause for breath. "I knew Philippe would marry you because he stared at you so at the Congo dances."

"Odette," her brother reproved to the unrepentant chatterer.

"You did," she declared defensively, unconscious of the glances the couple exchanged above her head. "Whatever Papa says about disowning you, Philippe, Claire and I can still be sisters, can't we?"

"Of course, you can, *ma belle,*" Philippe answered softly, without taking his eyes off his wife.

"*Très bien.* May I call you sister?" she petitioned her brother's wife.

"I should be delighted if you did." Claire smiled.

"I want you to call me sister, too. Come, you must meet our parents." Odette seized her newfound sister's hand to lead her toward them.

"*Non,* Philippe is right. It would be better if we didn't disturb them today."

"Oh, all right," Odette agreed carelessly. "They're coming over here, anyway."

Philippe watched in amazement as the docile Clothilde, flanked by René and the unwilling Pierre, led the way. Her thin face, framed by her bonnet, was determined as she reunited her family.

"Ahem...*bonjour,* Philippe," Pierre trumpeted, made more pompous than usual by awkwardness.

"*Bonjour,* Père, Maman, René." Philippe shook hands with his father and brother and kissed his mother's cheek. Clothilde clung to him as if she thought she would never see him again.

"You must be Claire." The woman turned a watery gaze on the girl and smiled tremulously. With an uncertain glance at Pierre, she added doggedly, "Welcome to our family, daughter."

Pierre scowled and took over the introductions. "This is my wife, Madame Clothilde Girard, young lady. I am your... er...father-in-law. And this is René, my eldest. Odette, I believe you have already met."

"How do you do." Claire curtsied. "I'm happy to meet you all. And please, call me Claire."

"Very well." His hands clasped behind his back, Pierre bounced on his heels, obviously ill at ease.

"Philippe," René interjected in one of his characteristic efforts to break the tension, "you didn't tell me your bride was such a beauty.

"If ever he doesn't treat you right," the handsome older brother informed Claire teasingly, "I'm the person you should tell. I've had plenty of practice at keeping him in line."

"Perhaps I should take lessons from you." She smiled, glancing meaningfully at her husband.

Good-naturedly, Philippe ignored the exchange. "I'm glad you could make it to the races today, Père," he said to his father. "My new filly is running."

"Well, while I'm not a betting man myself, I could hardly deprive my family of one of the social events of the season. Odette would never let me hear the end of it." Softening for the first time, the stout Creole smiled down at his impulsive daughter.

"Oh, Papa." Odette giggled. Suddenly, her eyes widened as an idea occurred to her. "Oh, can Philippe and Claire come tonight? It would be such fun! We're having a special dinner," she explained. "I got to pick everything we're having. Please, they can come, can't they?" she appealed prettily to her father.

"Well, ahem…" Pierre was nonplussed at being put on the spot. His distress deepened when Clothilde dared answer for him.

"Of course, they can come," Philippe's mother replied firmly, amazed by her own temerity. "It is a family dinner, after all." She eyed her husband uneasily, but there was a stubborn set to her jaw, so like her son's, as she defied him to disagree.

"Of course," the eldest Girard sputtered. "Dinner will be served at eight, *mon fils.* Can you join us?"

"We'd be delighted," the astounded young man accepted.

"*Très bien.* Come, Clothilde, Odette." Bowing stiffly, Pierre herded his family toward the grandstand.

As if in a daze, Philippe led Claire to their private box. A canvas roof sheltered them from the sun as they located their seats and made themselves comfortable.

On the other side of the track where the slaves and *gens de couleur* milled on the grass, Lila Broussard stood apart, her embittered yellow eyes on the couple who talked, their dark heads close. What had happened to Philippe? she wondered sadly. She had sent for him. She had bought special charms and candles, even a bag of come-to-me powder, but he had not come. The octoroon knew who was to blame. She turned a gaze of pure hatred on Claire.

Across the track, Claire's rapt attention was captured by the hubbub around her. She waved sociably when she spied Skylar and Nancy Prentiss.

"Philippe," Skylar bellowed over the heads of the crowd, "can we join you?"

"Please do," Philippe called back, smiling as the big Virginian escorted his wife through the press, one arm thrown protectively over her round shoulders.

"Good day, Claire." Skylar bowed formally, then wrung her husband's hand. "Good to see you, my boy."

"Hello, you two. My, what a madhouse." Nancy puffed, settling her plump posterior in the chair next to Claire's and fanning herself. "We have a box down the way, but it's simply overrun with young people. Leland and Bettina's friends are a most vexing group, always chattering. They never let a person get a word in edgeways. And I must be able to get a word in somewhere. You know how I like to talk," she concluded with a twinkle in her eye.

"No one's going to argue that, old girl," Skylar joshed, taking a chair by the rail. "But at least you know when to talk and when to cheer. That mob doesn't understand that horse racing is serious business."

At that moment, a ragged fanfare heralded the first race, and the American practiced what he preached, hunching forward silently to scrutinize the horses at the gate.

Hours slipped by as the horses thundered past in race after race. Claire forgot about the heat as Philippe's horses won virtually every contest in which they were entered. Taking a cue from the jubilant Nancy, she rooted for Girard Stables's entry in each event. Her cheers were sometimes drowned by Skylar's elated whoops as his stallion, Sweet William, left the pack in his dust.

Philippe was as pleased with his wife's excitement as he was with the outcome of the races, but he said little. Restlessly, he awaited the running of the big race, the race Touch-me-not would run. He glanced at Skylar, who seemed remarkably unconcerned, although his filly Rose of Sharon was also running.

The horns sounded to announce the main event, and the spectators watched as at least twenty horses crowded together at the starting line. With so many animals running, riders jockeyed desperately for position, knowing their start might dictate the outcome of the entire race. The horses reacted to the tension in the air, prancing edgily.

The starting gun went off and the pack burst from the starting line with Prentiss's Rose of Sharon in the lead. Alain

Comeaux, Girard Stables's new jockey, fought to control the skittish Touch-me-not, who reared at the sound of the shot.

"Come on, girl," Philippe murmured fervently as his filly bolted down the straightaway a full three lengths behind most of the racers.

"Come on, Touch-me-not, you can do it," he almost chanted. Her legs flashing with a graceful rhythm, the filly passed the body of the pack and began to shorten the gap between Rose of Sharon in the lead and Alouette, Neville Johnson's mare, as the close second. Effortlessly, Touch-me-not drew even with Alouette and left her behind in the blink of an eye.

Touch-me-not and Rose of Sharon pounded down the homestretch past clamoring spectators. Desperately, Prentiss's jockey looked over his shoulder at Alain as the little Cajun cooed encouragement into Touch-me-not's ear. Grim determination on his face, Rose of Sharon's jockey urged his steed to a narrow victory.

"Go, Touch-me-not, go. . . ." The words died on Philippe's lips as Prentiss's horse crossed the finish line seconds ahead of his filly.

"Congratulations." He offered his hand, but his good wishes were drowned by the Virginian.

"What a race, by damn!" Skylar was on his feet, shouting exuberantly. "Well run, my boy! Your new filly is going to give me some stiff competition next season." He bailed out of the box, headed toward the winner's circle.

"Yessir, a helluva race." His voice drifted back to the three he left behind.

"Ah, Sky," Nancy said, sighing in mock exasperation. "He won't be fit to live with for a week." She squinted shrewdly at Philippe and asked, "Now do you understand why he sold you the filly?"

"I believe I do." The Creole grinned impudently. "And the next time we'll give him a run for his money."

"Nothing he'd like better," she answered cheerfully.

With Nancy on one arm and Claire on the other, Philippe escorted them through the crowd of merrymakers. The trio arrived at the winner's circle just in time to see the ebullient Skylar lift a glass and say, "Here's to my dear wife, Nan, who's around someplace." He gazed around distractedly. "I thought she was."

"Here I am, Skylar," she yelled, jostling her way gleefully through the crowd with Philippe and Claire in tow. The couple stayed for a glass of champagne before they made their excuses and left the celebration.

Pushing their way through the throng of well-wishers, they found themselves beside the flagpole. Most of the carriages had departed, leaving dusty tracks on the hard-packed field, but Claire's rig waited under a nearby tree.

"I'll see you to the carriage," Philippe offered.

"Where are you going?" Claire balked, looking up at him.

"I must see about my horses."

"I'll go with you. Then we can ride home together."

"Are you sure? It's been a long day."

"I'm sure."

The stable yard was quiet as grooms led freshly rubbed, blanketed horses toward the barns and owners reviewed the races with their trainers. Claire trailed behind as Philippe and Billy visited each stall, discussing the inhabitant's performance at great length. At last, the Creole wrapped an arm around his wife's waist and called to Xavier, "An extra ration of oats tonight for all of them!"

As the couple walked to the carriage, Claire glanced at her husband in the waning light, concerned that his face showed signs of exhaustion.

"You look tired," she murmured.

"I am tired," he admitted, handing her into the vehicle. "But what a glorious, surprising day," he announced with satisfaction. He sprawled in the seat across from her and pulled his hat down over his eyes. All Claire could see beneath the brim were his lips, and they curved in a lazy smile.

Chapter Seventeen

Nero watched from the veranda as M'sieur Philippe and his bride alit from the carriage in front of Bonté. The young master had never looked so handsome and prosperous, he noted approvingly. And—did he dare hope it?—happy.

Almost as tall as her husband, the new Madame Girard resembled a beautiful flower. Her soft lips appeared to match her rose silk dress naturally, contrasting with dark hair and creamy skin to make a most engaging picture. Her bearing proud and regal, she seemed to glide into the house on Philippe's arm.

Nero stole a moment in the foyer for a whispered greeting. "Welcome home, M'sieur Philippe."

"It's good to see you, Nero. I want you to meet my wife." Philippe's tone caressed Claire.

"A pleasure, madame." The butler bowed respectfully, the network of wrinkles on his face melding into one blissful smile. Then, remembering his duties, he announced briskly, "This way now. The family is waitin'."

The couple followed him to the parlor where Clothilde, Odette and Tante Delaney sat in a half circle, their full skirts carefully arranged on the stiff horsehair furniture. Pierre and René stood nearby, their wineglasses in hand.

"*Bon* . . . Philippe and Claire! I was afraid you wouldn't come." Odette bounced in her seat, calmed promptly by her mother's quieting gesture.

"And miss your birthday cake?" Philippe teased his sister. His eyes swept the room as he greeted the rest of his family. "*Bonsoir,* everyone."

"*Bonsoir,*" Claire echoed nervously, her eyes firmly fixed on Tante Delaney's encouraging smile.

"Come in," Pierre said gruffly. Then he instructed Nero, "Tell Cook we'll have dinner immediately."

Offering his arm to Odette, Pierre's manner changed. "Come, *ma petite,* I shall escort the birthday girl," he invited jovially. "And you, Madeleine." He offered his other arm to his sister. The trio led the way into the dining room.

"May I have the honor of escorting the new Madame Girard?" René requested gallantly. Claire smiled at her brother-in-law warmly and accepted his arm.

"Well, *ma mère.*" Philippe smiled down at Clothilde tenderly. "It looks as if we must bring up the rear. As always, the best is saved for last."

"Ah, *mon fils.*" He was rewarded with a rare chuckle. "It's good to have you home. You always make me laugh." In that moment, she seemed almost flirtatious, and her son was given a glimpse of the carefree Creole girl Clothilde Breaux had been. Smiling broadly, Philippe escorted his mother to the dining room.

Odette's birthday dinner was a stiff, formal affair. When everyone was seated, her presence was nearly forgotten as the conversation swirled around her. A well-behaved Creole child, she did not mind. Her gifts had been opened at breakfast and now she let the adults talk while she imagined riding like the wind on Desirée.

Pierre, with René on his right and Philippe on his left, reigned at one end of the table, dominating the conversation as course after sumptuous course was served. Clothilde sat silently at the other end. Although she had several thoughts about the exchange, Claire followed her mother-in-law's lead and listened while the men talked of Bonté and business, of horses and hunts, and of plans for a new medical school soon to be built in the city.

By the time dessert arrived, Tante Delaney was tired of discussion that excluded females. "Medical schools, hotels. The Americans even have a new theater!" she exclaimed. "New Orleans has certainly changed in the past few years." Disregarding Pierre's annoyed frown, she continued blithely, "In spite of what some said at the time, I made no mistake holding on to my property in town. I believe there will be a building boom here soon."

"We all know of your business acumen, Madeleine," her brother retorted sarcastically, "but I don't know where you get some of your outrageous suppositions."

"What I say is not outrageous," she maintained. "I hear from reliable sources that part of the Quarter of the Damned is to be drained. And that'll be just the beginning."

Pierre snorted disbelievingly. "Nonsense, the city has no funds to drain marshland at the back of town."

"But speculators do." Tante was unfazed by his disagreement.

"Think of what that would mean," René chimed in earnestly. "Better sanitation would be possible. We wouldn't be plagued by so many flies and mosquitoes. Perhaps we wouldn't even have outbreaks of yellow fever and such when the weather is like this."

"You have a point," Philippe agreed soberly. "People are talking about yellow jack again."

"Dr. Perez has told me of rumors of several cases already," René added quietly.

"Perez is an alarmist," Pierre snapped. "Always has been."

"Maybe not, Pierre," Tante Delaney disagreed sadly. "I've heard the same rumors."

"If *le bon Dieu* is willing and the heat lets up, there will be no epidemic," Clothilde contributed, almost desperately, to the conversation for the first time.

Everyone fell silent as Clothilde glanced worriedly at her daughter, but Odette was paying no attention to the conversation, content to shovel unladylike quantities of Italian ice into her dainty mouth and daydream.

"Well, this is no way to celebrate a birthday," Pierre boomed, shattering the gravity of the moment. "I propose a toast to Odette Madeleine Marie Girard, the belle of all New Orleans!"

Rising, the family saluted the prettily dimpled girl with raised glasses. When they had drained them, they adjourned to the veranda for coffee.

Claire sat with the women while the men stood in a cluster at the bottom of the steps, smoking and talking, slapping occasionally at a bothersome mosquito. The fragrance of their tobacco mingled with the aroma of fresh chicory coffee and the sharp scent of citronella candles.

Flanked by Philippe's mother and aunt in bentwood rocking chairs, Claire and Odette shared a glider and talked quietly. Pleased to have her family around her, Clothilde contentedly stared out into the darkness while Tante Delaney dozed in the corner, snoring softly, a counterpoint to the men's muffled voices. Claire's gaze continually drifted to where Philippe stood.

"This is so romantic, just like at the Congo dances," Odette murmured sleepily, struggling politely to stifle a yawn. "Only this time, you're watching Philippe. Last time he watched you. It must be grand to be in love."

"*Oui*, grand . . ." Claire smiled down at her young sister-in-law.

"Odette." Clothilde's hushed voice interrupted their chat. "Do you not think it time for bed? It's been a long day."

"*Oui, Maman*," Odette replied meekly. "Good night, Claire." She squeezed her newfound sister's hand, then went to kiss her mother. She bade the men good-night before stopping in front of her aunt's chair. "*Bonne nuit, Tante*," she piped.

Tante Delaney woke with a start and glared at the little girl with piercing black eyes. "*Mon Dieu*, Odette, don't creep up on an old woman that way." Then she softened. "Good night, my child. Come and give me a kiss before you go."

Obligingly, the girl bussed her aunt's wrinkled cheek and went into the house. Their discussion interrupted, the men joined the women in the flickering candlelight on the porch.

Pierre and René pulled chairs into the circle as Philippe lowered himself onto the glider beside Claire.

"Did I tell you, Claire," Pierre asked as he sat down, "that I knew your uncle?"

"Did you?" the girl responded politely.

"Etienne was one of his stiffest business rivals," Tante Delaney interjected from her shadowy corner.

"I thought you were asleep, Madeleine," the man fussed, giving her a hard look. "*Oui*, we both traded in cotton. Etienne Fortier was a fine businessman, one of my greatest competitors.

"But I wouldn't expect you to know of those things, my girl," he added hastily. Then he mused, "Let me see, my old friend Prosper LaBiche was the Fortier attorney, was he not?"

"*Oui*." The girl nodded, unsure where the conversation led.

"Then he is managing things for you now?"

"Monsieur LaBiche has been invaluable as an adviser," she said diplomatically, "but Philippe manages the Fortier interests."

Pierre snorted disparagingly. "Philippe...what does he know of business?"

"He has done a fine job with the stables, and he's doing well with the Fortier family interests as well." Claire defended the son while trying not to lose her temper with the father.

"I manage everything but the Mercantile," Philippe corrected modestly. "Claire manages that."

"Claire manages the Mercantile?" Pierre gasped disbelievingly. "And you let her?"

"Originally I didn't have a lot of choice," the young man responded mildly. "It was a part of the agreement we made before we were married."

"A lot of people have prenuptial agreements these days, Pierre. After all, it *is* 1832," Tante Delaney contributed, earning another murderous glare from her brother.

"Yes, but those agreements usually do not stipulate that wife will work in business. It's unthinkable for a Girard to work in an office." He spat out the words as if it were an unpleasant taste. "Furthermore, a Creole woman should never have to worry about such common things."

"Perhaps Claire enjoys the challenge of commerce, *Père*...at least until the first child is born," René suggested placatingly.

Claire glanced at her handsome brother-in-law, unsure whether to thank him or to kick him in the shin. But her course of action was never decided, for Pierre exploded in anger.

"A challenge?" he roared. "She has Philippe. God knows, that's challenge enough. In the meantime, what will people say?"

"You know by now that I don't care what people say," Philippe drawled. Resigned to the fight that was coming, he goaded his father. "Claire worked in the office before her uncle's death. If she wants to work there again..." His shrug was eloquent.

"You must stop her, Philippe. Damn it, be enough of a man to put your foot down."

Pierre turned to his daughter-in-law appealingly. He had been opposed to this marriage and quite prepared to dislike

Philippe's new wife, but she seemed a quiet, docile girl. Certain she would listen to reason, he said patronizingly, "You must understand my point of view, my dear. Believe me, I know best and I advise you not even to consider going back to work. Now, surely we have said enough on this subject."

A long pause followed during which an intake of breath was heard from the two in the company who knew Claire. Tante Delaney leaned forward avidly in her rocker, while Philippe groaned inwardly and prepared for the worst.

"I fear I do not understand your point of view, sir," Claire dissented quietly, "but I do agree enough as been said about it. In fairness, however, I should tell you," she continued as Pierre stared at her dumbly, "I'll try to operate the Mercantile with as little public notice as possible. I have a good manager for the day-to-day work, but I can't run a profitable business without going to the office at least occasionally. Since you're apparently unaware that I've already resumed my position there, you see discretion is possible."

For a moment, Pierre's mouth opened and closed wordlessly, then he lashed out at his son, unwilling even to address the girl. "*Mon Dieu,* Philippe, sometimes I think you're determined to be a deliberate embarrassment to this family. You set out to make a bad reputation for yourself—drinking, gambling, carousing, dueling with Kaintocks. You choose an occupation of questionable repute. Then, to further aggravate me, you marry an outlander!" he raged.

"Enough, Père," Philippe warned the older man.

But Pierre would not be silenced. "She has no respect for me, for family obligations or for honor. And now—" his voice continued to rise "—you stand by as she defies me, the head of the family!"

"You are not the head of my family, *Père,*" Philippe interrupted his father's tirade quietly. "I am."

"Then be the head! Tell your wife what she must do."

"That she must not manage her own business because you say so?" the young man asked stonily.

"Exactly that." Pierre grunted and waited expectantly.

"I am sorry, *Maman.* We shouldn't have come," Philippe muttered as he rose, drawing Claire up with him. "*Bonne nuit,* everyone." He nodded to the others on the dark porch.

The angry young Creole led his wife to their carriage without a look back. Climbing in beside her, he settled back, not speaking until they were nearly home.

"You might at least have told me that you'd returned to the office." Philippe's hoarse voice held no anger.

"I didn't have a chance," Claire said apologetically. "We've not talked for a week."

"I know." He sighed as the carriage stopped in front of Fortier House. "We have many things to discuss, you and I... tomorrow. But tonight I'm tired and my head feels as if it will split."

"You don't look well." Claire studied his pale face, concern evident in her eyes. "Come, let's get you into bed."

Philippe smiled lopsidedly, embarrassed by his obvious weakness, but he preceded her into the house without protest. Pausing in the foyer, he touched her cheek reassuringly. "I'm fine, *chère*. I must have gotten too much sun today. But I'm perfectly capable of putting myself to bed. I'll see you in the morning."

"All right," she agreed, frowning worriedly as she watched him trudge up the stairs. *"Bonne nuit."*

Later, in her room, Claire threw open the doors and windows and prepared for bed, rejecting the nightgown Beady offered her in favor of one Lucene had made for when the nights became unbearably hot. It was a scant shift, two panels of sheer white batiste sewn together and held up by narrow lavender ribbons that tied at the shoulders. The gown barely skimmed her ankles and each side was split to the knee to allow freedom of movement. It could hardly be considered modest, but no one but Beady ever saw her in it, Claire reasoned, and Beady had seen much more than her legs.

Clad in the gauzy white sheath, she pulled her hair back and splashed tepid water from the basin on her face and neck. She climbed into the bed, still dripping, and stretched out atop the coverlet. Beady arranged the *baire* around the bed, then left her.

Claire tossed and turned, searching for a comfortable position, but it was too hot to sleep. She willed her body to relax until, gradually, drowsiness began to overtake her.

All at once, her eyes opened and she listened carefully. On the other side of the wall, Philippe was thrashing in his bed and mumbling in the throes of a nightmare. She lay still until a loud thump and a muffled curse brought her to her feet and sent her racing into the next room.

Near the bed, Claire almost tripped over a heavy brass candle stand in the darkness. Philippe had not even awakened when he knocked it to the floor in his flailing. She returned it to its position on the bedside table and looked down at her husband through the sheer *baire*.

Flushed and feverish, he slept fitfully. Below his bare chest, the tangled bed sheet, one corner still tucked under the mattress, was wrapped tightly around his torso and one of his legs. His other leg had escaped the linen shackles and protruded from the netting. Wadded bedclothes trailed across the foot of the bed and lay in a pile on the floor where he had kicked them.

Muttering in his sleep, Philippe flung one arm over his head as Claire gently returned his uncovered leg to the protection of the *baire*. He was not just having a nightmare, she realized when she touched him. He was feverish. His skin was dry and hot. Drawing back the netting, she put her hand on his forehead.

"Claire . . ." Philippe's glazed, unfocused eyes opened.

"I'm here," she whispered reassuringly.

He shook his head as if trying to shake off sleep, to collect his muddled thoughts. Nothing was clear but one thing: she was here, leaning over him, her cool, soothing hand on his brow.

The delirious man did not question what luck had brought her to him; he was simply glad of it. Even in the darkness, he could see the outline of her trim figure beneath the transparent nightgown. Her dark, sweet-scented hair tumbled to slender shoulders, and when she bent over him, he had the most enticing view of rounded white breasts.

"You came to me, *mon amour*. I knew you would someday." He smiled triumphantly. Moving quickly, he caught her hand before she could change her mind, unaware that in his delirium, he crushed her wrist with unnatural strength.

"Philippe, please, I just came to see about you." She struggled to pull from his bruising grip.

"This is what I've wanted from the beginning," he muttered, drawing her toward him. "I've waited for you to come. Come, Claire, let me love you as a husband should."

He pulled her down on the bed and kissed her, his lips searing hers. Trapping her wrist against his muscular chest, Philippe slid his other arm around her shoulders and held her tightly against him. He twined his fingers through her hair, pulling her head back, exposing her throat to his scorching kisses. Along the entire length of her body, she could feel the heat of his skin through the thin fabric of her nightgown.

Her pulse quickened as his hands fumbled with the ribbons at her shoulders. They came untied in an instant, freeing her breasts for his caresses.

"No, Philippe, please," she gasped desperately when his mouth left hers to rain kisses on her face, her neck, her shoulders.

"Oh, yes." His response was muffled as he breathed in her sweet fragrance, dipping his head lower to trail a molten path of kisses downward to one of the breasts he cupped, setting her entire body on fire.

She moaned, fighting the sensations he kindled deep within her. This was wrong. He was out of his head with fever. He did not know what he was doing. But passion ignited in her as his hands followed the contours of her body. Through the sheet, she could feel the hard bulge of his growing arousal.

"Philippe," she panted, clinging to the last remnants of self-control, "you must let me go."

"I'll never let you go," he murmured, his hand finding its way under the hem of her gown to stroke the length of her smooth, firm thigh. The garment bunched up at her tapering waist as his fingers glided around her hip, molding to the curve of her buttock. His grip tightened and she could feel his insistent hardness against her flat belly.

"Listen to me, Philippe." Her protest came in ragged gasps. "I must send for the doctor. You're sick."

"Only from the want of you, my own," he responded teasingly, his voice thick with desire. Panic-stricken, Claire realized the corner of the sheet had somehow worked its way free. No longer encumbered, Philippe ripped the sheet away from his body and wedged his lean, sinewy leg between hers, spreading them gently but relentlessly to his tender exploration. Skillfully, his hands stroked and probed, bringing her to new heights of pleasure as her willpower slipped away and she forgot all but his touch.

With one swift move, he tucked her body under his. A sharp pain stabbed through her, but Claire's cry was lost as, murmuring endearments, Philippe covered her mouth with his. Gradually, she relaxed as the physical pain ebbed, only to be replaced by the pain of pure, aching need. The heat of his fevered flesh was matched by her hot fluid passion as Claire yielded to desire and moved to the ancient sensuous rhythm, arcing her body upward to meet his.

The precious intensity of her surrender penetrated the man's delirium and awed him as he thrust deeper into her warmth. Her musky sweetness filled his senses, enveloping him in a warmth and tenderness he had never known. Together, they soared until spasms of release shook them to the core of their beings.

"Claire, *mon coeur*..." Philippe lifted himself to gaze down at her wonderingly. Then, with a groan, he collapsed, unconscious.

Her heart pounding, Claire could barely move under his dead weight. She placed her hands against a broad shoulder and rolled him slightly to one side so she could slide from beneath him. His skin was still hot and dry and his breathing shallow. Struggling to free her legs, which were entangled with his, she sat up and peered at her husband anxiously.

"Philippe," she whispered. "Philippe, are you all right?"

His only response was a moan as he thrashed, rolling his head from side to side.

"*Non,*" she sobbed. Tugging the hem of her nightgown from under the man's inert body, she raced into the hall to shout for help.

Chapter Eighteen

"So hot," Philippe mumbled, tossing. "Hot for so long."

Claire leaned over him, bathing his fevered body to ease his discomfort. Dipping a towel in a basin, she squeezed the water from it and ran it gently over his lean torso and down his long, powerful legs. All the while, she reviewed her recent actions. She had sent Greer for the doctor and Beady for fresh water and towels. She had gotten word to the servants in the slave quarters to stay away. What more could she do?

Forget, she told herself firmly, forget what just happened. Philippe had not known what he was doing. But she was plagued with questions. Would he remember? Did she want him to?

Her thoughts were interrupted when Beady returned with clean linens.

"Help me change the sheets," she instructed the maid. "These are soaked."

Together, they rolled Philippe gently from one side of the bed to the other.

"Holy saints, is he dead?" Beady gasped, her horrified gaze fixed on the bloody sheet, evidence of Claire's lost virginity.

"He's not dead or even dying. That's my blood, not his," her mistress snapped.

"You mean—"

"Are you going to help me or not?" Claire scowled at her.

Beady bent to the task, dodging Philippe's delirious blows while they labored to change the linens. When he was resting more comfortably, Claire pulled a light cover over him and arranged the *baire* around his bed.

"Lock all the doors," she instructed the maid. "I don't want anyone coming into the house by mistake. You can let Greer and the doctor in when they arrive."

"Yes'm." Beady bustled away, pointing to a wrapper that hung on the doorknob between the rooms. "I brung that for you. Best put it on before they git here."

Never taking her eyes from her husband, Claire numbly obeyed. Then she pulled a chair close to the bed and sat down to await the doctor. What was wrong with Philippe? she fretted. Too much sun? Something he ate? Let it be anything but yellow jack, she prayed.

What had been said at dinner? She struggled to remember the conversation. René had said a few cases had been reported. Surely it could not be yellow jack, she tried to convince herself. If only Dr. Perez would arrive...

After what seemed like hours, she heard horses on the shell-covered drive and Beady called, "Here they comes, mam'selle."

Claire heard anxious voices in the foyer, then footsteps on the stairs. Dr. Perez hastened into the room, his elegant clothes looking as if he had slept in them. His sunken cheeks bristled with stubbly whiskers, and behind his spectacles, his tired, bloodshot eyes took in the girl's concern.

"Sorry to be late," he apologized, going immediately to Philippe, "but it took poor Greer some time to find me."

Reluctantly, the butler explained, "We have the beginning of an epidemic. Fortier House is Dr. Perez's sixth stop tonight."

"What are his symptoms?" the doctor asked efficiently.

"A headache earlier," Claire replied. "He thought it might be from too much sun. Then he started running a high fever. He's been out of his head for several hours now."

Completing his examination, Dr. Perez turned to Claire. "I fear it is yellow fever."

As Claire swayed on her feet at the news, he took her arm and propelled her to the nearby chair. "Don't panic," the doctor said kindly. "The disease is not always fatal. I must tell you, however, Philippe is already running a high fever and that's not good. But he's as strong as a bull and, with good care, he may recover."

"I'll care for him myself." Claire's voice was low. "Just tell me how."

"Très bien, I'll tell you what we know about yellow fever, which is not enough. But at least you'll know what to expect.

"First," he began, "Philippe will run a high fever for several days. He'll be nauseated. Some black blood may show up in his vomit or other excretions. Try not to be too upset. This happens as the fever runs its course.

"By the third or fourth day, his temperature will drop and jaundice will set in. His skin, even his eyes, will be yellow. It will look fearsome, but there's nothing you can do. It may seem, then, but for the jaundice, that he's on the road to recovery. Keep a close watch, for his heart rate may drop dangerously low," he warned.

"By the sixth day, he'll be in a decline and there's likely to be a relapse into fever, but if you can nurse him through it without pneumonia or complications, he'll live. By the ninth or tenth day, the worst should be over.

"About what to do," he continued, "bar everyone from the house, except for those who have already been exposed. Understand, my dear, all you can do for Philippe is to keep him quiet and as comfortable as you can in this heat. Give him fluids, perhaps some broth, but make sure your water has been boiled first.

"I see you've already been bathing him." The doctor nodded approvingly. "That's a good way to hold the fever down.

"I have some medicine here that may ease him somewhat," he muttered, rummaging in his bag, "but it doesn't work on everyone. Use it...and pray." He smiled encouragingly. "I'm sorry to leave you, but I have other calls to make. Try not to worry. I know you'll do fine."

Claire was back at her husband's side before the doctor was out of the room. She stayed with him through the night and the next day without a moment's rest. She did not know what went on in the city as the epidemic swept it, taking victims from every third household. Locked in Philippe's chambers, she knew nothing of the quarantine, the tent hospitals hastily set up in the Place d'Armes or the temporary morgues on barges moored in the river, where bodies were kept until they could be burned. She was not even aware of the black ribbon—the yellow fever sign—hanging on her own front door.

All she knew was Philippe's valiant fight for life. Hour upon rigorous hour, she attempted to force liquid between his lips, bathed his fevered flesh and held his head while he retched black bile.

When the medicine began to work, he settled into a restless, tormented sleep. Although he tossed and turned in the heat, he slept through most of the day.

On the afternoon of the second day, Greer sent Claire to rest, insisting he would sit with the master himself. At last, she surrendered, realizing she would be no good to Philippe if she became ill herself. Going to her own room, she fell asleep, still clad in her bedraggled dressing gown.

When she awoke, the girl bathed in tepid water and dressed in her coolest dress. Between bites of cold meat, cheese and bread Beady brought her, she rolled up her sleeves and plaited her hair to keep it out of the way. Thus fortified, she returned to Philippe's room to resume her vigil through the night.

After fighting back the *baire* around his bed for the hundredth time, she instructed Greer to remove it and stretch it across the open window. Unimpressed with the idea, he complied nevertheless and tacked it into place. The French doors had to be closed, but the room was cooler and free of insects, and the patient was not separated from his nurse by netting.

While Claire admired Greer's handiwork, the faint report of a rifle reached their ears. "What was that?" she asked.

"Someone trying to get out of New Orleans, or trying to get in," he said hesitantly. "The militia set up barricades to keep the disease from spreading. The guards are diligent. They shoot first and ask questions later."

"Will the doctor be back, Greer?"

"I'm afraid not—at least, not for a while, Miss Claire."

"Then it's up to us."

When the butler withdrew, she sat on Philippe's bed and tried to feed him. He opened unfocused eyes and squinted at her without the slightest glint of recognition.

"I've wasted so much time," he rasped urgently, struggling to lift his head. "Do you think it's too late?"

"Of course not," she soothed him, brushing back a stray lock from his gaunt face. "You'll be well soon, I promise."

Appeased, he lay back weakly, unaware of his wife's fierce determination. She would not let him die, Claire resolved. She had not learned she loved him only to lose him to yellow fever.

Philippe was violently ill for the next two days, vomiting until his empty stomach had nothing further to eject, the heaving racking his weakened body. He ranted deliriously for hours on end, flailing at invisible foes, until at last he slipped into unconsciousness. On the fourth day, to Claire's relief, his fever broke and he slept peacefully for the first time.

She slept in a chair beside the bed, awakening the next morning when Beady entered the room, a heavy bucket in one hand.

"*Bonjour,* Beady," she greeted her. "Thank you for bringing more fresh water."

"How 'bout some breakfust, mam'selle? And don't tell me you ain't hungry, 'cause I know you ain't been eatin'. You cain't tend th' master if you don't take keer of yourself. You eat, then git some sleep while I sit with him."

"After we change the sheets," Claire acquiesced wearily. "These are drenched."

When they completed their chore and the maid went to get her breakfast, Claire dipped a clean cloth into water and moistened Philippe's lips, dried and cracked from the high fever he had run. Her heart ached at the sight of his emaciated form. His eyes were sunken and circled, and under his growth of beard, his skin had the yellow tinge the doctor had predicted.

He was resting easier and his skin felt cooler, but Claire could not leave him, even for a nap, for this was the time she must increase her vigilance.

Claire ate the breakfast Beady brought, mostly to please her, but she flatly refused to go to her room to sleep. She washed in a basin, replaited her hair, then returned to Philippe's side. There she sat all day, instantly alert to his slightest stirring.

"She sure do love him," Beady whispered each time she and Greer met in the hall outside Philippe's room. "Too bad she don't know it."

"Too bad, indeed," Greer rumbled disapprovingly. He opened the door a crack to watch Claire worriedly from the hall. The mistress's thin face was haggard and pale. The lackluster braid hung limply down the back of her wrinkled, sweat-stained dress. At times, she seemed unsteady with exhaustion. Certain she would be forced to succumb to fatigue, Greer prepared to take her place beside the master's bed, but she did not leave her post. Claire's will and determination kept her going; her will and determination kept Philippe alive. She would not let him die.

When she awoke at dawn on the sixth day, the morning was strangely silent. Not even the now familiar sound of sporadic gunfire broke the eerie stillness. Smelling smoke on the stagnant air, she went to the window and looked out at a thick black haze hanging over the landscape. It seemed to be coming from the other side of Esplanade. The sun, an angry red ball in the eastern sky, could barely be seen as it fought to send its rays through the suffocating fog.

"What's burning, Greer?" she asked without turning when she heard the butler's heavy tread behind her.

"Smudge pots, ma'am," he reported. "They burn them in the intersections of the Vieux Carré to keep away flies and other pestilence so the fever does not spread."

"I was afraid—"

"No, ma'am, don't even think it," Greer interrupted gently. "The bodies are burned downriver, away from the city. This smoke is from smudge pots. Come now," he urged compassionately. "I brought broth for Mr. Philippe and some food for you."

During the afternoon, the sick man's fever shot up. Out of his head, he thrashed wildly and raved at the inhabitants of his nightmare world.

"Claire!" he shouted suddenly. "Claire, where are you?"

"Here," she quickly reassured him, kneeling beside his bed. "I'm here, Philippe."

His eyelids fluttered open and he turned his head, straining to see her. She gasped, shocked at his appearance despite the doctor's warning. Philippe's eyes were completely yellow, their dark irises glittering from the fever.

"Non..." He rolled his head in delirious denial. "You're not Claire.... Night Storm. Sometimes...hot. Sometimes...ice queen...beautiful."

Disconcertingly aware of her haggard appearance, she tried to calm her husband.

He closed his eyes and lay still for a moment, panting from exertion. Then he mumbled so that she had to bend close to hear him. "Cold, beautiful Claire...warm in front of the fire...exciting as the storm. Remember the cabin?"

"I remember," she choked.

"You *are* Claire, aren't you?" he sighed.

"Yes, my darling."

He smiled feebly, his dry lips cracking and seeping blood. He whispered disjointedly, "Your skin...soft. Lips...sweet. I wanted you...so many times...but I couldn't have you."

Suddenly, the man's eyes flew open and he sat bolt upright in bed. His weird, unseeing eyes glared furiously at her as he seized her shoulders with fevered, inhuman strength and lifted her from the floor like a rag doll.

Dragging her onto the bed, he leaned over her menacingly and thundered, "Why didn't you love me?" He shook her until she thought her neck would snap. "Why?"

"Philippe, I did love you," she shouted to make herself heard over his ravings. "I do love you!"

"You do?" His abrupt release nearly unseated her.

"*Oui,*" she whispered, slumping wearily at his side.

"You love me?" he whimpered like a small boy, his wasted face brightening incredulously for a moment. Then, wrapping his arms tightly around her waist, the sick man buried his face in her bosom and wept great gulping sobs.

Her own emotions in turmoil, Claire gazed helplessly down at him. Thrusting her own confusion aside, she cradled him tenderly, smoothing his tousled hair. "Of course, I love you, Philippe," she murmured, rocking him gently. "I love you more than you will ever know."

At last, his tormented sobs subsided and his arms became lax around her waist. Gently, Claire freed herself from his embrace and laid him back on the pillow.

He stirred in his sleep and said weakly, "Lila...I must tell her...."

Claire jumped to her feet, staggering with the force of her retreat, and collapsed heavily into the chair, aching with grief and shame and weariness. She nursed Philippe, willing him to live, to live for another woman.

She would not let him die, because she loved him. But she would never be such a fool again as to think there could be anything between them, she vowed sadly. Painfully, she recalled the passion of their lovemaking—lovemaking he would never remember. Just moments ago, she had experienced his embrace, had felt the heat of his skin, the rough stubble of his beard through her thin dress. She had assured him of her love. He would never know, and she must never let it happen again for she could not live with the shame.

In the silence of the sickroom, Claire was forced to face facts. She loved a man who did not love her. She had never admitted that love to him until now—when he could not know. And now it was too late. What she would do about their sham of a marriage she did not know, but the decision could wait until he recovered.

Over the course of the next few days, she nursed her ailing husband, listening almost against her will as his fevered mind traveled deep into his past. Following the train of his incoherent words and phrases, she shared the pain and longing of a lonely boy. When his fever dropped slightly as it sometimes did just after dawn, he reached into the past to talk fondly of Odette, Tante Delaney and Thor Povich. Though his wife listened with dreadful fascination when his voice softened and he spoke of dear ones, he never mentioned Lila's name again. But Claire was not cheered when he called her own name. She knew he sought only his nurse.

The days blurred into one another, made the same by the never-ending toil of caring for a helpless invalid. So this day had progressed into evening. Claire stood beside the window, her face mirroring the dark countenance of the weather outside. The overcast sky bore down on the breathless twilight heat as, in the distance, storm clouds roiled and distant thunder rumbled.

Pale and drawn, the exhausted girl stared out at the murky sky and tried to hope. Until yesterday, Philippe's illness had followed the course Dr. Perez had described, but today was the eleventh day and his fever showed no sign of abating.

She glanced over her shoulder to where he lay, the sheet over his motionless body like a shroud. She had worked so hard to save him; surely she could not fail.

Lost in her painful musings, Claire did not see when Philippe opened his eyes and blinked away the long, tortured sleep. She did not realize when beads of perspiration formed a glaze on his forehead and rolled unchecked into his hair, dampening his pillow. He turned his head to see his wife beside the window, her slender back to him. His mouth worked, but no words came. Tentatively, he tried to lift his hand to reach toward her, but had not enough strength. It dropped feebly, ashen against the white sheet.

Hearing him stir, Claire turned and found his dark eyes fixed on her.

"Claire," he croaked through cracked lips.

"Philippe!" His name welled up joyfully from her very being. Rushing to him, she fell to her knees beside the bed. "Thank *le bon Dieu*, the fever is past!" Wetting a corner of a clean towel, she dabbed at his parched lips and shouted, "Beady, quick! Fetch some fresh water for the master to drink—and some broth."

"Yes'm." The maid blubbered in the doorway from pure gladness.

"How long have I been unconscious?" the patient rasped, grimacing with the effort of talking.

"Ten days."

"Yellow jack?"

"*Oui.*"

"An epidemic?"

She nodded silently.

"Any word from the city?" he asked laboriously.

"No one is allowed in or out, so we don't know what's happened there," she answered hesitantly. "But don't worry about it right now. Lie still, Philippe. You mustn't tire yourself."

He acknowledged her request with a weak gesture. "Just one thing... How badly have we been hit? Have provisions been made?"

"Everyone is being cared for." She smoothed his hair. "You were the only case in the main house. Two field hands died and Xavier was stricken—"

"I must've given it to him," the man berated himself.

"Don't fret, Philippe, he lives," Claire comforted him. "As for the ones who died—there was little we could do without a doctor. He wasn't able to come back after the first day."

"So you nursed me yourself?" he questioned wonderingly.

Their conversation was interrupted when Beady returned with a tray bearing a pitcher of water and a bowl of clear broth.

She set the tray on the table beside the bed and grinned shyly at Philippe. "I'm glad you're better, m'sieur. I bin burnin' candles for you."

"Votive or voodoo?" he joked wearily.

"Both," she replied seriously and departed.

"I seem to have had the best of care," Philippe remarked thoughtfully, watching Claire pour a cup of water for him. The expression in his eyes was odd, made odder by the jaundice. Flustered by his scrutiny, she refused to meet his gaze. She sat nervously on the edge of the bed and helped him drink.

Wrapping his hands around the cup so they covered hers, he drank greedily, never taking his eyes from his wife.

"Not so fast," she muttered. "Sip a little at a time. You don't want to make yourself sick."

"*Non*, madame, I do not."

She lifted her eyes to his unwavering stare, but looked away quickly. The air around them seemed to be charged.

"This is a heartening picture," Dr. Perez declared hoarsely from the hallway. Looking even more rumpled and bloodshot than the last time Claire had seen him, the exhausted man regarded the surprised couple with weary satisfaction. "Not all of my patients are recovering so well, but they didn't have such a determined young woman to nurse them."

"She has done well," Philippe agreed with a tired smile.

"She has saved your life," the physician replied positively, coming to his patient's bedside. "When I left here, Philippe," he teased with a twinkle in his eye, "I wondered if you'd be around long enough to give us a houseful of little Girards. I can see that Claire was determined you would."

Her face flaming red, the girl withdrew to the window and watched the clouds swirling on the horizon.

"You're going to be fine, *mon ami*," Dr. Perez pronounced when he finished his examination.

"In a day or two, he'll have as much devilment in him as ever," he assured Claire, "but you must get some rest, my dear, or you won't be able to enjoy it." With a pleased chuckle, he departed to finish his rounds.

Claire returned to the bedside to feed Philippe. After a time, he leaned back and closed his eyes, fatigued by the simple task of eating.

"Rest now," she advised softly. Rising, she pulled the sheet over him.

"If you promise not to go away," he said without opening his eyes.

"I'll be right here."

Her heart stood still when Philippe murmured drowsily, "You know, my love, I had the most wonderful dream about you...." His head sagged against his chest before he could finish the sentence.

"Yes, *mon amour*, a dream," she whispered, gazing down at the sleeping man, "only a dream."

Pulling her chair near the window, Claire listened to the wail of the rising wind and pondered her situation. A few feet away, she could see the even rise and fall of Philippe's chest under the sheet. Offering a wordless prayer of thanksgiving, she reflected that whatever happened, at least he was alive.

Suddenly, the dam of pent-up emotion broke free, sweeping away her reserve. As the howling storm broke over New Orleans, Claire wept. Her shoulders heaving silently, she cried, weariness, relief, joy at her husband's recovery spilling out.

But all other feeling was overshadowed by the desolation of losing him. Outside, lightning struck, accompanied by a deafening thunderclap, but in the depths of her sorrow, she did not hear.

"What's wrong?" Philippe's voice came faintly over the tumult.

"Nothing," she answered, her voice thick with tears. She turned her face resolutely toward the window.

"Are you crying?" he asked bemusedly.

"No." She shook her head violently and stared unseeingly at sheets of rain that began to pound on the dry ground, making small craters in the dust.

"You are crying," he accused incredulously. "I thought you said I would never make you cry."

"So I did," she snapped, her voice cracking as she tried to stem the uncooperative flood of tears.

"Come here, Claire." Despite his weakened condition, Philippe managed to command her in a voice that would brook no argument.

Reluctantly, she approached the bed.

"Sit down." He tugged on her skirt to pull her down beside him. "Cry, *chère*," he ordered. "Shed the tears you must—for me, for you, for all the time we've lost."

What remained of Claire's composure crumbled, and she doubled over on the bed, burying her face in her husband's shoulder. He enfolded her tenderly in his arms while she sobbed.

"That's right," he whispered, smoothing her tangled hair, "cry. But cry for joy, too, because we're together."

Philippe held her until her tears ran out and she heaved with dry, racking sobs. At last her crying ceased and her body re-

laxed on the bed beside him. Exhausted, they nestled together, lulled by the gentle rhythm of the rain. The violence of
the storm had passed, taking with it the past and the stench of
smoke and death.

Chapter Nineteen

How strange it had been, waking in Philippe's bed, Claire thought. She had awakened, still clad in her wrinkled dress, to discover his lean, hard body separated from hers by only a thin coverlet. Carefully she inched her way to the edge of his bed, her breath catching when he stirred in his sleep. She fled to her own room, knowing she could not face him yet.

Now, perched on the railing of the damp balcony outside her room, she savored the rain-washed morning and delayed thinking of the future. Perhaps she must soon make decisions that could change her life, but now she reveled in knowing the man she loved would live. That he loved someone else, she would consider later.

"Here we are, mam'selle," Beady called from inside the house. Claire stepped inside to find a procession of grinning house servants laden with bathtub, towels and bucket after bucket of hot water.

"*Bonjour, maîtresse!*" they greeted her gladly. The shadow of death no longer hung over Fortier House.

"Y'all gonna wake up M'sieur Philippe," Beady fussed, rushing to close the door between the rooms. Then, shooing the other girls from the room, she helped her mistress undress.

Claire unplaited her hair and eagerly stepped into the bath, emitting a sigh of pleasure as she sank to her neck in the hot water.

"Reckon we better burn this ol' thing." Her maid picked up Claire's rumpled dress with a distasteful look on her round face.

"*Oui* . . . and the sheets we used on Philippe's bed."

"Yes'm." Beady poised at the door. "Oh, Greer say to tell you th' Girards sent a boy over to find out how we doin'."

"That was good of them. Are they well at Bonté?"

"*Oui*. They was hardly hit at all. The boy said M'sieur René bin in town, helpin' Dr. Perez. The doctor told th' Girards 'bout the sickness here and Madame Girard sent word she been prayin'. I hear Tante Delaney and M'sieur Philippe's baby sister wanna come right away, but ain't nobody goin' nowhere till th' militia goes home," the little maid concluded sensibly.

Guiltily, Claire realized she was grateful they were keeping to their posts a little longer. If she was not yet ready to talk to Philippe, how could she deal with his family?

"Claire," Philippe called from the adjoining room.

She sat up with a splash, causing Beady to shoot her a warning glance.

"You stay here and rest yourself," the maid ordered. "I'll see to th' master." Dropping the soiled garment she held, she hurried to Philippe's room.

"*Bonjour*, m'sieur," she greeted the patient cheerily.

"*Bonjour*, Beady. Where is my wife? She was here when I fell asleep."

"She in th' bath. Kin I help you with somethin'?" the servant asked politely.

"You can tell me what a man has to do around here to get fed," Philippe growled good-naturedly. "I could eat a horse."

"Thought you liked hosses," Beady teased.

"Not to eat . . . usually." Despite the weakness of his voice, Claire was pleased to note he sounded as if he were in good spirits.

"A good appetite's a good sign. Reckon you'll be well in no time. I'll fetch your breakfus' right away, but don't you try to git up."

"Never fear," he answered wryly. "I don't believe my legs will hold me."

Before setting out on her errand, Beady paused in the doorway between the rooms to say, "I'll be right back, mam'selle."

"Take your time." Philippe could hear his wife's murmured reply as the maid started to close the door.

"Don't close it," he bade swiftly. "Leave it open so we can talk."

This was the moment she had dreaded, Claire thought on her side of the wall. She listened as Beady departed. In his bed, Philippe listened, too, for sounds of his wife's bath. Finally, he called through the open door, "Claire, are you there?"

"I'm here." Her soft answer floated to him, an echo from the recent past accompanied by a vague wisp of memory—Claire standing by the bed, her slim, lithe body visible under a transparent white nightgown. Intently, the invalid tried to separate fevered fantasy from fact.

"Perhaps I should ask, are you there?" she teased after a long moment, interrupting his reflection.

"*Oui,*" he answered, his brow knit with a preoccupied frown.

"How do you feel this morning?"

"Battered and beaten. Do you kick in your sleep?"

"I do not," Claire laughingly assured him.

She heard a rap on the door of the adjoining room as Beady returned with a tray bearing a teapot, a steaming bowl of broth and two slices of dry toast.

"What's this?" Philippe grimaced at the meager fare. "I asked for breakfast."

"This is breakfust. Doctor's orders—broth and toast for th' first few days, then you kin git back to andouille sausages and deviled crabs."

Sausage? Crab? He gulped deeply, fighting back unexpected queasiness at her flippant retort. Meekly, he sat up and accepted the tray, dipping an unsteady spoon into the broth.

"How 'bout if I feed you?" Beady hovered over him, watching the shaky progress of the broth toward his mouth.

"Let me," Claire requested, emerging from her room. Wrapped in a lavender satin dressing gown, her damp hair pinned up, she was fresh from her bath. Her face was pink and shiny and delicate tendrils framed her face.

"I can feed myself, *merci*. There's no reason to treat me like an invalid," the weakened man grumbled.

"You wish to sleep in puddles?" She pointed to damp splotches on the sheet where he had dribbled broth.

"Accidents happen," he protested, but he surrendered the spoon. As she sat down beside him, stirring the broth in the bowl, he touched the cuff of her robe. "Have I seen this before?"

"I don't think so."

"I like . . . the color," he muttered with a distracted frown.

While Claire fed Philippe, she shared the news she had managed to garner. His family was well, as were the Héberts; Marguerite Ledet had been stricken, but was recovering; and there had been no word from Billy Barron or Robert Mc-Connell. The American side of the city had been hard hit. Dr. Perez estimated that three in ten had died on the other side of Canal Street. The Prentisses had lost both Leland and Bettina.

"Poor Skylar and Nancy," Philippe mourned. "At least, they have each other."

"*Oui,* they have each other," his wife echoed, oddly saddened. Excusing herself, she returned to her own room to dress.

During the next week, Claire spent virtually every moment with Philippe, retiring only when he had fallen asleep for the night. At first, she did everything for him—fed him, bathed him, shaved him, read to him when he was bored. Gradually, he was able to sit up for longer periods, reclaiming many of the duties she had performed. Under her watchful eye, he rapidly regained his strength.

The days blurred into one another, and Philippe did not bother to count them. He was pleasantly surprised that, when word came that the barricades had been removed to allow traffic in and out of the city, Claire did not leave his side. Nor did she leave him in the days that followed. Instead she thoughtfully dispatched one of the grooms to the racetrack to find out how Billy Barron fared, and sent Greer into town to check on the Mercantile.

Although she wanted nothing more at the moment than to be with her husband, Claire the businesswoman still felt guilty of neglecting her responsibilities. When the big butler returned, she met him at the door and bombarded him with questions.

Yes, Greer informed her, the quarantine had been fully lifted. Yes, he had told McConnell that Claire would return to the office as soon as Philippe recovered. And yes, the Scotsman looked fit, he confirmed, handing over an envelope addressed to her.

McConnell's scrawled note assured his employer that all was well on the waterfront. Though they had lost a warehouse man and business had ground to a halt during the epidemic, the Mercantile was once again operational.

The groom returned with word that Billy and the stables were fine. Satisfied with the news her servants brought, Claire hurried to tell her husband.

Throughout his convalescence, Philippe was content to have Claire by his side, but something disquieted him—something indefinable, an elusive fragment that skimmed across his memory. At first, he feared his mind had been affected by the fever. He recalled little of what had happened during his illness. He knew he had dreamed, vividly remembering visions of family and friends, of creatures that lurk in nightmares. Strange dreams still troubled him and he awakened some nights in a cold sweat, trembling at what his sleep brought. But there was something more that bothered him—something nearly remembered.

At last the answer came, through another dream.

He tossed in the throes of a nightmare. Was he waking or sleeping? He must be awake, but when he willed his eyes to open, they would not. Someone was there, Philippe hallucinated, his heart pounding. Someone lurked in the doorway to his room.

Determinedly, the weakened man forced his leaden limbs over the edge of the bed and laboriously sat up. With a hoarse shout, he launched himself on unreliable legs toward the shadowy intruder. Swinging his fist wildly in his sleep, he pitched forward, catching the bedside table and knocking the candle holder to the floor. Fully awakened from his nightmare by the clatter, he found himself swaying in the middle of the room.

Claire materialized from the night and supported him with her body, pulling one of his arms around her shoulders. His hand resting on her smooth skin brought a thrill of recognition. Tentatively, he moved his fingers against her bare shoulder and traced the thin satin strap that held her nightgown in place. Philippe gazed down at her, ethereal in white, and he knew. He *had* made love to Claire. It had not been a dream.

"What are you doing?" she panted, steering him toward the bed.

"Getting up," he answered weakly, "but I knocked the candlestick over."

"You would make a habit of it, m'sieur," she said with a sigh, never guessing what her words revealed. Helping him into bed, she observed him keenly through the darkness. "What did you need?"

"I—I thought I heard a noise."

"Just a bad dream, *cher.*" Shaken by the similarities to another night so vivid in her memory, Claire struggled to keep her voice steady. "Sleep now, you need your rest."

Pausing only to right the table and retrieve the candlestick, she fled to the safety of her own room, leaving Philippe to ponder his revelation.

He lay awake for hours, dredging his memory, nearly groaning aloud as that night came back to him in bits and pieces. She had not come willingly, he realized, but Claire had been in his bed, wearing the same provocative nightgown she wore tonight. How well he now remembered her complete shuddering surrender as she gave herself, her virginity to him with fierce passion. He summoned the feel of her smooth skin, of her slender body moving rhythmically under his.

He had wanted to love and possess her, but he had done exactly what he had vowed he would not, Philippe realized guiltily. He had taken her against her will. It made no difference to him that he had been delirious with fever when he did so.

Why had she said nothing of that night over the past few weeks? he wondered. Did she hope he would not remember? Or did she hope to forget? *Mon Dieu,* did she hate him for it?

Surely she did not. His recuperation with his wife at his side had been one of the happiest times of his life. Claire seemed genuinely fond of him. If she cared a little, he would make her care a great deal, Philippe vowed. He would win her love.

When he awoke from a deep dreamless sleep, the Creole stretched pleasurably, feeling better than he had felt for a month. His lean body still showed signs of the ravaging illness from which he was recovering, but he was confident of his returning strength and his spirits soared when he recalled last night's discovery.

He did not know that Claire lay on the other side of the wall, drained and exhausted after a sleepless night. It was time—past time—to deal with her troublesome feelings for Philippe. She had wrestled with the problem and made her decision: she would hold to her bargain. But if he did not love her, she must learn not to love him.

She was gone by the time her husband rose. Called into town, Beady informed him, on urgent business. The man rambled around the huge house until late afternoon, when boredom overtook him and he decided to test his strength by going for a ride.

Philippe strode to the barn, disregarding the servants' protests and a bank of blackening clouds moving swiftly overhead. His step quickened as he neared the stable yard and heard a shrill whinny piercing the babble of excited voices. Rounding the stand of palmettos that separated the barn from the main house, he saw the grooms scatter before Lagniappe's flashing hooves, deserting Xavier, who strained at the huge beast's bridle. They watched from a safe distance while the boy fought for control of the great beast.

Xavier looked even skinnier than he had before his illness, if that was possible, Philippe thought wryly. He watched approvingly as the young groom talked softly to the rearing horse while gently taking in the slack in the halter rope.

"How come you so cantankerous, Lagniappe? You and me's friends, ain't we? C'mon, settle down," he wheedled.

Slowly, the huge black stallion responded to his coaxing. As he calmed, his bucking lessened, until at last Lagniappe stood uneasily in one spot. His nostrils flaring, the big horse pawed and snorted. Grudgingly, he allowed the groom to give his nose a conciliatory rub. Philippe waited to be certain the animal had quieted and Xavier was fully in control before he went to congratulate him on his accomplishment.

"Good job, Xavier!" he called loudly so the other grooms heard.

"*Merci*, M'sieur Philippe." Xavier beamed delightedly at his hero. "Glad to see you well again, sir."

"The same to you." Philippe nodded, rubbing Lagniappe's flank in response to the horse's welcoming nudge. He looked the boy over appraisingly. "You seem to have recovered well enough," he joshed, "but you could still use more of Toolah's cooking."

"Reckon both of us could." The groom grinned even wider and hitched up his baggy trousers. "You and me got into a passel of sick, didn't we?"

"A passel of sick, indeed," the Creole agreed with a laugh. "But I feel well enough to ride today."

When Xavier had saddled the now calm stallion, he said, "M'sieur, I oughtta tell you Tati come here yesterday with a message for you." He fished a wrinkled envelope from his pocket and attempted to smooth it before he handed it to the man.

Philippe tore it open and read,

Cher Philippe:
How unkind of you to stay away. I heard weeks ago that you had recovered. I have waited, but still you do not come to me. Have you forgotten your poor Lila? I am alone, without a protector. Do you no longer think of me? Perhaps I must find someone else who will care for me. You know I have many admirers, but I have always loved you best. I am sad to say this, *cher*, but you must come within three days or you will lose me forever.

I remain,
Your faithful Lila

His handsome face sober, Philippe wadded the paper and thrust it into his pocket. "I'll be back, Xavier," he said, taking Lagniappe's reins. "I have unfinished business in town."

Swinging onto the stallion's back, he galloped down the *allée* in a cloud of dust.

The bell tinkled when the door opened and Lila glanced up from behind the counter where she was consulting with Madame DuBois, a particularly difficult customer. Triumph flickered in her amber eyes at the sight of Philippe. When she faltered, the bonnet she held in her hand momentarily forgotten, the heavy, florid-faced matron turned to see who intruded.

Philippe flashed a brilliant smile and bowed, flourishing his hat. "*Bonjour,* ladies."

"Monsieur Girard, *bonjour,*" the Creole woman greeted him warmly. "How are you? I heard you were ill."

"Much better now, *merci.* Who wouldn't be on such a beautiful day? Although it is not nearly so lovely as you this morning.'' Slipping easily into his familiar role of rake, Philippe fairly leered at the stout middle-aged matron.

The flattered woman turned even redder and dissolved into coy titters behind a tiny fan. Behind her, Lila fixed Philippe with a stony stare.

''A moment, m'sieur, and I shall be with you,'' she said crisply. Pointedly, she returned her attention to her customer. Philippe wandered around the shop, looking in showcases, fingering ribbons and veiling.

''I cannot choose.'' Madame DuBois wavered helplessly. ''I like them both so very much.''

''May I be of service?'' Philippe stepped to her side, ignoring the octoroon's warning glare.

Madame DuBois offered two improbable hats for his inspection. ''I can't decide which is more my style.''

''They're both very... er... fashionable.''

''Then you think I should take both of them?'' She seized upon his comment eagerly.

''I think you would look ravishing in either. Why not have both?'' He settled the question with the wisdom of Solomon, then watched with an arrogant smile as Lila placed both hats into boxes.

''*Merci*, Monsieur Girard, for the man's point of view.'' Madame DuBois smiled sweetly at Philippe as she lumbered out of the shop. ''Give my best to your wife.''

''I shall, madame,'' he promised.

Lila busied herself arranging merchandise, refusing to look at him until she was sure the other woman was out of sight and earshot.

''What's the meaning of this, Philippe?'' she hissed through clenched teeth.

''You didn't want to sell two hats at once?'' he jested with feigned innocence.

''You know very well what I mean—coming here while I had a customer.'' She whirled to face him, her tawny eyes flashing.

''You sent for me, remember?'' he said impatiently.

''But I thought...'' She floundered, then gave a brittle laugh. ''*Non*, I should've known you wouldn't honor my cottage with your presence. Months ago you promised to call on me. Do your promises mean nothing to you?''

She broke off her tirade abruptly as a window-shopper paused in front of the store. Snatching up a bonnet, she passed it to Philippe and said smoothly, "*Oui*, I'm certain *madame* will like it—the large brim is the very latest fashion from Paris."

So only Lila could hear, Philippe mocked, "You see, you don't have to worry so much about appearances. I could be just another gentleman out to buy a chapeau for his bride."

He boomed amiably for the benefit of the passerby, "Yes, it's quite fetching."

The shopper wandered on, and Philippe leaned across the counter with a look so intense that it caused the woman to step back.

"In answer to your earlier question—I keep my promises, but in case you hadn't heard, I've been ill. You remember... the yellow jack epidemic? So inconvenient for everyone.

"You said in your note," he went on, "that you wanted to talk to me. Well, I want to talk to you, too, and it can't wait."

Flustered and angry that the man affected her so, Lila held aside the curtain over the door to the back room. "We can talk in the workroom."

He bowed and gestured grandly. "After you, mam'selle."

Drawing herself up disdainfully, she swept through the door. Philippe followed, the hat she had handed him still held in his hand.

In the midst of the cluttered room, filled with silk flowers, bolts of ruche and spindles of brightly colored ribbons, stood a sturdy worktable. Lila leaned against it, half-sitting, yet poised for action.

"I suppose you've come for an explanation," she said, coolly expectant of the scene to follow.

"An explanation?"

"Of why I've been seeing other men." The octoroon's smile was cruelly confident.

"You said in your note you might have to seek another protector."

"Since you haven't seen fit to offer me your protection." She shrugged.

Philippe stared at her through narrowed eyes, gauging her readiness for his news. "Protection, no. However, I can offer assistance. Is there anyone you would like for me to talk to?"

"What?" Lila gasped. "Surely you're not serious, Philippe. It's a joke, *oui?* You've always been able to make me laugh." She threw back her head and chuckled, a note of desperation making it sound hollow. She went to him and placed her hands on his chest, almost playfully.

"It's not a joke, Lila," the Creole answered gravely, removing her hands from his shirtfront. "You and I are finished. We won't see each other again. Don't expect me at the cottage. Don't send messages to my home. And do not visit Claire and stir up any more trouble. It upsets her and I don't like it when my wife is upset." His voice was cold and hard.

Lila drew back, stricken. Her amber eyes searched Philippe's impassive face, trying desperately to understand.

"She may be your wife, but I'm your woman. I'm the only woman for you. You told me so yourself."

"That was a long time ago. Things change." Philippe frowned down at her.

"Love doesn't change. Mama Dédé says you and I belong together—we were meant to be."

"Gris-gris cannot tell what is in the heart."

Lila recoiled at his words, so like the voodoo queen's prediction. "You don't love Claire," she gasped. "I know that."

"And how do you know?" His question stung Lila visibly, but she refused to surrender.

She moved close to Philippe, tiptoeing to wrap her arms around his neck, and molded her body to his. Using her passion as a weapon, she kissed him with parted lips. Like the last time, he felt nothing. This time he did not even attempt to return her kiss. Abruptly, the *placée* pulled back, her face a mask of hatred.

"So it's true," she spat. "She's turned you against me."

But in the space of a breath, she changed her tactics and her manner. Clinging to his lapels, she buried her face in the whiteness of his shirt.

"What's to become of me?" Lila whimpered forlornly. "You are my world, *cher*. Nothing else matters. I didn't mean it when I said I'd find another protector. I love only you. I love you as no one else can." Her voice rose hysterically. "I'm more of a woman than that girl can ever be. You know you love me. Why don't you admit it? You love me."

Her final words, nearly a wail, dissolved into a pitiful sob. Philippe let her lean against him as she wept inconsolably, then he grasped her firmly by the shoulders and pushed her away. Taking her hand, he pressed a wad of money into it.

"You think I can be bought off?" she screeched, throwing it in his face.

His mouth tightening, Philippe sauntered toward the curtained passage to the front of the shop. Pausing in the doorway, he twirled the bonnet on one finger and said casually, "I think you should keep the money, Lila—for the hat." Then he pivoted and left the shop.

Sobbing, her lovely face contorted with hatred, the octoroon stumbled to the front door and flung it open. From the banquette, she could see Philippe astride Lagniappe, the bonnet tied to the pommel of his saddle. Overhead, murky clouds crowded toward the sun, throwing an unnatural yellow light over the scene, and the wind was beginning to rise.

"I hate you, Philippe Girard!" she shrieked over the wail of the wind. Uncaring that she was making a scene, she screamed after him, "Stay with your wife if you love her so much. Don't ever come back. I don't care. I can have any man I want," she declared with an arrogant toss of her head.

Philippe rode away without so much as a glance over his shoulder.

Lila turned and began to walk toward her shop. A little ways down the banquette poised a still figure that neither she nor Philippe had seen.

Claire Girard stood, her hat held against the gust that would have removed it, her skirt whipping around her legs, and she stared after her husband with a curious expression.

How much had she seen or heard? Lila wondered. Set on vengeance however she could wreak it, the octoroon schooled her face into a pitying smile.

"I'm sorry that you had to see Philippe coming from the arms of his lover," she said sympathetically, "but I did warn you."

"Do you always tell your lovers that you hate them and never to come back?" Claire asked coolly.

So she *had* seen, and heard. Lila drew herself up proudly and snapped, "Only the ones I'm finished with. You can have Philippe. I don't want him anymore." Her head held high, she swept inside her shop and closed the door.

As Claire walked to her carriage, the rain began in torrents. Chilled and soaked to the skin, she brooded all the way home. Lila and Philippe were finished, that much was clear. She felt a faint glimmer of hope, for Lila's haughty declaration was overshadowed by the memory of the words the octoroon had shouted after him, "Stay with your wife if you love her so much!"

Did Philippe love her? She wanted to believe it was true; she wanted to believe with all her heart. But how was she to find out?

Greer went from room to room, lighting the lamps against the gloom of the afternoon. He peeped into the library but did not enter, unwilling to interrupt Philippe as he paced, a worried expression on his handsome face.

Where the hell was Claire? the Creole fretted. Halting to peer out the window, he tried to calm himself. There was no reason for alarm, just because she was not home yet.

The rain had begun only an hour ago, but the streets were probably already nearly impassable. Swift currents made it dangerous to traverse the narrow bridges over the bayous that laced the area. Perhaps she was not out in the storm at all, he told himself reasonably. Perhaps she had delayed her return from town until it passed.

Running his fingers through his hair in a harried gesture, he began to pace again. Reason be damned. He was worried and he wanted his wife safe at home.

As if in answer to his agonizing, the sound of wheels could be heard over the patter of the rain. Philippe raced immediately for the foyer, reaching it ahead of the servants.

Wet and bedraggled, Claire was already stepping from the carriage when Philippe threw open the front door. He snatched an umbrella from a rack and ran out into the fury of the storm to meet her. A savage gust of wind turned the umbrella inside out before he even reached the edge of the veranda, nearly tearing it from his hand. With a curse, he released it and it somersaulted over the sodden lawn, coming to rest against a leaning, windblown trellis.

Stripping off his jacket, he threw it over his wife to shield her. He did not see her look of gratitude as he wrapped an arm around her waist and whisked her toward the house, steadying her when she slipped on the uneven shell-covered drive.

Greer, Beady and Lucene poised anxiously in the doorway, each laden with warmed towels. When the couple hurried up the steps to the veranda, the babble of the servants' voices reached them. Before they had even reached the shelter of the foyer, Beady was scolding her mistress in a voice made sharp by relief. Lucene took Claire's dripping cloak, while Beady draped her with towels.

Accepting a towel from Greer, Philippe mopped his face and regarded his dripping wife apprehensively. "I've been worried sick about you out in this weather. Are you all right, Claire?"

"Just cold and wet." Smiling wanly, she shivered.

The urge to lecture her was chased away by concern. "Take her up and get her out of those wet clothes before she catches a chill," he ordered her maid at once.

"Lucene, see to some bathwater—good and hot." Greer took charge as Beady led her mistress upstairs. "Mister Philippe, you must get out of your wet clothes, too. I built a fire in your room earlier, but I suggest you crawl into bed until you're thoroughly warmed. You're scarcely past your fever and we don't want you to come down sick again."

"*Merci,* Greer." Philippe grinned and obeyed.

Shedding his sodden clothes in front of the fireplace, he dried himself. All gooseflesh from the chill, he followed Greer's suggestion and got into bed, drawing the covers up around his chin. Slowly he began to warm, as he lay listening to the noise from next door. It sounded as if a veritable parade of servants were hauling hot water to Claire's room.

A rap sounded at his own door and Greer entered with a cup of hot coffee, liberally laced with whiskey. Philippe accepted it gratefully, feeling better with each sip. At last the furor in the adjoining room died, and the man heard the familiar sounds of bathing through the closed door.

In the adjoining bedchamber, Beady stoked the fire in the fireplace and asked, "You warm enough now, mam'selle?"

"Much better, *merci,*" Claire murmured.

"You musta bin chilled to th' bone," the maid chattered. "I laid out a nice warm gown for you here on th' bed, and a robe. How 'bout if I bring your supper up so's you can rest?"

"I'm not sure I even want dinner."

"You gots to eat and keep your strength up," Beady protested.

"I was only wet, not ill," Claire countered wryly.

"Don't wanna see you git ill," the servant argued. "We done had 'nough sickness here."

"I agree, but I'll be fine. Leave me," her mistress instructed. "I'll call when I need you."

When Beady had gone reluctantly, Claire settled back in the tub with a sigh, considering the scene she had witnessed earlier. Did Philippe care for her? Their entire marriage seemed to be built on doubts. Their relationship had all the aspects of a duel, filled with skillful verbal lunging and parrying. And neither of them had emerged unscathed.

Could love grow between two people who had hurt each other again and again, who were unwilling to trust each other? Was she strong enough to trust Philippe first? What would she do if he rejected her as he had so many times in the past? She did not think she could bear it.

In the next room, the man listened to the quiet sounds of his wife's bath, barely audible through the closed door. He could almost smell the scent she used and imagine how she looked in the deep tub, white breasts bobbing up through the water's surface. His groin tightened at the mental image and he shifted restlessly in his bed.

After a while, the sounds told him she had finished her bath and was stepping out of the tub. He pictured her slender body in his mind's eye, feeling heated desire rising. He would not take her against her wishes again; but he had to know if she wanted him. Then he would know if she loved him, for Claire would not have him if she did not.

There was one sure way to find out. A purposeful gleam in his dark eyes, he jumped to his feet. Without even taking time to don a robe, he strode to the adjoining door and threw it open.

Silhouetted against a roaring fire, she stood, dripping, beside the bathtub, her towel draped loosely around her back as she dried. Her shocked eyes met his and she hastily wrapped the towel tightly around herself.

"Is anything wrong?" she gasped.

"*Non*, nothing." He lingered in the doorway, his dark eyes hungrily taking in her scantily covered form.

"I thought you were lying down." Her eyes widened in alarm as her gaze took in his state of undress for the first time. Her husband stood gloriously naked in the shadowy doorway, but his lust was clearly visible. Involuntarily, she retreated, only to find any hope of escape blocked as her calves pressed against the side of the bathtub.

"There is something I would discuss with you." Deliberately, he stepped into the lamp-lit room.

"I'll be happy to talk with you, but can't it wait until I'm dressed?" she requested evenly. She struggled to keep her gaze from drifting downward.

"It's waited long enough." He advanced another step, enjoying her discomfiture immensely.

"I insist you return to your own room," she said haughtily and clutched her towel tighter, accidentally affording him a magnificent view of her breasts swelling against the restraining fabric, threatening to burst free at any moment.

"I suppose I could leave," he allowed reasonably, showing no intention of doing so, "if you promise to come and talk to me in a moment."

"I promise," she pledged, relief apparent in her voice.

His eyes flitted to the bed where a voluminous nightgown was spread. "I'd like it better if you'd wear a different nightgown," he suggested with a rakish smile. "I'm particularly fond of the sheer white one—you know, with the lavender ribbons."

Her eyes widened in dismay. "Lavender ribbons . . . You remember?" she whispered.

"*Oui*, I remember." Suddenly serious, he held her eyes, but he stayed where he was for fear of frightening her. "You must have thought me a cad."

"You didn't know what you were doing," she muttered, hanging her head in mortification.

"Do you think I had to be out of my head with fever to want you?" Philippe asked gently. "I would've taken you anytime if only you had come to me. I always wanted you." He watched her closely, trying to gauge her emotions.

"*Oui*, you wanted me," she echoed bleakly. Fighting back tears, she refused to look at him. He spoke of desire, Claire thought miserably, never of love.

"You wanted me, too," he reminded her quietly.

"That's not why I came to your room that night." She met his gaze defiantly.

"But it's why you stayed," he countered bluntly.

"*Non,* I—"

"Don't try to deny your response to me, Claire. I remember it vividly now." He crossed the space between them in two steps and captured her in powerful arms. Holding her tightly against his bare chest, he bent so his face was close to hers and murmured insistently, "As vividly as I remember you holding me in your arms . . . and telling me that you love me."

"No—" She struggled in his embrace, unshed tears glinting in her eyes.

"Yes," Philippe whispered, lowering his mouth to hers.

For a moment, Claire fought the sensations he aroused in her, but her body responded to his caresses. Her mind reeling, poised on the edge of white-hot passion, she returned his kiss eagerly, her hands sliding over his muscled chest, up his neck until her fingers entwined in his thick hair.

Drawing back slightly, he looked down at her, astonished at the passion his kiss had awakened in her. Eyes closed, her face tilted toward him invitingly. His eyes swept her face and came to rest on the pulse fluttering below her delicately chiseled chin. His lips traced her jaw, lingering on the sensitive spot below her ear. She whimpered with pleasure and shifted against him, the towel dropping unnoticed to the floor.

Sweeping her into his arms, the man cradled her against his broad chest and carried her to the bed. Laying her down gently, he stood over her for a moment. "*Mon Dieu,* you are beautiful," he whispered. "I never realized it more than tonight. You were made for love."

"Then come and love me," she invited huskily.

Nearly overwhelmed by long-restrained desire, Philippe lay down beside her, his lean hardness pressed against her hip. Propping himself on one elbow, he spread her hair on the pillow, savoring the feel of the silky locks in his fingers. He traced her cheekbone with his thumb as he gazed down at her tenderly.

She smiled up at him, her eyes dark with desire, and reached out to touch his cheek. As if drawn, he bent to kiss her. The heat of his mouth on hers was at first tender and exploring, then passionate, sweetly demanding.

Philippe's dark head dipped lower, trailing hot kisses along her shoulder and down until his lips closed on one coral-crested mound. Under his teasing tongue, her breast seemed to swell with aching longing. Claire felt as if liquid fire ignited in her body, coursing through her veins to the very core of her being. His hand traveled in loving exploration, moving downward along the curve of her hip, stroking the warm flesh of her thigh, gently invading her most secret, sensitive place.

Her hands gripped his broad shoulders tightly as her hips rose to meet his tender probing. Experimentally, she feathered shy kisses along the corded sinews of his neck, down to the mat of hair on his chest. Her exploring hands traced delicate circles around and down his chest and taut stomach, slower and surer until she found and held what she sought, surprising even herself. Philippe moaned at her caress, as if suffering exquisite pain.

Urgently, he rolled, pinning her lithe form against the mattress, covering it lovingly with his own. Claire gasped, but welcomed his weight upon her, his sudden heat. Her breath came in ragged swallows as she felt him, burning and hard, work himself gently between her thighs and inside her.

The man was sorely in need, yet his lovemaking was slow and sensual, prolonging the sweet union between them. With strong, knowing hands and lasting kisses, he reveled in the joy of discovery. His relentless, tender movement impelled Claire to move beneath him and, without design, she gave Philippe pleasure more complete than any he had ever known. In return, he guided her expertly, insistently, almost wantonly to tap the long-denied wellspring of desire and response within her.

Spent at last, the lovers lay with legs intertwined, their bodies coated with a sheen of perspiration. Philippe lay on his side, contoured to his wife's body, one arm flung under her breasts, his face buried in her hair.

"Claire . . ." His breath on her neck sent tingles down her spine.

"*Oui?*" she squirmed reflexively closer to him, causing his arm to tighten around her waist.

"I love you."

Turning in his embrace to face him, she stared at him incredulously. "Do you, Philippe?" she breathed, her face illuminated with love.

"I do," he confirmed tenderly. Then, taking for his own the words she had spoken while he was delirious, he whispered, "I love you—more than you will ever know."

Epilogue

For three days, the December weather had been gray and dreary, and the houseguests assembled to celebrate the marriage of Anne Hébert and Gaspar Boudreaux were confined in the gracious halls of Belle Grâce, the Hébert plantation. But early on the morning of the wedding, the sun broke through the overcast, illuminating droplets of water glistening on the bare branches of the trees surrounding the big house. Although the wind was raw and cold, the dazzling display seemed to beckon, drawing two of the guests to stroll in the wintry garden.

At a window in the wing that had become the women's quarters for the duration of the house party, the lace curtains were drawn back and a trio of curious female faces peered out, fogging the glass with their breath.

"I vow I've never seen such a changed man as Philippe Girard," Yvonne Ledet announced almost petulantly. She flounced over to sit in front of the fire, abandoning the window to her daughters.

"I've never seen such a happy couple," Marguerite declared positively. "I don't think Philippe has left Claire's side since they arrived three days ago. I think it's terribly romantic, don't you, Isabelle? Just like a—"

"Just like a French novel?" Petite, lovely Isabelle sniffed disapprovingly. "You're becoming as bad as Anne.

"Perhaps it is romantic," she muttered, staring out at the garden through narrowed eyes, "but it's terribly gauche. Just look at them out there, holding hands like schoolchildren and telling secrets."

"You're envious," her younger sister charged tactlessly.

"Perhaps," Isabelle admitted with uncharacteristic candor. "I certainly would like to know what he is saying to her."

Lingering determinedly near the fountain, its surface glazed with a thin layer of ice, Philippe smiled down at his wife. "But I am not ready to go back inside, *mon coeur*," he murmured insistently, his breath hanging in the air in a vaporous puff. "There are too many people in there, too much going on—parlor games, recitals, amateur theatrics. Too many people," he repeated emphatically. "I'd rather have you all to myself."

"I'd like nothing better, my darling, but we're to be at the church in a little more than an hour. I must still change clothes," Claire reminded him smilingly.

"I don't see why," he murmured, stealing a kiss. "You're beautiful just as you are—with your pink cheeks and your red nose."

"Philippe—" she began patiently.

"I know," he conceded gloomily, "and I suppose you're right. We must go in sometime."

Holding her gloved hand in his, the young Creole led her along the frost-hardened path toward the house. "You know," he confided, "last night at Gaspar's bachelor party, he asked me the secret to a happy marriage."

"And what did you tell him?" Claire shot him an indulgent sidelong glance.

"I told him our secret." He paused dramatically.

"Aha, so you do like the theatrics, after all," she said with a grin.

He stopped in his tracks and fixed her with a playful, baleful stare while she tried not to laugh. Throwing a quick, furtive glance at the house, he stepped behind a hedge, pulling Claire with him so they could no longer be seen from the house.

"This is much better for a serious conversation," he said, drawing her into his arms behind the shrubbery screen. "As I was saying, I told Gaspar our secret."

"That in the beginning he and Anne should ignore what their hearts tell them and do nothing but fight?" she asked teasingly.

"*Non,* fighting is not fun. Making up is fun," he replied, nibbling on her ear. "Look what a good time we've had together for the past few months."

"What did you tell Gaspar?" Claire looked up at her husband curiously.

"That they should never have locked doors between them," he answered seriously.

"Excellent advice, *cher*," she approved, sliding her arms around his neck.

Philippe's arms tightened around her and she could see the flare of passion in his dark eyes as he looked down at her.

"Promise me, Claire," he said huskily, "now that the door is open between us, we will never close it again."

"Never, my darling," she whispered, her face aglow in the winter sun as she lifted it gladly for his kiss.

*　　*　　*　　*　　*

HISTORICAL

CHRISTMAS

STORIES · 1991

Bring back heartwarming memories of Christmas past
with HISTORICAL CHRISTMAS STORIES 1991,
a collection of romantic stories
by three popular authors.
The perfect Christmas gift!

Don't miss these heartwarming stories,
available in November
wherever Harlequin books are sold:

CHRISTMAS YET TO COME
by Lynda Trent
A SEASON OF JOY
by Caryn Cameron
FORTUNE'S GIFT
by DeLoras Scott

**Best Wishes and Season's Greetings
from Harlequin!**

HARLEQUIN
Romance

A Christmas tradition...

Imagine spending Christmas in New
Orleans with a blind stranger and his aged
guide dog—when you're supposed to be
there on your honeymoon!
**#3163 Every Kind of Heaven
by Bethany Campbell**

Imagine spending Christmas with a man
you once "married"—in a mock ceremony
at the age of eight!
**#3166 The Forgetful Bride
by Debbie Macomber**

*Available in December 1991, wherever
Harlequin books are sold.*

HARLEQUIN

Romance

**This December, travel to
Northport, Massachusetts,
with Harlequin Romance
FIRST CLASS title #3164,
A TOUCH OF FORGIVENESS
by Emma Goldrick**

Folks in Northport called Kitty the meanest woman in town,
but she couldn't forget how they had duped her brother and
exploited her family's land. It was hard to be mean, though,
when Joel Carmody was around—his calm, good humor
made Kitty feel like a new woman. Nevertheless, a Carmody
was a Carmody, and the name meant money and power to
the townspeople.... Could Kitty really trust Joel, or was he
like all the rest?

Back by Popular Demand

A romantic tour of America through fifty favorite
Harlequin Presents, each set in a different state
researched by Janet and her husband, Bill. A journey
of a lifetime in one cherished collection.

In December, don't miss the exciting states featured
in:

Title #21   **MASSACHUSETTS**
            That Boston Man

     #22   **MICHIGAN**
            Enemy in Camp

Available wherever
Harlequin books are sold.

JD-DEC